The Sol Empire
Volume 5
Genetic
Engineering

Vic Broquard

The Sol Empire Volume 5 Genetic Engineering
First Edition
Copyrighted © 2021 by Vic Broquard
ISBN: 978-1-941415-86-3

This is a work of fiction. All characters, organizations, and events portrayed in this novel are products of the author's imagination and are used fictitiously.

Thank you to my colleague, Lisa Walker, for her many useful suggestions and corrections.

What isn't fictional is the work that Humanity and Inclusion (formerly Handicapped International) is doing to help those who have suffered:
http://www.hi-us.org

Published by:
http://www.Broquard-ebooks.com
Broquard eBooks
1055 Brandy Lake Rd
Woodruff, WI 54568
author@Broquard-eBooks.com

For Morgan and L. Ron Hubbard

Table of Contents

Chapter 1 Unexpected Clues

June 1, 2368
Hoffdorf, Cass-C, Federation of Planets

"Molly, we've been going about these robot murders backward," Dirk Bennet said over tea in my apartment at Soros University.

Years ago, Galactic Robotics Chicago built ten robots, indistinguishable from humans. But engineers had not programmed five with the robotic laws when those robots disappeared and went rogue during the Sixth Invaders' attack. Now one lived on Cass-C, murdering those who uncovered its identity. It had killed my first husband Ted and several others.

"Huh? We exhausted clues years ago," I said.

I'd come back to Cass-C six years ago to find that robot and terminate it, but I'd come up just as empty-handed as their Investigation Division (ID). The Federation's ID Commander had ordered us to cease, insisting this was their case.

Dirk said, "We looked for the robots by tracing the path that Bonita Valdez and her two detectives traveled before they were murdered. Likewise, with Senior Ambassador Aaron Strawn."

Dirk used to be a member of the elite Galaxy Detective Squad, charged with solving crimes throughout the Sol Empire—a space-faring detective. That was before an ancient race known as the Third Invaders took him along with another thousand as part of their deal to save Earth from the aftermath of the Sixth Invaders.

As I watched Dirk's robot assistant lift his teacup to his lips, memories of that massive betrayal returned. The Sixth

1

Vic Broquard

Invaders created the armless telepath Galactic Doll mutation agent in their attempt to conquer Earth. Unscrupulous people saw this agent as a way to earn fortunes: make telepaths and sell them off-world to the highest bidder. But when that agent mutated people native to other Federation worlds, the Federation of Planets had to prevent its spread. They threatened to destroy Earth to protect their human-inhabited worlds.

At that point, the Third Invaders offered to cure everyone if in return they could have a thousand of our people to found a new human colony on Domes. We had no choice but to agree. A thousand people versus three billion. But instead of curing them, the Third Invaders re-mutated them into armless telepath Galactic Dolls, impregnating them with twins, thus forming a breeding colony of telepaths to be sold.

When others and I found this colony and kicked the Third Invaders out, the Berktold Soros Group from Hoffdorf, Cass-C, promised to help the victims. Their revised mutation agent removed telepathic ability preventing them from being kidnapped. The Soros Group provided robot assistants to handle their basic needs. My arrival on Domes forced them to speed up their plans. Hence, Ashton Soros mutated my daughter Nikita and me into armless dolls, too, and transported sixteen hundred eleven of us to Cass-C.

"Right. Backtracking," I said, using my formal PI term. "That's always worked for me."

"Maybe so. But it got us nowhere. We should approach it the way Bonita might have. Remember, she had a robotics doctorate."

Cleo, my robot on wheels, lifted my teacup for me. Our arms looked like matchsticks. Only months ago, my sister Eve and dwarf friend Lara Axehead—both top geneticists—developed a full cure for all sixteen hundred of us. But our arms needed a year to develop.

2

"Yeah, what're you saying?"

"I've been pretending I was Bonita looking for that robot. I've been doing that for months. Never stopped thinking about it and following hunches. Least I can do for you for saving me with that therapy thing of yours. Mind you, I put little stock in those past lives traumas. Anyway, most hunches led nowhere until this one. What do these human-form robots have?"

"Mechanical arms? Mechanical legs?" I asked. "Are you saying Bonita looked for manufacturers of robot parts? There could be zillions, what with Cleo and the thousands of personal helper robots."

Cleo and the other helper robots rolled along on wheels, unlike the rogue human-forms.

The other five human-form robots, which did have the robot laws installed, secretly aided us. One of these, Bishop, had been my security guard for many years.

"You're getting closer. Positronic brains. That's what separates industrial robots from human-form robots and robot assistants. I checked into the brains of Cleo and Walt. They have the cheapest, least complicated positronic brains. I checked for companies building the most sophisticated ones. Bingo. There are four companies in Hoffdorf producing them."

"Perhaps you're on to something. Four?"

"Right. I cheated. Used Bonita's old clearance code to request sales records going back eight years for their top-of-the-line brains. Two have responded. They'll make their records available, but only if we show up in person."

"Dirk, I'm a moron. I should have thought of this. Well done. When do we pay them a visit?"

"Now. If you have nothing planned. Summer classes won't start until next week."

Funny how a word triggers memories. Classes. For the last six years, we'd been taking university classes. I enrolled in subjects I wanted to know more about. In the past, various situations popped up highlighting my ignorance. Electronics and robots, for example. I swore I'd not be that stupid ever again. Thus, that first year I enrolled in Space Navigation 101, Calculus 1, Physics 1, Federation Common 101, Robotics 101, and Piloting 101. I hadn't finished Piloting 101 when I was first here. I had always relied on Sam, my second husband, for navigation. With his death, I had to learn to do it myself.

I'd met Dirk Bennet that first day of Space Navigation 101. He was one of sixteen hundred armless Galactic Dolls. At first, I thought he was a woman since he looked like any of us armless Galactic Dolls, monster breasts, long hair, and distorted feet. Our class of twenty students contained six dolls. We sat together in the back of the classroom, accompanied by our robot helpers.

Our professor said, "I see we have Galactic Dolls. Welcome. Everyone, start your recordings."

Cleo started my computer recording of the lesson. The professor spoke Federation Common. If we couldn't understand him, our computers recorded what he said but translated it into our language. Clever.

He called roll, and I answered, "Here."

"Dirk Bennet."

Ah, the Doll sitting next to me was a man. In a soprano voice, he said, "Here."

When the class ended and our robots stopped the recording, he said, "Are you the person I'm supposed to visit tonight? The one who will approve my request to die?"

"I don't know who's scheduled, but yeah, we're giving everyone therapy sessions like we did to the victims on Earth. Molly Parkinson."

"Guess I'll see you tonight."

His voice sounded apathetic. Hope gone. His long brown hair and piercing blue eyes caught my attention. He stood six inches taller than me, but he looked the perfect Galactic Doll, minus arms.

He showed up just after supper, his robot, Walt, at his side. "I'm here. Can't you tell them it's okay to kill me? I can't live like this. No point in living. What's the use?"

That was six years ago when I desperately wanted happiness. Someone had murdered my husband and son. A month later, someone had murdered Bonita Valdez and her two detectives from Indrani-C. That ignores being fired from my jobs of Senior Investigator and Senior Judge for no reason. I'd given my all to save Earth and the Sol Empire and to help establish a good governmental system. I'd salvaged countless lives with Celeste's therapy.

My dual rewards: had my body mutated many times and sent forty light years away to be governor of the newly discovered, barely inhabited world of Domes and then fired a month later. Yes, I needed a change and fled halfway across the galaxy to Cass-C, home of the Federation of Planets.

But, no escape for me. Celeste and I faced salvaging sixteen hundred lives using her therapy. I began with Dirk.

"Have a seat. Good. Close your eyes. Let's return to when you first suspected something terrible was about to happen to you. Was it when you landed on Domes or before that?" I asked.

"Before. My group is loading our possessions and getting strapped in."

Ugh. Slow going. Massive betrayal. After the flying saucer lifted off, they released the mutation gas. He awoke to his never-ending nightmare. The massive betrayal and hopelessness still crushed him.

After three evenings, we'd taken the edge off the betrayal. He felt relieved and relaxed. Dirk no longer wanted to die and hoped Eve and Lara would soon develop cures. We became friends.

Later, I continued delivering therapy sessions to him until he'd erased his entire series of traumas. Dirk began helping me track the rogue killer robot.

I smiled. "You're right. We've lots of free time. Let me text Bishop. He'll meet us here. I don't go anywhere without Bishop."

"You place a lot of confidence in that security man. Not sure I do. But okay. I hope he's packing a weapon," Dirk said.

The non-descript Bishop arrived, a gun in the holster at his side. The more powerful weapons, such as blasters and disintegrators, were illegal for civilians to carry—far too dangerous.

As we crossed the university's Rectangle, I called out. "Hey, guys. I'm still wearing these damned heels. Slow way down."

The university campus comprised a giant Rectangle. Class buildings surrounded its longer edges. The married dorms comprised one narrow side; the unmarried dorms the other, making a long stroll from one set of dorms to the other.

The problem: Hoffdorf's dress code. All females from the age of five wear tall heels. They teach children the Three Bests. "Look your best. Feel your best. Be your best. A professional appearance promotes self-worth and instills confidence in others." And everyone wears black and white.

When my daughter asked why, Professor Heli explained, "The heels make us amble so we can observe, appreciate, and enjoy the world. Our world's dress code is black and white. Women wear white blouses with knee-high black skirts. Black polymer stockings encase our legs. In fact, they're an incredible engineering feat—designed to massage our legs, making them feel fabulous with each step. Our knees need it. Men wear white shirts, black pants, jackets, and shiny black shoes.

"University students must follow a strict dress code. All female attire is identical as is all male clothing. The only variation shows marital status. Married students, regardless of sex, wear black ties, while unmarried students wear red ties. Non-student women dress similarly, but have a wide variety of white tops, black skirts, and tall black heels."

Because of the dress code, I had my security human-form robot change gender. Back on Earth, the robot's identity was Sherry Cooper. I had it revert to its former male Bishop persona because wearing such tall heels inhibited it.

Dirk flushed. "Sorry. I forgot you still wear them. The freedom of movement I've gotten back is—well, let's say it sometimes makes me giddy. Bishop, we'll make frequent stops at the benches along the avenues."

"I've calculated that," Bishop said. "Always it's women who sit on them. Curious that women living on the Southern Continent don't wear such heels. There are no benches on their streets. Women there work in the factories, mines, and commerce. Like two different worlds."

"Fascinating. So, Dirk, what's our first stop?" I asked. I wanted to race to the company but had to be content with my three-inch steps, each carefully placed. "Best rest a spell at the next bench."

While sitting and relieving my knees, Dirk showed me his latest gadget. "It's a geo-tracker. I've entered the coordinates of the four companies. It plotted the shortest path to visit them. The Blaue Robotik company is our first stop in one mile. About two miles further is Krauss Robotik. A mile from there is Ostermann's Robotik Imports. Then it's two miles to Unger Robotik Umsatz and four back to campus."

"Oh, my aching feet and knees!" I gushed. "I'll need a long massage when we return."

"It wouldn't make any difference if you dropped out of the university. All women have to wear them." Dirk, the master of stating the obvious.

"Apply the same laws to men. Laws would soon change," I said.

Dirk grinned. "I planned to take a long lunch timeout between the second and third company. It's a shame they insisted on in-person access. No choice but to respect their requested privacy."

"Still, great insight. Could prove a big breakthrough. I wish we'd of thought of this six years ago."

We chuckled, and I headed for the next bench, occupied by two other women. They smiled as I sat.

One said, "University students?"

"Yes. Glad they have these benches."

"If they didn't, Cass-C women would rebel," the other woman said with a wry grin.

The original woman added, "Keeps men in their places." She nodded with a mischievous grin to Dirk and Bishop.

Both women rose and left while I massaged my knees.

Four bench stops later, we entered Blaue Robotik. Dirk handled the details while I used my telepathy to verify the veracity of what they said. I hadn't told Dirk or anyone other than my family I still had my telepathic ability. Ashton's genetic mutation left mine intact, unlike the sixteen hundred others, including Nikita's, my daughter.

The manager hesitated. "You're wearing university student clothing."

"We're working undercover," Dirk said. "Let's see your listings."

"Highly unusual. I don't want any ID troubles. Only the top-of-the-line positronic brains?"

"Right."

The manager brought up the list on his virtual monitor, the list appearing in the space between Dirk and me. He snapped a photo of the list using his Earth-based phone.

"As you can see, such sales are to Cass-C government facilities."

"Yes, thank you. Sorry to have troubled you, sir," Dirk said, smoothing our interference.

Once on the street, he blew up the captured image. All seemed in order.

I added, "He wasn't lying, either."

Dirk gave me a strange look. I leveled with him.

"Still have my mental skills. Ashton's mutation didn't work on me."

Dirk smiled. "Rather thought so, but best keep that a secret."

"Damned right," Bishop said. "It's hard enough protecting Molly without dealing with telepath traffickers."

Many bench stops later, we entered Krauss Robotik. A half hour later, we headed off to have lunch. No luck thus far. Most of their sales had been to Cass-C government agencies. But via our clandestine receipt copies, we had a few sales transactions to pursue.

We dined at Denger's Strudel, famous for their apple confections. Invigorated, we set off on the trek to Ostermann's Robotik Imports.

"How strange you should ask about sales of our best positronic brains. Several years ago, a young woman and two men made similar inquiries. She doesn't look like the woman who was here, though her ID number matches what that woman gave me. I've a notion to call the ID about this," Herr Ostermann said.

Dirk lowered his head and fiddled with his belt.

I took charge. I touched Ostermann's mind, spotting what he tried to hide from me.

"Please. Let's call them," I said. "I'd like to hear how you explain extorting the Cass-C government out of a million credits."

His face reddened. "That—that will not be necessary. Here's the listing you desire. Copy it to your computer and get out of here. Don't come back."

"Nice doing business with you," I said and walked out, followed by Dirk and Bishop bringing up the rear.

Once away from the store, Bishop said, "I detected three armed men hiding in the background but had no way to tell you."

"Thanks," I said. "Let's see that listing. If they're doing one illegal thing, they might do more."

"Bringing it up now," Dirk said, activating his portable computer attached to his wrist.

Its display opened in the space between us, a three-foot square projection. The same four buyers kept showing up. Three appeared to be government projects. At least they had such names. One customer had purchased fifty-three positronic brains during the last eight years.

Dirk commanded, "Find Huber Electronics address." His computer returned a map. "Hey, it's not too far from here. Let's check it out. It's on the way to our next stop."

"Okay," I said. "What're they doing with top-of-the-line brains? I learned in Robotics 101 that our helpers use a far cheaper and simpler brain."

Bishop said, "I suspect one would have enough computing power for human-form robots."

"Scary, Bishop, scary. One rogue robot is deadly enough. Fifty-three more. Jeesh," I said. "Come on. Let's do this before my knees give out."

Bishop said, "At least these avenues are level. They aren't level in the Southern Continent."

Chapter 2 Blaze of Glory

Early afternoon crowds streamed along the broad avenues we traveled. Women kept right on the sidewalks since we moved much slower than the men who always seemed in a rush to get somewhere. As expected, every few hundred feet, benches beckoned. Soon, I stopped at each just to give my aching knees and feet a breather.

I sensed Dirk's desire to rush on ahead and check out this clue. Bishop, too. I couldn't sense robot minds. Besides, I wasn't about to pry into Dirk's mind. We filled our stops for rest with a continuing discussion about potential uses or misuses of such sophisticated brains.

After a mile, Dirk led the way down a side street. The widths of the main avenues varied from two hundred feet to five hundred. Most of the more frequented shops lay alongside these broad avenues. Far narrower side streets branched off, though other large avenues intersected. Dirk guided us via his wrist nav unit. The first side street narrowed to about a hundred feet, benches fewer and farther apart.

We took another side branch. Fifty feet wide at most, this street had no benches. I spotted a few women walking, but mostly men hustled along. Dirk veered right and said, "Getting close."

As the streets narrowed, the tall buildings blocked sunlight making the narrow street spooky. We paused a minute and let our eyes adapt to the dingy light. Few pedestrians walked ahead of us.

Small storefronts opened onto the street. The smell of chocolate drifted in the air. I paused allowing my eyes to follow the lone woman walking in front of us. She ducked into Ludwig's Schokolade. Oh, how I wanted to stop there.

"Guys, we have to come back and visit this shop!"

Dirk teased. "Yummy."

Bishop smiled and continued his slow walk down the dark street. Automated trash bins sat near storefronts. A man carried a large sack from his store and tossed it into the bin. A crunching sound followed a whirring noise as the sack vanished from the bin, presumably taken below ground. They had a garbage collection method much like Earth's.

"Great way to dispose of a body," I said. "They have surveillance cameras on most buildings. We should check the videos."

"Ah, there's the place." Dirk pointed to a small store just ahead of us.

A tiny blue and white sign announced Huber Electronics. We passed the store's garbage bin and approached the door. Without warning, the door flew open. Two giants armed with guns rushed out, followed by an ordinary-looking man wearing the usual black suit with a white shirt. The giants wore their own suits, brown tweeds, which I recognized as being akin to those worn by the giants who immigrated to Earth a few years ago. A flurry of action followed—almost too much to follow.

The man yelled. "Kill them. Toss them into the disposal."

My attention focused on him. I sensed no mind. Blam. Blam. The giants drew guns and fired at us. Dirk trailed as he consulted his wrist device, verifying we had the right store. Bishop stood behind me when the giants burst out of the door. The attack happened too fast. I had no time to react.

Bishop did. He grabbed my arm, jerking me backward. The first four shots should have struck my chest. Bishop's lightning reaction yanked me back so fast that only one bullet struck me. Unfortunately, it hit my head. Pain!

For a moment, I reeled from a gigantic wall of pain and blackness that forced me out of my body. Then out-of-body vision turned on. Bishop had me behind the garbage bin, his left hand applying pressure to my head wound. He tossed his gun to Dirk.

Dirk snatched it and dropped prone. He rolled out from behind the dumpster and fired. Twice. Then twice more. The giants hadn't expected his move or that we might be armed. Both dropped to the ground. Dirk fired two more times. I saw the human jerk first to his right and then left as the slugs slammed into his body. He didn't drop but ducked back inside the building.

"Molly!" Dirk yelled. He glanced my way and stopped shooting.

"Call for help," Bishop said. "I'm trying to save her life. Did you hit the man?"

"Got him twice, but he ducked inside." He used his phone. "Help! Molly's been shot. Send emergency medical help." He rattled off our location. Dirk looked over at Bishop's squatting body.

Bishop continued applying pressure to my head wound, though I couldn't sense it any longer. He injected me. Four syringes. No, five.

"What're you giving her?" Dirk asked.

"Trying to save her life. I got her out of the way of three bullets, but I wasn't fast enough to avoid the fourth. Sorry. Make sure he doesn't come after us."

"Already on it. I know I hit him twice. Shit! They're sending in an army," Dirk said.

The ID unit arrived along with emergency medical teams. No one could miss their sleek black ships. Instead of gawking onlookers, the appearance of the ID unit sent fear into many. Foot traffic on the street vanished!

"She should be dead," a man said.

"No, the regeneration ability of the mutation agent will kick in soon. Keep her on life support until it does," Bishop said. "Do it!"

I sensed confusion on the emergency medical team, but Bishop's command authority overrode their concerns. "Keep pressure on it," one said. "We'll get her into the vehicle."

"What happened here," barked a man in black, an ID agent.

I heard Dirk explaining the two-minute event. Had it even lasted two minutes? I doubted the attack lasted one minute.

"Good shooting. These giants are dead. You say you hit the man twice?"

"Once on each side. I saw his body jerk, but he ducked inside."

"Door's locked." He signaled, and two ID men in black rushed up with a battering ram. What happened after this I later learned from Dirk because the emergency vehicle shot off bringing me along with it.

Wham. The door splintered. Armed men in black rushed into the building. Told to stay outside, Dirk obeyed, content to examine the ground for blood splatter from his two hits on the man. He intended to collect a DNA sample. Instead, he found traces of a yellow-green fluid. Dirk took a sample and then headed inside after the ID men. Many "All clear's" echoed from above.

The main floor was one large empty room. An elevator and stairs led to upper floors. An ID agent came down the steps.

"Whoever was here has cleared out. No sign of him. In fact, this whole place is empty. You sure he ducked in here?"

"Yeah, but maybe it was that robot who killed Senior Ambassador Aaron Strawn, Bonita, and the two detectives. I know I shot him. There's this goo beside the door. Look there.

14

Traces here just inside the door. That's not any kind of blood I've ever seen."

"Say, didn't we order you not to investigate that rogue robot?"

Dirk's cheeks radiated, but he didn't reply.

"Okay, I have to take you to HQ for questioning, while we gather up surveillance. Mrs. Parkinson is probably dead. That's a nasty head wound. Should have listened to us. Leave investigations to us professionals."

Heck, I was a PI and so was Dirk, but that didn't matter to ID agents.

Dirk said they put him inside their windowless vehicle and took him to a secret location, likely underground. They grilled him. He explained what we did wasn't illegal, mostly. They released him when surveillance video backed up his story. Clever Dirk snagged a copy of the brief video of us walking up to the store and being shot. I later got to see myself being wounded. Dirk and I both marveled at the reactive speed of Bishop. I should have had been dead four times, not once. Thank the gods they didn't use blasters or disintegrators or laser guns. My body might not have survived those.

Once at the hospital, I doped off, drifting into the pain-filled blackness around my head. I still sensed voices, but soon even that awareness dimmed. I was in another mutation coma, which I later had to erase. Eve knew how to deliver Celeste's therapy, since Celeste had returned home a few years back, though Nikita could have assisted me, too.

I lost the entire month of June before I regained consciousness. The blackness gave way to a dull gray. My mouth felt like I'd swallowed sandpaper. I mumbled something.

"Mom's waking!" I heard Nikita's voice.

I tried to sit up, but my new arms failed to function. My chest felt heavy. An arm slipped behind my shoulders, lifting me. Dirk, Eve, Nikita, and Lara faced me, smiles on their faces.

Bishop stood behind them, expressionless as usual. One glance at my body told all. To save me, Bishop must have injected me with armless Galactic Doll mutation agent. I didn't complain. I was alive.

"What happened? A drink. My throat. Parched."

Nikita held a cup of ice water to my lips. "Slow, Mom. The doctor said take it easy. He's never seen anyone survive a head wound like yours. Bishop saved you. The robot got away. Again. Dirk's got a video of you getting shot. Pretty cool video, Mom. Bishop moved like lightning. Glad he had that mutation agent with him."

Eve interrupted her. "Molly, this time it took five adult doses to start the process. Each time, it's taking more agent to produce mutation. Your DNA is scrambled even more. It'll take Lara and me longer to invent your cures. Still, given enough time, I think we can do it again."

"Thanks. Everyone. Thanks. Did we get the rogue robot?"

Dirk said, "I shot it twice, but it only leaked hydraulic fluids. Bishop confirmed the chemistry as did the ID agents. It got away. Robot's impossibly fast moving. That store was only a delivery front for parts. ID agents are investigating where the robot shipped the brains. My guess is the man at Ostermann's warned the robot about us. I told the agents about him. If they found anything, they aren't sharing with us. Was told to stay away from an ID investigation or they'd kick us off-world."

The doctor entered, shooing everyone out, and tested my mental facilities and reflexes. "It's a miracle you're alive, Mrs. Parkinson. Cleo will help you dress. Then you can leave. If you experience any difficulties, please let the university clinic know. With head wounds, you may have side effects later on."

"Thanks. Hi, Cleo."

"Hi, Molly. Time to get dressed. We have larger blouses for you."

As the robot helper got me dressed, I felt a surge of helplessness again. I'd only had my arms back for a short while. Now, I missed them, particularly knowing I'd be without them for a long time, assuming Eve and Lara could ever find a cure for me. I felt sick at my stomach. My distorted feet forced me to wear tall heels even if I returned to Earth. Plus, as I stood up, my heavy boobs almost caused me to topple. And I needed a haircut. My raven locks, thicker and darker than before, touched my calves.

With Cleo at my side, I walked out of the hospital room, joining the others in the hallway. Together, we walked back to the campus. Me feeling vulnerable again.

Chapter 3 Vogelmenschen

July 1, 2368

"Do you really have telepathy?" "Aren't they awfully heavy?" Acquaintances at the university asked such questions. While I was in the mutation coma, word had spread across the campus. Fortunately, none asked if I felt helpless.

Once in my apartment, Eve said, "Bath, food, then therapy."

I chuckled. "I'm no longer cooking, but a bath sounds heavenly."

While Eve and Nikita helped me bathe and washed my hair, Lara fixed supper. Over dinner and as Cleo fed me, Dirk joined us and outlined details I didn't know.

He ended with, "Now we know much more about this robot. Unfortunately, it's not leading us anywhere. Can't tell where it came from, where it sent the brains to, or where the robot is today. Between us, their ID agents don't have a clue and are waiting for the robot to attack again.

"Bishop and I staked out the store several times. Spotted ID agents doing the same thing. The robot appeared to have abandoned that store."

Eve said, "Okay, everyone, take a walk. Molly needs her therapy session."

As I ran through the long incident, the pain from my withering arms exceeded the intense head pain from the bullet. Two hours later, I desensitized and confronted it, erasing the whole trauma. A slight feeling of helplessness lingered, and Eve promised to return in the morning to help me erase that, too.

When Eve let the others back into the apartment, Bishop asked, "Molly, did I do the right thing in giving you that mutation agent?"

"Absolutely. I can't thank you enough. I'm not ready to end this life and start over in a new baby body. Too many loose ends. Thanks. Don't get caught with the stuff."

Bishop grinned. Unless someone knew where the secret compartments were within his body and how to open them, no one could discover his stash of mutation agent.

"I see why you always want Bishop as your security guard," Dirk said. "He's unbelievably fast. One second he's pulling you from the line of fire, the next injecting mutation agent, and the next, tossing me his gun.

"He has great reflexes," I said.

"Another thing. If I take a bullet that should be fatal, do *not* use mutation agents on me. Let me die. That's the natural way of things."

"Okay. We promise we won't. But don't go getting yourself killed." I changed the subject. "Any luck tracking down the hydraulic fluid that leaked from the robot?"

"Not yet. It's a special blend not found on Cass-C. Bishop and I suspect our search will lead us back to Earth."

"Crap," I said. "I can't fire my Glock now. I wanted to exterminate that rogue robot myself."

With a straight face, Dirk said, "Leave something for the rest of us."

That cracked me up, but exacerbated my helpless feeling.

"Mom," Nikita said, "I'm sixteen and taking summer classes. By rights, I should live in the Single's Dorm with my classmates. I know you need me now you're armless again, but it's strange living in the Married Dorm."

Sixteen, looking twenty-one; and me, thirty-three looking twenty-one. These mutations stretched credulity. My daughter—so grown up. Too soon. I sighed.

"Yes, honey, you can move into the Single's Dorm. You're old enough. You'll be happier staying with other young students."

"Thanks, Mom." She gave me a big hug. "And if you need help, just call. I'll send you my new room number. This'll be loads of fun. Coming here has been the best thing for us." She bounded off to pack her things.

"They grow up," Dirk said. "Maybe too fast." We both chuckled.

***

At ten the next morning, I sat around the breakfast table sipping hot tea. After stopping by to help me with breakfast, Dirk departed for his morning summer school class. Nikita had moved into the Single's Dorm and was also in class. Because of my month-long coma, I missed June's enrollment and classes. If I wanted to continue my studies, I had to wait for the fall sign up. Celeste had long ago returned to Domes. I was alone, so alone, dependent upon Cleo to help me. Sure Bishop, Eve, and Lara were a call away. Still... That I felt helpless made matters worse. I'd only had my arms back a short while before I lost them again. Not fair. Not after all I'd done for others.

Someone knocked on my door and entered. The bird-woman maid entered. I flashed a forced smile. The Vogelmenschen entered our rooms when we weren't there and cleaned up for us. I'd forgotten these aliens existed. They excelled at not being visible to us.

Years ago, while returning for a left-behind laptop, I'd accidentally discovered them.

"Oh! Excuse me," I had said, watching the person dusting the furniture. She turned. I gasped.

From the rear, the person appeared almost human, except for her feet, which looked like those of a giant chicken. Instead of hands, the end of her arms sported giant claws, like

20

a crab or lobster, a dust cloth pinched between them. Instead of a mouth, she had a bird's beak extending six inches from her face. She couldn't talk, but I glimpsed her bird-like tongue. She had human eyes and hair and wore a black and white maid's outfit.

Shocked, I had Cleo retrieve my computer. As we left, I sensed a flow of sympathy towards me coming from her. Was that water in her eyes? Once headed to class, I had asked Cleo what she was.

"She is one of the Vogel people, hired to clean dorms and dry clean your clothes. Others maintain the lawn, but no one is supposed to see them. They can't talk."

I had accepted Cleo's explanation but wondered how she could even eat. Did she have to peck at food? What kind of food? She was the first bizarre alien life form I'd seen.

As she walked in, I understood why they hid themselves. The beak, located where her mouth should have been, reminded me of woodpeckers. That she managed cleaning duties with her giant lobster claws amazed me. She wore no shoes, not with such large, sprawling chicken feet. And she walked much like those I'd seen at a petting zoo when I was ten.

"Sorry, I can leave if you'd prefer," I said. "I've awakened from a long coma. Too late to start summer school. Nod if you want me to leave."

How could we communicate? I tried Federation Common and had success. On Cass-C where many aliens spoke disparate languages, Federation Common proved a vast improvement over the language translator units.

She shook her head and waddled up. Looking into my eyes, she gestured with a lobster claw, pointing to her head and then over to my head. She repeated the motions several times. Telepathy? That's what her gestures suggested.

"You want me to use my telepathy to pick up your thoughts?"

Her beak opened a little. She nodded vigorously. Otherwise, I couldn't read her bird-like face.

In Federation Common, I said, "Okay. Think your thoughts. I'll pick them up and tell them back to you to make sure I'm getting them right."

Again, she nodded.

I've never probed the mind of an alien or a Vogel person. I focused and made contact. Surprise. Her mind felt like any human mind.

"I'm seeing a bunch of humans. In a village."

She nodded energetically. The images moved, much like a movie. Masked men rushed into the village, shooting men and women. I watched as one woman screamed. A man shot her. I perceived waves of electricity flooding her body and darkness. Oh, crap. I had viewed the start of her trauma.

"Men came into your village." She nodded. "They shot people. Did you get shot too?" She nodded, reinforcing the truth of what I saw. I presumed there was more because she pointed to her head.

She woke up in a white room, strapped to a table. When she turned her head, she recognized others from her village tied down to other tables. Men wearing white laboratory gowns walked in. They spoke. She didn't know their language. She and others cried out, protested, and squirmed. The men injected their arms. Crap. I viewed another major trauma event happening. Her world turned black.

She awoke and tried to scream, but could make no sound. She brought her hands up to her face. I perceived the wave of terror flooding her essence. Lobster claws replaced her hands. A six-inch, narrow beak replaced her mouth, while her nose rested on the back of the beak. She tried standing, but saw giant chicken legs and feet had replaced hers. She screamed—silently.

22

Men came and dressed her. Others brought in a bowl of water and food that looked like compressed pellets. She watched as others like her tried eating and drinking. She mimicked their motions. Head down, peck a pellet, head up, swallow. Over and over. Later, she saw her face on a shiny steel wall. Her narrow, long tongue flicked wildly, but she made no sounds.

Before I could relay what I'd seen, the images changed. Men led her and many others onto a transport ship, which landed here in Hoffdorf. Ashton Soros met them and brought them to the university. At first, the arrivals spent hours learning Federation Common and performance of maid duties. The images ended.

"Wow. Let's see if I got this right. Someone kidnapped you and others in your village. They mutated you into this bird-like form and brought you here to work."

She nodded before slumping into a chair. I sensed enormous relief. Someone human now understood what had happened to her.

"Has this happened to others?" She nodded. "Many times?" More nods. "Is this continuing now?" Her head continued to bob.

"Dear God! I'll see what I can do about it. Will others like you share their stories? Can you take me to them? I don't know where you Vogel people live."

She nodded before glancing at a clock. I took the hint.

"Not the right time?"

Bingo.

"Well, I don't have any classes. I can wait until you think it's the right time. I should visit other Vogelmenschen here on campus and find out if this happened to them, too."

She returned to her cleaning duties. I tried not to stare. But fascinated by her appearance, I couldn't help but study how she accomplished things. The lobster claws handicapped her, reminding me of how Celeste, Eve, Randi, and Ted had done things without their hands after the Padella doctor cut them off.

Around four that afternoon, she motioned to the door.

"Time to leave?"

She nodded. Cleo trailed along behind me as I followed her to the elevators. In the sub-basement, we stopped at a door. Its sign read: Vogelmenschen Only. The woman waved a key card at me. I didn't spot any reader device, but as she approached, the door automatically opened. As Cleo and I followed her inside, I spotted more Vogelmenschen arriving on another elevator.

A hundred Vogelmenschen stopped their activities and stared at me. Boy, did I feel out of place. Several waved their claws at the door and me. I didn't need telepathy to sense how unwanted I was.

"I'm Molly Parkinson. I have telepathic abilities. She's shared what happened to her. I'd like to hear everyone's story. Have you all been kidnapped and mutated into these bodies?"

The hostilities evaporated. Many heads nodded. Several motioned for me to sit.   "Okay, anyone who wants to share their story with me, come sit in front of me. As I observe your story, I'll relate it aloud to make sure I'm getting it right. Perhaps I can do something about it. One at a time."

I chuckled. Dozens rushed to sit in front of me. I focused on the first person, a male.

"Recall the memories you want me to watch."

I felt the loss of my arms. I wanted to jot notes but didn't have my computer. I asked Cleo if it could remember some facts. After it said it could, I had it record the planets mentioned by these victims. As I repeated what I had witnessed, many others cried. Via telepathy, I observed hundreds of similar stories.

Kidnapped by men wearing masks, knocked unconscious by stun guns, taken to an unknown laboratory, and injected with something, they awoke to find their bodies mutated into this Vogel form. Men transported them to another place and taught them Federation Common. During the transition, they learned to dress and eat, which proved difficult. Men often became groundskeepers while women handled maid duties along with laundry actions for the fifty thousand university students. All showed me an image of meeting Ashton Soros when they arrived on campus.

Four stories shocked me even more. They were from Philadelphia taken during the terrorist mutation attacks. I'd long known after one attack a hundred victims went missing out of the thousands of comatose people. Now, I'd found a few.

"Everyone, thank you. I promise you I will investigate and stop this from happening to others. I'll see if they can restore your bodies."

Hundreds of bird heads nodded. I walked to the door but had to wait for Cleo to come to open it for me. Damn, what a rotten time to be handicapped again.

When I entered my apartment, I smelled supper. Dirk called out, "About time. I was about to call campus security. Wanted: abducted telepath. Oh, what's happened?"

My solemn face must have registered.

"Dear God! I've stumbled into the worst humanitarian crisis ever. Dish out supper, and I'll tell you a horror story. Hundreds of them."

With dinner done, I had Cleo repeat the stored names of the Vogelmenschen home worlds. Dirk wrote them down for us and stored them in our computers.

"Crap. Hundreds really did go missing from those terrorist genetic mutation attacks. I thought the GMed people miscounted the victims. Someone snuck in there and kidnapped them while they were in mutation comas? Wow. Instead of selling them as telepaths, they re-mutated them into alien Vogel creatures. Unreal. I had no idea, Molly."

"Hey, I didn't either. I never had time to search for those missing people. Just trying to deal with the thousands of victims as they woke up to find their bodies like mine is now took everything I had. Dirk, courses can wait. We've got to put an end to this horror. Let's put them out of business."

"Count me in. Probably should talk to Ashton tomorrow."

"Talk to Ashton about what?" Eve asked.

Eve had arrived to give me another therapy session. I needed erasure of my recurring surges of helplessness. It had struck again while I was handling the Vogelmenschen. Yeah, I know such is a natural response from losing one's arms, but...

"Sit. You will not believe what I discovered today!"

While Dirk brewed tea, I related what I'd discovered.

"Four came from Philadelphia, taken during the terrorist attack that mutated thousands."

"The missing hundred are real? What's the next step? Get DNA samples. Then Lara and I can determine if there's any way to restore their bodies. Crap. I'm not heading home soon. Genetic engineering has gone off the rails big time," Eve said. "But first, your session."

"Maybe we should wait and try catching Ashton tonight."

"Nope. We need you in top form. Excuse us, Dirk. We'll take our tea and get started."

She ran me through the recent times I'd had an uncomfortable feeling of helplessness. These light incidents didn't erase. I knew something lay behind it; that feeling swamped me. Eve asked for an earlier similar incident. Boom. I ran smack into it.

"I think it happened four hundred years ago. I'm climbing a tree. I lose my balance. I fall. Yeeoh. I break both arms—like really bad. I lay there trying hard not to move a muscle. The pain. I pass out. I wake up in the hospital. They

26

have me in a full upper-body cast. Helpless. I can't move anything above my waist. My nose itches. I'm helpless to scratch my nose. Someone tells me I'll be in this cast for months. I can't imagine surviving that long being this helpless."

She had me go over it several more times as I filled in details and erased the intense pain.

"Oh! The doctor says, 'You'll be helpless for at least two months. Then you'll be okay.' Only I wasn't okay. When the casts came off, my arms were weak and sore. Can't hold a fork. Oh crap! Since I wasn't okay and didn't think I'd ever be okay, I swallowed a whole bottle of painkiller pills. Wow! That's why I get edgy when I feel helpless. I don't want to die. Feeling helpless equals dying. Well, that's a stupid decision." I laughed and Eve ended the session.

When we joined Dirk in the kitchenette, he had a fresh pot of tea waiting. While Cleo assisted me, he showed us a sketch he'd made.

"I plotted the approximate locations of the worlds the kidnapped people came from. Unreal. They're all over the known Federation but none from the Cass-C area. I had thought they'd all come from one locale but nope. What's wild is there are over a thousand worlds or empires in the Federation of Planets. Some empires contain dozens of worlds. Plus, there are about two hundred worlds on the 'Let Them Develop' list. You know, the ones whose civilization is in a Stone, Bronze, or Iron Age. Even some that are industrializing—pre-spaceflight civilizations on the watch list."

"Any pattern?"

"The victims come from space-faring civilizations. None come from the Let Them Develop list," Dirk said. "Random places, including Earth."

Eve said, "Helps prevent discovery of how vast the number of missing people is. Age when they were abducted?"

"Sorry," I said. "I was floored with what I saw that I didn't pay attention to that detail. Most seemed young though. Probably in their twenties. No kids, teens, or older folks."

Chapter 4 An Explanation

The next morning, Dirk and I sat in Ashton's waiting room, our feet tapping. He had agreed to meet us at ten. Ashton rushed in at 10:20 out of breath.

"Sorry. Bit late. Come in. Kaffe, tea, water? Oh, Cleo's not with you. Is he malfunctioning?"

"Yes, I left him behind," I said. "We're fine. We need to talk about the Vogelmenschen."

He chuckled. "Ah, the Vogelmenschen. Did one fail to keep itself hidden from you? Rather shocking visual appearance. They are taught to understand Federation Common. I trust one didn't harm you or cause a problem. They haven't harmed you?"

"No. Nothing like that. What do you know about them?" I asked. First, establish what he knows. My PI skills kicked into gear.

"Oh, I hire them. Long story. Years ago, Soros University needed to save credits. We'd been too generous helping others. Anyway, Jensen Temps approached me with a proposition. He had several aliens needing employment. 'Good workers. Can't make trouble.' He showed me an image of a Vogel. Frankly, I was shocked. I'd not seen many true alien life forms.

"Anyway, he said they'd work for half what I paid locals for domestic duties and grounds work. I agreed. He was right. Never had more dependable workers. They saved the university tons of credits. I've put the savings toward supporting many handicapped people, including those sixteen hundred from Earth.

"They've worked out well. I'll continue hiring Vogelmenschen, replacing higher paid local workers. Running a university this large requires devising ways to cut expenses. We keep their visibility to a minimum. You drop your dirty clothes down the laundry chute. Volgelmenschens launder them for you and return them while you're scheduled for class. They have copies of your schedule.

"Plus, the men tend to the campus greenery and gardens at night, often when the automated weather control activates the rains. Mind you, I still keep handymen around for daytime emergencies, like plugged toilets or defective power storage cells. Did you know the roofs of our campus buildings are solar power producers? Self-sufficient we are.

"Vogelmenschen are my best workers, despite their handicaps. Their food preparation proved interesting. They peck food like birds. Our nutritionists formulated a meal that meets their dietary needs. They mix the prepared ingredients and compress it into pellet form. Clever. Similar to meals provided for those on long-duration spaceflights. I believe your Sol Empire makes stuff like it. Blue goo? Our pellets make it easier for the birds to eat. Does that satisfy your curiosity? I've ordered another two dozen Vogel maids for the fall term. We're accepting a few more students."

While he talked, I sensed his mind. Ashton wasn't lying. Time for the bombshell.

"As everyone knows, my latest mutation gave me telepathic ability. Word of that spread to the Vogelmenschen. The woman who cleans my apartment insisted I read her mind. She wanted someone to know what happened to her."

"Oh dear lord. She wasn't sexually assaulted was she? I've always worried rowdy young men would do that. They can't tell us if that happens, because Vogelmenschen can't communicate."

"No. It's much worse. She was a normal human woman. Masked men came to her village, used stun guns on them, and whisked them off-world. There, inside a laboratory, men in

30

white gowns injected them with a mutation agent. She woke from a coma to find her body as it now is. They moved the mutated people to another facility, where they gained an understanding Federation Common, learned to dress and feed themselves, and taught the housekeeping skills Soros University needed."

The more I said, the whiter Ashton's face became.

"I interviewed over a hundred in their restricted living area in the sub-basement. Imagine my shock when four of them revealed themselves as four of the missing terrorist attack victims from Philadelphia, a large Earth city. Dirk plotted the worlds on which they lived. All are space-faring worlds, spread out over half the galaxy, from as far out as Earth to almost Cass-C, which is near the center of the Milky Way."

"This—this can't be happening! On my watch. Oh lordy. We thought they were just a strange alien race. Human? Good lord. Vogelmenschen also work as maids and gardeners for wealthy aristocrats. I must get the ID involved. Don't go anywhere. This has never happened. Stay put. Help yourselves to whatever."

He motioned toward drinks in a well-stocked cabinet as he raced out of his office, taking out his phone as he ran.

Dirk said, "I'll make us tea. He was telling the truth?"

"Did you see the color fade from his face?"

Dirk chuckled. "For a moment I thought he might faint."

"I'm glad the university isn't to blame. I love this place. I don't think I could continue here if they were. Then again, Ashton and Professor Heli re-mutated the sixteen hundred on Domes and brought them here. At first, I believed that treachery. The way it's turned out, it isn't black and white."

"Have to agree with you. I respect this institution. What's our next move? If it was me, I'd pay a visit to the company that Ashton contracts these victims from. Work backward from there. Love to get my hands on those genetic engineers."

I laughed. "Of all the courses I've taken, genetic engineering isn't one. Somehow, I can't confront that subject. Don't know how Eve and Lara do what they do. Darn. I should've brought Cleo."

Dirk prepared our tea, but considering I had no hands, he carried the cup to me and added a straw. "Hope the straw doesn't melt."

We chuckled. Before we finished our tea, Ashton returned with two ID agents, dressed in their signature, attention-grabbing black suits. Both were tall, burly men with chiseled features that exuded a zero tolerance for disobedience to their wills.

Ashton said, "These are ID agents Jarvis Gerlach and Eric Von Klausburg. I've told them what you've told me."

Agent Gerlach glared at me. "Oh, it *is* you again." He pointed his index finger at me before turning to his partner. "Klausburg, it's those amateurs I told you about. Gotta meddle in everything, don't you? What's with these tall tales you've been telling Mr. Soros?"

"It's simple," I said. Their condescension irked me. "Perhaps it's too simple for you gentlemen to grasp—with such limited comprehension. But these Vogelmenschen were once humans. Men kidnapped them, transported them to a laboratory where others injected them with a mutation agent that turned their bodies into these bird-like creatures. After being taught to understand Federation Common, someone hired them out as maids and groundsmen here at Soros. Is that simple enough for you?"

Agent Von Klausburg turned to Agent Gerlach and said, "Have you heard one of these Vogelmenschen say that? I can't recall ever hearing any bird creature making any noise at all. They aren't human."

32

Both men chuckled. Agent Gerlach said, "Next, she'll be telling us she used telepathy on them." He faced us. "Look. Stop meddling in things you know nothing about. Leave investigations to the ID. If you don't, well..." With one finger, he swiped a line across his neck making a cutting noise. "Get the picture?"

"Dirk, I didn't realize they hired morons in the Intelligence Division. I guess ID stands for Idiots Division. You don't want to know details of the most monstrous crimes I've ever heard of?"

"Leave crime solving to the professionals. We have warned you for the last time. Go home," Agent Gerlach barked. The two pivoted and marched out.

"Come on," I said, following them. But I paused for Dirk to catch up since I couldn't open the damned door.

Dirk said nothing during our walk to my apartment. Neither did I.

Once inside, he said, "I wish we had our own transport. We could follow up on our own today. Since I look like a man again, I can talk to members of the Galaxy Detective Squad and see if they'll lend a ship or take the lead. Some of these victims came from Earth. They'd have jurisdiction because of that."

"That's a good idea." I suggested, "While you're at it, see if you can get your old position back. Anyway, Ashton said he gets them from ABC Shipping on Delius-C. We could take a commercial transport and visit that company. Based on what we discover, take another flight if necessary. But I'd feel better if we had our own ship. I could see if the Friendship is available." The Friendship was my billionaire sister's transport ship.

Dirk said, "Good idea. Take a commercial flight and check this first lead. I'd bet anything whoever Ashton is dealing with, they only teach the Vogelmenschen Federation Common and help them adjust to their handicaps. They think their work is a humanitarian endeavor. They might lead us to the actual culprits. This chould be a case for our Galaxy Detective Squad. Let me get a hold of my old boss. See what he says. With luck, they'll meet us on Delius-C at this ABC Shipping and take on the case. Besides, they have the big guns, not puny Glocks. I think we'll need blasters before this is done."

"Sounds like a plan. Check if they're interested in the case. If they aren't, I'll rent a transport or take a commercial flight. It shouldn't take long to track these fiends," I said.

The next day, Dirk sent a long-distance communication to his former fellow investigators. The comm delay across half the galaxy was hours long. Glad I didn't have that task, I focused on checking transport rental costs and commercial flights.

Rentals: prohibitively expensive. I booked a flight on a commercial liner for the three of us. One-way. Five hundred credits each.

That settled, I had Cleo dig out my Earth apparel from duffle bags. I'd forgotten how much I'd loved my sister's gown designs. The satin dress fitted tightly around my shoulders, leaving no doubt what I lacked, but showcasing my curves. Leslie had style.

"Cleo, we're taking a trip. I want to wear my Earth-style clothes."

"I don't know how to dress you in them." After a pause, it said, "I can learn."

We spent the next two hours practicing. Cleo found dealing with the back zippers easier than the buttons on the school blouse. Once I slipped on my old pumps, I regained the use of my feet and toes. Imagine my surprise when I realized how much I missed doing things myself and not depending on Cleo and others. I laughed for minutes over that realization.

Bishop dropped by. I explained what had transpired with Ashton and the ID agents. He asked, "We're going to Delius-C?"

"Yes. I've ordered three tickets. Leaves tomorrow."

"Excellent. What if Ashton is more involved than he's admitted? We could be walking into a trap."

"Too many what if's, Bishop."

"True. Have you considered motivation? Why would any genetic engineer create this bird-like mutation? For what purpose?"

"Darn good question. It's been bothering me ever since I found out the Vogelmenschen are mutated humans. There's nothing beneficial in this mutation. They're barely able to function. I doubt they could make their own food. The only aspect that makes any sense is they are low-wage workers. Normal maids and grounds keepers are low-paying, unskilled jobs on Earth. Here, the university pays the Vogelmenschen about half what they'd pay humans for the work. That's the only benefit I see. Hardly a reason to invent this mutation."

"I concur with that calculation. What if the Vogelmenschen isn't the only mutation these engineers have created?"

"I see where you're heading. Excellent point. If someone can mutate a human body into having chicken feet, lobster claws, and bird beaks, what else have they engineered? And why?"

"They'd market the other mutations, too. Is there an underground market for mutations?" Bishop asked.

With a straight face, I said, "Excuse me, sir. Could I have the catalog of mutations that are available? I'd like to choose the best one for my needs."

Then I roared with laughter. Bishop smiled.

It said, "Molly, that's not farfetched. Suppose these genetic engineers are black-marketing mutations. They'd need a product catalog and sales personnel. Might I suggest you pretend you're in the market for mutated personnel when we arrive on Delius-C. See if you can acquire a catalog. Maybe meet with a salesperson."

"Brilliant, Bishop! I'll bet anything making Vogelmenschen is not the focus of these people. What's that ancient saying?"

Bishop said, "Tip of the iceberg."

Chapter 5 A Slight Problem

Seven reported to Six via his scrambled comm line. "Yes, Ashton Soros alerted the ID about the Vogelmenschen's discovery."

Six asked, "Who found out?"

"That pesky PI from Earth. Mrs. Molly Parkinson. Her security guard kept her alive when someone shot her in the head. Mutation agents at work. She's acquired telepathy. Again. Ashton assured us his new mutation removed that ability, so we allowed her attendance at Soros. It did on the other sixteen hundred. Now she has given the Vogelmenschen voice with that ability."

"Be precise. What is she aware of? Does she suspect Ashton?" Six asked.

"That they were once humans, kidnapped, mutated, taught Fed Common, and given to Ashton and the university. The whole damned story."

"How unfortunate. Ashton?"

"He's convinced he's outplayed her, and Parkinson doesn't suspect a thing. That he thought he was aiding them by giving them jobs. But he had to reveal he picks them up from ABC Shipping."

"Good and bad. Okay, what about the ID?"

Seven said, "They sent two agents to get her story. I gave them little choice. We must protect Ashton's role. They rebuffed her and demanded she stop interfering in their investigations. While they didn't resort to physical violence, they warned her they would if she continued. She got the message."

"All right. For appearances, we'll have the ID poke around a little. Alert our agent in Kistna. He's to take whatever action he thinks required if the ID agents get too carried away with this," Six said. "I talked to Five. He doesn't want this escalating. Hell to pay if One gets involved."

"If he does, we're as good as dead. Okay, but what about the Parkinson woman?" Seven asked.

"For now, have ID watch her. She's darn near helpless. Five doesn't think she's a real threat. Still, watch her."

"All right. I hope One hasn't heard about this!"

Six chuckled. "I'm certain he'll have our butts if this venture is exposed. He's focused on our enemy, the Imperium, and they're continuing expansion."

"Are they sticking to their half of the galaxy?" Seven asked. "I haven't heard much."

"Neither have I. Don't worry about the Imperium. It's above our pay grade." Both men laughed.

***

The ID Commander growled. "More shit's hitting the deck. Seven called. You know how I *hate* such calls. It's that infernal Parkinson woman again. Because of that rogue robot attack, her telepathy's restored. Now you're telling me she's uncovered the source of the university's Vogelmenschen."

"Commander, we told her to stop," ID Agent Gerlach said.

"Aye, threatened her," Agent Von Klausburg said. "I think she got the message. They've not done any further investigation into the rogue robot mess. I'm sure she'll leave this alone."

The Commander said, "Seven wants her tailed. He doesn't trust her. Hell, a telepath wandering the streets of Hoffdorf equals major trouble for everyone. No secret is safe with that woman around."

"Want us to off her?" Agent Gerlach asked.

"I wish. But no. That'd raise ten times more problems. Worse, she'd probably survive by being re-mutated. Anyone

38

else would prefer death, but not Parkinson. Prefers helplessness. I'll assign a clandestine observer to her. Seven's orders. But he wants the pretense of an investigation into this Vogelmenschen situation. Ashton and his big mouth."

"Has he told her the whole story?" Agent Von Klausburg asked.

"No, just verified what she had already discovered via telepathy. Ashton's damn good at psych stuff. He can fool anyone. I've tried recruiting him a dozen times."

The men laughed. Just then, the recruit ID Agent Wanda Hammerstein walked into the room. She glanced at the two senior agents before saluting the Commander.

"You wanted to see me, sir?" she asked, her mellow alto voice forming a sharp contrast to the men's.

"Yes, agent. Here's the assignment. That Parkinson woman and her telepathy has created a huge problem for Seven. She's discovered the secret of the Vogelmenschen—that they're humans—victims who were mutated."

"I didn't know that," she said, frowning.

The Commander said, "Precisely. Seven has ordered me to conduct a follow-up investigation, but do *not* dig too deep. Just go through the initial motions with this. Then we can say we're on the case. Ordinarily, we wouldn't even bother, but that fool Ashton revealed he's been picking up the new Vogelmenschen from ABC Shipping on Deluis-C."

The two agents groaned while Wanda frowned and looked confused.

"So," the Commander continued, "I want you three to go to Delius-C and question ABC Shipping. Lightly. Lightly, mind you. We don't want to raise suspicions. But we want to say we checked out that lead. Got it? Seven wants the matter ended there."

He glared at Agent Hammerstein. "Are you ready for real fieldwork?"

"Yes, sir!" she saluted.

Women didn't get many actual assignments within the Intelligence Division. Most worked at menial positions. Rarely did one achieve Agent status. Wanda had worked harder than the men for the last four years, leaving the Commander no choice but to acknowledge her status as a full field agent. But that had been as far as it'd gone. Month after month, she'd watched men going off on assignments. But she received only documentation duties, the last being documenting the robot attack on Mrs. Parkinson.

"We gotta take her?" asked Agent Gerlach.

The Commander glared at him. "If I must have a bad day, then you do, too. Dismissed."

After the Commander left them, the men relaxed. "Whew," Agent Jarvis Gerlach said. "He had me worried there. Don't worry, Wanda; we'll keep you safe. This shouldn't be a dangerous mission. Now that rogue robot one—that's an entirely different matter. Thanks for running the 3d Tracer on the scene for us. Haven't had the chance to say so."

"I'll watch your backs. But what's this about the Vogelmenschen, anyway? They're just strange mutated bird people," she asked.

Agent Eric Von Klausburg said, "You don't know? Well, they're imported from an outfit on Delius-C. Rumor is they were humans that got mutated."

"Why aren't we supposed to do a complete investigation?" Wanda asked. "Impressive that Seven calls our Commander directly."

Eric shrugged. "Probably because the Imperium is a huge threat to the Federation. Priorities. That'd be my guess. And yeah, I suspect Seven knows the Commander."

"Interesting. But has anyone ever met any of the ruling seven?" she asked.

Jarvis said, "I heard an agent once did, and they found his body the next day. From the Commander's hints, none of the seven knows any of the others. Safer that way. If someone gets to Seven, he can't be tortured into revealing Six or any of those above him."

"Hey, once One called the ID Director. Shit hit the pedals after that."

"Oh, yeah? Tells us about that one," Jarvis insisted. "We can't get a transport for three days. Time to kill."

"Please, tell us," Wanda said.

"Well, it's like this..."

Chapter 6 Chance Meeting

My yellow satin gown encased my shoulders, broadcasting my lack of arms. After six long years, I enjoyed the freedom of attending my own needs using my feet and toes. Though I'd taught thousands of mutation victims independent living, a taste of Cleo's help made a burden out of the same self-care techniques I'd taught others. After a taste of how Cleo could help me, I had moved here six years ago.

On this trip, Cleo accompanied me to aid me in difficult tasks such as eating in the deep space transport's cramped seats.

The Wandering Soul could carry a hundred passengers, but the line of waiting passengers departing the spaceport nearest Soros University suggested half that number. Bishop and Dirk carried my duffle bag while I handled the tickets. I'd made the reservations electronically and had my phone with the receipt in one of my concealed dress pockets. The line moved much like a snail.

When we reached the front of the line, the attendant looked up and gaped at me.

"One second. I have my receipt here," I said. "Three plus my robot assistant." Cleo retrieved my phone and displayed my receipt to the attendant.

"The baggage weight limit is..." She rattled off. The guys weighed our bags and Cleo. We made the weight limit, though had we gone over, buying a ticket for Cleo would have been cheaper than paying for the extra weight.

Each side of the main aisle held three seats. Cleo guided us to our seats before storing my phone in my dress pocket. A bronzed-skinned young woman sat by the window. I sat next to her and had Cleo take the aisle seat.

"Wow! Do you need any help?" she asked. "Rina Pappas."

"Hi, Rina. Molly Parkinson. My robot assistant Cleo. My friend Dirk and my security guard." I motioned to them with my head. "We're heading to Delius-C."

"Same here. Say, are you the student who just got telepathic abilities? I attend Soros U. Rumors."

I smiled. "Yes, but don't worry about it. I'm not spying on anyone. Dirk and I have spent the last six years at Soros U. My daughter is in summer school."

"Glad to meet you. My degree is in a new field: astro-history, with minors in astro-chemistry and linguistics. I'm from Kalak, Zeta Minori-D. That's in the Sagittarius Arm. What's your major?"

I laughed. "To be honest, a little of everything. Space navigation, space piloting, history, politics, math, physics, and a dab of astronomy. I study what interests me."

She had coal black hair, shoulder length, and charming black eyes. She wore the Soros University white blouse and black skirt but had changed into sensible black shoes from the high heels women wore. Something about her impressed me.

Rina smiled. "Ah, a professional student. Students go to the university to become—fill in the blank—and get a job. Historically, that is. I'm just starting fieldwork for my doctorate. Haven't you ever wondered why many worlds in the Federation have humans like us? As opposed to say the Third Invaders and the ugly Sixth Invaders?"

"Yes, I have wondered."

"What's more interesting is the Federation of Planets has one thousand three hundred nine worlds in it. Many of these are members of various smaller empires, like the Varouna Empire and their Empress Kalindi Amandani on Indrani-C."

"Or our own Sol Empire," I said. "I've met Empress Amandani. She's quite a person."

"You have? Wow! Tell me all about her. She's a human being, isn't she?" Rina asked.

We lifted off, interrupting our conversation for a minute. She stared out the viewport as Cass-C shrunk below us. Then, heavy metal covers slipped down, encasing the sides of the transport and protecting the viewport from space junk.

I told her about my visit to Indrani-C. She seemed eager to hear about the powerful empress. That's when I remembered what Empress Kalindi Amandani had told me. She insisted I had to be the empress of the Sol Empire—that I alone could ensure its survival. She'd said empires are built upon a hierarchical bureaucracy, often corporations. Yet in a crisis, one individual must lead. Since Earth's corporate leaders dismissed me from my posts, I ignored her advice. Until now, I'd forgotten what she'd told me.

"Oh, I was telling you about my thesis research project. The Federation protects almost two thousand more worlds. Their people have primitive cultures, like those of a Bronze or Iron Age. We have representatives assisting those in more modern civilizations, guiding them towards an eventual space-faring society. Non-humans live on some of these worlds. About ten percent are alien species, like the snake people of Scythian-B. Another twenty percent are human-derivatives, like the gill breathers of Papillon-D, who almost pass as humans, and even the Third Invaders.

"What's amazing is that we classify seventy percent as Homo sapiens. True, wild skin color variations abound, such as your unusually white skin. Some faces are flatter than others. Little differences, but all can interbreed with each other."

"I've often wondered," I said, "about finding many humans on these worlds."

"Exactly. Astro-chemistry plays a role. Did you know most of the complex organic molecules in space are carbon-based? You don't find silicon forming these kinds of molecules. One would expect developing life forms on worlds to be carbon-based and use these original kinds of organic sugars in their life cycles. It's not surprising to find humanoid life predominating. But—here's the critical point—why are they so close that they can interbreed? The same Homo sapiens species? Now that's the zillion credit question."

"I've wondered that, too," I said.

Rina grinned, "But in academia, no one cares. They've good theories of planetary development worked out. Zillions of protoplanets. Heck, it's rare that a star doesn't have planets. But habitable planets with water and air takes billions of years to evolve from a coalesced mass. Various processes create an atmosphere of oxygen and oceans of water. Astronomers visit and document these processes on newly developing worlds.

"But what I want to know is why are seventy percent of the space-faring worlds populated by us? Home sapiens."

"Your plan?" I asked. Honestly, Rina intrigued me.

"That's the beauty of astro-history. Each world has had its own unique development, documented by its inhabitants in local history books. Most are available as electronic docs. I'm gathering the most comprehensive history books from these thousand plus worlds. I have good data for about half of them. I'm on a quest to discover more. For example, I know Delius-C has a large depository of ancient history volumes from many worlds in the Sagittarius arm. I'm headed to Dropock, their capital city, to see how many more I can get. Then, it's on to Kristna, Kali-D. It houses a huge archive. I'll pay a short visit to my father; my folks divorced when I was little. Anyway, once I see what holes I can fill from these two, then I'll head to other worlds in the Federation."

"Boy, you've got quite a project. The language barrier—you'll have to be able to read all those docs, too," I said.

"That's where my linguistics training becomes useful."
Rina sighed. "At least a couple years of reading before I see if
I've found anything. I'm making a 'settled' timeline. Here's
what I've got going thus far."

She pulled her microcomputer from her bag. A 3d holo
display appeared in front of us. The spiral arms with their gas
and dust lanes looked spectacular. Various colored dots
popped up.

"I've color-coded the known dates. Blue dots represent
civilizations going back only a few thousand years. At the other
end are the red dots whose civilizations go back thirty
thousand years. The other colors represent gradients in
between these two extremes. Homo forms go back much
further in time.

"At first, I thought astro-archeological data, such as
when the local Stone Age began, the local Iron Age started,
initial agriculture, first written language, and similar events,
held the answers I sought. However, those early developments
are poorly documented in histories. And not all space-faring
worlds went through such evolutions. I've settled on their first
space explorations because they are well-defined, well-
documented points in world histories."

"I think I see a pattern in the dots. There's a lot of red
there in the outer arms." I tried pointing to what I saw but
couldn't. "Lots of blue closer to the inner arms."

She grinned. "You see it, too! Yes, it's suggestive that
our ancestors migrated towards the inner arms from the outer
arms. Isn't that just intriguing? Examining the past."

"Sure is."

"Oh, do you need help?" Rina asked.

A hostess arrived with in-flight snacks.

"No. Cleo assists me."

As we dined, she said, "Must be awful not having arms.
I can't imagine living without mine. Soros University is in the

forefront helping those with physical challenges. My roommate has a mechanical leg, but unless you listen carefully for its motor's whir, you'd never know."

I found Rina charming and intellectually stimulating. We continued chatted all the way to Delius-C. Dirk pointed out that ABC Shipping was also in Dropock.

***

"Eoo! It stinks!" Rina covered her nose as we stepped out of the transport.

We landed at Dropock, Delius-C, around local noon. A layer of smog draped the city. Acrid fumes burned my nasal cavities. Even Dirk covered his nose, but I had no choice but endure it. After a short tarmac walk, we entered the main terminal and went through their customs office. Here, someone overdid the pot-pourri; an over-sweet, unpleasant odor attacked our noses.

"We need to visit ABC Shipping," I said to the Entry Information Officer.

She suggested we rent a wheeler for a hundred credits a day and pointed us toward the rental section. We each signed an open-ended contract for a wheeler. The salesperson handed Dirk the wireless key. "Its number is visible on the vehicle's hood. Next..."

"It's a car!" I declared when we stepped outside to the wheeler lot. "Well, sort of." I still owned my grandfather's tiny electric car, but in Chicago, there were few places left I could drive it.

The automatic wheelers used fossil fuels and didn't even have a steering wheel. Dirk sat up front along with Bishop, and they entered our destination via a dashboard nav system. After experimentation, Bishop activated his language translator unit and solved the mystery. It converted English into the local language. The nav system only needed the name of the company before it responded.

The wheeler's computer said, "Thirty minutes to your destination. Press Start when ready; Abort to change destinations."

Rina waved at us. From her smile, I guessed she'd gotten her wheeler ready to go. We'd exchanged contact numbers and promised to visit when we could. While I wanted to wave, I watched her wheeler drive off, puffing a cloud of blue smoke from a pipe in its rear.

Our wheeler activated with a dull roar, belching similar blue smoke behind us. We pulled out onto a large avenue, filled with wheelers. Many were very large with attached huge boxes. Bishop pointed out they called these wheeler-trucks. He'd seen the same road ad sign I did.

Dirk said, "This place is unbelievably dirty! Crudest space-faring world ever."

"And smelly!" I said.

Skyscrapers with many parking decks holding countless wheelers drifted by. My nose stopped registering the stench, but my sinuses throbbed. Here and there, giant cones rose atop the buildings. Gray smoke billowed from them and descended onto the city, assuring a steady smog supply.

The wheeler pulled into the visitor's lot of ABC Shipping. The company's one-story warehouse covered at least forty acres. Wheeler-trucks parked in long rows lined the sides with a giant door at each stall. Later we learned they'd expanded at the back, adding another twenty acres under roofs.

Ten minutes later, a receptionist led us into the CEO's office. From the moment we entered the double set of entrance chambers, the air cleared. Inside, proper humidity and temperature replaced the putrid air. Like magic, my nose discomfort cleared up. The polished linoleum reflected outside light through the only windows of the building. My heels clicked, announcing our arrival.

A plump man wearing a typical black business suit rose from his desk. Papers littered his desk. I presumed we interrupted him.

The receptionist said, "CEO Cronus. This is a party from Hoffdorf, Cass-C." She turned and left us.

"Well, I'll be! You must be one of those armless Galactic Sex Dolls! Welcome to ABC Shipping. I never dreamed a Galactic Doll would visit our company. Please, have a seat. Do you need any help?"

The man nearly fell over his feet trying to please me. Hadn't he seen a shapely woman before?

"I'm Mrs. Molly Parkinson. Yes, I'm one. From Earth, Sol Empire, originally. My friend, Dirk Bennet, and my security guard, Bishop."

"Cronus. Just call me Cronus. Jaffe? Tea? Water?"

"We're fine. I'm here to talk about the Vogelmenschen you send to Soros University, Cass-C."

"Ah, the bird people. Yes, they make excellent menial workers. That's what Ashton Soros tells me."

"Do you realize they are mutated humans? But masked men kidnapped them, took them off-world to a laboratory where they transformed them into their present bird-like forms, and then sold them into slavery." Ought to be up front about our visit.

"This a jest, a joke? Well, it isn't funny," he said, sitting back down and glaring at me.

"No joke. I'm a telepath. I interviewed hundreds at Soros University. Every one of them told me a similar story."

"But they can't speak or make any sounds. They have little control over those large claws. We gave up trying to teach them to write. They couldn't have told you that."

"Not in words, but in mental images in their minds. Telepathy. I read minds."

"Wait. Are you saying you are one of those armless telepath Galactic Dolls from the Sol Empire? One of those the

Federation has tried to prevent from spreading to other worlds?"

"By stopping the spread of those mutation agents. Not us people." I corrected him.

"It's not that I don't believe you, Mrs. Parkinson, but everyone knows there's no known technology capable of turning a human into a bird-like creature."

"Sorry to burst your bubble, Cronus, but someone knows how and is doing it. You are guilty of trafficking in these mutants—probably carries a lesser penalty than the fiends who kidnapped and mutated them."

"But—but I had no idea. I thought myself a humanitarian. Honest. Look there," he pointed to a large plaque behind him. "I got a Delius-C award for humanitarian of the year two years ago for all the work we've done on behalf of these bird people.

"From time to time, Mr. Naraka Salad of Kistna, Kali-D sends our company new bird people they've discovered. Rescued from terrible calamities I'm told. We do our best to feed, clothe, and teach them an understanding of Federation Common. Once I'm satisfied they can survive on their own, I find positions for them. It's true. Mr. Soros takes every one that comes our way, providing them gainful employment, housing, food, and credits for their work. I've assisted in over a thousand bird people recoveries. That's why they gave me that award. I'm not making any profit on these people. Mr. Soros covers the expenses incurred in prepping them for survival.

"If you like, I can show you our facilities. My staff is working with six bird people right now. Come. I'll show you. We're helping these poor people."

As we followed him, his muscles appeared to relax.

"Say, since you are one of those Galactic Dolls, perhaps you could show them your humanity."

"What do you mean?" I asked, growing curious. I'd detected no lies. His humane treatment jived with what the Vogelmenschen had shown me.

"Three children came with this latest batch of bird people from Kali-D. I'm tasked with finding them proper homes. Apparently, their parents died. They're unable to speak, and no one's found any living relatives. They brought them here, because they recognize we are good at helping the less fortunate."

"I didn't know bird people could have children," I said.

"They told me their mother was an armless Galactic Sex Doll and their bodies would mature into that, too. Without arms and unable to speak, we haven't any idea what we can do for them. I hoped Mr. Soros would take them on his next visit. His university accepts handicapped students. Between you and me, I'm not too hopeful, since they can't speak. I've no idea how they can survive on their own. Since you're like them, perhaps you could take them with you and help them. But I've no idea how anyone can help them. Ah, here we are."

We stood outside an inner wall with one-way mirrors and watched workers teaching six bird people to read simple Federation Common. Over in one corner, three young children sat staring at the floor. They wore sack-like clothing but looked otherwise clean.

"As you can see," Cronus said, "we're doing our best for the bird people. We know nothing about their origin. We want them to survive. The children are in the corner. Please, if you have any way to help them... We are out of ideas."

Dirk asked, "When did they bring the children to you?"

"Three weeks ago."

"Molly, we can't leave them here. We just can't. Maybe Eve and Lara can help them," he said.

"I agree. I'll temporarily adopt them," I said. "Let me speak with them. Alone."

"Adopt them? That's generous of you. Thank you. We have a small interview room. I'll have them brought to you. Follow me."

He opened a door for me. Inside the rather sterile room, I spotted four chairs. For a moment, I regretted not bringing Cleo in with me. I pushed chairs about until I got them in a crude circle. Then, another door opened. A woman ushered in the children.

Although they sat down, their eyes riveted me, moving up and down my body, pausing long at my shoulders where Leslie's gown hid them.

"Hi. My name is Molly Parkinson. Can you understand me?"

Blank stares. I wished my eldest daughter, Isabella, was here. She's a linguist. I couldn't change settings on my language translator box. Telepathy was my only option.

'Hi. I'm Molly Parkinson.' I placed that into each mind. Their faces lit up. Smiles told all.

'What's your name? How old are you?' One by one, I sent that to each.

'I'm Annette Leroy. I'm thirteen. My sister is Gemma. She's ten. That's my brother, Henri, who's eleven. Do you know where our mother is? She's Amalie Leroy.'

'No, I don't, but I'll bring you with me. Let's try to find her. What happened to you? Have you always been unable to speak?'

Tears trickled down cheeks. Annette thought, 'No. We used to talk and had arms. But then masked men raided our house. They knocked out Mom. We kicked and screamed, but they held rags over our noses. We woke up like this. No arms. No voices. No Mom. We're scared. A guy told us we'd grow up to be Galactic Dolls and showed us a picture of one. Dad died two years ago. We did all the chores since then. Men brought us here, but we can't understand what they're saying. Can you help us?'

'Dirk and I will try. For now, I'll adopt you. What is the name of your world? Where you lived before the men came?'

'Dad called it Rousseau. That's all we know,' Annette thought. 'Can you fix our feet? We can barely stand.'

I glanced at their feet. They had the same mutated feet as me. Only their toes could lie flat on the ground. Having learned all I could, I wanted to leave but couldn't open the damned door. I sent a telepathic message to Dirk.

'Will I look like you when I grow up?' Henri asked.

'Yes, unless my sister and a dwarf friend find cures for you.'

He cried.

"Cronus, we'll take the children today."

I told him what had happened to the kids. His skin paled. Sweat beaded on his forehead.

"Good rats! We had no idea, and I don't know where this Rousseau is. Isn't a Delius-C word. I'll order you a second wheeler and have them carried out to the vehicles. They aren't able to walk without someone's arm around them. Thank you. Thank you."

I took Annette and Gemma with me. While they sat in the back, Cleo and I issued orders to the wheeler through our translation units.

Henri rode with Dirk. Bishop issued the control orders to the wheeler. Our initial plan was to return to the spaceport, buy three more tickets for the return flight. While I wanted to continue on to this Kali-D world, the children's needs took precedence. With no flights for two days, we took rooms in a motel at the spaceport. As we signed in, Rina walked up.

"Hi. You're staying here, too? Who are these children?" To the children, she said, "I'm Rina. I met them on the transport."

"Sorry. They can't speak and don't understand Federation Common. We're rescuing them. Maybe you can help. They're from Rousseau, wherever that might be. Not sure if it's a world or a city. I have used telepathy to reach them. We must clothe them right away."

"Wow! Okay. I'm meeting with the archival person tomorrow. I have the rest of the day to kill. Once we get our rooms, I'll come by and see if I know their language."

Later, the three sat on the edge of the bed, while Rina and I sat on chairs in front. I sent to them, 'Rina will speak in several languages to see if any of them is your language. Nod if you understand one.'

Annette's smile melted my heart. At first, Rina spoke an opening round in all the languages she knew.

"Incredible. You speak ten different languages!" I said.

Rina grinned. "Yes. Now we'll try the language translators." One by one, she tried this language and that. Soon Annette nodded.

I picked up her thought, 'I got a word or two from that one.'

"Good, now I know the language family. Let me zero in on it," Rina said.

After another ten minutes, she produced a setting that allowed the children to understand what was being said. Rina explained Earth's French was a derivative. I had Dirk set my unit to that setting.

"They need clothing. Tall heels are critical if they're to walk," I said.

She looked at their feet and agreed. "Well, we can't carry them into the stores. Let me take their measurements, and we'll shop for them."

"Thanks, Rina. Sorry I can't help with that."

I felt frustrated with my disability but dared not show it in front of the scared children.

"Kids, when you want to say something, get my attention by pushing into my body. Okay?"

Three large smiles responded. Gemma pushed into me. I contacted her mind.

'I don't want to be a Galactic Sex Doll. Do we have to be that?'

"No, Gemma. You don't. I hope Eve can restore your bodies to what they were. No matter what, you'll go to the same school as my younger daughter, Nikita. Be patient a while longer."

Rina, Cleo, and I went shopping, spending several hours at it. Since I intended to take them back to Soros University, we chose black and white outfits as close to the school's styles as possible. We spent hours finding heels in the right sizes and height. After returning with Cleo and Rina carrying the packages and me frustrated, I put everyone to work.

We bathed the children and dressed them in their new clothes. Once we slipped on their heels, I had them stand and try walking. Great big smiles rewarded us.

Annette's bosom had already blossomed, though much smaller than mine. Her long brown hair shone after Rina finished with it, and her blue eyes displayed her appreciation. Annette now looked pretty, which pleased her.

Gemma looked much like her older sister: long brown hair and light blue eyes. Henri's hair had grown quite a lot during the mutation process. Dirk gave him a haircut. Dressed in shirt and pants, he looked like a boy again. But we knew that would change in a year at most as his body matured into that of a Galactic Doll.

We ordered room service. They took turns feeding the children while Cleo helped with it. I had a notion to show the kids how to do things with their feet and toes but decided against it. Soros University would provide them robot assistants.

Rina said, "After I collect the data I came here for, I'll return to Cass-C with you. You need my help."

I bought her ticket to thank her. We departed the next day for home. I paid for a long-distance call from hyperspace to Ashton Soros. I explained what we'd found and asked for his help.

"Yes, I've adopted them," I said.

I sensed a reluctance in his tone, but he agreed to help with their education. I then paid for a second call to Eve, telling her what we'd done and asking for her help.

Thus, when we arrived, Eve and Nikita stood waiting for us, along with Ashton Soros, who presented the three with their helper robots.

He said via his translation unit, "They will help you get dressed, fix meals, feed you, and help you as much as possible. The robot will guess what you need. Nod when it guesses right."

He asked Eve, "Is there any hope for these young armless Galactic Dolls who can't speak?"

"Lara and I will try. First, we need medical checkups," Eve said.

Rina helped Eve and Nikita get them settled. Rina and I booked passage on the next transport to Kali-D. I paid for her ticket as thanks for her help. Since the next flight wasn't for two days, I dropped by her place in the Single's Dorm just to chat. Then she visited mine to see the children.

Once more, the sophistication of these helper robots impressed me. They proved excellent guessers, often getting it right on the first try.

I had to make a tough decision about our travel. We couldn't leave them alone. Eve would be in the lab inventing cures. Nikita spent hours in summer classes. Either Dirk or I must stay behind. I decided Dirk should stay, much to his dismay.

"Look," I said, "we're dealing with very unethical people who think nothing of mutating people against their wills. Your body is restored to male. Let's not chance it."

Immune to mutation, Bishop couldn't be knocked out. He still carried a concealed supply of mutation agent in case I fell victim again.

"I'll be safe with Bishop. You've seen his reaction times. We can't just abandon these kids. In the meantime, see if you can locate Rousseau so we can try finding their mother. Then we can next try to find their mother. Find any records dealing with Amalie Leroy. Records exist somewhere, particularly if she registered as a Galactic Sex Doll. You've got the more challenging assignment."

Reluctantly, Dirk agreed to play father. Though he knew Bishop's reactions were faster than his own, I sensed he didn't believe I was safe without him. His arms still hadn't regained their full strength. He agreed to stay behind.

Chapter 7 Sales Brochure

Bishop, Rina, Cleo, and I headed for the spaceport. Bishop had rigged up a line so I could tow my bag behind me. Clever. I felt pleased.

Rina and I chatted, making the fifteen-hour trip pass swiftly. The return flight from Kali-D to Cass-C wasn't for three days. We checked into a hotel at the spaceport just outside Kistna, this world's largest city. Rina headed off in search of her research documents.

What a difference in worlds. Clean, almost sterile. Kistna surprised us. Automated shuttles flew about the city. A computer controlled flight was as simple as entering the desired destination.

Like Cass-C, people out shopping thronged the great avenues. Only a few parks offered a respite. No periodic benches. But then I didn't spot many women wearing tall heels. The fashion appeared professional. Suits for men and women, some women choosing skirts and low heels.

We rented a shuttlecraft at two hundred credits per day. From Cronus we knew the name of the place that sent him the bird people. That was our first stop. Salad's Supplies resided in the suburbs of the sprawling city. From the craft's windows, we observed people walking the avenues below us with little variability in apparel. The cleanliness of the city still bordered on sterileness.

Soon, the tall skyscrapers vanished behind us, as small office buildings fought each other for dominance. Then, even those yielded to single scattered buildings. As the buildings thinned, trees appeared, and the shuttle landed in a small lot.

As we stepped off, Bishop pointed out the simple sign that said: Salad's.

From the outside, the windowless structure revealed nothing. Inside, a simple room, a simple desk, and a receptionist. Crap. She's a robot. Clever.

"Would you like to see our catalog before you meet with Mr. Salad?"

"Yes," I said.

"Please step into that room. The catalog will appear," the robot said in a monotone.

As we walked through the door, I noticed a silent switch activated the fancy video presentation. I asked Cleo to record it.

"Welcome to Advanced Genetic Engineering where the impossible is possible. Modern Genetic Engineering: the perfect match to your needs. We custom engineer solutions to your problems. We offer solutions for primitive cultures through advanced space-faring people. Walk along and view our existing collection of Genetic Engineering solutions. If one interests you, note its number. A salesperson will meet you when the presentation ends."

Images illuminated on our left. "Here are existing solutions for primitive cultures. Winning a fight means survival. Make sure your force wins! Engineer them to victory. Number One and Number Two models come in four or six arms. Number Two models come in two strengths."

A hologram of a robust man wearing primitive armor appeared. With his four arms, he carried two swords, a spear and a shield. A second, the six-arm version, carried an additional whip and javelin in his arsenal. Both looked formidable. Two other models looked like a giant on steroids and a dwarf with super muscles. The presentation showed both men breaking steel rods like they were toothpicks. A caption added the life span of the super strength version was half that of the lesser strength one.

We moved forward and watched six more versions. I gasped. Some had a human upper body grafted onto an enormous snake. Another appeared to be a gigantic scorpion with a human upper body grafted onto it. They guaranteed the stinger's poison would kill anything alive. I swallowed hard. Another mutation brought the mythical Greek Centaur into existence.

"For water worlds, we offer gills and stock-model mermaids and mermen. Our Mers can dive to over a hundred feet and farm oyster beds. Let Advanced Genetic Engineering help you bring home the pearls!"

The next images showed giant men. I'm familiar with the race of giants since many immigrated to the Sol Empire. But these made real giants look like dwarves. This mutation had two down sides: voracious appetites and short lifetimes.

I expected the next set. Tiny people, six inches tall— guaranteed spies read the promo. I shook my head in disgust.

Then we entered the modern era. I saw what I expected to see: various forms of Galactic Dolls, including males that looked like female dolls. Only the promo called them Great Ladies. One set had arms, and another set lacked them. The third set of armless ones carried the label Sex Dolls. Fine print showed these dolls lacked voices. Voice removal was an optional feature on all models of Great Ladies. A fourth set had breasts twice the size of mine, and mine were as large as my head! Fine print stated: voice boxes and blindness optional. At least deafness wasn't a choice.

The Vogelmenschen came under the heading of hardworking, voiceless workers. A disclaimer alluded to their special dietary needs.

Next came the Sex Toys Collection. Here, men and women's bodies glistened in the light, exuding sexual attraction. "These fine mutations crave sex. They emit irresistible pheromones. Have the male or female toy of your heart's desire. You may bring in your own person for the mutation or choose from our fine selection."

Yet another set showed attractive men and women who had no legs. They labeled them limited-movement sex toys.

I said, "Next, they'll show us some with no arms or legs! Shit!" I was right. That was the next offering. Again, voiceless versions were optional.

The next images showed a studious man and woman. "This mutation boosts IQ to genius levels." Another mutation increased one's physical strength to half that of a dwarf.

The next display was more of an "I can't believe that's possible." Contortionists who could squeeze their bodies into a suitcase or duffle bag displayed their abilities in the video. Then, some posed in sexual positions, locking both legs behind their heads.

Cleo asked, "Is that even possible?" I didn't answer it.

Then came normal appearing bodies, only with ten fingers on each hand. Then, bodies with four arms, two attached mid-torso. Next came very tall men and women wearing running attire. Their legs were twice as long as normal. They carried a label of "fast runners."

Another display offered giant lip disks like those worn by Senior Ambassadors to the Federation of Planets. Unlike the official ones which fitted only the upper lip, this version split both lips. It expanded the lip loops outward to eighteen inches and held the disks parallel to the ground. These men and women reminded me of a platypus.

Fine print suggested available other options. No hands or feet or eyes or teeth. Disgusting. Then came one I found intriguing.

These models had super long hair that touched the ground. The speaker said, "Nerve cells with axon connections to adjacent nerve cells within the length of the hair prevent cutting it. Any attempt creates intense pain that shoots through the body. Thus, the person's hair is always long, lustrous, and thick. Add the sense of touch to your sense of style."

Next, they showed humans turned into Sixth Invaders and Third Invaders. I was familiar with both species. Commander and Ambassador L'Grina and Edyta came to mind. With these modifications, you could pass as one.

Next came the "unusual looks" versions. Besides seeing the wild, made up creatures of the 3d movies, some options showed women with almost no waists at all. Okay, I exaggerate. Very tiny waists. The ad claimed fourteen inches around. One could add optional tails to many of the mutations. One added an eye in the back of your head.

What wasn't among the offerings were telepaths.

At last a sane panel. "Submit your DNA for analysis. We can remove any birth defect and propensity for illness, such as dementia, via your own specially designed mutation agent."

"Ah, one that is useful," I said.

The final panel issued a warning. "Not all forms can reproduce the form of the parent. For example, children from the Great Lady mutation will inherit the Great Lady mutation from either parent. Children from the giant mutations will not inherit their parent's large size. If reproduction is a needed factor, check with the salesperson before ordering."

"Hello, Mrs. Parkinson. My name is Mr. Vijay," a tall, thin dark-skinned man with slicked black hair said as we walked into the next section of the displays. "I scanned your ID card as you toured the display. It isn't often we have an armless Great Lady visiting our esteemed facilities. Never from Earth, Sol Empire. Your bank account entitles you to additional offers we make only to our exclusive clients."

He clicked his fingers. Another display activated, which hadn't when we entered the room moments ago. I'd thought we'd seen everything.

"Some love their bodies. Some love their lives. Some love their pets. If only you could cheat death. Save a beloved Fido?" A lovable image of a dog licking a woman's hand appeared. "Have the fountain of youth? Never to grow old? Sorry, we can't reverse the aging process, but we can prevent death or damage to bodies.

"Salad Industries can clone your body or that of your pet, keeping the body in stasis until needed. A simple, painless minute later and your mind is transferred into the youthful clone body, identical to your own. Yes, live life until your body gets too old or ill, then swap your mind into the new youthful body, and extinguish your old one. Live another fifty years or more if you desire.

"There's no limit to the number of clone bodies you can hold in stasis, subject to your finances, that is. We ship clones to all medical facilities in the galaxy. Buy multiple clones, stash them across the galaxy, insuring any encounter with illness or accident is but a blip in your day.

"To build your clone, we take a small DNA sample. Many options are available for customization of your clone bodies, such as the Great Lady form, tiny waists, and so on. The cost includes the first ten options. You may add additional options for a small fee. We'll create your ideal body. When finished, we can transfer you into the finished product or store it in stasis until you need it.

"For those advocating a rugged, challenging lifestyle, Salad Industries recommends purchasing three clones. With your DNA on file, you may order more clones on demand, but construction times approach a year. Plan accordingly. You don't want to run out of bodies."

During the talk, life-sized images of gorgeous young women and handsome men flashed on the 3d holo display—so real that one couldn't resist touching them. Bishop did and watched his hand pass through the image. He grinned.

"Is the body swap machine provided in the cost?" I asked, hoping to take Mr. Vijay by surprise by showing him my familiarity with part of the technology. I'd body swapped several times. Besides, my body was a clone.

His eyebrows rose.

"Why, yes, we offer a unit. Few worlds are familiar with or possess mind swapping technology. How perceptive of you."

"I'm not a dummy Great Lady," I teased.

"Of course, you're not. How could you be and have the bank account balance you have? I'm honored you thought of us for your needs, Mrs. Parkinson. Did you see modifications or options you'd like done to your magnificent body? Or are you interested in purchasing clones? Perhaps modifications to your man there? A male Great Lady perhaps?"

"Oh, he's just my bodyguard. Never leave home without one. You know how it is for us Great Ladies, especially those of us who are wealthy. I heard of your company from Amalie Leroy, who recommended you."

I'd hoped to see a reaction to the name of the children's mother. But I saw none. His mind glossed over it though I picked up one clue: they had six stores on Delius-C. I continued playing the game.

"I need a list of your options. Some minor ones intrigue me, like the new style, long hair. I'm rather partial to my hair, but that's obvious. And the clone concept fascinates me. If I had a clone made, might I have last minute modifications made just before I swapped my mind into it?"

"Oh, absolutely. Salad Industries is always inventing new options. When the time of swapping approaches, pay us another visit and see if any of the new options interest you. Most optional features take only about eight days to implement. In your case, I've taken the liberty of checking your Earth's DNA database while you were enjoying the presentations."

I must have looked surprised, for he explained. "Yes, Salad Industries has received a copy of your world's massive compendium of DNA. As we say, you never know when a Sol Empire Earth person might show up desiring our unique services. If you prefer, we can manufacture one or more clones based on that original DNA. You may then pick which options to apply to the clones. Or we could take a current DNA sample and use that to create your clones, adding whatever options you might wish. Ultra-flexible for our best customers."

I said, "I could have you make me a clone using that old DNA in the database and then add on the marvelous options of my choice."

"Precisely."

"When I'm ready to use my new body, can I add on more options?"

"Yes, because they're always inventing new options. I might add that if you have an idea for a modification we don't offer, please let me know. I'll pass it along. Perhaps our scientists can invent it for you. Additional cost, of course."

"How interesting. If I had the stasis body shipped to Earth, could I ship it back for further modifications later on? You know how fickle we women can be. Never can make up our minds."

He faked a chuckle. "You can always send the body back for changes. Extra shipping costs apply."

"Naturally. You must have a large—does one call it a factory or a laboratory? Just what does one call it?"

Mr. Vijay laughed. "I've never seen it. Top secret. I believe it is both a laboratory and a factory. Have you seen options you'd like for this body or can I interest you in a clone?"

Sometimes you have to think at light speed. This was one. Just how many of these sales offices did they have? One might have handled Amalie Leroy's mutation. How else could I discover what happened to their mother? I'd seen no clues to the location of the actual laboratory or factory or unethical scientists. I couldn't fault Mr. Vijay for selling these modifications. He wasn't forcing anyone to do anything. I sensed he wanted to improve lives. Plus, I found having a new clone body based on my original DNA long before this body had undergone so darn many genetic mutations very appealing. Eve said my body now had three competing DNA profiles, making new cures more difficult to invent, to say nothing of the time delay.

"May I see more information about the new hair modification?" I said, stalling to think.

"Of course. We've only added this one last year. Show Number 106."

The holo monitor displayed another video. While showing images of women with long hair, the voice described the modification. "Your sense of touch culminates in your fingertips. Now imagine each strand of your lustrous, long hair with that same stimulating sense of touch. Your hair can feel the wind, the breath of your lover." The voice rattled on touting the benefits of this modification. While it played, I reached a decision. I had to uncover more information and locate the laboratory.

"Okay, you've sold me. I'd love a spare clone body. Base it on my Earth DNA sample, but add the hair option. When the time comes to swap my mind into this new body, I may request other options. I'm uncertain what I want in a new version of me. You know women," I jested. "I'd like a few days to decide about having the hair option done on my body. How long would I be in the mutation coma if I had it done?"

He looked it up in his handheld computer. "Two days, but it says to allow a month for your new hair to reach its maximum length of five feet. During those two days, it says your existing hair falls out, and the new touch-sensitive hair grows in."

"Oh, my. Will I be provided a wig for that month? I can't go around looking bald. That's not how a Great Lady should appear."

I feigned seriousness, but I wanted to laugh.

"I can ask a lab technician about that. Since you want a few days to decide on options for your gorgeous body, I'll check and have the answer for you when you return. How about the clone body? Can we work on that order now?"

"Yes, that will be perfect. Use my old Earth DNA database. I'll work out what other options I want later on. When it's ready, ship it to the Galactic Medicine center in Chicago, Earth, Sol Empire."

We went over details for several minutes. The ordering software had read my ID card, retrieved my basic information, and inserted it into the order form. He had to enter the shipping destination data and my request. The last step brought up a payment screen. I used five hundred thousand credits from my old account on Earth. I entered my security code to authorize the payment, after Bishop guaranteed me the transaction was secure.

"Payment received" flashed on the screen. Mr. Vijay submitted the order and sent a receipt to my phone.

After jotting a note about my hair question, he said, "When you drop by in a couple days, I'll have that information for you. We'll have a potential delivery date for your clone when you return. Subject to any further modifications you might desire. You may wish to consider the giant breasts modification, the tiny waist, and the no-voice option. My wife is herself an armless Great Lady. She loves the enormous breasts and contrasting waist. Everywhere we go, everyone admires her incredible form, but stunning doesn't do her justice. She wanted the no-voice choice, although I didn't. She claimed her shrill and tinny voice was grating to hear. Changing a voice isn't an option. Now me, I overlooked that because everything else about her is absolute perfection. But she insisted. Consider what modifications we can make to enhance your incredible beauty."

Chapter 8 Treachery

"Damn it! That meddling Parkinson has been here ahead of us!" ID Agent Jarvis Gerlach said.

The two agents left ABC Shipping and Mr. Cronus and stomped back to their wheeler. They insisted Agent Wanda Hammerstein stay on board their small transport, monitoring their comm and recording the interviews with those at the shipping company.

Wanda had complained. "We both know the system is automated. I want to come with you."

But the two men were insistent. In unison, "Follow orders, Agent Hammerstein."

She fumed, ending the recording and waited for their return. Wanda thought about the key information they'd received from Mr. Cronus. Mrs. Parkinson had been there yesterday and revealed the truth about the bird people. He'd told the two agents what Molly had told him, while sweating. The man told them he'd informed the party about Salad's on Kali-D. Wanda suspected the two agents would go there next.

She found Molly's adoption of helpless orphans curious.

Why bother? From the images Mr. Cronus showed the agents, these three would never be valuable people in society. They couldn't even take care of themselves.

She checked and saw they'd made large clothing purchases that same afternoon. While she waited the return of the two men, she hacked into hotel security feeds and observed how the three children looked in their new clothes.

At least now they can walk. But they're still helpless. Perhaps she plans to bring them back to Soros University and get helper robots.

She found Molly had bought tickets for the children's return with them to Hoffdorf. Wanda leaned back. At last, Molly's actions made sense.

"Well, that Parkinson has done it again!" Jarvis cursed when he boarded their ship. "You got that all recorded, Wanda?"

"Yes, sir. Also Mrs. Parkinson adopted the children, bought them clothes, and purchased them tickets back to Soros University. Assuming Ashton gives them helper robots, three lives are salvaged."

"Oh, don't be stupid, Hammerstein," Eric said. "They can't even relay their needs to the robots. Without arms and a voice, they're useless. They should've been put out of their misery."

Wanda bit her lip. When the urge to retaliate passed, she said, "The world needs more kindness."

"Well, keeping them alive isn't kindness in my book. A bullet to the brain would be a real act of kindness. Think about it, Wanda. What life could those kids have? None. No, what's really annoying is Parkinson's meddling!"

Wanda tried ignoring his callousness. "Lay in a course for Cass-C?"

"Those were our orders," Agent Jarvis said. "But that was before Parkinson butted in. Once she dumps the kids, I bet anything she'll head to Kali-D to check out Salad's. Wanda, lay in the coordinates for Kali-D. For once, we'll be ahead of that nosey woman. We can check what's there. I suspect we'll find nothing at all. Then, we can report that to Seven."

"But our orders..." Wanda said.

Agent Eric Von Klausburg broke his silence. "Lay in the coordinates. Parkinson is likely to pay them a visit. Best we know what she'll find before she does. A fool's errand, but Seven will have our hides if she finds out something nefarious."

After Wanda executed the jump into hyperspace, she said, "Twelve hours until landfall."

"Hey, make us supper," Jarvis said.

Make your own, damn it. Best keep quiet. I've waited four years. Don't blow it. Ah, I'll make them wish they'd never asked. With a wry grin, she over seasoned it.

When the two men cursed and spat out their first bites, she said, "I told you I don't know how to cook much."

The men glared but didn't ask her to cook after that.

Later, she said, "Okay, guys. There are six Salad's offices across Kali-D. Which one do we visit?"

Wanda parked their sleek, black ID transport at the spaceport at Kistna, Kali-D, which held two of the Salad offices, both located in the suburbs far from the spaceport.

After buckling his gear, Jarvis said, "Doesn't matter. Pick one. And rent us a shuttle."

Again, she held her tongue. Once the rise had passed, she chose one location and left to rent a shuttle. This field assignment wasn't turning out the way she imagined it. She tossed the electronic key fob to Eric and sat back in her comm center chair, knowing they'd not let her accompany them.

"Monitor things. Record everything. Both the Commander and Seven are gonna want a full report," Agent Jarvis said.

She nodded, again pressing her lips tightly together. Once the two men left the ship and the door shut, she cursed and smashed her fist onto the desktop. That only brought another curse. Wanda headed to the cramped galley, fixed herself a tea, and microwaved a breakfast snack. With a sigh, she sat at the comm controls, hitting record once the men arrived outside the Salad office.

"Maybe I can pick up tips on field operations. We're not supposed to be here. Our orders didn't include drilling down into this outfit. We have no jurisdiction here." She wiped away cheese that had dripped down the side of her mouth and sipped her tea.

She watched both men enter Salad's and flash their Intelligence Division badges.

Hell, if anyone knows anything about the ID, their black suits are a dead giveaway. Fools. We should use disguises.

Jarvis said, "Look. We want to speak to the boss." Soon, another man entered. "Now we're getting somewhere. We've reports you're kidnapping men and women from other worlds, mutating them into bird people, the Vogelmenschen, and then selling them. Plus, you're kidnapping women and children turning them into armless Great Ladies who can't speak. This has to cease."

Nothing subtle about Jarvis, Wanda thought.

The cagey manager said, "Wait a minute. I'm not saying any of that is true. Where's your proof? And if they can't speak and lack arms, how can you know what happened to them? What kind of con are you running?"

Oh, now that is clever! This guy is sharp. Bet he asks about jurisdiction.

"We've got a telepath. One of those Sol Empire armless Galactic Doll telepaths. She's read the minds of the Vogelmenschen at Soros University, Cass-C, and the three children you dumped on ABC Shipping on Delius-C. What type of life can armless kids have if they can't even speak?"

"I see. You must talk with our director about such accusations. Please wait here while I contact him and have him discuss this with you. Help yourselves to refreshments while you wait."

Wanda watched the two agents enter a side, windowless room. Both headed to the cabinet with drinks. They passed up the kaffee and tea dispenser, opting for bottles of alcohol. Then they sat down to wait.

Damn bad idea, fellows. What if they doped the booze?

She monitored the boring scene of two men knocking down what might be whiskey. Then, she noticed something yellowish in the air, drifting down from two jets near the ceiling.

"Guys, get out of there. He's gassing you," Wanda yelled into her mike.

Too late. She watched as Jarvis raised his head toward the jets and gas. Then, his head dropped. Both men slumped unconscious in their chairs. Wanda gasped, holding her breath as though the gas might reach her. She shook that idea away.

What now? Head over there? Another shuttle rental and travel time. At least an house before I could reach them. Wait.

Men wearing gas masks entered the room. Wanda watched as they stripped the men. Their concealed cameras continued to function though they now lay on the floor. They carried the men away. After a few minutes and still wearing a mask, one attacker returned and stuffed their clothes and weapons into a bag. The video appeared black for a time, but just as she considered ending the recording, the cameras glimpsed the apparel's drop into an incinerator. The melting cameras provided distorted images for a couple seconds. She ended the recording.

"Now what?" Wanda asked the surrounding air. "I don't dare call for backup."

Being on Kali-D wasn't in their orders. After careful consideration, Wanda decided she should search for the two missing agents. Surely they'd return the pair—dumped naked in a back alley. She'd hear from them soon. Maybe she'd hear from them in an hour. She glanced outside. Maybe in the morning. Sun's setting.

Following overnight protocols, she activated exterior surveillance cameras and locked down the ship.

The next day, Wanda paced the ship, awaiting the men's return. Then, she reviewed the procedural manual to kill time.

One entry reminded her of the men's failure. They didn't research their opponents before embarking on field actions. Jarvis and Eric had violated a major ID protocol.

Wanda spent the day scanning through public files concerning Salad's. She discovered exotic rugs and genetic engineering lay behind the company. Further, based on the amount of taxes the company paid, their gross income was gigantic. She uncovered six off-world shipping companies receiving infrequent shipments from Salad's, but she didn't know what they shipped. Records suggested a hundred six people worked for the company, but these six offices accounted for only eighteen. Where did the others work? That remained unknown.

A reverse search yielded more information. She had the onboard computer scan through the tax records of the billions living on Kali-D looking for anyone who recorded pay from Salad's. That program, she concluded, would need days to complete. It spat out curious details, displaying each person as it found them.

Some, Wanda discovered, were low-level criminal types. Thugs, more or less. Others were top geneticists. The disparity in salaries paid to these two types didn't surprise her. But what did this Salad's do? How did it make its money? For it must make a fortune, she reasoned.

By nightfall, the two agents hadn't returned. Since her program hadn't completed, she took no action but tossed and turned all night. The next morning as she ate breakfast, her exterior motion sensors activated. Another ship landed near hers. She watched the video and choked!

She stared at Molly Parkinson, Bishop, and the assistant robot, Cleo, walking across the tarmac. They'd just arrived, along with another young woman. "What's she doing here?" She decided to spy on the woman who disobeyed orders.

74

Molly wore a bright yellow dress with matching heels, a style of gown not seen on Cass-C. Her own black uniform announced she was an ID agent, unsuitable for spying. She changed into street clothes opting for soft sole instead of the tall heels that Parkinson wore. Satisfied she looked as native as she could, Wanda left the security of the ship, locking it down.

Molly went through customs and rented a shuttle. Wanda ran into them as they headed into the hotel by the spaceport. She backed off and observed. Satisfied they took a room, she did too, hoping her room might be close to theirs. Just as she entered her room, Molly, Bishop, and Cleo walked out of the room next to hers.

Wanda waited a moment before tailing the trio. From a distance, she watched them rent a shuttle. Trouble was, one had to enter the coordinates or speak the name of the destination. Computers controlled the flight of all shuttles. How to follow them?

The ID agent reasoned Molly intended to visit Salad's, but which one? She rented a shuttle and watched Molly's shuttle head to the right. Jarvis and Eric's shuttle had headed left. She spoke the word Salad's. A menu appeared, showing the two locations. She chose the other one, relaxing when the shuttle lifted off, veering to the right.

A half hour passed before the shuttle descended, landing in a lot next to the other shuttle. No sign of Molly or the others. She slipped out of her shuttle and over to Molly's. After glancing around, she slipped inside and attached a recording bug in the ship. She returned to her ID ship at the spaceport, retrieved a portable radio, and more bugs. Next, she landed her shuttle in the hotel lot. She set up the radio in her room but heard silence. She installed a bug on the wall between their rooms. With luck, she could pick up anything Molly and Bishop might say when they returned.

"You spent a half million credits for a new clone body." That had to be Bishop's voice. "Why? Do you trust them? I can't believe what they're doing."

"I don't trust them at all, but we need facts. Plus, if there's any chance I could get a new body to replace this one, I'll take it. Probably won't happen. Eve said my DNA is really messed up now. Three conflicting DNAs. Eve tried sounding hopeful she and Lara could invent an arm regrow solution for me, but the dismal truth is I might be stuck like this. Yeah, I'll take the chance. Besides, I'm trying to find their mysterious laboratory."

"I think I grasp your angle," Bishop said. "Look, I've just spent a half million credits. Can I see the lab and my new body being made?"

Wanda heard a female chuckle. "Bingo, Bishop. In case that fails, that's why I said I wanted options for this body. I like the hair mutation, but the others. Hardly. These boobs are far too large as it is. I can't imagine walking around with some twice this size. Why would anyone desire a tiny waist? No, if I must get a modification, it'll be the hair. Perhaps that will get me a trip to their secret lab or factory or whatever it is."

"Was Vijay lying?" Bishop asked.

"Not as far as I could tell. He seemed little more than a salesman. What floored me is that they read my ID card, found my DNA in Earth's database, and retrieved my bank account balance. All without my consent."

"Amazing what computers can do these days," Bishop said.

"Anyway, I've got lots of credits. No biggie if the deal goes south. What do you think the chances are they'll let me see the clone body being made in their labs?"

"I can't calculate the odds. Insufficient data. Probably not good."

"You think I stand a better chance if I get the hair mod done? Won't they need me in the lab for the procedure?"

"I don't know. Insufficient data."

"Well, we must find that lab or we'll never locate the kids' mother."

That ended the relevant conversation picked up by Wanda's bug.

What is she up to? I think she discovered a lot of key info. But what to do? Jarvis and Eric still aren't back. Wanda sighed. Pay them a visit and gain their confidence. No choice. She waited until they entered their room before knocking on their door.

Chapter 9 Working Together

"I'm ID Agent Wanda Hammerstein. May I come in?"

I let her in, introducing Bishop and Cleo.

"I think we have enormous problems," Wanda said. "Originally, Seven requested we follow up with ABC Shipping and not delve deeper. When we got there, you'd already been there and adopted those three children. You've met my two fellow agents, Jarvis Gerlach and Eric Von Klausburg. I know, they're sometimes pigheaded. Anyway, after checking out that shipping company and learning about Salad's here on Kali-D, we should have headed back to Cass-C. We have no jurisdiction or authority here. But you've met Jarvis. Infuriated that you were interfering again, he decided to check out Salad's. Eric agreed, but over my protests. That it wasn't in our orders.

"They barged into the other Salad's here in Kistna. Not the one you visited, but the other one. I discovered they run six offices on this world. Anyway—no, best if you watch this for yourselves."

She played back the video recording of their encounter. I watched as the two men slumped in their chairs. The video showed showed their clothes being stripped away and deposited into an incinerator. I envied her wristband video display device.

"I'm unable to locate them since then. Rather hoped they'd be dumped in an alley and have made it back to our ship. It's been days now. I was researching the company and its personnel, but when I noticed your arrival, I followed you. I'm in the room next to yours. I followed your shuttle to Salad's, but you were already inside when I arrived. I bugged your shuttle. I needed to make sure you were safe and if you knew anything about my missing ID agents."

I said, "Those two weren't nice. But Wanda, I think they're in big trouble. After what Bishop and I saw today at Salads, those mutations are worse than what the Sixth Invaders did to Earth."

Bishop tried to blend in. "Yes, Mrs. Parkinson, far worse than the Sixth Invaders. But Agent Hammerstein—"

"Wanda, please. We've no authority out here—not yet, anyway."

"Molly, we should illuminate this ID agent on what we saw," he said. "At least the Sixth Invaders were humane, more or less."

I sighed. "Wanda, this is shocking." I launched into a detailed description of what we'd seen, following the order that we watched the audio-visuals. The more I said the paler Wanda appeared. I had Cleo replay what it recorded of the audio-visual presentation.

I ended with, "Based on our experiences on Earth and now at this Salad's office, I would bet your agents have been mutated. They're likely in lengthy mutation comas. Considering the wide variety of mutations these people can do, I can't predict what their bodies will look like. But I doubt someone will kill them."

Bishop said, "Molly, my calculation is either the armless Great Lady mutation or the Vogelmenschen mutation. Expect they'll lose their speech. Trouble is: we don't know where their lab facilities are. Perhaps they have more than one."

"That's why I ordered a new clone body based on my original DNA taken years ago before any of these mutations appeared on Earth. I hoped a half million credits would gain me a tour of their labs. As a hedge, I told them I'm interested in their new hair modification. Perhaps I can get a look that way, but they may give me a shot of the agent in my leg, instead."

Bishop said, "We still need to find the children's mother, Amalie Leroy. Even if you get inside, will you find that information? We must shut these people down, right?"

"Yes, we do, Bishop," I said. "Wait!" I smiled. "Didn't they kidnap and mutate four of our people, turning them into Vogelmenschen? Possibly a hundred of our people? I was the Senior Investigator and Senior Judge for the Sol Empire when they were abducted and mutated. I have the authority to arrest these fiends."

I had doubts. That was years ago.

Wanda laughed. "Molly, that's stretching your authority just an ant's worth. Still, it's enough for me. I can say I am backing the justice arm of a Federation world. That allows me to act on your behalf. But what can we do? You're helpless. That leaves Bishop and me against who knows how many. Since Seven ordered the ID not to get this far, I don't think I dare request backup."

Bishop said, "If I may be bold, they're prepared for a frontal assault. Look what happened to your two agents who barged in. Undoubtedly, they have other mutation gas attack setups to stop intruders. I would guess they employ a significant number of armed guards. I would. But I worry about your going in there alone, Molly. We can't trust these people. They might turn you into a Vogelmenschen."

Wanda said, "More digging into Salad's? I've already identified Salad's personnel. It's a combination of thugs and scientists. There should be a way to locate their lab or factory. They need basic supplies. I wish we had a geneticist who could tell us what those might be. We might track shipments to their lab."

"Eve and Lara might know, but I don't have access to an LD communications system to call back to Cass-C," I said.

"I do. On our ID transport. Come on. Let's make that call," Wanda said. "If we can find the factory or lab, I've got invisibility devices on the ship and two personal defense shields we can use. We must be darn cautious. I couldn't live with a mutation like yours."

An hour later and back in our room, Wanda studied the list of supplies. We were barely able to pronounce them, much less guess at their use. She returned to her room to see if she could discover anything useful from this list.

Someone knocked on our door. Bishop opened it for me.

"Surprise. I'm back," Rina said. "Took forever, but I got the ancestry logs. What have you been up to? You're pale. Something wrong?"

"Come in. Yeah. We uncovered a nightmare," I said. "We found Salad's. You won't believe what we found!"

"Salad's?" she asked sitting down. Her face formed a curious look. "Like the galaxy's fanciest rugs?"

"Hardly."

"That's my father. Salad Naraka. Runs one of the largest rug import/export businesses anywhere. Collects top quality rugs from many worlds and resells them. Makes a fortune. I'm having lunch with him tomorrow. I haven't seen him since I went to Soros U. Mom never wants to see him again. Bad breakup."

"Must be a different man. This Salad's is beyond belief."

"Jeesh. What did you find out? Can you tell me?" Rina asked.

"I can do better than that. I had Cleo record Salad's audio-visual presentation. Cleo, play back the recording. I warn you, Rina, what you are about to watch might be upsetting."

Cleo projected the recording, making a three-foot square virtual 3d holo screen.

Rina cried out, "Wait! That's dad's company logo. This can't be right."

"I don't know about that. It gets worse," I said, preparing her for the shocking mutations to come. Shit. What have I done?

She put her hands over her mouth and stared at the presentation. I don't think her eyes could open any wider than they did.

"My gods! This is what they used on those children!" Rina said.

When the lengthy presentation ended, Rina's face held no color. Her bronze skin had turned almost white.

"This—this can't be right. Dad's into rugs. Not these terrible things. Must be an awful mistake. Come with me tomorrow for lunch. You can meet him. I'll ask him about all this. It just can't be true. He'd be the monster of the galaxy. Please, come with me. This has to be wrong. Please."

I agreed. Rina promised to pick me up at eleven. After Bishop closed the door, I heard her break down, sobbing in the hall as she presumably headed for her room. Just then, another knock jarred us.

"It's me," Wanda whispered. Bishop let her in. "I heard. Is she really the daughter of Salad?"

"Yes. Her mother divorced him when Rina was quite young. You heard she's taking me to meet him for lunch?"

"Yes. Don't go. He is dangerous if he's behind this. And I can't imagine he isn't. I checked legal records. Salad Naraka is the owner of Salad's Offices and Salad's Rugs. He's quite diversified and a billionaire, too. Can't imagine where he's made his money," she said.

"I've shocked her with this. She left sobbing. I'm certain she knows nothing of her father's black side. I have to go with Rina to meet him."

Wanda ran her hands across her face before speaking. "Okay. Either Rina is lying to you or she knows nothing about her father's involvement. But if this man is behind these

82

horrific mutations and kidnappings, when he finds out you know, he'll come after you."

Bishop agreed. "Her point is valid. I'm sure you can take Cleo with you to this luncheon. A bodyguard won't fit in. Besides, he may order my elimination before abducting you. The less threatening we can make this lunch date the safer you'll be. Remember, this man is a billionaire. He's not likely to get his own hands dirty and probably has this world's law enforcement in his pay."

"Not a chance he's innocent," Wanda said. "The real question is has Rina been playing you? If she has, then you're walking into a trap."

"But if she isn't, then I need to protect her from this fiend of a father," I said.

"I'm worried they'll kidnap you. Drug your food. Bishop, we must take precautions," Wanda said.

Chapter 10 Lunch at Timin's

Rina knocked on our door at eleven. She wore her school black and white clothes, including the stockings and tall heels. That surprised me.

She said, "We're dining at Timin's, only the most expensive restaurant in this world. We need to dress up. I tried wearing comfortable clothes and heels these past few days. The leg pain got to me. Wearing tall heels for too long has negative side-effects. Anyway, your yellow dress looks good on you. Everyone can see your lack of arms and your figure is to die for."

"I don't know about the figure bit. Is this outfit acceptable? I must bring Cleo along. Hope that's okay."

"Oh, sure. You must bring Cleo. How else can you dine? Come on. I've got a shuttle rented."

Ten minutes later, I gasped. We stood just outside the entrance facade of Timin's, rather a cross between an ancient gothic cathedral and a Roman temple with its myriad columns. A uniformed doorman opened the ornate doors with golden fixtures. I followed Rina, Cleo rolling along behind me. The man stared at me as I passed.

I almost stumbled when my feet hit the thick, blood-red carpet. Rina did too, but she had arms to aid her balance.

"We're meeting Salad Naraka," Rina said. "He's expecting us."

"Yes. This way," said the hostess. She wasn't the least surprised at my appearance, surprising me. I spotted other Great Ladies sitting at secluded tables, but they had arms, except one. Our hostess led us to a private table lit with candles. A brown-skinned man rose as we approached, his eyes scanning my form before a broad grin responded to seeing Rina. He had black eyes and hair, which Rina got from him, though her bronze skin must have come from her mother.

"Dad, this is my friend from Soros University, Mrs. Molly Parkinson. This is my father, Salad Naraka."

Since I estimated Rina to be around twenty-five, I wasn't surprised to see a fifty-year-old man. We exchanged cordialities. He helped each of us sit, beginning with me.

He had already ordered the meal for us. My first observation yielded a man who liked control over all aspects of a meeting.

"I'm glad you've made the acquaintance of a special Great Lady, Rina. Molly, here on Kali-D, special Great Ladies are considered the absolute finest role models for women, especially those of means. Rina, I promised you that when you turned twenty-five, I'd cover the expense of forming your body into that of a gorgeous special Great Lady. You're thirty now, and with such incredible looks, why, you can go anywhere and be anything you wish. Have the man of your dreams. Let me tell you, men appreciate a stunning woman. It's a ticket to class. Isn't that so, Molly? I presume I may call you Molly. Mrs. Parkinson sounds formal."

"Molly's fine," I said.

He charged on, thwarting my planned question.

"Rina, look at Molly's fantastic dress. Comes from Earth, Sol Empire, I believe."

"Yes, my sister designed it." I tried continuing, but Rina interrupted me.

"She did? I didn't know that. I agree. She has incredible sense of fashion. I've seen others on campus. We hosted sixteen hundred, Dad. But Molly's gown is striking. Did you see the doorman's eyes when we walked in? I thought they'd pop out!"

"That's why I'm importing their full line. Getting a contract with her to manufacture her gowns here in Kistna.

Make them far more affordable. Then they can adorn many more incredible women. Add to the beauty of our world," Salad said.

He continued, "This is your school dress?" Rina nodded. "I received a snapshot from your headmaster, Ashton Soros. He's related to the school's founder, I'm told." Turning to me, he added, "Only met the man once when I verified Soros University was worthy of my Rina.

"Nothing is too good for my oldest daughter. Say, how is your mother? I haven't heard from her for twenty years. I've remarried. Wonderful special Great Lady. Anala. One day, Rina, I'd love for you to meet her. She's an armless Great Lady, just like you, Molly. A beautiful, charming, amazing woman. When you're not at the university, do you have a personal assistant? I heard Ashton provided these helper robots for you.

"Nothing against robots, mind you. But undignified. Crude. But perhaps you're not wealthy enough to afford a personal assistant. If so, please accept my apologies. No affront intended."

Rina stuck up for me. "Dad, they don't allow human personal assistants on campus. Independence is stressed. Robots are assigned to those who need them. They provide the finest prosthetic limbs. My astro-history professor lost both legs, but I never knew until I saw him out running one day. Soros U has a long history of aiding the handicapped. But I want to meet Anala. Sorry I couldn't come to your wedding. Mom forbad it."

"Well, now you've grown into a beautiful, educated, professional woman. You can do as you wish, right?" He winked at her.

Rina flushed. "Well, yes. I'm traveling worlds collecting research data for my doctorate." She launched into an explanation of her theory and thesis.

86

I watched her father's reaction. Bored, but he nodded and smiled as needed. I sensed he didn't care about her work. I broached the key topic.

"So, Salad, I visited one of your offices and watched the lengthy audio-visual presentation of all the genetic mutations your company offers."

"Oh, you have? Wonderful. I mostly sell exotic rugs though. The genetic mutations are my gift to humanity, like Ashton Soros and his helper robots. Wait a minute. Someone told me an Earth special Great Lady just ordered a clone body. Was that you?"

"Yes, I told them I would return in a couple days. I might want the new hair modification. To feel with hair sounded interesting."

"Oh, you must have that one. Anala loves hers."

"I'd like a tour of your lab or factory where all this is done."

"Absolutely. We should do it later this afternoon."

"I'm a telepath. I used telepathy to communicate with the Vogelmenschen that Ashton Soros has working for the university. A hundred told the same story."

He interrupted. "You mean the bird people? Sometimes I don't follow Cass-C language."

"Yes. Masked men kidnapped them and mutated them into bird people in your labs before selling them to Ashton as menial workers. Some years back, someone kidnapped several from my world—from Philadelphia, Earth, Sol Empire. My friend and I just returned from Delius-C and ABC Shipping. They told us your lab kidnapped a woman, Amalie Leroy, and her three children, mutated them into armless, voiceless Great Ladies, and dumped the three helpless children there. They don't know where their mother ended up or if she's alive. Since ABC Shipping didn't know what to do with them, I adopted them. With Rina's help, we got them clothed. We took them to Soros U where they're being cared for at the moment."

Rina held back tears as I talked. "Dad, how could you do these things? Mom said you were a monster, but this..." Her voice failed her.

Salad raised his arms in protest. "I didn't do this. We're providing humanitarian aid to those in need, same as the Great Ladies. There must be an awful mistake. Maybe confusing Salad's with someone else. We run the most advanced genetic engineering laboratory in the Federation. At least that's what I'm told. Surely there's been a huge mistake."

"But I saw those three kids, Dad. I helped them," Rina said, wiping her eyes.

"I'm sure you saw the children, Rina, but this telepathy thing. What do you know about it? Is it reliable? No one I've met has encountered a real telepath. Many quacks out there. I'm not blaming you, Molly. There must be a mistake here.

"For years, Salad's has helped women become flowers of perfection. I understand we assist developing worlds by providing mutations. You know, making stronger, more robust male bodies to better aid their worlds in moving into a space-faring era. But they are volunteers from those worlds. Besides, I'm told we make very few of them. Most of our work comes from enhancing the beauty of women.

"Speaking of that, Rina, remember I promised you I'd arrange your special Great Lady mutation when you were ready. Are you ready for it now? Take a little time off your thesis research and pamper yourself. Plus, if you moved back to Kali-D as a special Great Lady, you could have your pick of the most eligible, wealthiest men on this world. Forgive me. By now you must have your own boyfriend on Cass-C. Still, it's been my experience that all men love a gorgeous woman. Do it for him."

I watched Rina's face for a reaction. At first, she looked surprised, possibly as though she'd forgotten he'd ever made the offer. Then, her eyes glazed. "Special Great Lady" caused that reaction, one I'd seen several times today. Moving back to Kali-D produced a distinct tightening of her face, but at the mention of a boyfriend back at the university, a slight flush replaced its tautness.

"Not while I'm in the middle of my research. I still need archive copies from six more worlds. Then I must study millions of documents. Thesis work is a bear, Dad. Hardly have time to eat."

"I wanted to remind you my offer still stands whenever you're ready. Meanwhile, I will speak with my lab manager about these ridiculous charges, which can't be true. Say, tonight Anala and I are hosting a twenty-year anniversary party. We've been married twenty years. You must come, Rina, and bring your school friend. In fact, I insist Molly comes too. There'll be music and dancing. Anala wants to meet you, Rina. She's only seen images I've found. And Molly, Anala will insist you come, since you two share much in common. She only wears stylish gowns like yours imported from your world though she prefers red not yellow. And lots of sequins. She'll drown you in questions about your sister's fashions."

Rina chuckled. "Okay, we'll come on one condition. We'd like to see this lab or factory where all these mutations are done. Molly has ordered a clone of herself. She's paid for that assurance, considering the exorbitant purchase price of her clone body."

"Deal," he replied without hesitation. He added, "Since our party is a formal affair, your robot will be unacceptable. I'll send a personal assistant by your hotel room to attend your needs, Molly. Expect Padma to join you around four this afternoon. I'll let you ladies return to your rooms and freshen up while I visit the lab and sort out this mess. What you've said about illegal activities can't be right. I'll come by later and pick you up for a tour. My manager will disprove these terrible allegations."

***

Back in my room, I said, "Great thinking, Rina. Now we can see his genetic mutation lab."

She chuckled. "Yeah, that's what I thought. He denied it. But Mom always claimed he's a monster. I don't know what to believe. I've never met his new wife, Anala. I heard they had a daughter. Guess she'd be my half-sister. We should be safe enough at their party, don't you think?"

"Probably. But Bishop and Wanda should tail us and keep watch."

"Right. Wouldn't think of letting you go into the wolf's den without backup," Bishop said. "We'll follow you to this secret lab."

"Maybe my missing agents are in there," Wanda said. "That'd be enough proof for me to alert the ID."

I bit my lip. "Something else is bothering me. Your Dad said they had these special Great Lady modifications over twenty years ago."

"Yeah, Mom divorced him because of that." Rina had our full attention and grinned. "I was four when it happened. He forced Mom to have it done—the armless Great Lady version. When she woke up, besides doing a lot of screaming, she filed for divorce. She and I returned to her home world, Kalak, Zeta Minori-D. Those first years were awful, but Mom met a wonderful man, Gregoros Pappas. I took his sir name when Mom married him. I haven't seen Dad since we fled. I'm thirty now, and he mutated Mom when I was four. That means his genetic modifications have been in operation for at least twenty-six years. Is that important?"

"I think so. The Sixth Invaders claimed to have invented this special Galactic Doll mutation on Earth as part of their plan to make my civilization into one like theirs. Sixteen years ago, they mutated every woman on Earth into a Galactic Doll. I helped stop them from unleashing their newer agent, the armless telepath version. Yet, you're saying that same

90

mutation has been in use on Kali-D for twenty-six years, only here it's called special Great Lady. I wonder if the Sixth Invaders got the genetic mutation technology from this world. If so, how and when? And why? Where did this world get it? Did they invent it?"

"I read the report," Wanda said. "That Earth invented the armless telepath Galactic Doll agent. Rina, is your mother a telepath?"

Rina laughed. "Hardly. No, just damned handicapped is all. Looks beautiful. Like Molly, she always has an assistant."

"Is there a program to make every Kali-D woman a special Great Lady?" I asked. "Could the Sixth Invaders be active here like they were on Earth?"

"They're an alien race. Gray skins," Wanda said. "I think everyone would know about them if they were active."

I said, "Unless they used their body swap devices. One could be living in your father's body. Just saying. Not implying one is. That's how they infiltrated Earth. Swapped their leaders into our leader's bodies."

"That's frightening," Rina said.

"They almost conquered Earth."

Chapter 11 A Visit to the Lab

Salad picked us up in his rug company shuttle. I took Cleo with me. Bishop and Wanda followed us.

While the autopilot navigated to his secret lab on the north edge of the city, he explained, "I talked to Jivin, my manager, about these allegations. He swears nothing like that happened. But I took the presentation tour. I'm appalled at some genetic mutations, but he assured me those are engineered for a limited number of primitive cultures. The four-armed person and similar ones. A few worlds demand strength in their men and women if they're to survive. He claims we rarely make bird people and then the subjects mutated have a zero chance for a productive life. So we're giving them a chance at survival. Soros University hires many of them.

"He promised us a guided tour. Your clone body is gestating. You'll view it inside the stasis pod. That part of the facility is automated. I have clone bodies in stasis for Anala and me, just in case. Best to be prepared. Rina, if you want one, just tell me. I'd be honored to have one made for you. Accidents happen. I'm told the body swap procedure works even shortly after death. It's the best insurance policy in the galaxy."

"Dad, I don't know if I want to live forever. That's not natural."

"That's understandable. If you decide against using the clone body, we donate it to a needy person, such as a security person maimed in the line of duty. Gives them another chance."

I said, "Have you found giving injured women your Great Lady mutation heals them?"

"Well, now you mention it, I recall Jivin telling me that's happened a couple times."

"But no similar cure for men, unless they want four arms or something," I said.

His mouth twitched before he chuckled. "I'm not up on these genetic mutation things. I'm a rug baron. We can ask Jivin if one of his genetic engineers can answer those kinds of questions."

That ended any significant conversation, though Rina continued to chat with her father, asking questions about her half-sister, Lanka.

"She's eighteen and stunning. But fathers always think so. She has six wealthy suitors dying to marry her. I insisted she not marry until she's eighteen, but that happens next week. She wants to become a special Great Lady before marrying. She likes to shop for fancy gowns. Guess I've spoiled her. Anala and I expect to go through the empty nest syndrome. You can talk Lanka about going to Soros University after she becomes a Great Lady. That is, if you think she needs to do that."

Again, I noticed Rina's eyes fog out when he mentioned that phrase. Strange.

We landed beside a long, narrow single-story building surrounded by a tall fence topped with barbed wire. A guardhouse and gate blocked the single entrance. I counted a dozen gun-looking weapons mounted on the roof, providing complete defense of the grounds. Five security guards patrolled the vicinity of the gate, while six more converged on our shuttle, which landed on the parking pad where six other shuttles sat.

When Salad stepped out, the guards lowered their weapons. I'd never seen their specific weapons, but I guessed they were blasters. No doubt about how guarded this secret facility was. I hoped Bishop and Wanda exercised extreme caution.

A fake smile plastered on his face, the brown-skinned Jivin walked up. Covert hostility emanated from his being.

Jivin said, "Ah, welcome back, Mr. Naraka. This must be your charming older daughter. And Mrs. Parkinson. I recognize you from Earth's DNA database. I'm pleased to tell you that your clone body is forming as we speak. It won't mature for at least six more weeks. We prefer monitoring it for half a year to assure its stability, though a year is even better. This way."

I felt an instant dislike of Jivin. Enough that as we entered the gigantic facility, I lightly touched his mind, but pulled back. A flash of recognition shot through me! Jivin wasn't human. No, that's not correct. His body was like the denizens of Kali-D, but his mind and the being occupying that body was a Third Invader. My many unpleasant experiences with that alien race had given me a feel for their thought patterns.

A body swap or a disguise device such as the Sixth Invaders Ambassador L'Grina often wore to blend in with humans? I decided a body swap was more likely since he'd held this position for at least a quarter century. But why? I paid close attention, touching the minds of those we met along the way. I uncovered a second Third Invader in the body of the operations manager. The other employees checked out as human.

"Here's where the production genetic mutations are mixed," Jivin said, pointing to a huge machine with countless dials and switches. "You dial in the combination the person has ordered. That computer brings up the person's order, and the corresponding switches to flip. Then, a syringe filled with the mutation mixture comes out there. A simple injection is all that's needed, along with proper care of the body undergoing mutation. We take them into this next room and hook up the comatose patients to life support units that provide proper nutrition and waste removal."

"Where is the clone manufacturing part?" I asked.

"At the back end of the facility. Next is the pure research department. Our genetic engineers are always working on new cures, new mutations. We test each new mutation on mice and other animals before it's used humans."

A dozen men and women wearing white lab coats worked at computerized stations. I'd never seen such a well-equipped lab. It made Eve and Lara's lab look primitive. None paid any attention to us.

Jivin said, "Here is the clone wing. First is the machine we built to convert a DNA sample into a physical body. Getting a copy of Earth's huge database revolutionized our processes. Your new body came out of that machine yesterday. This way."

I wondered how they even knew about Earth's massive DNA database, let alone retrieved a copy. We entered a gigantic warehouse containing stasis pods stacked floor to ceiling. Miles of plastic tubing and wires connected to a computer installation controlled each pod.

Jivin said, "We can manufacture one thousand clones at a time. Yours is in this one." He pointed to one on the ground level. I looked through the plastic canopy and saw myself as I used to appear, though more like a filmy ghost.

"The body solidifies in a few weeks. When it's finished, we'll ship the stasis pod to your designated location. Once the device in the other room manufactures the body, this whopper computer controls every aspect of the clone growth process."

Since the tour ended, I asked the serious questions. "Days ago, I rescued three young children being kept at ABC Shipping on Delius-C. Their mother is Amalie Leroy. All four were abducted from their home, brought here, mutated into armless, voiceless Great Ladies. Then someone took their mother somewhere else and left the kids to fend for themselves. Rather an impossible task. Do you have records of who purchased their mother? I'd like to reunite the family."

As I asked this, an image of a computer screen flashed in Jivin's mind. "Mr. Naraka already asked me about that and other awful things. I assure you we kidnap or abduct no one. Our business is on the level and legal. I've never heard of this woman. We don't mutate children that way. Someone's fibbing."

"ABC Shipping swears the four came from Salad's. I saw the shipping manifest."

"Must be another Salad's. Anyone can fabricate false shipping information," Jivin said. "Now, if you'll excuse me, I've much work to do."

As Salad took us back to our hotel so we could dress for his anniversary party this evening, I asked several key questions. "I bet this company cost a fortune to build."

"Yes, staggering. But we keep adding on more each year. Operational costs are gargantuan, but I still make a tidy profit. We service many worlds with our genetic mutations."

"How many facilities like yours does the Federation have?"

Salad laughed. "We have the only one. A monopoly on genetic mutations. That's why we can turn a profit despite the huge operational costs."

When he dropped us off, my promised personal assistant, Padma, stood waiting outside my door.

Chapter 12 The Anniversary Party

Rina ducked into her room. Padma used my electronic key to open my door. Padma wore an elegant gown with heels. The brown of her dress matched her skin tones. Like me, she had long, straight black hair.

"I'll be your personal assistant at tonight's anniversary party. I'll be Lanka's assistant in a few weeks when she becomes a Great Lady like her mother."

As she pampered me, I asked, "Did you always want to be a personal assistant?"

"Oh, yes. Very much so. One of the highest paying jobs. You get to live in the mansions and wear fabulous clothes. The latest fashions and all. I'll meet many Great Ladies and the wealthy men in their lives. It's quite an honor to be selected as a personal assistant."

She explained, "I'll be in the background, but close by and ready to help. We're drilled on picking up the small signs you need something. We don't speak at these fancy affairs."

I probed, seeking a better understanding of Kali-D society. "Do you wish to become a special Great Lady yourself one day?"

She pressed her lips before answering. "Wish? Or desire? Even if I kept my arms, I don't have enough money for such a lifestyle. But should I one day fall in love and marry a man who wanted to provide for such a life, then yes, I would want to please him and elevate our status. That's what Lanka is doing. She wants to become a special Great Lady and marry a wonderful man who can afford a luxury life like Salad has given to Anala. You'll meet her tonight. She's a wonderful person. Anala hosts a charity ball each year, donating millions in aid to the poor of our world."

"Most women of your world don't want to become special Great Ladies?"

Padma laughed. "Hardly. Such is a fairy tale dream."

"How different our worlds are. On Earth when the Sixth Invaders invented this Great Lady mutation, all women wanted the procedure. Fanatics. Something like one and a half billion women had it done over a couple years."

She let out an exclamation that sounded like "wow."

"Here, getting the Great Lady modification is affordable. I could have it done today. Most women can afford it, but few can then afford the luxury lifestyle demanded of Great Ladies. What's the point if you can't live in luxury? Anala's gown for tonight costs as much as my yearly salary.

"No, Lanka has been smart. She dated wealthy boys throughout her school years. Lanka's been planning this for years. She's reached eighteen and graduated. Soon she'll marry a man who can support her as a special Great Lady and have me as her personal assistant."

Just then, Bishop and Wanda returned. Padma let them in.

"Oh, hi. Padma, these are my security guards: Bishop and Wanda." Both nodded to her while eyeing me.

"She will be my personal assistant at tonight's party. You two can take the night off. Padma, I'd like a private word with these two. Then you can take me to the party."

After she stepped outside, I outlined what I'd found out. "Yes, Jivin and the manager are Third Invaders occupying these men's bodies. Like the Sixth Invaders did. The others I saw at the lab are normal humans. Be careful. Something's going on, but I've no idea what. More when I get back."

Wanda opened the door, allowing me to join Padma, who had already collected Rina. As our shuttle flew us to Salad's mansion, Rina grew worried.

"Molly, I don't trust my father. Maybe because Mom's always calling him a monster. Still, I feel like we're heading into a den of snakes."

Padma said, "You're worried over nothing. I've been training with Lanka. I've been around them. Anala is a wonderful person, embodying all the traits of a Great Lady. Your sister wants to follow her example and has a beau lined up to marry as soon as she transforms. Mr. Naraka has always been most kind and generous to them and us assistants. Perhaps your mother still has ill will against him over their divorce."

Ah, ha. They trained personal assistants in diplomacy, too. Rina sighed and agreed that might be the case.

The Naraka mansion occupied many acres. A stone fence encircled the land near the edge of the city. The shuttle landing pad lay in the southwest corner surrounded by rolling grasslands. A quaint paved path led from the guardhouse of the pad up to the main entrance portico whose roof rested atop ten stone pillars. In our heels, the walk took several minutes, all the while admiring the mansion. Padma provided a continuous stream of details. I figured we'd triggered a silent alarm because Salad joined the guard at the door.

"My daughter and guest," he said to the security man.

The stained glass doors opened as we approached, a feature no doubt designed with Anala in mind.

"Ah, here you are, Rina. Salad has many images of you. I'd recognize you anywhere. I'm glad you came. I've always wanted to meet you. So has your sister, Lanka."

A mellow alto voice spoke, but slowly, and came from a small device around Anala's waist. Brown-skinned, she stood as tall as me. Her black hair shone in the light, both long and straight. Like mine. She lacked arms and had a similar large bosom, though the circumference of her waist was half that of mine. Perhaps I exaggerate. Her red gown had my sister Leslie's stamp all over it. Like my yellow satin gown, hers encased her shoulders too, but hers had hundreds of eye-dazzling rhinestones. A small video camera affixed to an almost invisible mesh four inches from her mouth read her lips, converting her attempted speech into the sound we heard. Anala had no voice of her own.

That she could speak surprised me. "After I became a special Great Lady," she explained to Rina, "I had to do something about my voice. I couldn't stand my voice—shrill, tinny, and grating. Thanks to modern science, this micro device reads my lips. Don't you like my new voice? I love how I sound. But I'm pleased you've brought a fellow special Great Lady from Earth, Sol Empire. I see you have similar tastes in gowns as I do. A woman named Leslie makes all my dresses."

Again, I watched Rina's eyes glaze but had no time to pry into her mind. I chuckled. "Yes, that's my sister. And I love how they wrap around my shoulders. You don't have any voice."

Anala smiled. "No. I must speak slowly or the device doesn't pick up what I'm mouthing. Rather hard at first, but now I'm used to it. We have much in common, Molly. We've a giant swimming pool out back. I go swimming every day. You must visit and join me. But you must tell me about Leslie."

After pressing into my body in our unique way of hugging, she turned her attention to Rina.

"I've heard much about you. We followed your progress at Soros University as much as possible. You look much like your father. After the party, you must tell me about this astro-history of yours. Mind you, I'm not a scientist. No big words. Salad says you are traveling about the galaxy doing thesis work. You must tell me about that.

"Forgive me. I've been dominating the conversation," she said, nodding to her daughter. "This is Lanka. She's just turned eighteen and will soon undergo her conversion into a special Great Lady and marry Chandra, who comes from a

100

prominent family here in Kistna. Padma will be her personal assistant."

Lanka had her mother's facial features but her father's hair and eyes. She wore a knee-length cherry red gown that flared at her waist, the same exotic black stockings worn by all Soros U women, and matching tall heels. Knowing she wanted to become a Great Lady, I thought her wise for wearing the same height of heels we wore. Her mind's surface thoughts suggested she'd done everything she could in preparation for the mutation's effects on her body. I sensed a hint of jealousy over my own curvy shape. She didn't show the same attitudes toward her sister though.

"About time you paid us a visit. Dad's been paying your university tuition all these years, Rina, and yet this is the first time you deign to pay us a visit," Lanka said.

I sensed Rina's ire rising and intervened. "She's not had the chance, Lanka. I've been at Soros U, too, for the last six years. They work us to the bone. We don't get the summers off. Constant study. At last, Rina gets to travel doing the research for her thesis. She couldn't pass up this chance to visit you. I'm lucky because I have six sisters, including Leslie who is into fetish fashions. She and her husband Felix run Costumes R Us in Chicago on Earth, Sol Empire."

"Really?" Lanka asked.

I sensed I'd melted the ice. I hoped that was true or this evening would suffer.

Rina said, "Yeah, I've had to work hard to get the degrees I have. I'm on the last step. Doing the thesis. I must impress all the professors or try again. It's like having a huge failure mountain resting above my head held up by a thread. Talk about stress. Glad you won't suffer that. Congratulations on your upcoming wedding. Did you meet him at school?"

Rina turned the conversation around to what interested Lanka, who now couldn't stop chatting. Meanwhile, Anala led us on a tour of her mansion while Salad remained near the main entrance to welcome guests due to arrive within an hour.

The mansion occupied a single story with no stairs for Anala to navigate. One locked door led to the basement offices of Salad where he did much of his oversight work, but Anala had never been down the stairs. Her assistant didn't have a key to the door. Out back, colored lanterns cast a rainbow on the paved garden surrounding the giant pool. An abundance of flowering plants scented the air adding to the evening's ambiance, In one far corner, four musicians tuned up stringed instruments, akin to those I'd seen in Earth's museums.

I walked at the side of Anala while Rina and Lanka walked just behind us. Unpretentious. That's how I'd describe Anala. While she commanded great wealth, she didn't flaunt it. I made the mistake of asking about her formal balls for charity. She chatted about all she did until the other guests arrived.

"Excuse me. I must greet my other guests. We'll talk later. Tonight, you'll meet dozens of us special Great Ladies."

She left me standing beside the pool.

Lanka asked, "Molly, do you swim? Mom does. Every day."

"I floated in the ocean when I was a young girl, but no, not really. It's rather scary with my handicap. You're facing quite a transition."

She chuckled. "Well, Mom's never cooked. In fact, I don't think she's ever cooked a meal in her life, let alone swept floors, made beds, or done the laundry. She'll give her assistant all those chores, often issuing a flood of orders. Her assistant smiles and ignores them. Padma and I've talked about that lots.

"It'll be scary at first. But what new position isn't? Even being married can intimidate at first, sleeping with this person you've known for a short time. But being a special Great Lady

102

gains a woman the highest respect on our world. And money—though I would never lack for funds. Dad's wealthy if you didn't know."

"Are you choosing the option of no arms like your mother and me?" I asked.

"Of course. I can't see doing things halfway. But I'm not about to lose my voice like Mom. She's right. Her original voice—it was so bad no one could stand listening to her talk. Dad made several recordings of her speaking before she underwent that minor mutation. I know. Now she talks slow, but the voice box sounds mellow. My voice is just fine. But if Chandra wants me to do that, I will. Padma can aid me either way. Mom hopes that one day science can implant her new voice into her body. Then she could do away with that video camera.

"It gets bumped a hundred times a day. When it's off a little, it doesn't pick up anything she says. Now that's scary, but her personal assistant always watches for that, except at night. I've always wondered how Mom and Dad manage in bed."

She giggled. Rina rolled her eyes while I smiled.

The rest of the evening became one big blur of people. While most of the women were armless Great Ladies, a few had kept their arms. I noticed they received far less respect than the majority. The men wore expensive suits. Their shiny black shoes reflected the colored lights. Once guests arrived, the musicians provided relaxing background music. Later, many slow-danced. Chandra and Lanka insisted on introducing Rina and me to every available bachelor in attendance.

Chandra said, "These wealthy men can afford a special Great Lady. Molly, you can have your pick of men."

During lulls, I lightly touched the minds of everyone. I sensed no other Third Invaders. What a relief. Third Invaders weren't taking over the bodies of Great Ladies or these rich men. What were the Invaders trying to achieve with genetic engineering?

Salad, Anala, and Lanka invited Rina and me for a return visit the next day or when we could. He suggested we be present when Lanka underwent her mutation into a special Great Lady.

"Oh, please come. You must, Rina," Lanka pleaded. "Molly, too. I insist."

"It is rather a shock when you wake," Anala admitted. "I'm sure Lanka will appreciate our support. If nothing else, Molly, you and I can go swimming."

Padma escorted us back to our hotel. There, Cleo took over for her, and I thanked her.

When she left, Wanda said, "Well, did you find more Third Invaders?"

"No. I saw many special Great Ladies and wealthy men, but no Third Invaders occupying their bodies. I had expected to find many. It's just those two at the lab."

Wanda returned to her ship. Bishop plugged himself in for a recharge. Cleo tucked me into bed.

But I had bad dreams. Really bad dreams. I woke up dripping with sweat, having seen potential futures again. I felt bad I'd brought Rina into this mess with the Third Invaders. Her life might be affected, too.

As I sat up in bed, I realized what bothered me. No hesitation. These Third Invaders hadn't the slightest hesitation about mutating the two ID agents who accused Salad Industries of these crimes. Since they knew I had told the ID about the crimes, they might try silencing me and those with me, including Rina.

I knew I should be around Lanka when she awoke from her mutation coma. She would be terrified. And why did Rina's eyes glaze over whenever someone said "special Great Lady"? Was Rina tempted to become one, too?

What to do? And what did these Third Invaders want from running this genetic research and development laboratory? Why one thousand pods for clones? Who even had clones these days? Such was illegal on Earth.

That Anala who had no voice could still speak fascinated me. This world had invented a brilliant bit of technology: automatic lip reading. I wanted to send one of these devices back to Earth. Many could benefit from regained speech. Sure beats undergoing the Galactic Doll mutation for restoration of hearing and voice.

In the morning while Cleo fed me my room service breakfast, Rina dropped by.

"I got a text from Dad. Lanka is going to the lab today to get her special Great Lady mutation. She really wants us to come with her for moral support. Dad thinks she's getting nervous about it. She should be. I can't imagine why anyone would want to lose their arms. No offense, Molly."

I chuckled. "None taken. I agree we go. Now more than ever she needs a sister and friend. We should be present when she wakes up. I've seen people waking up from these mutations finding their lives destroyed. It's bad for men. Imagine a fellow waking to find his body indistinguishable from any armless Great Lady."

"You've seen that happen? Tell me about it while I take us to Dad's place," Rina said.

I told her about a few of my experiences back on Earth. I rather overdid it. When we landed, she was pale as a sheet. Her hand trembled.

She didn't know I had Bishop and Wanda tailing us. Before we departed, I told Wanda if there was any suggestion of mutation agents in the air, she should get out fast. Leave me to Bishop, who was immune to the gas. She asked why, but I refused to explain further. Not my place to reveal Bishop's robot-hood.

Once inside their mansion, the relief on Lanka's face told me we'd done the right thing. Her nervous twitters faded. She relaxed.

"Guess I'm ready to become a special Great Lady. I'm glad you both are coming with me and Dad. Mom wants to come, but she's way old."

I chuckled. "I know what you mean. We've got your back. That's what sisters and friends are for. But are you sure you want this? There's no going back. At least not easily. These boobs are heavy and annoying."

"But you look stunning, Molly. Quite beautiful," Lanka said. "On your world, don't beautiful women have more options in life than plain women?"

I sighed. "Point taken."

Rina laughed. "That's true on Mom's world of Zeta Minori-D, too. Maybe it's universal. Handsome men and gorgeous women have more options. It's a biological thing."

"But should it be that way?" I pointed out.

Salad ventured his viewpoint. "Look, I wanted the best woman I could find, best looking, best personality, best mind. Best everything. Anala and I have had twenty of the happiest years of our lives. We look forward to the next twenty. It's universal. Everyone wants the best mate they can afford."

"Money isn't everything," I said. I thought of Ted and Sam. No, money meant nothing in my choice of mates.

Lanka laughed. "But it damn well helps a lot."

Her father glared at her choice of words but said nothing.

Chapter 13 Strike Back

Salad parked in the staff lot of his genetics research lab. He assisted us out of his shuttle. Cleo rolled along at my side, as we headed inside. Jivin met us with a shifty smile plastered on his face.

"Ah, Miss Lanka. I'm pleased you have chosen the life of a special Great Lady like your mother."

Lanka beamed. His words appeared to sooth her fears. If she only knew how fake they were.

"Follow me. We'll program the computer for your perfect body."

As we walked, he turned to Rina. "And are you ready to become a special Great Lady like your younger sister? You can share this special time."

"Well, not really," Rina said. Again, her eyes unfocused. She hesitated, which Jivin picked up on.

"With a special Great Lady mutation, all options are your choice, Rina. You choose your body's appearance. And what about you, Molly? Ready for that new hair modification?"

"Not today," I said. "Still thinking about it."

"Ah, here we are. Lanka, let's go over the options. Ready to make your choices?"

While we sat back, Lanka made her selections. She opted for armless, like her mother and many Great Ladies. But added the tiny waist and the new hair, skipping the "jumbo breast" option. I wondered who in her right mind would want breasts that gigantic. Then again, who seeks to be handicapped? Yet, Anala, Lanka, and many others did. I wondered if the Third Invaders carried out a mass implant like the Sixth Invaders had done on Earth. Their hypnotic suggestion had women of earth lining up for a Galactic Doll mutation. I made a note to run therapy sessions. Lanka was an excellent candidatem as well as Anala. Here only wealthy women became special Great Ladies, unlike Earth.

To my shock, Rina said, "Okay, I'll do it. I'm meant to be a special Great Lady, too."

Before I could counsel her decision, Salad praised her, and Jivin rattled off the options. She chose only the basic Great Lady form. One after the other, syringes appeared in the dispenser. Jivin had both ladies lie on comfortable couches before injecting them. As he spoke smooth deception, cloaked as words of encouragement about how beautiful they'd be when they awoke, they drifted into their mutation comas.

Jivin said, "You two stay here. Watch over them while I get stasis pods ready. We must provide proper nourishment during their mutation periods."

After he stepped out, Salad sighed. "This is all I ever wanted for my girls. Beautiful women can marry rich men who can give them all they deserve. Now I can relax. Both will be Great Ladies and can have their choice of men. Rina always worried me. After her mother psyched out and split. Now Rina can have her pick of men and the rich life she deserves."

"What's wrong with letting them make their own choices?" I said.

"Now they can make their own choices but from among the best men Kali-D has. I can't give them anything better than that, but I'll see Rina has no financial worries. Do you hear a hissing sound?"

I looked up. Already gas shot into the room from vents in the ceiling.

I yelled, "Mutation agent!"

Salad dove for the door, yanking with all his might, but Jivin had locked it from the outside. Jivin's voice came from speakers embedded in the ceiling.

"You two, pay attention. If you ever divulge what goes on here at this lab, we will find you and mutate you into bird people; you can clean toilets the rest of your lives."

Salad screamed, "This is my company. You can't do this..."

His body slumped to the floor, but the gas didn't affect me. I recalled something Bishop telling me that when he had injected me with the mutation agent to save my life, he had had to give me five times the normal adult dose before it took effect. A plan formed. I sat down on a couch and feigned unconsciousness. I suspected spy cameras focused on me.

A fan activated, sucking fumes upwards, while fresh air slipped in from floor vents. The door opened. Jivin and his compatriot, the office manager, wheeled in gurneys with stasis pods on them. From the corner of my eye, I watched as they undressed the two women before placing them in the pods and attaching the tubes and electronics. They wheeled them off.

"Molly, are you awake?" Bishop whispered from the doorway.

I peeked with one eye and saw nothing.

"Yeah. It's not affecting me. Knock both men out. I want them alive."

"Wanda wants them dead. She's found her two ID men in stasis pods. They're morphing into special Great Ladies."

"We must uncover what's going on here. Keep them alive. Better yet, turn them into armless Great Ladies. Look out. Someone's coming back."

The manager returned, undressed Salad, and rolled him into the stasis pod. He left with the body, presumably to hook Salad up to the machinery. I rose and pressed against the wall by the door waiting for his return.

"What the..."

With the man's attention on me, Bishop conked him on the head. He dropped like a rock. Bishop clicked off his invisibility shield.

"Wanda is watching the other man hook up Salad to the machine. She'll take him out after that. What are we to do now? She says we don't have jurisdiction here."

"I need to question him, but I don't want Jivin escaping."

Wanda appeared, dragging the unconscious Jivin with her.

She said, "Bishop said not to kill these alien fiends. After what they've done to our two agents, I say shoot them."

"You found your agents?"

Wanda said, "Yeah. They're hooked up in pods like Lanka and Rina. I think their arms are vanishing, and they're looking like those special Great Ladies. These two have to pay for what they've done."

"I agree. Bring them in here. Bishop, dial in Great Lady and bring up the options. I want them armless and unable to speak."

"Oh, you fiend!" Wanda said. Her smile spread to her entire face. "That's far better than killing them."

While Bishop operated the controls, I cautioned her. "These two Kali-D bodies are being operated by Third Invaders who've body swapped into them. We've no idea where these bodies' original owners are, probably in stasis pods somewhere. I want these aliens imprisoned and helpless in mutated bodies. Then I can probe their minds and find out what's going on. The Sixth Invaders body swapping technology requires a nearby electronic station that emits the white energy that causes the transfer. Perhaps it's in their offices."

Bishop said, "No one has questioned us. But what do we do when other workers question us? Should I inject them now?"

"Yes, inject them and put them into stasis pods. Leave the staff to me. I have an idea. Wanda, have you found Jivin's office yet?"

"I think so. Follow me."

"Cleo, come with me," I said. "Oh, Bishop, you wear Jivin's ID badge and bring the office manager's badge for Wanda."

We walked down a long corridor with stasis pods lining the sides. She paused by one pair.

"There lie Jarvis and Eric."

I studied them. "Your analysis is right. They're becoming armless Great Ladies. Let's hope they don't lose their voices. Can't tell until they wake."

Once in Jivin's office, I observed while Wanda searched for clues. I spotted a metal plate about a foot square in the ceiling.

"Up there. That's likely the receiver unit for their body swap machine. We don't want to let Jivin or the manager sit in this chair. There's likely to be another one in the manager's office."

Wanda continued rummaging but kept her head as far from beneath that square as possible.

"What's that? A comm set?" I asked. "I can't read the writing."

She laughed. "I can't either."

That gave me an idea. "Found any official company paper?"

"Yeah, why?"

"Start writing in your own language, not Federation Common."

"Huh? Okay, but I don't follow."

"To Employees of Salad Industries," I began.

"This is to inform you I granted Jivin and his office manager their fondest desires to become special Great Ladies along with me. While we are recovering, I have appointed Mr. Bishop to run the laboratory. Later, I'll hire replacements. Sincerely, Mr. Salad Naraka."

111

Wanda chuckled and finished up. I had her lay the official-looking document on Jivin's desk. Next, I had Cleo read the writing on what I thought might be the comm center. It was. Following Cleo's instructions, I hoped I had Wanda speaking to the entire lab.

"May I have your attention?"

Her voice echoed from either direction from the hallway outside Jivin's office. I nodded.

"This is Wanda Hammerstein, assistant to Mr. Bishop. Mr. Salad Naraka wishes me to read this letter to all who work here." She rattled off what she'd written.

"Those who doubt this may come to Mr. Bishop's office, formerly Jivin's office, and inspect the official letter. You can view the three men on their way to widh fulfillment, becoming special Great Ladies. Mr. Naraka's daughters are doing fine. I give you Mr. Bishop."

She handed the mic to him. He gave me a curious glance as if to say what do I say? I smiled.

"Hello. I'm Mr. Bishop. A big thank you for the excellent work everyone has been doing. All work will continue as before. Management doesn't wish to make changes, not until Salad hires a permanent replacement for Jivin. Thank you. Keep up the superior work."

Bishop flipped off the comm. "How's that? I didn't know what you wanted me to say."

"Perfect, Bishop. That was excellent. You stay here. Wanda, take me to see the girls in their pods. I'll keep up the illusion."

I stood before the pods containing Rina and Lanka. Nearby Salad and the two lab men lay in their pods. I noticed what looked like a countdown clock attached to each. All displayed eight days. Two men in white lab coats rushed up to us.

"Hi," I said, putting on my welcoming smile. "I'm Rina and Lanka's friend. Isn't this just wonderful? Today, they're becoming special Great Ladies together like sisters should."

"What's going on?" one asked.

"Molly Parkinson. This is Wanda Hammerstein, the temp office manager, I'm told. When we came this morning, I didn't know Mr. Naraka wanted to join his wife and sisters. I guess he and your two men had this planned for quite some time."

"Badal Haldar, Chief Geneticist. Why did they order us out of this section this morning? Are you from Soros University? That's one of their robot helpers."

"Yes, I came with Rina. Cleo. They don't allow human personal assistants at the university, just these helper robots. I don't know why Jivin did that, but I can guess. Can't you?"

I gave them my coyest smile.

"No, I can't."

"I suppose Jivin was embarrassed, Didn't want you witnessing his transformation into a special Great Lady. Men don't often do that, at least not on Cass-C."

"He never gave any hint..." Badal's voice trailed off.

"Excuse me. Mr. Naraka neglected to tell us what clothing arrangements are needed. They wake from their mutation comas, in," I glanced at the countdown clocks, "about eight days. Should we bring some here?"

"No, when they wake, we provide one outfit. Part of the service. But I still don't understand," Badal said.

I shrugged my shoulders. "We love being special Great Ladies. It's not only the province of women. I suppose you should meet Mr. Bishop. He seems like an okay fellow. Say, if I understood Mr. Naraka, he will let Mr. Bishop choose replacements from those who are already working in this lab instead of bringing in outside people. He says everyone here is doing a good job running the company. Why look elsewhere?"

"Well, we are doing groundbreaking work here. I'm glad Mr. Naraka sees that. Jivin often didn't."

"I think that's why Mr. Naraka is making these top-level changes, giving your rank-and-file personnel a chance to run this company. Rina and I were wondering if you ever have geneticists from Cass-C and Soros University visiting here. I know geneticists who would leap at the chance to study what you're doing here. They invented the arm regrow mutation. Perhaps you've heard of that."

"How interesting! We've wanted to share our findings for years, but Jivin wouldn't allow it. If Bishop has the authority to allow that, we'd love to have them visit. We can pick their brains. Re-growing limbs and organs are critical applications of genetic engineering."

"Let's go visit Mr. Bishop and ask him," I suggested.

We found him showing the letter to other employees. I let Badal make his case for visiting geneticists.

With six men and women listening, Bishop said, "Now that's the best idea I've heard. Yes, Cass-C geneticists, those at Soros University, have created a mutation that regrew the arms of over two thousand people. We should bring them here and work on an exchange of ideas and technology. Let's make it happen. I'll get word to Ashton Soros later today. Any other bright ideas?"

Several clapped. One explained, "We've been begging for an open exchange with other geneticists for two decades, but Jivin wouldn't allow it. This is great news. We'll spread the word."

After they left, I asked Bishop and Wanda to search company records for clues about what the Third Invaders plans might have been and if they could find Amalie Leroy.

"I had best pay a visit to Anala and arrange for another personal assistant for her husband. I'll send word to Eva and

114

Lara. I want them here as fast as possible. Rina might need a robot assistant."

"Want me to fly you back to the hotel?" Wanda asked.

"No, I'm hoping I can manage with Cleo's help. It's vital we find out what the Third Invaders wanted from this lab. Keep me posted."

"Cleo, hang on to this visitor's pass for Molly," Bishop said.

We had left the bay door open on the shuttle. I walked in and up front to the controls. Cleo buckled me in. Menus controlled these vehicles. I spoke the destination, though Cleo was ready to press buttons for me if voice commands didn't work.

Once back at the hotel, I sent a message to Eve and Lara via the hotel's hyperspace relay system. Then, I called Anala and got her permission to drop by after lunch. I ordered room service. As Cleo fed me, I relaxed. I hadn't realized how tense I'd become doing all this on my own without Bishop, Wanda, or Rina close by in case I needed something. I proved that with Cleo I could visit other worlds by myself. And if Rina wound up like me, a lack of arms wouldn't stop her thesis work. Amazing how much tension eased.

Anala welcomed me though her assistant met me at the door and led me to her poolside table.

"Salad isn't here yet. Tea perhaps?"

"No. I have both good and bad news. The good news first. Lanka is in her special Great Lady mutation coma. At the last minute, Rina became one, too."

"Oh, that is such wonderful news. Salad was worried Rina wouldn't take advantage of this opportunity. He wants her to have the best in life."

"Yes, I've seen both in their stasis pods. At the moment, we don't know what options either sister chose."

"That is as it should be. It's a very private choice. Padma expects to be Lanka's assistant. I don't think Lanka liked the enormous breasts option, though, but I hope she went with the tiny waist like mine. It displays our impressive curves, don't you think?"

"Well, yes, it does. Now for the bad news. It seems a pair of Third Invaders had been body swapped into Jivin and his operations manager for many years. They've conducted some illegal actions."

"Oh, dear me! Salad will be angry. What can they do at a simple genetics research lab?"

"He knows. It seems they sent goon squads to other worlds, kidnapped adults and children, brought them here, mutated them into bird people and other creatures, and sold them into slavery."

"Dear Lord! Salad will fire them at once. We must tell him."

"I already did. After they handled the girls, Jivin unleashed that mutation agent on Salad and me. They locked the door. Salad's in a mutation coma now. He's safe but in a stasis pod beside the girls. Because I've been exposed to many mutation agents, I wasn't knocked out. At least that's what we think. Anyway, my security man, Bishop, and a Federation ID Agent Wanda Hammerstein arrived and captured the two men. Since the authorities need to question them, Jivin and his manager have been mutated, too. Wanda wanted to kill them because several days ago those two men mutated her two field agent companions turning them into special Great Ladies. We can see their mutating bodies in the stasis pods."

"Oh, Salad! What's he going to become? This is horrid. Is the Federation ID investigating now? Can I see the girls and Salad?"

"I thought you might like to visit them. I can come by and pick you up tomorrow morning. By then, we hope to know which mutation Salad's undergoing. I've left Bishop and Wanda there searching their records. I don't think Jivin's

116

mutating Salad into a bird person. Probably a special Great Lady like yourself."

"Oh! You—you mean he'll look like me? A woman?"

"We won't know for sure until morning. But you should prepare for that. It's not a death sentence. Terrorists mutated my first two husbands into special Great Ladies. I admit life was strange, but our love kept us strong. If that's what they did to him, I'm sure you both will still do just fine, though he might need his own personal assistant."

"Dear me. Dear me, but I suppose that's true. Salad will be angry."

"One other thing. While you are lining up a personal assistant for Salad, you might purchase several more sets of this video device that reads your lips. I'd like to take one back to Soros University. Perhaps they can make some for the three children that Jivin turned into voiceless, armless Great Ladies. Then, they can at least speak."

"We'll do that today. Will Rina need an assistant and a voice box, too?"

"We don't know yet. Best be prepared. If she loses her arms, Soros University will provide her a robot helper like my Cleo here. They don't allow human assistants on campus. But as you can see, I'm getting by okay with Cleo."

"All right. But I might just see about lining up one for Rina, anyway. Will you stay for supper? Go for a swim with me? Or perhaps have a stiff drink with me. I think I need a very stiff drink. Salad as a special Great Lady. That will take getting used to."

I chuckled and turned down her offers.

When Cleo and I returned to my hotel room, a hyperspace relay reply from Eve waited for me. She promised she and Lara would be on the next flight to Kali-D and would bring another robot assistant. I relayed the news to Wanda and Bishop.

Cleo helped me take a long, soaking bath. I turned in early, exhausted.

When I awoke, I sat up on the edge of the bed as I always did. I gasped. All my lovely long black hair lay on the bed. Cleo rolled in and stared.

"Molly. What happened to your hair? It fell off."

"Shit. That mutation. Guess it affected me anyway. My head feels funny. Put my shoes on. I want to see myself in the mirror."

During the night, my body grew mutated hair. My new hair was short, thicker, and still black. It shone. Plus, I had a strange tactile sensation coming from every strand. As Cleo dressed me, we noticed another change. My waist had shrunk some though I could still wear my yellow gown.

I had certain cravings for food and indulged myself via room service, figuring the body was telling me what it needed. As I ate, Wanda dashed into my room.

"Molly, something's happened at the lab during the night—what happened to your hair?" Her pale face yielded to one of surprise.

"I think the mutation is affecting me without putting me in a coma. What's happened? I'm supposed to take Anala to see Salad and the girls this morning. Is Bishop okay? What happened?"

"Bishop's okay. He recorded the attack. Six masked men shot the night security guards, broke in, and killed Jivin, the manager, and my two ID agents. Everyone else is okay as far as we can tell. Bishop has the local police on the scene and has the engineers checking for any other sabotage or damage. Let's pick up Anala and get there soon. I've notified the ID and they're sending backup."

Later, Wanda landed our shuttle in the lot, now swarming with local police vehicles. Guards checked our ID badges. We headed straight for Bishop's office. Anala's face suggested she'd gotten little sleep. Her assistant walked behind her while Cleo rolled along behind me.

"Is Salad all right?" Anala asked the moment we entered Bishop's office.

"Please have a seat. Much has happened," Bishop said. He tried to project sympathy; he had gotten better at mimicking human responses.

"Salad is in his stasis pod and wasn't harmed during last night's attack. Neither was Lanka and Rina. With the help of our genetic engineers, we identified the mutations. They exposed all three to the Great Lady mutation. Lanka and Rina's options include loss of arms, tiny waist, and sensitive hair. Salad's options include those three and no voice."

He looked at my short hair. "It appears Molly was exposed to the same mutation agent as Salad. Only her hair is affected. You still have your voice, right?"

"Er, yeah. Seems I'm still okay otherwise. Well, my waist is shrinking a little. I should take Anala to see her family. Then, I must see what happened last night."

As Anala stood looking at Salad in his stasis pod, tears trickled down her cheeks. Already his breasts had enlarged; his arms looked withered. I saw new, thick hair had already replaced his and was about as long as mine. The pods holding Lanka and Rina lay next to his, a pile of discarded hair lying beside each woman's head. All four of us had similar thick new hair about four inches long.

"Oh, Salad, what have they done to you? Will he survive this? Will he be okay?"

"He's healthy. Bishop queried the engineers this morning. All say he's doing well. Physically, he'll be like you. Mentally? Well, he will need a lot of support and encouragement from you, Anala. He told me how much he relished spending the next twenty years with you. He loves you."

"It will be hard for him, won't it?"

"No denying that, Anala. Very hard. He'll depend on you."

"Oh, Salad. I won't let you down. Guess I best get him the things he'll need when he wakes up. Salad told me they would give us Lanka's final measurements. Then we can purchase clothing before she wakes."

Wanda checked on that. She returned all smiles, handing three documents to Anala's helper.

"Here you go. The genetic engineers calculated their final measurements. They said they'll provide one set of clothing when they wake up, but those won't be fashionable."

Anala thanked Wanda and left, her assistant guiding her. I heard them discussing what they needed to buy for the three. Meanwhile, Wanda and I returned to Bishop's office.

"Okay, what happened last night?"

Bishop said little, preferring to replay the videos. He had combined the recordings from several cameras into one stream. The jerky gaps resulted when the men were beyond camera range.

Six men rushed out of a shuttle. Wearing battle armor and carrying blasters, they killed the night guard before blasting through the main doors. Since they darted here and there before stopping by the rows of stasis pods, I concluded they weren't familiar with the lab's layout.

Too bad it didn't record sound. Various men pointed to various pods before they fired blasters. First, they destroyed Jivin and his pod, then his manager's. Then they killed Jarvis and Eric. As they killed these two ID agents, an armed guard walked up. They shot him and left the way they came. The camera stayed focused on the rows of pods. A blaster shot made an eight-inch hole through the plastic pod cover and the chest of the body inside. Blood spatter covered the remaining plastic cover. Gruesome.

120

Wanda's soft voice intruded. "The murder of two ID agents turned this into an official ID investigation. A whole unit is on their way. They'll want to interview us. Molly, are you sure you're all right? Voice still there? I'm worried you'll end up like Anala and Salad, unable to speak."

"So far, so good. Hair is mutating for sure. Possibly my waist, but I'm still talking. Any idea who these men were? Where they come from?"

Bishop said, "One fact is certain. The Third Invaders didn't want us questioning Jivin or the ID agents. I've not yet calculated the odds that they'll send a hit squad after you, Molly, and me, since we uncovered them."

"Maybe they see me as just a special Great Lady, not a threat."

"Stick around until I can leave. I'm not leaving your side," Bishop said.

"Seven days until they wake from their comas. Then, we'll have our hands full," I said.

With a straight face, Wanda said, "But Molly, you don't have any hands."

Chapter 14 Theories and Recoveries

Eve and Lara arrived along with Nikita's old robot assistant, George. I met them at the spaceport and got them rooms at my hotel. While they unpacked, I brought them up to date on what I knew.

Lara said, "I believe we can regrow the children's arms. We are mutating them into Galactic Dolls, hoping that restores their voices. If so, next we'll work on their arms. Any idea where their mother is?"

"Well done. None, yet, but Bishop is searching their records," I said.

"I like you with shorter hair," Eve said. "It's what? About a foot long now."

"It's growing at least six inches a day. Each strand has a weird sense of touch. The overwhelming amount of sensation around my head feels strange."

They chuckled.

"My dresses don't fit right, but it's not too noticeable yet. Is their special Great Lady mutation the same as our armless Galactic Doll version? Less the telepathy. I think these mutations predate those of the Sixth Invaders. And that can be a big clue."

Later, Wanda took us to the lab.

After welcoming everyone, Bishop said, "I've found clone bodies in storage. Salad has a youthful duplicate of himself. There's a copy of Anala and one of Lanka. None for Rina. And your new clone, Molly, is growing fine according to their computer readouts. Should we body swap Salad into his new clone body?"

We discussed their cloning operations for a time before heading out to check on my new body.

"My body will be normal for once," I teased. "I'll leave you to consult with the genetic engineers while I chat with Anala. Don't swap Salad into his male clone body just yet. Something doesn't feel right."

Lara said, "Why are they wearing earbuds?"

The head genetic engineer walked up to meet Eve and Lara and overheard her question.

"We play positive re-enforcing words during their comas. It lessens their trauma when they first wake. It's not necessary for the basic Great Lady mutation. Even though women wanted the armless modification, they woke with fear bordering on terror. Since we cannot undo this option, we found positive re-enforcement eliminates wild reactions. Women tell us this is a difficult modification to get used to."

If I had had arms, I might have slapped him silly. Instead, I asked if we could hear what the patients heard. He sent me to Room Ten. I headed off to find out while Lara and Eve joined the other geneticists and engineers.

A woman played the recording for me. She said, "It's not long and is repeated while they're unconscious. It almost eliminates their emotional reactions when they wake. From our studies, it aids adjustment to their new lives as special Great Ladies."

This was implanting. The pain of the mutation buried these words below the person's conscious recall. The pain gave the words their force or control over the person's actions and reactions. After hearing them, I knew we had to wait on swapping Salad's body.

```
I'm now the perfection of beauty. I
love my body. I am proud and honored
to be one of the beautiful and
special Great Ladies. I'm very happy
and totally content. I am perfect.
```

> There is nothing better than being a
> special Great Lady. I am a role
> model for others, and I must show
> everyone how wonderful it is to be a
> special Great Lady. There is nothing
> I cannot do though I must depend
> upon my personal assistant. I will
> always be faithful to my spouse.

By definition, playing these words repetitively for eight days while the person was in a mutation coma and experiencing massive pain is an implant. At least drugs and electric shocks weren't involved. It could have been worse. But...

My hunch about Salad's body swap proved correct. He'd been given this implant. When he awoke, these concepts would become part of his view of life. I tried to imagine his internal conflict with his clone body being a normal male while his mind believed he was a special Great Lady. Awful. Might cause a psychotic break.

If he received Celeste's therapy and erased the implant and the mutation pains, then he'd be free to body swap without ill effects. Otherwise, perhaps in time, the control value of the implant would lessen enough allowing Salad to body swap into the new clone body.

I relaxed a little. Since Lanka and Rina both were losing their arms, this implant might ease their fear upon waking. While they had chosen that option, nothing would prepare them for such a shocking new reality.

With little I could do at the lab, I visited Anala to make sure she was coping.

"Hi, Molly. Yes, we're okay. Padma is off buying a half dozen voice machines and arranging for a new personal assistant. I hope we're not causing more problems for Salad.

All personal assistants are women. He'll still be a male, won't he?"

"Yes, but his body will appear that of a special Great Lady. I checked. He's got a male clone in a stasis pod, but..."

"I recall him telling me he had one made for each of us. Should we transfer him now?"

"I don't think that's a wise idea." I explained about the implanted words, watching for any adverse reactions from her. By my reciting the implant words, I risked restimulating her.

"You know, I seem to recall hearing something like that. That's what I felt when I first woke. Scared. Terrified. But that only lasted a moment. I just knew I was perfect, that I was a proud, beautiful special Great Lady. Right away, contentment replaced that terrified feeling. I'm a role model for others because life is wonderful as a special Great Lady. Besides, I'm always showing everyone there isn't anything I can't do. But we need our personal assistants."

She glanced up, meeting my eyes. "I see what you're suggesting. When Salad wakes, he will have the same feelings I did. Couldn't that cause him a mental problem if he's in that new clone male body?"

"My thoughts. Best be safe. He can always swap bodies whenever he desires."

She smiled. "That's settled then. I became a special Great Lady after Lanka was born. I tore rather badly, and the doctors believed undergoing this mutation would repair me. They were right. Say, would you care for a swim?"

"No, but could we share a cold drink on your patio by the gardens?"

Sharing an iced tea, I asked, "Do you care for the plants yourself or do you have a gardener?"

I spent a relaxing afternoon with Anala. Later Padma returned and gave me two sets of the voice machine. She'd hired Kasi to be Salad's personal assistant. Kasi dropped by to familiarize herself with the home. I headed back to my hotel.

The next day, ID agents swarmed the lab like ants on the prowl. I relayed my version of events six times. They swept for bugs and other electronic spy devices and found two in both Jivin's office and that of his manager. By nightfall, they declared the lab alien-free. They installed software that allowed them remote access to the main computer system so they could search company records for any significant details.

One agent, Otto Stein, must have known Wanda. He took her aside for her statement while another grilled me.

Before departing, Wanda said, "Otto hinted I might be in trouble—what with two agents dying on my watch. They want answers. He'll back me up, for whatever that'll do." She gave me a hug and said goodbye.

Eve and Lara disappeared with the genetic engineers. Bishop and I returned to our hotel.

Giving his best attempt at displaying annoyance, Bishop said, "The ID agents have very little . Not like the kinds of investigations you and I have done."

We talked while Cleo fed me supper.

"You're right. I have questions. Who invented their Great Lady mutation? How is it related to the Sixth Invaders' Galactic Doll agent? Why have the capacity for a thousand clones? Why invent all those weird mutations? Why the bird people? How many secret labs do the Third Invaders have? How long were they inhabiting the bodies of Jivin and his manager? Plus, we need to find the children's mother."

Bishop said, "Another thing. I've been calculating the impact of Rina's thesis work. I consulted all the databases I can find. Nowhere is there any reasonable explanation for why humans inhabit many worlds in this half the galaxy. By my calculations, we'd expect many other humanoid species, such as those on Dingle-D or Rutgers-E. And I would expect more strange species such as the Vogelmenschen."

126

"Good point. Her research may yield valuable clues. I admit I don't know astro-history. What she's doing interests me. Plus, I'd like to know why Homo sapiens are widespread, too. Then, we have those rogue robots to locate." I exhaled. Many avenues needed exploring.

On the morning of their coma's eighth day, I picked up Anala, her personal assistant Jaya, Padma, and Kasi and chauffeured them to the lab. Bishop welcomed us as we landed, bypassing the heavy security forces that now guarded the lab. When we reached the stasis pods, the engineers had already unhooked all three and had them lying on portable cots.

"We provide a simple set of clothing for them unless you've brought what you'd prefer they wear," one said, glancing from Anala to me.

"We brought dresses in their favorite colors if that's all right," Anala said.

She nodded, while Padma and Kasi unpacked the suitcase they'd brought. George rolled up beside Cleo.

George said in his mechanical voice, "I brought a proper Soros University dress for Miss Rina Pappas. Should I dress her now?"

The engineer said, "No. First, they should see themselves in a mirror. Ah, here they come now."

Several workers rolled in tall, full-length mirrors on wheels, positioning them beside each of the three naked bodies.

"When they wake, their personal assistant should stand beside them. They will need help to sit and then stand while looking at their perfect bodies."

Now, we waited. I expected the girls to wake first, which they did at the same time. Sensory and emotional overload. That's what I imagined they felt as they regained consciousness and realized how much they'd depended upon their arms and hands.

127

My first husband, Ted, said it best. "It's like waking up and finding the space you control has shrunk from about three feet all around you to that of your nose and monster boobs. Helpless."

Because of the many terrorist attacks years ago on Earth, I'd seen thousands of people waking from mutation comas. Fear, shock, terror.

Even though both Lanka and Rina had knowingly chosen this option, waking to experience an armless life brought instant fear, nearing terror. Their faces twisted in shock and fright, and each shrieked, startling Anala and the personal assistants.

As the assistants helped them stand and look at their new forms, I noticed the implanted words kicking in, particularly with Lanka.

"Oh! I really am *perfect*! I'm proud. I *am* a beautiful Great Lady. But I'm nervous and scared. No, I'm happy. I *am* perfect. Padma, nothing's better than a special Great Lady. But I depend on you. I have to be a role model like Mom. It's wonderful to be a special Great Lady. Mom, there's nothing I can't do, is there? Oh, I'm naked."

While Padma dressed her, Rina reacted similarly, except she added, "Oh, gods! What have I done? I'm helpless. No, I'm perfect." She rattled off the phrases of the implanted words she'd heard over and over for the last eight days.

George dressed her in the standard Soros University white blouse and black skirt outfit, tailored to accommodate her new, larger bosom and tiny waist.

Once dressed, the initial terror drained away. The implanted phrases dominated their thinking. But dressed, they noticed each other and then their father, who hadn't yet woken.

"Rina, you look beautiful, too," Lanka said. "Now we really are sisters and special Great Ladies."

A hesitant smile appeared on Rina's face. "We are beautiful and perfect, but I'm scared. How can I do my thesis work? Oh, I must depend on my assistant."

George said, "I am here to serve your every need. Please allow a week for you and me to synchronize with each other."

"Is that Dad?" asked Lanka.

I said, "Yes, sit. Let me explain what happened after you slipped into your mutation comas."

That sobered both girls, but then Salad woke up, quite confused. He tried screaming but had no voice. Combined with everything else, he passed out from the shock. An engineer roused him. While he tried to scream again, his body shook, radiating terror, before he vomited on the cot.

Anala introduced Kasi to him. While Kasi cleaned him up, I saw the implanted words kick in. The others believed he had calmed down, and that all was now well. Hardly. Kasi faced a challenge getting him dressed for the first time. Once done, she brushed his long hair, while Padma did Lanka's hair and George did the same for Rina. Kasi attached the voice machine, adjusting the camera for maximum focus on his lips.

Salad spoke too fast. The device caught one word in a dozen.

Anala said in her slow mechanical voice, "Salad, remember, you must speak slow like I do."

"What. Happened. To. Me? I. Am. Perfect. No!" He rushed through the implanted words, which became an odd word here and there.

Again, I explained what had happened. His eyes grew wider and wider. He tried speaking but again went many times faster than the machine could handle. I suggested he go home with Anala and Lanka and adapt to his new situation.

"Rina and I will come by tomorrow for lunch. We have much to discuss," I said.

"Scared!" he said. "Terrified. No. Perfect. Happy. No. Yes."

Salad had many struggles ahead. I couldn't even run Celeste's therapy on him until he gained effective use of the voice machine. Giving him time seemed a good start. At least he hadn't yet tried killing himself like many terrorist victims had on Earth.

"Come on, Rina. Let's get you back to our hotel. I had them move your things into my room. We can bunk together."

"I'm frightened. I'm perfect, but scared. Why did I ever do this? But I'm supposed to be a special Great Lady. I'm helpless. George, don't let me fall."

"I'll keep a steadying arm around you, Rina," George said.

With Cleo rolling along at my side, I led the way to our shuttle. I felt annoyed at Rina, but she had agreed to this path. Now she had to walk it. Still, I couldn't turn my back on her. Her implant insisted she could do anything she wished but had to depend on her assistant. That evening, I allowed her to do just that, learn to depend on George.

Once in our room, Rina said, "I've always done everything for myself. I now depend on George, but I'm scared and nervous. And happy and perfect. How can I be all four? And I need to get going on my thesis travels. Can I even do that now? Oh, depend on George."

My heart understood her confusion, how the two opposing positions tore her in half. But time didn't allow me to spend a week or more giving her therapy sessions.

"Have George get your stuff in order. What's your next destination?" I asked.

Rina tried reaching for her computer and the bag of documents. With tears seeping down her cheeks, she sat back and gave George instructions. Well, I could help. I had Cleo get my computer out and running. Time to decide what I should do.

Bishop entered. "Molly, I've uncovered more about those thousands of clones. Their database is extensive. During the last ten years, the lab produced ten batches of a thousand clones, each group sold to a company on Goringy-E, Staszak Import-Exports."

"Excellent. No word on where they took Amalie Leroy?"

"Not yet."

"Goringy-E?" Rina interrupted. "That's one of the worlds I must visit. Their oldest records aren't digitized." Fighting frustration, she ordered George to bring up her schedule. "If you're going there, may I come with you?"

I didn't need telepathy to sense how desperately she wanted our company on her trip.

"Of course, Rina. Bishop, make travel plans for us, please."

Someone knocked on our door. "Expecting anyone?" I said, glancing from Bishop to Rina.

Bishop opened the door. A young man wearing a black, felt cowboy style hat looked in at us.

"Is Rina Pappas here? The desk said this was her room."

"That's me," she said. "Come in."

"Maybe you don't remember me. We went to preschool together. Our homes were next door, and every day we played together. I'm Adri Kedar. I haven't seen you since you and your mother moved away a lifetime ago, but your father has shown me clippings of you at Soros University."

"We played together. Yeah, a lifetime ago," Rina said, her voice wavering. "Didn't I give you that stone spear point I found?"

Adri smiled, as he removed his hat. "You remember that? That stone tool launched my career in astro-archeology. I'm an astro-archeologist. The last I heard you ended up on Zeta Minori-D. But I ran into your dad last year. He told me

131

you were on Cass-C at the university. I didn't know you'd become a special Great Lady."

"I came out of the mutation coma today. Rather scary. This is George, my Soros U helper robot." She then introduced Bishop and me. "I'm working on my thesis, going for a doctorate in astro-history, but with minors in linguistics and chemistry."

"Yeah, that's what your dad said. Did you get that packet of ancient documents you wanted? I helped put them together."

"You did? Small world. Yes, I picked them up last week. Haven't had time to study them. Been in the mutation coma these past eight days. Thanks for collecting them."

"I'm exploring ancient human civilizations. Have you noticed many Federation worlds have our species on them?"

Rina and I laughed. She said, "Duh, no kidding. My thesis is on the origin and distribution of Homo sapiens. At least in our half the galaxy. I'm working on gathering the earliest appearance dates on all worlds inhabited by humans. Not all worlds digitized such records. I'm on Kali-D retrieving physical copies."

"Wow, our investigations overlap. I'm off to Goringy-E to pick up samples for Carbon Dating. Professor Levitsky has been kind enough to get samples from their earliest known human settlement site.

"This season, that's what I'm doing—collecting samples for dating."

"You're right. That data can help me too. Goringy-E is where I'm heading next. Molly's going there for other reasons. If I can figure out how George can run my thesis stuff, maybe we can compare notes and dates. This is all very new and frightening, but I know I'm a perfect special Great Lady now. I must depend on my assistant."

Adri chuckled. "Rina, you are gorgeous. Both of you are beautiful special Great Ladies. I didn't expect you'd have that done. You're stunning. No doubt about that."

She flushed. "Many professors at Soros U used to lack arms. They all had helper robots, like Molly. And sixteen hundred of her people were there too, only they called themselves armless Galactic Dolls. Molly's sister Eve and friend Lara invented arm regrow cures. Now there are only a few professors like me. I can do this, only..."

"Only it must be terrifying," Adri said. "Your father didn't say you were married."

She flushed. "I'm not. Too busy studying."

"Oh," Adri said, his face flushing. "I just assumed. No, I'm not either. Too darn busy with school and digs. You're both going to Goringy-E?"

We nodded.

"Then, if you don't mind, I'll go with you. I can be an extra set of hands. Besides, I'd love to compare notes. When are you leaving?"

"Bishop, get an extra ticket for Adri," I said. "If Rina doesn't mind, having extra arms will come in handy. Besides, I'm interested in what you're discovering, but for other reasons. Have you heard what happened to Salad Naraka and the genetics laboratory?"

He hadn't. While Bishop headed off to buy tickets, I outlined what had happened. In detail. He asked many questions. I explained the Sixth Invaders and their attempts to conquer Earth. By the time I finished answering his many questions, Bishop returned with our tickets.

"Flight leaves at noon in three days. That's the soonest I could get a transport."

"It's getting late. If it's all right with you, Rina, I'll come by tomorrow morning and bring my research notes with me. We can use these three days to share our data. It's lucky I ran into you after all these years. Honestly, you look spectacular,

133

but I can't imagine how you can cope. Anyway, until tomorrow."

After he left, tears trickled down her cheeks again as she and George struggled to get her undressed and ready for bed.

"I can't even brush my teeth," she said.

"I can't either without a stool by the sink and my stockings and heels are off. Relax and let George help. These robots work well. You'll get used to it in time. Back on Earth, I did everything using my feet and toes. Awkward. Took forever. Now I use Cleo as my arms. The hardest part is keeping your balance. No arms to help keep us steady on these heels. Expect life to seem daunting for a time."

"Thanks. I feel helpless, but I know I'm perfect and have to depend on George. Still..." She heaved a deep sigh.

Implants—I hate them.

Chapter 15 Clues

Three days passed. Adri arrived by nine and didn't leave until nine each night. He shared his preliminary findings and helped store the data onto Rina's computer. Adri showed patience, giving Rina time to figure out how to best use George to accomplish what she wanted. We both saw a frustrated and nervous Rina. In fact, he lent her more encouragement than I did. By the third day, Rina relaxed a little, becoming more accustomed to her limitations.

"What our display shows is a complete mess," Adri said. "There's no pattern here."

Rina and he used different colors to represent the earliest known dates of the appearance of Homo sapiens on a world where "world" might include moons and asteroids. Blue represented the appearance within the last five thousand years. Each deepening color added more years with the red dots representing their arrival over fifty thousand years ago. I added a red dot for Earth since I knew the rough archeological dating for the first appearance of Homo sapiens, not the Neanderthals.

Their display showed the spiral arms with their massive clouds of gas and dust—our half only. A giant space-faring civilization called the Imperium owned the other half. The various colored dots looked as though someone had put them into a cup, shaken them, and then tossed them out across the stars. I saw no pattern. Rina's initial findings suggested they originated in the outer arms and moved inwards. Adri's additional data suggested a random pattern, conflicting with Rina's beginning observations.

"No," Rina said, "as it stands, the pattern isn't visible. Not yet anyway. But there must be one. Let's use Molly's Sol

Empire as an example. It began on Earth with the red dot. They've added worlds of Pylon and Brussels, but those are blue dots. Earth's civilization has expanded out to neighboring habitable worlds in modern times."

I asked, "Are you saying that these other old worlds, the red dots, expanded out populating nearby worlds? How can we tell if that happened?"

Rina said, "Linguistic spread. One would expect a world whose people developed in situ independent of other worlds would have a distinct set of languages. Languages evolve. Yet I'm finding remarkable similarities. Languages spoken on some worlds are related, almost as though they evolved from a common version. Earth hosted a big linguistic conference a few years ago. I couldn't afford the transport cost from Cass-C. Anyway, I'm collecting linguistic data of the earliest humans, where known."

"Ah," said Adri, "I hadn't thought of that angle. Do the developments show a spread in colors from red to blue?"

"I haven't gotten that far yet. Still collecting volumes of data. We should attempt DNA analysis, but I've not had time to learn that subject."

I laughed. "Small universe. My younger sister, Eve, is a geneticist. Last year, she told me something she and Lara had discovered. She said DNA studies showed all humans on Federal worlds had a common ancestor that existed a hundred thousand years ago. She claimed that proves DNA can't aid evolutionary research. The common Homo sapiens ancestors would have had to live simultaneously on planets scattered across half the galaxy and at a time they'd be crude hunters and gatherers, not space-faring people."

Adri said, "Well, it's egocentric to think across all these worlds, evolution always ends up with Homo sapiens. There must be a reason behind the spread of our species."

"What about an outside influence?" I asked. "Suppose someone kidnapped a bunch of people from one world and used them to colonize a new world. That could account for the linguistic traits and the random patterns."

"Like the Third Invaders?" Bishop asked.

"Yeah."

Adri said, "But why would an alien race populate new worlds with humans? Wouldn't they prefer their own people?"

Rina said, "Outside influence. Like mice experiments. Perhaps that's what the Third Invaders are doing. If they can somehow get themselves into the minds of human clones, they could become an outside influence."

Adri grew excited, latching onto Rina's idea. "To promote uprisings, unrest, civil disobedience, revolutions. But how can that work? You said two were inside Mr. Jivin and the manager. How is this possible?"

I knew I'd have to explain in more detail. They had given me an entire new angle to consider, one that made sense.

"We are composites. We have a physical body that needs food and sleep. Next, we have a mind that can think. But it has a dark side that can adversely affect us. Last is the real person, the spiritual being, who has the mind and for a brief time occupies that body. As a telepath, I sometimes sense another's thoughts and can place a concept into another's consciousness. The being is immortal. My sister Celeste has invented a mental therapy that erases trauma. Sometimes today's pain and worry come from a trauma experienced in an earlier lifetime."

"Did I undergo trauma while in that mutation coma?" Rina asked.

"When we have a block of free time, we can explore that. Meanwhile, back to Adri's question. The Sixth Invaders first used their body swap machines on our top corporate leaders. One of my friends reverse engineered the machine and produced a body swap machine for herself. It saved my life more than once. Point is that it works.

"You attach the head harness to each body. The machine slides each person and mind into the other body."

"Wow. Can't they slide back on their own?" Adri asked.

"As far as I know, that's never happened, despite intense desire to swap back. It's only done via another use of the machine. We latch onto the physical body like glue."

They chuckled. And a new idea flashed.

I said, "Those clones in the stasis pods—there's no being or mind in them. It's just a human body vegetating in the pod."

"Wait," Rina said. "If you say we're all beings, what's preventing one of us from taking one of these new clone bodies as our own? Moving into it or whatever."

"When a body dies, the being and mind abandon it and search for a new baby body. It's unlikely a being would spot the clone body in the stasis pod inside that genetics lab. We seek babies in hospitals and med centers, at least on Earth."

Adri rubbed his forehead. "Then, these thousand clone bodies are useless on their own. I've seen people who can't live without total help with everything. No personality. No intelligence. They live as long as someone feeds them and takes care of them. Zombies, more or less."

I said, "While those clones are alive, they have no intelligence and can't do anything for themselves. Maybe the Third Invaders are body swapping into them. They'd have a perfect disguise and could infiltrate any human society. I think we may have stumbled upon something key."

"You mean like Jivin," Rina said. "He controlled Dad's entire genetics lab."

"Good heavens!" Adri said. "They could be our top leaders, our generals, our admirals. Holy basin rats! That's damned scary."

"Is there any way to detect them?" Rina asked, dark lines creasing her face.

"Telepathy."

"But telepaths are rarer than grasslands in the desert," Adri said. "Isn't there another way?"

"Well, right after they swap into another's body, they show unfamiliarity with those who were closely associated with that body, like wives, children, co-workers, and relatives. That soon passes, given time to become familiar with them. One could perhaps detect a huge change in personality or likes and desires. Before and after kind of thing. I recall now that Mr. Hardy, one of our CEOs that the Sixth Invaders occupied, always had this quirky hand gesture, which I later learned was their officer salute. Overall, though, it's tough to spot them unless you have telepathic abilities."

"Unlimited weapon," Adri said.

"They can be anywhere. They could be in anyone. Even Adri. Or Bishop," Rina said, her body trembling.

"Relax, Rina. Adri's not a Third Invader, nor is Bishop. Trust me on that. And you aren't either."

She relaxed and then laughed. "Not sure one of them would choose me."

"But you're gorgeous, Rina. Stunning." Adri smiled and gazed at her, causing her to flush. "Oh, the arms thing. Well..." He shut up.

"Thanks. You've given me a whole new angle to these missing thousands of clone bodies," I said, getting back to the key topic. "Using them as spies makes the most sense."

"But why? The Third Invaders occupy only a few planets here in the Sagittarius arm and aren't a military threat, as far as I know from school," Adri said. "They aren't even in the Federation of Planets. The Sixth Invaders out on the rim in the Perseus arm aren't in the Federation either, but they do invade other worlds."

Rina laughed nervously. "There are at least a thousand worlds with human Federation members and double that of worlds inhabited by humans who haven't achieved space travel. You don't suppose the Third Invaders are messing with these primitive hunter-gatherer worlds?"

Adri asked, "What's being gained? Iron Age agriculturalists can't be critical to the survival of the Invaders. Maybe an industrialized modern world that hasn't yet ventured into space might have stuff they want. Still..."

Just then, Eve dropped by. After introductions, she gave me an encouraging report.

"Well, we have restored the voices of the children you rescued. Soros University has provided them with robot assistants and enrolled them in their children's school since you adopted them."

"Just their voices?" I interrupted.

"Yes. We gave them another mutation using the one Ashton used on the sixteen hundred. It's restored their voices. But what's more important is that Lara and I have finished our initial mutation agent comparisons. This world's special Great Lady mutation agent is almost identical to Earth's armless Galactic Doll agent, except telepathy is missing, as are the Padellas' unique identification sequences. The odds are high— ninety-nine percent—that Chief Science Officer G'Karn developed Earth's agent from Kali-D's special Great Lady agent."

I asked, "Does that mean the cures you've developed will work on this world's Great Ladies?"

"Likely."

"But I'm the perfection of beauty. I love my body. I'm perfect just the way I am," Rina said, looking confused.

"Of course, you're gorgeous; you are perfect, Rina," Adri said. "Anyone with eyes can see that. You'll have men fighting each other to win your affections. Wait, what cures are you talking about?" His eyes moved from Rina over to Eve.

"Little things such as fixing our distorted feet. Then we can wear flats instead of these tall heels. Reduced breast sizes. Even re-growing arms is possible though that's been more difficult. Little things," Eve said.

I picked up her intention to not restimulate Rina's implanted words by implying she needed body repair.

"But I don't need my feet repaired. You know that," Rina said. Turning to Adri, she added, "Women attending Soros U must wear the outfit I'm wearing now. Besides all Cass-C women wear tall heels. That's a wasted cure."

Eve changed the subject. "One of the genetic engineers found out where they sent the children's mother, Amalie Leroy. They sold her to a mail-order bride company called Pinski's on Goringy-E. Since you're heading there, you can follow up in person."

"Thanks. Will do. Send the data to my phone," I said.

After Eve left, Bishop used our guest room's computer for locating this company and making our plans for the visit.

Meanwhile, Adri said his goodbyes. "I best head home and pack for tomorrow's trip. See you in the morning, Rina."

"I'll show you to the door," she said, moving over to him and the door.

She faced him and pressed her body into his, then kissed him. I glanced over and saw them. His hands came up and slipped up her waist until they reached her shoulders.

"That feels fantastic, Adri. Hope you don't mind me being so forward," she whispered.

"No, I didn't know if you still liked me. You're beautiful, intelligent—a terrific woman. Never let someone tell you otherwise. Cya tomorrow. This'll be a wonderful trip for us."

Later, Rina asked me, "He's really cute. Don't you think? I wish I had gowns like yours. You and Anala look classy and sexy. I look like a silly school girl."

"We can buy some first thing tomorrow. Besides, I need more, too."

"You do? Great. I think Adri likes me."

"I do, too. Especially since he kept that stone point you gave him when you were five. That says a lot."

She grinned. "And inspired him to become an astro-archeologist. My body felt electrified when he slid his arms up my sides. Wish I could make him feel that way, but without hands..."

Chapter 16 A Step Back in Time

Rina and I added half-dozen outfits to our wardrobe. She wore her new Leslie- designed red satin gown home. It displayed her incredible form.

"You'll hit a home run with this dress," I said.

After spotting her confusion, I had to explain my idiom. By noon, we finished packing, ready to head to the nearby spaceport, though Cleo and George did the work. Right on time, Adri arrived.

"Wow! Rina, wow. You look fabulous! Incredible. I see what you meant about the drab school garb."

She flushed. "Thanks. Molly's sister designed these dresses for her. Now, our world imports them."

"How many sisters do you have?" Adri asked.

"Seven still living that I know of. We best get going. We move slowly."

I took the lead at the spaceport because the closer we got to the building, the more nervous Rina became. Her comfort level dealing with life actions had yet to deal with much outside her hotel room. My ticket poked from a pocket along with my ID, in easy reach for Cleo. The robot had such operations well-practiced. From the corner of my eye, I spotted George emulating the actions of Cleo, and I relaxed a little. Still, this trip would challenge Rina.

The doors opened as I approached, pulling one bag on wheels behind me. Bishop lugged our heavier pair. While we were shopping, I had gotten a similar harness and rolling bag for Rina. Poor Adri had no choice but to struggle with three large bags, only one of which was his.

Once inside, Cleo presented my ticket and ID to the clerk who stamped the paper. I watched as our bags disappeared down the conveyor. Efficiency.

When we reached the staging area, a male voice called out.

"Molly! There you are. Almost thought you would miss the flight."

"Dirk, you're coming too?"

"You bet. Now that the kids can talk and are used to the robots and school, I had to come. I'm not letting you go up against Third Invaders alone. They've reinstated me. Got my old job back. Rina, what happened to you? You look smashing."

She flushed.

"She and her sister just became special Great Ladies," I said. "The Galaxy Detective Squad?"

He nodded, flashing me his badge. "Supposed to report back to Earth in a month."

I introduced Dirk to Adri. While we waited to board, I brought Dirk up to date. Once in flight, I planned to go into more detail about the possibilities we'd discussed last night.

Only ten passengers joined us on the ten-hour flight to Goringy-E. These looked like businesspeople or perhaps salespersons.

"What do we know about this world?" Dirk asked after the ship dropped into hyperspace.

"They're in the Federation," Rina said.

Dirk chuckled. "Okay, fellows. I did my homework. Goringy-E has only two operational spaceships, and how they managed that is dubious. The population is perhaps five hundred million, pretty sparse. Part is classified as industrial modern, part is agricultural."

"A frontier world," Adri said. "Anthropologically, speaking. But they claim to have Homo sapiens inhabiting

144

their world for fifty thousand years. I'm to get samples to verify that date."

"And I'm getting copies of documents that will cast light on the origins of their people," Rina said.

"It's a K-type star, rather orange appearing," Dirk said. "It's been around a while. What's interesting is that it's near the edge of a large dark cloud of dust and gas. It's rich in precious metals. They export tons of gold and silver each year. With many Federation ships trading with them, they need not waste their credits on building a space fleet of their own. A recent Fed survey showed this dust cloud is rich in these heavier elements. It probably formed from this cloud some time ago. That's the theory, anyway."

"Any cities?" I asked.

"Gutka is the largest and where we're headed. Half their population lives in Gutka and the surrounding hundreds of miles of burbs. The rest is spread out across the planet. They imported electromagnetic trains to haul cargo from Gutka and its surrounding towns out to several key mining and agricultural centers. According to the reports I found, they resort to primitive horse-drawn wagons to reach the actual mines and farms."

"Unreal," I said. "A Third Invader saucer landing in a remote area would go unnoticed. Great way to bring in a thousand clones or whatever. This world might be one of their transit hubs. What are they up to? What would an advanced race want on a primitive world?"

"Up to no good. Just look at how they betrayed us— mutating sixteen hundred against their wills," he said.

"Say," Adri said, "why did the Federation try to stop Earth and your mutations from spreading? I saw the news photos. Your armless Galactic Doll seems to be the same as our special Great Lady. Just look at Molly and Rina. No difference I can tell. Well, they're different but you know what I mean."

I sighed. "Telepathy. Our original version gave them telepathic abilities, which some put to good use. Others hated it. Unethical people tried to abduct and sell our telepaths to the highest bidders. Bad men even mutated thousands of people, planning a mass kidnapping and bringing in billions of credits when they sold them. The Third Invaders even tried to make breeding colonies of our telepaths."

"No wonder the Federation had to strike back," Adri said. "Always wondered why they took such a drastic action. I mean we've had special Great Ladies on Kali-D for as long as I can recall. Now things make more sense. Wait, you can read minds." His face flushed.

"Don't worry. I never do that without the person's permission. Otherwise, it's mental rape. My telepathy came as a byproduct of having had thousands of hours of Celeste's therapy. I erased tons of traumas, many of which I endured lifetimes ago. Her current theory is that anyone may develop telepathy if they received enough therapy sessions. Few have had thousands of hours of therapy."

Adri laughed. "That's why your dad hired armed men to guard Anala. He was afraid someone would kidnap her thinking she was a telepath. Much is making sense. Why didn't the Federation want to keep these telepaths? Until you, I've never heard of a real telepath."

"Because on Earth, we had no robot helpers like Cleo nor did we have a personal assistant job class."

"But don't you have to depend on your personal helper?" Rina asked. Her forehead creased; her eyes looked confused.

"We had none on which to depend. Because of the terrorists, there were tens of thousands of us, all created in less than a year. The sheer numbers overwhelmed all available medical facilities. Often we left the comatose victims lying where they were until they awoke. Grim."

146

"No pods. How did they get the nourishment and care they needed?" Rina asked.

"They didn't. You should call it brutal. In fact, it was. Later, when some got their telepathy, they couldn't control it and went insane from all the voices in their heads. At least Salad's lab handled the mutations humanely. With thousands of telepaths on Earth, the ruthless saw enormous profits. Just kidnap one, sell to the highest bidder, and make a fortune."

"Couldn't you stop them?" Adri asked, his face paling.

"With what? Like Rina and I are? What can we do to stop someone from picking us up and carrying us away?"

"Your personal assistant..." Rina glanced at George and Cleo. She had seen Bishop pick them up with one arm. Neither robot weighed all that much.

"But if you didn't have assistants, how did you survive?" Adri asked with a sympathetic glance at Rina.

"We used our feet and toes like hands. Often, I spent months teaching victims how to do things that way. I never had an assistant until I came to Soros University six years ago. But the Sixth Invaders left us a couple helpful machines. One handled our hair and toenails. Another helped us get dressed while a third robot cooked elementary meals for us. While we didn't need those machines, they made life easier. So, yes, Adri, we are handicapped. Rina has every right to be scared."

I chuckled. "We had a motto. Stop and think how. Our ways of doing things sure got stares. While we often took a lot longer to do something than a regular person, what mattered was that we did it. I found only a few things I couldn't do—such as firing my gun. I used to be a crack shot. Now, I can't even hold it. For me, the hardest thing is picking up things and carrying them. That's darn annoying, but if I give it time, Cleo does a good job for me. Yes, having Cleo around is wonderful. Don't become dependent on the assistant. These robots, for example, can only traverse level ground. They have to use elevators or escalators. They can't climb stairs. And what happens if their battery runs down?"

"George, you make sure you stay fully charged!" Rina said.

"Yes, I will," it said.

Since we three had four different places to visit, we rented rooms at the lodging closest to the spaceport. Adri took my hint and insisted he and Rina not split up. Adri and Rina planned to visit his professor and then collect her documents, meeting us back at the hotel. Dirk, Bishop, and I would check out this import-export company and then find Amalie Leroy, with luck returning to the hotel with her. Good plan.

After checking our IDs, the customs official said, "You must stay at the Visitor's Hotel. It's the only facility on this world where you have access to your off-world money. It's within walking distance."

Thank goodness for language translators. After walking out of the tiny spaceport, civilization moved backward on us. Wood formed the construction of their buildings, two stories tall at most. They didn't make the streets for pedestrian travel. Instead, endless streams of smoke-belching vehicles, akin to the electric car I had in Chicago, shot up and down the streets. They constrained us to walk on narrow sidewalks, dodging other people.

Many women wore plain, unappealing, cotton dresses, while men often wore leather shirts and pants. Every man and woman had a gun holster strapped around their waists.

Everyone stared at us as long as they could, often twisting their necks around. For once, though, it wasn't because we lacked arms.

We took a pair of rooms at the Visitor's Hotel but had to insist on ground-floor rooms, much to the manager's annoyance. No elevators. Adri and Rina stayed in one while we took the other. Since the manager had never seen a robot, he insisted on charging us for two more people staying in the rooms. That was a first.

We rented a pair of "steamers," the local name for the transportation vehicles. Each came with driving instructions and huge, folded maps. Four could fit in one.

"Do I get to drive?" I asked.

Rina gasped, but Dirk replied. "No, Molly. It's my turn. You drove last time. You get to navigate."

I gave him a playful, nasty look.

"I used to drive with my feet," I said, but I sensed Rina and Adri didn't believe me.

First, we took the instructions and maps to our rooms to study them. Dirk and Bishop found the location of Staszak Import-Exports and circled it. After an hour of map study and a visit with the hotel manager, we found the distant location of the farmstead where Amalie Leroy lived. He charged us for his help and converted some of my credits into local coinage, which I let the others handle.

Adri said, "These are pure gold!"

The manager said, "Of course. What else would money be made of? Well, there are silver coins, too, for tiny purchases. We are civilized here. None of those worthless pieces paper or numbers in machines you have. We have *real* money on this world."

We decided to find Amalie first because the import business could take a time to sort out and was on the return road from the farmstead. Cleo and I sat in the back, while Bishop held the map, directing Dirk. Because of the machine's loud racket, I figured I'd be deaf by the time we returned to the hotel.

The steamer used fossil fuel to heat water and make steam which propelled the vehicle, often at breathtaking speeds. A few streets allowed for high-speed travel. Bishop chose those.

Vic Broquard

I watched the colorful buildings and scenery fly by. Soon their numbers dwindled. An hour later, only a few isolated buildings and people flashed by the windows. Fields of crops replaced them until I viewed nothing but vast fields and forests dotting the rolling landscape. Still, we drove on. An hour later, we slowed to a crawl. The wide streets gave way to narrow streets, but now we followed nothing more than a dirt rut.

"Are you sure we're on the right road?" I asked Bishop for the tenth time. "Is this even a road?"

"If the map is right, yes. If the map isn't right, no," came the robot's dry reply.

The ruts ended in front of a quaint log cabin, surrounded by tall trees. A young girl, perhaps ten, came out to see what was making all the noise. Animals that looked like chickens and pigs scattered before us. That's what I thought the animals might have been.

"Papa, come quick! Real aliens are here!" she yelled.

A man wearing a leather outfit rushed out of the cabin, buckling his gun and holster to his waist while trying to plop his hat onto his head. He stopped and stared at us, dropping his hat to the ground.

"Hello. My name is Molly Parkinson. This is my friend, Dirk, my guard, Bishop, and my personal robot helper, Cleo. Are you Mr. Lukasz Warsky?"

"Papa, they talk funny. How comes their voices come out of their bellies? Are they really aliens?" the girl said, her eyes opened as wide as possible.

"That be me. My girl, Kamilli."

"Ah, good. We've learned that you recently got a mail-order bride named Amalie Leroy."

"Neva heard that name. But did git a woman. Called Al. Why? She's ma new bride."

"Can we talk to her?"

150

"Mind you, Al cain't speak none. Kamilli, you fetch her out here so's them can see her. Skedaddle!"

Kamilli ran back inside and soon escorted Al out onto the porch. She wore a crude, short, leather sack draped over her, as though someone stitched a sack and cut a hole for the head. It ended at her upper thighs. I realized this wasn't an accident. I guessed she could push the sack's bottom upward just enough for her to go to the bathroom by herself. She wore incongruous brown tall heels like those Rina and I wore. Her long black hair reached the middle of her calves. She stared at me.

"Thar she is. What of her?" he said.

"Lukasz, do you know what happened to her?"

He shook his head.

"Her name is Amalie Leroy. Hence, AL. Evil men killed her husband and kidnapped her and her three children. Then, they mutated her and the children into what you see now. No arms. Big breasts. No voice. Distorted feet. Just like I am. I've been mutated too. Then, those evil men sold her to the mail-order bride people, who sold her to you."

"That's preposterous. That ain't right, is it Al?"

He turned to her. Amalie must have understood me enough because she nodded, confusing Lukasz.

"I found her three children and took them to my home. Amalie, they are safe. My sister restored their voices. Soon, my sister will regrow their arms, making them normal people again."

She nodded while tears streamed down her cheeks.

"Is that true, Al?" Lukasz asked.

Amalie continued to nod. He tried to say something but hesitated.

"So, Lukasz, I had to find the children's mother and reunite them."

"But she's my wife now."

151

"Papa, let them have her. She's useless around here. I have to do everything for her. Instead of getting a new mom, I've got twice as much work to do," Kamilla said.

"I don't want to steal your wife, Lukasz. I want to help her, too, just like we're helping her children. If I could take her to my world and get her voice restored, her arms regrown, then I would return her to you along with her children. Then, you'd have four more sets of arms to help around here."

His dour face turned into a grin. "You'd do that? For her? For me? What's it gonna cost me? Paid dearly for her."

"It won't cost you anything. I only want to help them—to do what's right."

"She'll still look this pretty like, won't she? She's a real looker."

"Yes, only she'll be able to speak and have arms to help."

"Papa, you gotta let them do that. Please."

I said, "Amalie, would that be acceptable to you? I'll take you to my world, unite you with your children, and get your voice restored and arms regrown. Then, I'll bring all four of you back here to Lukasz and Kamilli."

She nodded vigorously. I thought she might injure her neck.

"Okay, ya got a deal," Lukasz said, extending his hand to seal the deal.

"Sorry, no hands to shake. How about a hug?"

I pressed into his body. His arms encircled me and squeezed.

"There, deal. Her arms will regrow rather slowly, but we will be back as soon as we can."

Kamilli darted to Amalie's side and helped her descend the steps. I'd forgotten how scary a set of steps can appear to us in our heels.

152

The girl hugged Amalie and said, "You make sure you come back, mama."

Amalie nodded and kissed the girl's forehead.

With Amalie and me tucked into the backseat with Cleo between us, Dirk fired up the steamer. With a racket, off we went. As we drove back into the city, I used telepathy to chat with Amalie, showing her images of her children to prove we'd rescued them. Cleo kept busy dabbing the tears streaming down Amalie's cheeks. Times like this, I felt I had made a difference.

***

Adri drove their steamer while their map rested on Rina's lap. George kept one hand on the map securing it in place. First stop, the archeological dig and Professor Levitsky.

Adri pulled up beside a group excavating a large site. City designers built part of this suburb on top of an ancient site. The rough, uneven ground with crude boards placed here and there over parts of the dig convinced Rina to stay in the vehicle.

"I can't walk over that. Neither can George," she said.

"Okay. Only be a few minutes. Ah, hello Professor Levitsky. I'm Adri Kedar. You have organic samples for me to date?"

"Ah, welcome, lad, welcome. Yes, yes, come see. We're making huge progress. Ancient site. Homo sapiens lived here. Come. Uncovered a dozen graves. Observe for yourself that I've identified the right species."

After verifying the skeletal remains were those of Homo sapiens, Adri collected a dozen samples of organic matter from twelve key locations across the site, including one grave.

"I'll have the results for you in a few weeks."

"Thank you. We don't have such equipment here. Very costly. Can't justify it. Took all my political pull just to make them halt their construction and allow us to excavate."

They shook hands.

An hour later, they met with the librarian who handed a box of documents to Rina.

"I'll take them," Adri said, defusing the librarian's embarrassment.

"This will help with my thesis. I promise I'll send you a copy of it when it's done. Thank you," Rina said.

They returned the steamer to the rental facility. With Adri carrying his samples in a backpack and lugging the box of record copies, the two walked along the narrow sidewalks back to their hotel.

The mile walk proved noisy, too many passing steamers. Without warning, three men stepped in front of them, guns drawn.

One man said, "We donna like aliens on our world."

"We're just leaving," Adri said. "Going back to the hotel and catching our flight."

"Yeah, well, we still donna like it. And we donna like no metal monsters like that'n. Do we boys?"

The two others said agreed.

"What da we do to metal fiends?" the original man said.

"This," the second man said.

All three opened fire on George. The guns produced vast clouds of smoke and noise, but many large caliber lead slugs hit George. The first one short-circuited the robot. When they emptied their revolvers, George no longer functioned.

"There. Take the lump of junk with you and donna come back, ya hear? We donna like creepy aliens even if ya look like a doll."

With that, they moved around the dumbfounded pair and vanished down a side street.

"Oh, my gods!" Rina gushed. "George? They killed George."

"Let me check," Adri said, his face pale. "It's not working. I don't know if they can repaired it. Guess we best bring him to the hotel and ask Molly."

"Adri, I depended on George. Now I am helpless. Adri, I'm scared!"

"I know. Try to relax. Let me see how we can haul him back."

Adri experimented a little. He could hold either the box of documents or George, but not both. Adri devised a solution. A glance at Rina's face suggested she might break down any moment. He dug out a length of twine he kept in his bag.

"Always be prepared," he said.

After attaching it to the inert robot, he discovered the robot still rolled along on its wheels.

"There, this will work. I'm sure they can repair George."

"But Adri, we must go back to Cass-C at least. Until then, I'm helpless!"

"No, not completely. See, you're walking fine. That's the first thing. We walk back to the hotel. After that, I can be your helper. But you must direct me. Maybe Cleo can help with your personal things."

His face felt hot, but his encouragement appeared to be working. Rina didn't break down but focused on walking.

"Back at Soros U, walking always was hard in these heels, but without arms, it's a thousand times worse. I keep trying to use my arms to catch my balance."

"You're doing just fine, dear. Just like a perfect special Great Lady," he said, hoping to encourage her further.

When they entered the hotel, the manager watched them.

He said, "We don't like aliens very much. Folks hate mechanical monsters."

Adri left George at the entrance for a minute. He got the bag, box, and Rina into their room, before retrieving the remains of George.

"Now, we wait for Molly to return. She'll know what to do."

"We've got to eat lunch. I can't even do that."

"Sure you can. I'll be your hands. Come on. I'm starving too."

***

We reached the more populated suburbs, but by now we'd missed lunch. My stomach growled. Although I peered out the windows, I didn't spot any pizza places or any convenience store where we could pick up lunch. Worse, I couldn't read their written language. Perhaps one of these buildings housed a walk-in diner.

Dirk pulled up at Staszak Import-Exports. We couldn't read the sign, but it looked right. A long single-story building occupied a many-acre plot. Though the structure hid much of what lay behind it, I spotted a tarmac, a perfect place to land spaceships. A tall fence topped with barbed wire enclosed the grounds. Two other steamers sat in the parking lot. A small wooden gatehouse manned by men with guns provided the only entrance.

"Bishop, you stay with the steamer and guard Amalie. I'll leave Cleo to help her. Dirk and I will try to gain entrance," I said. "But stay alert. Might be a trap."

Dirk checked his gun and then helped me get out the rear door. Together, we walked up to the gatehouse.

"What's the plan?" he whispered.

"Straightforward this time."

A guard stepped up. "Halt. This is a private company."

"I'm here to see the manager," I said.

"Do you have an appointment?"

"No. Tell him we're here to talk about the thousand clones delivered to this company from the genetics research lab on Kali-D."

"You' must make an appointment."

156

"No, you tell him that. If he doesn't see us, then I promise this illegal action becomes prime news on all Federation of Planets comm channels."

He turned and placed a call holding a handheld, black device to his ear and mouth. Just as I thought my bluff hadn't worked, he hand-signaled us to enter. The gravel path to the main door made walking treacherous for me.

"Hold me," I whispered to Dirk.

A middle-aged man surrounded by six local men in leather with drawn guns stood before us as we entered. The older man wore a business suit akin to what Dirk wore.

"I am Teos Staszak, owner and operation of this business. Would you like to explain what you're doing here? Clearly not to buy or sell something."

Dirk spoke first. "I'm Dirk Bennet. Molly Parkinson. We've just come from Salad's on Kali-D and know about the thousand clone pods. We know the dates when they shipped a thousand clones to this facility and that Third Invaders are behind this illegal operation. We want to know what you've done with these thousands of clones. By the way, we've put an end to the cloning and mutation operation on Kali-D."

'He's a Third Invader!' I sent the warning to Dirk. I'd touched Staszak's mind and found another just like Edyta.

"Preposterous. What silliness. If we had anything to do with that, what's keeping us from killing you where you stand?"

"You don't know who we've told. You can either talk to us or talk to the ID agents on Cass-C. Third Invaders killed two of their agents after mutating them. I'd expect the ID are close behind us."

"Ridiculous accusations. Now best you leave or I'll have my men take target practice on you. We're a wild-west world that loves to shoot things."

With that, the six waved their guns in the air, while two cocked their revolvers.

"As you wish," I said. "Let's go. We'll let the ID handle them."

Dirk and I turned and walked back to the steamer. I needed his steadying hand, and I sensed he held his breath. I hoped they wouldn't shoot us in the back. Only after he helped me into the rear seat did I relax.

"The owner is the man in the suit. A Third Invader occupies his body. He's just kicked us out. No info, but he threatened to kill us if we didn't leave. Nasty fellow."

Bishop nodded and stowed his own gun after Dirk got us rolling down the street again. We headed back to the hotel.

Imagine my surprise when we checked on Adri and Rina.

"I've been being her assistant this afternoon," Adri said. "Any chance they can repair George? I can't believe how backward this world is."

Red tinged Rina's eyes. Her body had slight trembles. I didn't need telepathy to know what she must be feeling.

"You can have Cleo until we get back to Cass-C," I offered.

I spotted a brief spark in her eye. "No, that's not fair to you. Adri promised to help me. You need Cleo as much as I need George. We'll manage somehow."

"Okay. We're next door if you need something. Let's get supper soon. I'm starving. Missed lunch," I said, smoothing this over.

"What did you find out?" Adri asked while we waited for the food to arrive.

"Not much. A Third Invader occupies the body of the owner who denied everything and threatened to shoot us if we didn't leave," I said. "I'll let the ID agents handle this case. We aren't welcome here. Does everyone carry a gun?"

Adri chuckled. "Yeah, everyone we saw. This place is gun crazy."

"We'll take the next available flight out of here," I said.

***

Later in their room, as Adri got Rina ready for bed, she cried. "I'm helpless, Adri. I'm supposed to be able to do anything, but I'm dependent on my personal helper. It's awful making you do everything for me."

"But I love you. Don't you know that by now? I'll always help you. You are a special Great Lady. I've never met anyone as beautiful as you are."

"I can't even hold you," she wailed.

"Hey, your mother couldn't hold you, if I recall. Wasn't she a special Great Lady when she divorced Salad and took you with her to Zeta Minori-D? And Anala couldn't hold Salad or Lanka. It's part of what a special Great Lady is. Perhaps that's the price women pay to be the ultimate in beauty and desirability on our world."

"Maybe that's too high a price to pay," she replied.

Adri wiped her cheeks again. "I think it's just a natural reaction to having lost your assistant. You've got me now. Please, marry me when we get back. I can't live without you."

"But Adri, I'm helpless like this. I'm not even a whole person anymore." Rina sobbed again, forcing him to get another tissue.

He helped her into bed, pulling her head onto his shoulders.

"There, it'll be fine. We'll get a new assistant. You can forget this ever happened. Will you marry me? I know I'm not the wealthiest man."

"I've never cared about money. If you're sure you want me, I will. As soon as we can."

They kissed.

***

When we entered our room, I held a brief council.

"I don't trust this place. Bishop, you stand guard tonight. If trouble comes, stay out of the fight until you can

159

rescue us. Tomorrow, find us the first available flight out of here. I don't care where. From there, we can catch a flight to Cass-C."

"What about our guest? Amalie?" Bishop asked.

"I'll have Cleo help her tonight like he did at dinner. Tomorrow, I'll check if my clothes will fit her. We're about the same size."

Dirk said, "We must find another way to tackle this Third Invader mess. I'm out of ideas."

"A good night's sleep might help," I said.

Bishop exited the room while Cleo helped get Amalie ready for bed. Dirk helped me though he slept on the floor.

I had a terrible nightmare. Someone forced a rag over my mouth just like the men did years ago when Casper Hugo had me kidnapped. I kept trying to wake up, but couldn't quite make it. Strange.

Chapter 17 Discussions

"Teos here. Got a problem. That infernal Molly Parkinson was just here. She's put it all together and traced it back here. She's threatening to bring in ID agents. Over."

He sat back to wait on the fifteen-minute delay in communications to Cass-C. Night had already fallen. Teos drummed his fingers on the desk.

"Seven here." When the reply came, Teos jerked. "Inevitable. That woman sticks her nose in more places. We can't have the ID involved in this. You've no idea how much trouble I had getting them to drop investigating the deaths of their two agents. No question. We must stop them. But killing them will cause too many problems. I'll bring up the matter with Home World and get back to you. Meantime, we must inhibit them. Do you know where they are staying? Over."

While it looked like Teos replied at once, Seven wouldn't get what he said for fifteen minutes.

"Yes, at the hotel by the spaceport. It's the only hotel aliens can use. There's a complication. They are with two others. An astro-archeologist and a Soros U student who is a special Great Lady. Locals got mad that she brought one of those mechanical robot things to Goringy-E and shot it up. Rather funny. They're staying with the Parkinson woman and her robot thing. They've brought back one of the voiceless special Great Ladies that we sold off to the mail-order bride store. What do you want done with them? Over."

Teos fixed himself a jaffe to help fight the boredom while waiting for the return call. He hated living on this world, but it had one great advantage. No one cared or witnessed their saucers landing on the concealed pad behind the warehouse. Perfect for clandestine operations these past two hundred years. He had swapped human clone bodies six times, but Seven had promised him a new position soon.

"Okay, here's what you're to do," Seven said. He outlined what he wanted done. "After you get it done, keep them in the stasis pods. I'll send a saucer to pick them up before the time's up. Just make sure you leave no trace of them at the hotel. We don't know who she's told about their spy trip. Contact me again when you have them in the pods. Over and out."

Teos grinned. "I like Seven's thinking. Best get the others together. We'll need six pods."

***

Seven hated to be forced to place a call to Home World. Hyperspace relay calls could be traced even though he took great care to keep his unit hidden in his office on the top floor. Long ago, he'd turned it into a Faraday cage. No outside spying could reach him. He had direct lines to Six, to the President of the Council of Admirals, and to the Intelligence Division's top commander. But he had no direct lines to Five or the others above Six.

Tonight, he contacted Home World. "Admiral Banszak, Seven here. Got a major problem. That Molly Parkinson woman again. She's uncovered the thousand-clone project on Kali-D. She's put it out of business for now."

He outlined what he knew of her actions, ending with what he had had General Teos do during the night. Now he had to wait an hour for the reply assuming the admiral would respond right away. More than likely, he'd take the problem on up to the Planning Committee for resolution. Hence, he might not get a reply for days. What he'd told Teos to do would handle any eventuality.

That comm finished, he placed another secure call to Captain Katya Binsk.

"Captain, I have a special mission for you. Take a saucer in stealth mode to Goringy-E and visit General Teos. He'll have stasis pods for you to bring back here. They're not to wake until I've made the arrangements."

"Understood. We'll leave in thirty," she said. He saw her huge smile on the monitor. These clandestine operations took their toll, he thought.

***

Teos said, "There's one robot machine with them. Before anything else, Tytus, you work your magic and turn it off; make damn sure you don't wake them. Then, we use chloroform. According to the manager, four in that room, two in that one. In and out. Keep it quiet. We don't want to attract the locals' attention. He'll send the night watchman off on rounds when we carry them to the steamer. On three."

He counted down. One picked the lock on the first room before moving on to the second one. Tytus slipped in, using infrared goggles. He spotted the robot plugged into the electrical outlet. Cleo activated as he neared, but Tytus flipped the emergency off switch. Cleo deactivated. He signaled the others and backed out of the room, his job well done.

Dirk struggled against the rag, slugging the man twice before he fell unconscious. The two women wiggled but offered no real resistance. How could they, Teos thought as he watched? He heard a whisper from next door.

"Excellent. Carry them down to the steamer. The rest of you, pack everything. Leave no trace they were ever here. Have we got them all?" Teos asked.

As soon as they carried out the victims, Teos turned on the lights. Now came the hard part, finding what likely belonged to these people. Men lugged clothes, bags, even the box of documents, and the inert robots out to the waiting steamer. Once his men signaled they'd finished, Teos visited each room, double-checking even looking beneath the beds.

Satisfied they'd missed nothing, they left, re-locking both doors.

Once he climbed into the steamer, it chugged off into the dark of night. It pulled into the parking lot of the very building Molly had visited that afternoon. At this late hour, no local guards were present. The men carted the unconscious into the huge building, depositing them in a secret back room, where stasis pods lay stacked though six lay open and ready for use.

"Doctor, are you ready?" Teos asked. "Got five for you."

"Yeah, all set. Put them down on the cots. Well, crap. You didn't say three were already mutated," the doctor said. "Which agent do you want me to use on them? These look like someone has given them the Kali-D version. If so, they're immune to it."

"Okay. Give them the Sol Empire version. That one there," Teos said pointing to Molly's body, "may be immune to that agent. But try it anyway. Be prepared to keep her knocked out if she doesn't fall into a coma. Likewise the other two."

"Tricky, but I can arrange a slow drip," the doctor said.

He began his work, beginning with the two men. Meanwhile, Teos had his men pack all the gear into shipping crates ready for the saucer.

After injecting the men, the doctor stripped them and placed each into the waiting pods. Next, he attached various tubes and earbuds. After double-checking, he closed the pods, sealing the men inside. He hit the play button. For the next eight days, the same recording played into the men's ears.

He put the three women in pods. Satisfied he'd handled them if the agent worked, he worked on a system to administer the knock-out drug to the three women if the agent didn't work. He did not attach the earbuds, figuring they'd already had that exposure. Rather, he needed to make sure they didn't wake up prematurely.

"All set, doctor? They can't cause trouble?" Teos asked.

"Nope. Even if they woke up inside the pods, they don't have arms to free themselves. Stop worrying," the doctor said. "Now, I'm going to bed."

Teos said, "Okay, boys, you can take off, too. I'll sleep in my office until the transportation arrives."

The men departed the secret room, shutting the door. Hundreds of dim LED lights from hundreds of empty stasis pods and life-sustaining equipment prevented total darkness.

***

Bishop switched off his personal invisibility shield and examined the five pods. When he found Dirk's pod, he disconnected the earbuds, but he left Adri's on, calculating the man needed the implanted words. He paused by Molly's pod, gazing down at her for a time, while he calculated the odds. Satisfied he'd computed the answer, he reactivated his invisibility shield and continued exploring the contents of the room. Five hundred six empty stasis pods concerned him. Where were the clones they once held? He found a stash of mutation agents stored in a refrigeration unit. The label proved his calculation had been correct.

But the room yielded no further clues and no weapons. He took up a position by the door waiting for the Third Invader's next move. Meanwhile, he continued to calculate how Molly had known they'd be kidnapped while they slept. She'd ordered him out of the room and to watch over them. He had watched an army of men led by Teos slip into the hotel, but they outnumbered him. Bishop could only watch them carry the unconscious out to a waiting large steamer. When he saw them go back to retrieve all their possessions, he slipped into the cargo bay. Later he followed behind the men who carried the victims into the warehouse.

Back on Earth, he had worked with Molly as a PI and as the Senior Investigator, but this human continued to surprise him. How had she known? Further, by sending him outside, she'd prevented his likely destruction. Chloroform wouldn't have worked on him. His only conclusion: Molly was exceptional.

Daylight came. The doctor entered and checked the five stasis pods and left. The light faded until only the dim LED lights remained. Footsteps approached. Someone entered and flipped on the floodlights. Blue-uniformed Third Invaders marched into the room, led by Captain Katya Binsk.

Though a little taller than a human, their heads identified them as non-human. Their heads curved back like a bird's beak, which seemed to stretch their facial features taut. Her muscular arms lifted a stasis pod. She wore a blaster and a disintegrator gun strapped to her waist, as did the five other soldiers in her squad. Her reddish skin tone and black hair looked alien.

"These five. Take them to Bay One. Then, get all their stuff. We're to leave no trace. Ah, Teos, good to see you again. Had trouble did you?" she said.

"Not my fault. It's that infernal Parkinson woman. She's undone the whole damn operation on Kali-D and traced the clones here. I don't know why they didn't let us kill them," Teos said.

"This matter went up the lines to Home World. Seven said so. Must be important. Are you sure your men got all their stuff rounded up? I don't want to return."

"Yes. No one will discover a thing about them. They vanished in the night like many aliens do who come to Goringy-E in search of easy gold or silver."

Both laughed.

As one carried the last pod out of the room, Bishop fell in behind him, moving like an owl. He stood in the cargo bay's rear and waited. The Third Invaders made several more trips, depositing all their possessions and the inert robot assistants. When the door shut, total darkness enveloped Bishop, who activated his infrared vision and braced himself for the flight to whatever world.

Based on travel time, Bishop calculated how far they'd traveled, presuming the saucer used hyperspace. The saucer's velocity became the wild variable in his calculations. Ten hours travel time suggested a long distance from Kali-D. But if this ship could travel several times faster than Federation ships as Molly once suggested, they might be anywhere within the entire galaxy! Bishop waited. He checked his ammo. Three spare clips. A little over sixty rounds. Not good for a lengthy firefight. If only this wasn't a saucer. He could navigate and pilot all smaller Sol Empire ships and many of the Federation. While he estimated he had good odds of taking out the crew, his calculations yielded no chance at being able to fly the saucer.

Bishop sensed a subtle shift in gravity, one that suggested descent. He opened the cargo bay door a crack and increased the sensitivity of his hearing. Bishop smiled.

"Cloaking activated. Descending onto the pad now," a voice said, likely a pilot.

He heard Captain Katya Binsk talking. "Good. Seven, we're landing now. Be another seven days before they wake."

A garbled voice responded. Bishop knew the speaker put his voice through a mixer making it unrecognizable by any known means unless one knew the precise filter and encryption code in use.

"Noted. Will contact Ashton for supplies. I've had the area cleared for your landing. No one will see you depositing the cargo. You'll have thirty minutes before their systems are back online. Don't get detected."

"What's Home World want with these humans? Why not kill them?"

"We follow orders, Captain Binsk. Something's up. That I can tell you. Something major. Goes far beyond our routine operations. What Intel do you have on them? Home World charged me with finding out what we can before they wake from comas."

"Seven, this is the strangest assignment you've sent me on. One is working on a doctorate thesis gathering ancient documents outlining earliest settlements. The male has a doctorate in astro-archeology. He collected organic samples from an archeology dig to Carbon date for the man in charge. One is a voiceless special Great Lady sold to a mail-order bride company and rescued by Parkinson's group. They already rescued the woman's children and have them at Soros U. As far as the meddler, she confronted Teos about the thousands of clones shipped there over the years. He denied everything and ran them off. One other thing, trigger-happy locals shot up the special Great Lady's robot helper. I can't see what all the fuss is about. We should have let the locals shoot them."

"I didn't have the authority to order that hit. Admiral Banszak called me personally."

"Well, *sheidt!*"

"That's what I said, only not to him. There's something big going down. That's why he wanted them mutated to stall for time. I think Home World is gathering further intelligence on them. From what little I've heard, Admiral Banszak thinks they might be useful. I get to keep them on ice for another six days. Later."

"Captain, touchdown in thirty," the first voice said.

Bishop felt the gentlest motion beneath his feet. He knew the technology used in these flying saucers dwarfed anything the Federation had. Molly had told him about the ship's quantum entanglement engine, an amazing piece of tech. He shut the bay door and waited.

Crew members entered, turning on the brilliant lighting. Each grabbed a stasis pod as though it weight mere pounds. Bishop followed the trailing man through the ship and down the ramp. The invaders sat the pods down against a far wall, and Bishop moved over to them, leaning against the steel wall. He was in a steel cargo hold. LED lights lined the upper edges of the four walls. The large flying saucer sat in the center on a slab of steel colored a little different. As he watched, they carried out the group's possessions, stacking them nearby. Then the ramp retracted. The steel slab moved upward, startling Bishop, who watched as a giant hydraulic piston raised the slab and saucer upwards. The steel ceiling retracted, allowing the ship to leave the box.

Once clear, the saucer shot upwards like a bullet, vanishing from sight in seconds, while the slab descended and the ceiling slid back into place. Where am I? What is this place? Isolated. Faraday cage. No electronic signals. I'm blind. Bishop looked around the container.

He spotted the outline of a door. A recessed keypad appeared when he moved his hands around it, feeling for a way to open the door. He heard footsteps and backed away, pressing himself up against the steel wall. The door swung open, and two men entered.

"Doc, check them over. Seven wants them in perfect condition when they wake," one man said.

The doctor moved from pod to pod. "Hey, three aren't in mutation comas, but two have lost their hair. Someone's hooked up a crazy-ass system to keep them unconscious. Risky."

"Well, do something. Keep them alive and healthy."

"I can induce medical comas."

"Make it happen."

Bishop watched the "boss" count the pods and look at the person inside.

He said, "Hey, one man is missing. Parkinson had her personal bodyguard with her. A man called Bishop. Those two are Dirk and Adri. Where the hell's Bishop?"

"Hey, not my problem," the doctor said.

While he continued altering the three women's pods, the other man left. Since the door was still open, Bishop slipped out to investigate. He almost bumped into a man talking on his phone.

"Yeah, one's missing. That Bishop security guard. Check with Captain Binsk and General Teos. They swear they got them all, but I have security video that shows Bishop going to Goringy-E with Parkinson. Odds are General Teos missed him, and he's still on Goringy-E. If so, have him killed. No loose ends. Call me when it's done."

He then headed down the metal hallway to a set of elevators. Soon, he vanished. Once more, Bishop tried connecting to comm or GPS satellites. Nothing. Still a dead zone. While Bishop stood calculating options, the elevator whined again. Bishop practiced his human reactions when he saw Ashton Soros step out followed by the original man. Bishop's raised his eyebrows and opened his eyes wider.

"Yes, I know—an unfortunate accident. But can they fix the robot assistant? Plus, we'll need three more robots for the others."

"And clothing," Ashton added. "Let me see the damage, please."

The two entered the container room, Bishop following close enough to overhear.

"Did it get into a gunfight?" Ashton said, bending over the inert George.

The other man laughed. "Sure looks like someone used it for target practice. Junk it or can your people fix it?"

"I'll take it with me. I think we can insert its positronic brain and memory cells into a new frame and have it work. Is Cleo unharmed?"

"Yeah, just emergency shutoff."

"Okay, I'll bring three more back with me. Wait, who's that woman? I recognize that face. Isn't that Amalie Leroy, the kidnapped woman? We have her three children here."

"Must be. The others had their ID cards on them when General Teos stripped them."

"What's the time frame for them to awake?" Ashton asked.

The doctor looked up. "Six more days, give or take. I suppose you'll want their measurements for clothing."

"If you don't mind, doctor," Ashton said. "Parkinson will be upset about this. But I'd rather see them alive and well than dead on some remote planet where the creeps shoot up helper robots. What happened to them? How'd they get here?"

The other man said, "I'm told a passing ship dropped them off. I'm not privy to the details."

"They should awaken in better surroundings. What is this place? Like a steel cage," Ashton said.

The other man's phone vibrated. "Okay," he said. "Ashton, Seven's on this line! Wants to talk to you. You must rate!"

Bishop watched Ashton's brows rise. Ashton's face displayed curious look.

"Hello. This is Ashton Soros. Is this really you, Seven? I'm honored. What can I do for you?"

Even though Ashton didn't have the phone on speaker phone, Bishop's sensitive hearing picked up the other voice.

"I'm told you're looking at the five now. Something major has arisen making these people extremely valuable. I can't tell you what that is. Yet. The last they knew they were sleeping. Men chloroformed them, kidnapped them, and have tried to mutate them. The kidnappers were idiots. Three can't be mutated since they already have been. Anyway, High Command wants to discuss issues of Federation security with them. Under such circumstances, one would expect them to be hostile. I want you to move them to a homey place. Attend to their needs. Do everything to make their lives better when they first awake and discover what's happened to them. I'll forward a few thousand credits to help cover their expenses. Ashton, I'm counting on you to make their recovery in six days both humane and kind. They must be friendly to us when the critical interrogation happens after they wake. I can't impress how vital this is to Federation security."

"You can count on me," Ashton said. "I'll make that happen."

Click. The phone went dead. Ashton grinned.

"I'll be back in a while. Have to arrange for their care. Escort me out."

The other man and Ashton left. Bishop remained with Molly. When the doctor left, he shut and locked the door. Bishop waited. He concluded they were on Cass-C, somewhere in Hoffdorf, perhaps close to Soros University.

Later, he heard faint voices likely outside the door.

"Send me that disgraced profiler Wanda Hammerstein. She had a rapport with Parkinson. A familiar face and all. Bye."

Conclusion: part of a phone call. What was Wanda's role in this mess? Although Bishop tried to extrapolate, insufficient data always resulted. While he waited, he reviewed all the galactic news he'd heard during the last few months. Nowhere did he find a hint of anything threatening Federation security. What was going on? We must be in an ID holding cell. If so, what is the Third Invaders connection? Insufficient data.

As days passed, the doctor checked on the patients every twelve hours. Then, men arrived and moved the pods and gear. Bishop followed them. Before long, they entered the open air. Overhead, the brilliant central bar of the galaxy illuminated the spaceport tarmac almost as bright as the sun. Although his invisibility device still cloaked his body, it cast a diffuse shadow. During the men's trips bringing up the gear, he dashed off. He spotted a Soros University shuttle landing. Bishop reached a calculated decision. Ashton would take good care of them. But he needed a plausible way to "not have been there."

He maneuvered to the outer fence and waited. Before long, a rabbit hopped along, triggering the motion sensors alerting a security guard. Via the surveillance system, he would spot the rabbit and ignore the false signal. Thus, Bishop seized this opportunity to jump the fence. Off into the night, he ran not stopping until he reached his own off-campus apartment. He entered, changed clothes, and recharged, planning his next move.

In the morning, he called on my daughter, Nikita.

"Hi, Bishop. Come in. Thought you were with Mom."

"I was, but I returned early to fetch documents for her. She was on Goringy-E when I left them. I haven't been able to reach her or Dirk or Rina or Adri."

"How long?"

"Several days now. I'm becoming worried something awful has happened to your mother and the others. Since three of them are university students, can you ask Ashton Soros to find out?"

"On it! Come on. Let's talk to Ashton right now."

Minutes later, precocious Nikita barged into his office, demanding to see him.

"Mr. Soros, Mom has gone missing. We think something terrible has happened to them. Bishop was with her on Goringy-E, but came back for papers Mom wanted. He hasn't been able to contact her for days. Rina and Dirk are with her. Since they are Soros U students, maybe you can use your influence to find them."

She put her hands on her hips, looking many years older than her sixteen. Bishop stood behind her.

"Bishop. Here you are. Others have wondered where you were. Relax, Nikita. Your mother and the others are here on our campus. There was a tragic event. I don't know the details, only that someone tried to mutate and kidnap them. ID agents interrupted them and brought them back here. I have a doctor monitoring them. They'll wake in two days. I was about to summon you to tell you about this and have you verify it is your mother."

"Oh, she's okay then? Mutated? I want to see her. Right now! Bishop, you come too. I want you to stand guard over her until they wake up. That's an order."

"Yes, Miss Nikita," Bishop said, trying to sound as meek as possible.

Ashton led them to the commons area near Molly's apartment. As they walked, he explained further.

"It seems your mother found Amalie Leroy. They brought her back with them. I've sent for her three children. I want them to see their mother even though she's still unconscious. My medical team tells me they'll be waking in two days."

Nikita looked at her mother and Dirk.

"Mom looks the same. They didn't turn her into one of those bird things. But Dirk. Oh, boy, he won't like what they did to him. Bishop, you stay here and guard them."

As she turned to leave, the three children walked in, their teacher standing behind them.

"Mom! That's Mom!" the eldest cried.

Nikita smiled and headed back to her summer school class.

Bishop took up a position in the back of the commons. At least, he thought, Amalie and her children will be happy.

174

Chapter 18 Explanations

I slept a century before I woke. We had to catch a flight to Cass-C and figure out what to do about the clone mess. I blinked.

"Nikita?"

"Hi, Mom. You're okay. You're in the commons by your apartment on Cass-C. Everyone's here. Cleo's got you dressed. Your body appears normal, but you had Bishop and me worried."

"What a nightmare!"

I heard Rina's voice and struggled to sit. I recognized my surroundings, which confused me.

"My kids!"

I heard a voice I'd never heard. Amalie could talk! How? Her three children pressed their bodies into hers, all four talking at once. Tears flooded down the woman's cheeks. Rina's and my eyes watered, too. What a wonderful feeling. We all wore identical school outfits, the white blouses with tiny sleeves, black skirt, stockings, and heels.

Two other screeches startled me. Turning, I almost didn't recognize Dirk. He wailed in a soprano voice.

"Oh, no! Not again!"

My foggy mind registered the fact someone had mutated him into an armless Galactic Doll.

"It'll be okay, Dirk," Nikita said. "You can handle this. They got your old robot assistant for you. See..."

Rina cried out. I turned around. There sat a terrified Adri, mouthing words. He'd been mutated just like Dirk. I recognized the words.

Although shaking from shock and fear, Adri said, "I'm now the perfection of beauty. I love my body. I am proud and honored to be one of the beautiful and special Great Ladies. I'm very happy and totally content. I am perfect. Nothing's better than being a special Great Lady. I am a role model for others, and I must show everyone being a special Great Lady is wonderful. There is nothing I cannot do though I must depend upon my personal assistant. I will always be faithful to my spouse. What's happened to me? Oh, gods! Rina?"

"I'm here," she said. "You're now a special Great Lady, too. It'll be okay. We are the perfection of beauty. We are perfect. You are perfect. Where are we? I must be having a terrible nightmare. This can't be real. We're on Goringy-E, aren't we? Has to be a nightmare. But George isn't all shot up. Rina, you must wake up."

Ashton said, "Your attention, please. Yes, this is real. You are back on Cass-C. Someone kidnapped and mutated you, but ID people rescued you and brought you back here. Rina, I've had George repaired. Adri, here's your robot assistant. Its name is Fred. Dirk, your old robot assistant Ben is here. Amalie, your new robot assistant is Wilma. For the new special Great Ladies or Galactic Dolls, trust your assistant. They'll handle your needs."

Adri's body shook, but he said, "I must be a role model. I'm perfect."

Rina said, "Adri, we can still get married. Like we planned. Can't we? I still love you. Ashton, we can get married, can't we? Adri, you're perfect, too."

Rina gasped. "Wait! What about the documents I've collected? What about Adri's organic samples? He promised to get them Carbon dated."

"I can't do anything. No, there's nothing I can't do. I depend on my assistant. How? I'm scared, Rina," Adri cried.

Ashton said, "Relax, everyone. Adri, I've sent your samples to our archeology lab for dating. When the results come back, I'll see Professor Levitsky gets a copy. Everything will be fine. Give it time. Yes, you can get married as soon as you like.

"Rina, I've talked to your thesis advisor and gone over the details of your project with them. They agree you have met their requirements for a doctorate, but you must write up the project and current findings. Do that soon. Then we can award your doctorate this semester. Adri can help with those details."

"Molly, what the hell happened?" Dirk asked.

I sighed, thankful he wasn't spouting the implanted words like Adri. He took this in stride, probably because he knew Eve and Lara would do everything possible to restore his body again.

"Dirk, I've no idea. We went to bed and woke up here."

Ashton said, "The ID wants to discuss the situation with the four of you, but I've convinced them you need time to adjust, especially Adri and Dirk. So, Rina, you take Adri to your apartment. Molly, you and Dirk go to yours. Clean up. Relax. Chat with your daughter and sister. Eve wants to see you as soon as you feel up to it. I'll arrange the ID meeting in a few days. Okay?"

Rina said, "We can get married? He proposed last night or whenever it was, and I said yes."

"Sure, Rina. I can arrange it later today, but what about sharing your special day with your mother on Zeta Minori-D or your father on Kali-D? And won't Adri want to share it with his parents on Kali-D?"

I spoke up, sensing their situation. "Why not get married now? Later on, visit Zeta Minori-D and have a second ceremony for your mother and then have a third on Kali-D for your father and Adri's family? That way you have additional time to adjust."

"Oh, yes. Yes. That's what we must do. Ashton, can you make it happen today?" Rina asked.

I guessed what she must be thinking. Because Adri looked like a special Great Lady, he might not want to marry her. Or anybody. Ever. She'd seen how her father had reacted.

"Ashton, I'll be her maid of honor. Dirk can be Adri's best man. We should get them wedding dresses. It's their special day."

With a wry smile, Ashton said, "I agree. Since I still have your body measurements, I'll see what I can find, as long as you'll be content with what I find. We'll conduct the ceremony at suppertime. How's that?"

Rina beamed, but Adri's body still shook. He continued to recite the implanted words, but that seemed to keep him calmer than I expected.

Ashton said, "Plus since you're marrying, I'll get you moved into the married dorm. Would you like to be as close to Molly's apartment as possible?"

Damn, Ashton's good. The instant smiles spoke volumes.

"While you dine and deal with the ceremony, my staff will move your things. Don't worry. I've already ordered a dozen school outfits for Adri and Dirk. Just remember to depend on your robot assistants. See you all later. I've much shopping to do."

"I don't know if I can even walk," Adri whispered to Rina. "I'm perfect, but scared."

"Tiny steps. I'm by your side. Our robot assistants can help," Rina said.

Dirk and I watched them make their slow way out of the commons.

He said, "I remember now. Keeping your balance in these heels is hard. Adri must be petrified. How come he's been implanted and I haven't been? Lord, I've many questions I don't know where to begin! But I feel dirty. I need a shower."

Dirk took this backslide in good humor. Six years ago, I spent countless hours giving him the therapy he needed to recover from having been mutated into an armless Galactic Doll. While this was a giant step back for him, he hadn't freaked out on me.

Once in my apartment, Cleo stripped me while Ben stripped Dirk. Together, we stepped into my shower, much as we once had years ago before Eve restored his body.

"Your hair is thinner and shorter," he said. "Otherwise you seem the same."

After the shower, our robots dried us off, dressed us in clean school outfits, and dried our hair. At that point, Eve and Bishop joined us. She made a pot of tea, which I appreciated.

Bishop spoke first. "When I counted over a dozen armed men led by Teos entering your rooms, I decided I couldn't take them. I used the personal invisibility shield and kept watch. That Teos fellow is a Third Invader general. They used a steamer to haul you back to the warehouse we visited. I followed them inside."

Bishop outlined all he'd learned and what had transpired.

"Molly, I'm sure one of the top rulers of Cass-C is aligned with the Third Invaders. Can't prove it, though. That steel cell is below part of the spaceport's tarmac. Oh, Dirk, I turned off that implant recording. Figured you didn't need it, but Adri did. He could barely hold it together back there."

"Thanks, Bishop. Your actions have been perfect. Well done," Dirk said. "I can see why Molly insists on having you around. One clever bodyguard. But we best keep quiet about all this."

"Yes, but if Third Invaders have infiltrated Cass-C..."

"My turn," Eve said. "Lara and I had lengthy discussions with the genetic engineers at Salad's lab. We learned key facts. First, they don't know how to grow or regrow arms. They faked those images of men with four and six arms. They faked the part human part animal ones. Even the mermaids were fake. However, they can grow gills for underwater breathing, necessary on several Federation water-worlds. About all they make are the various versions of the Great Ladies and the clones when someone orders them. And the Vogelmenschen.

"Lara and I shared our cures, though they didn't seem that interested in restoring the distorted feet, the monster boobs, or even re-growing arms and restoring voices."

"That's good news! Eve, when we saw that video presentation, I almost freaked out. But is their mutation agent the same as ours?"

Eve grinned. "Now the interesting part. Lara and I compared them. With minor exceptions, their Great Lady mutation is identical to our Galactic Doll, except the Padella markers aren't present. The other minor differences don't manifest observable features. Their armless version is similar to ours, but with one huge difference. Ours makes a telepath while theirs does not. Per their records, the original Great Lady mutation has been around for a hundred years. The armless option appeared about sixty years ago. Both were here years before the Sixth Invaders came to Earth. Lara and I suspect Chief Science Officer G'Karn somehow got a copy of the Great Lady mutation agent from Kali-D.

"Lara suggested if the Sixth Invaders acquired the Kali-D special Great Lady mutation agent, then others may have, too. We should expect copycats."

"Shit! That's scary," I said.

Dirk said, "If Bishop is right about the mutation agent used on me, then I will develop telepathic skills again. And what about Adri? Will he develop telepathy? And Rina and Amalie?"

180

Bishop said, "The women weren't exposed. The man claimed they were already special Great Ladies. But Adri might develop telepathy. Isn't that risky?"

Dirk said, "The man has enough trouble trying to survive this mutation. He doesn't need to worry about being kidnapped and sold off as a slave telepath."

Eve said, "He has a good point. But there's a way to deal with that."

"Make it happen," I said. "Dirk's right. Unless I can give Rina and Adri hundreds of hours of therapy, they have a tough path ahead of them. I don't have the time, and Celeste isn't here. Nikita has her classes. But..."

"What, dear?" Dirk asked.

"When George died, Rina became almost helpless. She freaked out. We could barely keep her somewhat calm, and then only because Adri stepped up and became her assistant. These robot helpers can be knocked out. I didn't even know Cleo had an emergency off switch."

"I didn't enjoy being turned off," Cleo said.

While smiling at my robot helper, I continued. "Now Adri depends on his robot. If they learned to use their feet and toes like we used to back on Earth, then when the robots get knocked out, they can carry on."

"Do you have time to teach them?" Eve asked.

"No. And we will need the laptops with videos and the three helpful machines. Still, if we get the chance, we should teach them how to be independent of the helpers, robot or human."

Just then, a deliveryman dropped off two new gowns and matching heels. Both were Leslie copies that encased our shoulders. The sky blue gowns highlighted our exaggerated curves and fell just below our knees. I had to give Ashton credit for picking out stylish gowns though perhaps his wife did it for him.

After getting us dressed, Dirk and I headed for the commons area for the ceremony. Eve and Bishop came with us, along with our robot helpers. A minister arrived along with Ashton. I worried when Rina and Adri hadn't yet shown up.

They arrived a half hour late. Adri looked terrified, but Rina did her best to appear calm and in control, though I detected a slight tremble in her legs. Both wore spectacular white gowns that enwrapped their shoulders. No one missed seeing what their bodies no longer had.

I moved beside Rina.

"You look perfect, Rina."

She smiled and whispered, "I am nervous."

Dirk stood beside Adri, who looked as though he might faint at any moment.

"Adri," Dirk said, "you're getting quite a wonderful woman in Rina. She's brilliant and gorgeous. Keep putting your attention on her and how fabulous she looks."

"I'm scared. I'm perfect, too. Okay. That helps. How can you be so calm? I'm helpless without my helper. How can I support Rina? I don't look male, but I am the perfection of beauty. I'm proud to be one of the beautiful and special Great Ladies. I'm very happy."

"Of course, you are, Adri. Rina knows that nothing's better than being a special Great Lady. She's marrying you knowing how wonderful and perfect you are."

"I'll always be faithful to Rina. But I don't know how I can support us."

"For starters, the helper robot is handling your needs, right?"

"Well, yes. But..."

"Yeah, damn scary. Give yourself time. Remember how we told you to give Rina time to adapt?"

"If the young couple will step forward, we'll begin," the minister said.

182

The ceremony took three minutes. Ashton signed the marriage documents for the couple while the two pressed their bodies together and kissed.

"Okay, let's go to the cafeteria where I've arranged for a special wedding dinner," Ashton said. "This way."

He had the diner done up in fresh flowers. Ashton's wife was there, super-tight corset and all. While we dined, musicians played. I monitored Adri, but he ate little. Much too self-conscious I presumed.

Once we finished, they played waltzing music.

Dirk said, "Miss Molly, may I have this dance?"

I grinned but picked up his intention. Our action forced Rina and Adri to rise.

"How can we dance? I can't hold you," Adri said to Rina.

"Like this," Dirk said. He pressed his body into mine, a collision of monster boobs. But we got our chins locked over each other's shoulders. In the tall heels, our minuscule dance steps didn't matter.

Emboldened, Rina and Adri copied us. A few minutes later, both seemed to enjoy it.

"May I have the next dance with the blushing bride?" Dirk teased, cutting in on them.

"Hey, I get the next dance with this handsome groom," I said, moving close to Adri.

He whispered, "I'm scared I'll fall. But I can do anything. We're perfect, aren't we?"

Damned implants! I hate them! "You've made Rina happy," I said. "She'll remember tonight as long as she lives."

Adri flushed. I felt much of his body's tension slip away.

Later, the musicians stopped, and the party ended. Ashton led them and their robots off to find their new temporary apartment next to mine. Most university couples moved out during the summer months.

As they entered their new home, I said, "Hey, send George over if you need any help."

Both Rina and Adri gave me a funny glance that said: you're like us; how can you help?

The next day, Eve and Lara took DNA samples from the four of us. Later, she confirmed that Dirk would develop telepathy, as would Adri, but not Rina.

Eve said, "Ashton suggests I re-mutate Adri like he did to the sixteen hundred, just in case someone found out he has it and well... Dirk, I can do that to you, too."

I pressed my lips together for a moment. "This should be Adri's choice. Coming from Kali-D, he and Rina appear to be special Great Ladies not Earth's armless telepaths. Why don't you wait a while? Unless you want that done, Dirk."

"She's got a point. Let's hold off. Everyone believes we're special Great Ladies. None of them have telepathy. We're safe," Dirk said. "Damn, and I just got reinstated to my former job as a Galaxy Detective Squad member. That didn't last long."

However, if Bishop was right, then some Third Invaders might know otherwise. But I concurred with Dirk's decision.

Nothing happened for another whole day. I got in a couple sessions with Dirk trying to erase the eight days of painful mutation. We got it desensitized somewhat, much to his relief.

That evening after supper, ID Agent Wanda Hammerstein showed up at our door.

"Well, hello. Didn't expect to see you again. Come on in, Wanda," I said.

She looked at Dirk and flinched.

"Go ahead. Say it." He teased her.

"You look... Well... Creepy. Sorry, but you do."

"Thanks, I think. What's up?"

"I almost lost my job as an ID agent. They blame me for losing Jarvis and Eric."

"That's dumb of them," I said.

"Anyway, they've given me a new assignment. I'm to escort you four to a high-level briefing tomorrow. I'll be by around nine, but I've no idea what it's about. Scuttlebutt says Third Invaders might be present. What have we stirred up? I hope not a war or something. I best go tell Rina and Adri. Dirk, you are freaky. Just want to be honest."

"No offense taken. I don't look like a man anymore."

Chapter 19 The Meeting

Right on time, Wanda knocked. Dirk and I, along with our robots, met her in the hallway. Soon, Rina and Adri joined us, their robot helpers following along behind them. We took the elevator down to the ground and out to the shuttle lot where Wanda had parked a large shuttle.

None of us said anything, instead focusing on watching where we were going. She took us to the spaceport. There, the ground lowered us, ship and all, into a vast underground labyrinth. Okay, I got lost within minutes, but Wanda led us without hesitation. We entered a spacious CEO-like office, had it been above ground.

Imagine my surprise when a female Third Invader wearing a blue uniform, suggesting an officer, walked in. Slightly shorter than us, she seemed human enough until you saw her head. Her head's rear beak-like protrusion made me wonder how she could sleep on her back. Her facial features appeared compressed as though the act of stretching out the back of her head and pulled in the entire face. She wore a blaster on her right side and a disintegrator on her left.

We took seats with our robot assistants to our right, necessary because tea and water cups sat before us along with straws. Without asking, our assistants moved our drinks closer. Wanda sat at one end of the table opposite the standing invader woman. The steel walls were otherwise bare, illumination coming from banks of LEDs on the walls close to the ceiling line.

"I am Captain Katya Binsk. I'm here to brief you four, after which I'm to request your immediate assistance."

Her tone suggested a loathing to ask for our help.

"I don't know you freaks, though I ferried you here from Goringy-E. Please introduce yourselves."

That done, she continued. "What I'm about to tell you is classified as very top secret. We trust you will not tell others about what we discuss." She snarled. "But no one will believe you if you blab. You aren't capable of much real action."

She wore an earpiece. She seemed to be listening to someone. I suspected she didn't like what she heard. When Captain Binsk continued, she sounded less sarcastic to us.

"History first. Our people, whom you call Third Invaders, came to this section of the galaxy many tens of millennia ago. We are long-lived compared to humans. Our lifespan averages about a thousand of your Earth years. We embarked on a major study of your species, which we found very suitable for our experimentations, primarily because of your short life spans and rapid breeding. What is the best system of government? What is the greatest population density? What is the degree of diversity within the species? They posed more questions.

"To answer these, we set up controlled populations on worlds in this side of the galaxy. We then nudged the cultures, especially along specific government lines such as a benevolent monarchy, kings, queens, democracies, and dictatorships. A very extensive list. Many societies developed religions, some worshiping a single unseen god, some a pantheon of gods. Such don't exist except where some other aliens landed and appeared godlike in the eyes of the primitives.

"It seems Rina and Adri are studying the earliest recorded appearance of your species on habited planets. In fact, both have data that outlines where we've been and when—at least roughly when. You have our permission to complete and document your work as it isn't relevant in today's experimentations with your species. Yes, we're still testing theories, and you are our test subjects.

187

"At first, we kidnapped a thousand humans, using them to establish the next colony on a new world. For many millennia that served us well. However, within the last millennia, the sheer number of space-faring worlds has grown beyond our ability to manage and control. As Parkinson discovered, our recent methods of observing our experiments involved constructing Homo sapiens clones. Then, to use your term, body swap a Third Invader into that empty shell.

"Indistinguishable from others of your species, our observers then studied the experiment, fostering changes when needed. The humans didn't know we intervened. Until Parkinson came along. Somehow, she can detect one of us who has body swapped into a human body. Perhaps she'd like to share how she does that."

I shook my head.

"Thought so. Anyway, often we need more host clones. We set up Salad's on Kali-D to provide us batches of a thousand at a time. Worked until Parkinson showed up and exposed us. We're working to contain that mess. With you and Salad now special Great Ladies, we are back in control."

Dirk's ire rose in proportion to how long she talked. Now he exploded.

"Your people committed treason on ours. You promised to cure all Earth men from the Galactic Doll mutation if only we'd donate a thousand of us to help you create a new colony on Domes. You took others and me. But you used the armless Galactic Doll agent on us. You impregnated our women with twins and tried to form a breeding colony of telepaths. But your promised cure lasted a month before Earth's men reverted to their Doll forms. Traitors. I heard your Home World suffered a debilitating attack for your treachery. You and your people are the fiends of the galaxy!"

She glared at Dirk before responding. "That was Edyta's mess. She was an influential psycho-sociologist, but a crazy

188

one. How she ever got Home World permission for that debacle I'll never know. Last I heard you still got her cleaning toilets with a brush in her mouth."

Well, that last was true. While Eve and Lara cured the other sixteen hundred, Edyta's DNA was different, and they hadn't invented a cure, though none had been sought.

"That's all I have for Rina and Adri. Wanda, escort them to someone who'll see they get back," the captain said. "Good luck on getting your thesis written. Our historians will check your accuracy."

Adri and Rina glared at Captain Katya Binsk but followed Wanda. When Wanda returned, Captain Katya Binsk continued, though she seemed more relaxed. I think our presence unnerved her.

"Let's move on to the present. It seems another alien invader has moved into this side of the galaxy. We've discovered its appearance in the Orion Arm. Specifically, it's invaded your Sol Empire, taking control of your people on Earth."

I sat up, following every word.

"The alien is a parasite, a worm-like creature about six inches long, four inches thick around its middle. It attaches itself to the belly of its human victim. Within minutes, it burrows its way inside, healing its entrance wound. It takes control of the person's thoughts and actions. What it wants is anyone's guess. But signs are it wants billions of host bodies.

"Once it has burrowed into the stomach, it's almost undetectable, except via the dramatic change in the person's personality. A stiff electric shock drives the alien worm out of its host. But the host doesn't survive."

"How do you know all this?" Dirk asked.

"We have our people operating clone bodies. That way we can observe Sol civilizations."

Why didn't that surprise me?

"We don't know where they came from, their numbers, or how many humans are infected. We need to stop them. They are ruining our experiments. Worse, they may spread to other human worlds. On behalf of the Third Invaders, we are offering you two an opportunity to join us on a joint expedition to determine the situation and exterminate these worms. The Federation of Planets is sending along ID Agent Wanda Hammerstein."

"Why us?" I asked.

"Damned if I know. You're helpless. Still, Home World considers Parkinson here the most dangerous human in millennia. Lord knows why. I think they're offering it to you because, out of the billions of humans, you two discovered our patterns of colonization of this side of the galaxy. Only an egocentric person would believe Homo sapiens would develop independently on every habitable world. If you two don't wish to tag along, that's more than fine with me."

"Dirk and I insist on coming along. It's our people," I said. "But we promised Rina and Adri to help them hold wedding ceremonies for her mother and then her father and his parents."

Captain Katya Binsk smirked. "You realize they're part of our experiments—Adri and that Salad man."

"Huh? What do you mean experiment?" I glared at her.

"Haven't you guessed? Our psycho-sociologists want to see if the behavior ideas implanted during their mutation comas work and allow the males to adjust to being helpless special Great Ladies. Will they be role models for other male special Great Ladies even if they keep their manhood? I'd say it's working. Parkinson, you and I both know most adults who underwent the armless Galactic Doll mutation on Earth found ways to die. They couldn't stomach living that way. We know about Professor Heli's machine that removes some power that implants have, but it's only a temporary fix. Doesn't last.

190

We've been curious about that therapy thing you and your sister use, which seems to work, though it takes hundreds of hours, making it impractical for our use. The scripts used on Salad and Adri appear to be working the moment they wake and with no other side effects. Time will tell."

"You're still trying to make telepaths?"

"Edyta had the right idea, just all the wrong methods to make it possible. Plus we thank that Sixth Invader science man for his contribution of the telepath genetic engineering mutation. We try to make use of the rare random discovery other species sometimes make."

I wanted to slap her condescending face. G'Karn was a kind Sixth Invader.

"Any implant is bad for the person. Have you noticed how Rina and Adri keep paraphrasing parts of the implant script?"

"Well, yes, but it helps keep their wild emotional reactions in check. They aren't trying to kill themselves. Isn't that a benefit?"

"Implants make the person less bright and with slower reactions and sometimes erroneous thinking."

"That may be, but nobody has hundreds of hours to devote to one of them using your therapy thing. Anyway, how long do you need for those weddings? What?"

Someone must have said something in her earpiece. She paused for a minute, listening.

"One month. You have a month to take care of your details. My people need time to prepare electrocution devices powerful enough to drive the worms out of the host bodies without killing the hosts. Wanda will coordinate with you humans. Meet in say a month on Kali-D at Salad's laboratory. We'll take a Federation ID ship from there. Can't risk humans discovering our saucers.

"Prepare yourselves, if that's even possible. You might make out wills. This is a very dangerous assignment. These worms aren't playing nice and don't care if you're a freak or not."

With that, the meeting ended. Wanda walked us out and into the shuttle.

While flying us back, she said, "I'll get you proper apparel. You'll be working as though you are official ID agents."

"We wear all black?" I asked with a grin.

"Of course."

"Do I get a badge?" Dirk asked.

"Yeah, but it'll be a fake one."

We laughed.

Wanda became serious. "They almost booted me out of the ID because I couldn't save those two agents. Then this came up. I think they're sending us on a suicide mission, but it *is* a mission. I have to try. It's not too late for you to back out."

"Hardly. It's our civilization that's being threatened," I said. "Make sure we have what we'll need to survive."

"Okay. I'll check with you tomorrow. We have your body measurements. I can get your gear. Catch you tomorrow. What I don't get is the sudden change in departure times. They told me we'd leave in a couple days. Now it's a whole month. Why?"

Once home, I walked the long Rectangle to the Single's Dorm to visit Nikita. She had to know our plans. On my way back, I visited Eve and Lara, telling them, too.

The next day Wanda returned with new apparel. Black blouse tops and black pants—yeah! The real hit turned out to be the shiny, knee-high, black boots. True, they sported the same super tall, spiked heel, but when Cleo tightened the laces, they fit tight against the slippery stockings. They contained steel braces that prevented accidental bending of ankles. After talking a few steps, I never wanted to wear any other shoes! They were that good. I ordered a dozen more pairs while Wanda laughed.

"Look, if we do any hiking on rougher ground than the flat avenues of Hoffdorf, you'll need ankle support," Wanda said. "I have to keep stretching my legs each night or I'll never be able to wear flats when I go on a mission."

She looked us over. "I can't get over how tiny your waists have become. I thought those pants wouldn't fit, but they're snug on you. Okay. I'll lay in a supply of these outfits. I've no idea how long we'll be gone. Unless we want to do laundry every day, we best have a fair number. I can't tolerate a stinky crew."

We laughed at that image.

After she left and our robots changed our clothes back into school attire, Dirk asked Rina and Adri to drop by.

Dirk said, "We're about to visit two worlds and your parents, Adri. You and I look like special Great Ladies, not men. How many like us have you seen on Zeta Minori-D or Kali-D?"

Adri's face turned crimson. "But I'm the perfection of beauty, proud and honored to be a special Great Lady."

He shook his head. A thin line of water trickled down his face.

"None. Only Salad."

He managed to admit those three words. Damned implants.

"Right," Dirk said. "We need to get our rationale and stories aligned. We can't say someone did it to us. We don't know who did or why. And that raises more embarrassing questions."

"We're happy, perfect. Nothing's better than being one. But they'll ask why? I can't answer that. Gotta be a role model. Show everyone how wonderful it is to be a special Great Lady. They won't understand, will they?"

I noticed how difficult it was for Adri to discuss his new reality. The implanted words continued to paint a different view, one he couldn't ignore.

"Exactly, Adri. We need a plausible reason we got the mutation. How about this? Special Great Ladies are the perfection of beauty. We want to honor our beautiful wives and show them how proud of them we are by being one. Show the world there is nothing better than being a special Great Lady. Be role models for others, showing them we can do anything we want. Show solidarity with our beautiful wives by being one ourselves. It's wonderful to be a special Great Lady.

"If they press us further, we can add that the famous rug merchant Salad Naraka is our role model," Dirk said.

"I like that," Adri said. "Not sure I can remember all that, but I can't write. Oh, Ben, write that in a note for me."

His robot did, then sent it to Rina's robot, Cleo, and Dirk's, too. It remembered Dirk's comment that we needed to get our stories straight. Clever robot programming.

Adri asked, "Are we sure we want to do this? I mean what's your mother going to think when she sees me? I'm proud to be a special Great Lady. Will she think I'm a freak? And my parents? What will they say? I know it's a great honor to be one, and it's wonderful to be one. But..."

His eyes drained down his cheeks. I sensed he fought a losing battle between reality and the implanted notion of reality.

"Dad will ask how I can afford to support a family, especially a Great Lady family."

"What did you used to do?" I asked.

"I teach at Linski University and run digs in the summer. But Dad—he owns Kedar Transports. They make the luxury transport spaceships. Wit is wealthy, and Jona's been a special Great Lady since just after I was born. He wanted a son before she became one. I have a younger sister, Celinka, who's nineteen, but she's been a special Great Lady since birth. There's nothing better than being a special Great Ladies. And it's because of Celinka that I know children of a special Great Lady are born this way—dominant genes that make us the perfection of beauty. Dad's been on my butt to take over his business when he retires, but I'm more interested in astro-archeology. We've often fought over this. What's he going to think? He'll disown me, but still, I must show everyone how wonderful it is to be a special Great Lady."

"Wit and Salad are neighbors?" Dirk asked.

"Yes."

"Then, Salad has already paved the way for you and me," Dirk said. "Wit must have seen Salad. That should help us. Will you be able to continue at Linski University? Perhaps you might work at Kedar Transports and teach too. There's nothing you can't do. That would give you many opportunities to show everyone how wonderful it is to be a special Great Lady. You'll have a bigger impact. Plus it's likely to make your father happy. He doesn't want to turn his company over to Celinka, does he?"

"No way. All she's interested in is buying more clothes and shoes. She is the perfection of beauty."

"Well then, when you make the arrangements for these two more ceremonies, tell your father you'll accept learning to run Kedar Transports."

That brought a smile to Adri's face. I didn't know how Wit would take having his son look like his wife and daughter, but Adri had to make peace with his dad. He needed support even though Rina and Adri wouldn't have said so because of their implants. God, how I hated implants!

Chapter 20 Weddings

Something Captain Katya Binsk admitted bothered me: that Rina, Adri, and Salad were part of a Third Invader experiment in behavior control via mental implants. Here, the pain experienced during the mutation comas powered the words. What did they hope to achieve?

I couldn't help thinking about the Sixth Invaders and their plans to conquer Earth. They used implants to convince every woman on Earth to undergo the Galactic Doll mutation, knowing any child they would later have would be a Galactic Doll, even males. With invention of the armless telepath Galactic Doll, unethical actions mushroomed. Even humans tried to profit from the misery of others, culminating in Edyta's several failed attempts to create breeding colonies. Once the implant technology became known, CEOs in Russian corporations experimented on humans trying to make victims want to be handicapped telepaths.

Granted, I'd only met a few of these special Great Ladies at Salad's party. Like Rina, they continued to spout the implanted phrases and displayed the desired behavior pattern, but at what cost? I watched Anala's eyes glaze over when she recited these implant phrases. Rina and Adri did too. But I now understood Rina better. When she was a child and before she left for Soros University, they must have implanted her to want to become one. I'd seen her eyes fog up when she heard the words special Great Lady. My guess is that Salad had somehow implanted her, perhaps playing a recording while she slept. It had worked.

From my point of view, implants and their desired behaviors squashed the person's actual reactions and responses. I'm happy while crying. I'm perfect while my body is shaking in terror. Dichotomies. These implants created a sharp contrast between two opposite realities. Like the two poles of an electric generator I studied in physics class, this created energy detrimental to the well-being of the person.

With the potential to create clone bodies, Rina and Adri could get body swapped back into normal bodies, assuming Eve and Lara didn't find genetic mutation cures. Yet the implant would prohibit them from getting the mutation undone by either means.

Why would the Third Invaders want to perfect such an implant? Other than Salad and Adri, no other males underwent the special Great Lady mutation. Though I have to admit I had only the sketchiest of data. Were they planning to do to Kali-D men what the Sixth Invaders had planned for Earth's men? Make them handicapped and look like women? Was there something important about Kali-D that the Third Invaders desired?

Too many questions. Worse, while I would have liked to deliver extensive therapy sessions to Rina and Adri, I didn't have the luxury of the time. Alien worms threatened the Sol Empire and my home. For unknown reasons, the Third Invaders chose Dirk and me to assist in a joint operation against them. While part of me wanted to promise the young couple that I'd give them the therapy they needed when I got back, I knew I must not make such a promise. Wanda made it clear we might not survive this mission.

"Back them as much as we can," I said to Dirk. "Help them smooth their relationships with their parents. See they have employment. That's all we can do in the short time we have. Are we packed?"

We each had two crates of apparel and personal items. Since we still lived on campus, we followed the dress code, our Leslie gowns stowed along with the fancy wedding outfits. At last, Rina and Adri joined us, their robots dragging three crates on rollers. I suspected both might not be returning to the campus, at least not soon.

I'd hired a shuttle to take us to the nearby spaceport, minimizing how far we needed to walk. The attendant loaded the crates though he gave us strange looks. An hour later, we dropped into hyperspace on our way to Zeta Minori-D and the large city of Kalak where Rina's mother, Lila, lived with Gregoros Pappas, a wealthy businessman.

Dirk and Adri reviewed their cover story, and Rina told us about her parents. Again, the dichotomy between their implant-caused happiness and their extreme nervousness far exceeded meeting the bride's parents.

As we dropped out of hyperspace, Zeta Minori appeared—a yellow star much brighter than the sun. Their main habited world looked Earth-like from the viewport windows as the transport descended. When the pilot announced Kalak ahead, Rina sighed.

"Coming home at long last," she said before her nerves triggered again.

Finally, a city that looked somewhat like Chicago. Tall stucco buildings painted in rainbow-bright colors lined a huge crescent of sparkling blue waters. A white sandy beach reflected puffy white clouds. Throngs of people mobbed the beach while many sailboats cut arcs farther out. My view shifted to the spaceport as we landed.

Once through customs, Bishop pushed a cart loaded with our crates, while Rina led us into the main lobby where her parents waited. Already, Cleo had adjusted our language translation units to the local dialect, but I hoped most spoke Federation Common.

"Mom!" Rina gushed.

Her family welcomed us. As expected, Lila had light tan skin just like Rina and Adri, but bronze-skinned Gregoros represented the locals. He stood tall and thin, but handsome.

His black eyes shone. A few streaks of gray lined his temples. He wore white shorts and a white shirt so thin I could see black chest hairs. He wore leather sandals.

Lila wore a thin white dress, held up by two tiny shoulder straps. Her short hair reminded me of Deanna's bob cut. Her empty shoulders caught eyes as much as her large bosom and tiny waist. Heck, we all had similar body shapes. Unlike us, she wore no stockings, just similar very tall spiked heels.

"Oh, no! Rina, you didn't..." Lila said as she saw her daughter now a mirror of herself, though we all wore our Soros U attire.

"I did it along with my half-sister, Lanka, when she turned eighteen. Now I'm perfect, too. And this—Mom, are you pregnant?" Rina asked.

Instantaneous smiles flooded Gregoros and Lila's faces.

"We thought I was too old. We've had an oops. But Greg always wanted a son. Now he'll get one."

He said, "Lila always refused to have children because she feared her genes would dominate mine. We forgot that her genetic mutation back on Kali-D so many years ago reset her biological clock. But we're happy. It's a boy. Three more months."

"Congratulations, Mom," Rina said, pressing her body into Lila's for a hug, and then doing the same with her step-father.

"Oh, sorry everyone. This is my husband, Adri. You remember—"

"Adri?" Lila interrupted. "I'd recognize that face anywhere. But the rest of you?"

"We ran into each other again. I couldn't let the most perfect woman in the galaxy get away from me this time," Adri said. He said what he and Dirk had practiced—that we wanted to honor our beautiful wives, showing them how proud of them we were by being one.

I watched how Gergoros reacted to Adri's justification. When Adri finished, a smile replaced his stoic acceptance. I picked up a flash from his mind. Adri might help his new son because the son's body would be like us. Adri didn't know it, but he got a big acceptance break.

Gregoros said, "Pleasure to meet you, Adri. You must come to visit us often, even live here."

"And these are our best friends from Soros U." Rina introduced us, including Bishop as my security guard.

"Do those robots actually help you?" Gregoros asked.

I said, "Immensely. Soros U doesn't allow personal assistants on campus. Instead, they give us with these robot assistants. They take a little getting used to but they get the job done. Beats using your feet and toes."

"Honey, your robots don't have feet. They'll have difficulties navigating our mansion. But don't worry. We'll get temp assistants to help during your stay. Greg, you make the calls while I lead them to the shuttle."

Lila's young personal assistant said nothing but helped Lila, anticipating her needs and being there for her. She helped us four get in while Bishop stowed the crates and robots in the back. Gregoros joined us, reporting that four others would be at their mansion to assist us.

After a sweeping flight over the spectacular city, we landed on a private pad beside a sprawling mansion, perched on the edge of a tall cliff overlooking colorful houses and the beach. The builders spared no cost on this mansion. Elegant woods, polished ceramics, even tapestries spoke of the wealth of this family, Gregoros in particular. Every room had its own elevation, often a mere step or two above or below the adjoining rooms. Everywhere, the opened large windows allowed the sea breeze to flow through the home.

Rina gave us a tour of her childhood home, including her bedroom. Adri beamed when he spotted the discolored print of Rina and him when they were playing around the backyard of the Naraka home.

"I can't believe you've kept that all these years," he said.

She flushed. "I never forgot my best friend."

The new assistants arrived and helped us change into the wedding dresses. Gregoros insisted the repeat ceremony take place on the open patio that hung suspended over the edge of the cliff. A tall outer iron fence made falling off impossible, even for us. The gentle breeze added much to the ambiance.

Two things became clear. First, Lila married the right man this time. He kept an arm around her, kissing her forehead several times during the ceremony and dabbing her cheeks. Second, even though his son would look like Adri and Lila, he already made plans for the boy. An unused room became the future boy's bedroom. He'd purchased toys and a walker on wheels that would help the boy learn to walk. That impressed me.

During dinner, Gregoros plied Adri with questions about how Adri was adapting. I sensed he wanted to gain knowledge about how to raise his new son. And he made Adri promise to come visit them often.

Lila pestered Rina. "Why didn't you wait until after you've had children? You know any children you and Adri have now will have bodies like yours. I wanted to get you away from that nonsense. Now here you are just like me, only with Adri being one, too."

"It happened, Mom. Lanka and I got along well. She had been waiting until she turned eighteen to get it done and married. I was with her. I got caught up in her elation and happiness. Now I am as perfect as you are, and Adri is incredible."

Lila sighed. "I guess I always thought you might get it done to be like me."

"Well, you are gorgeous, Mom. And Dad's fabulous. I can't believe I will soon have a baby brother. And he'll be perfect, too."

Dirk and I basked in the utter luxury and elegance that surrounded us. What a mansion.

When we left, I felt Rina and Adri would always have the support they needed here with her parents. But I didn't discuss the possibility the genetic cures Eve and Lara had invented might help Lila and her unborn child. It didn't seem right.

"I'm homesick already," Rina said as our flight lifted off, bound for Kali-D.

"But we just left." Adri chuckled. "I'm sure we'll be coming back often."

"Dad really liked you. I think he sees you're perfect, too," Rina said.

I didn't suggest otherwise.

***

We landed back on Kali-D at the spaceport in Kistna. This time, Adri's family met us. We wore our school dress, which was Rina's suggestion to help smooth the expected upsets.

"There's everyone," Adri said as we walked across the spacious terminal.

Wit wore a business suit that must have cost a month's salary. The black-gray material contained bits that sparkled in the light. His skin tones matched those of Adri, a light tan. His wife, Jona, stood beside him. She wore a cherry red copy of Leslie's fancy gowns that showed off her impressive curves. Her black hair shone and reached her knees. A young woman stood behind her, her personal assistant. Beside her Adri's sister, Celinka, stood, also wearing a scarlet Leslie gown. Both women wore the same black stockings we four wore. Her black hair almost reached her ankles, impressing me. Her personal assistant stood behind her.

Wit spoke first. "Rina, I'd recognize you anywhere. Lanka told me you both became special Great Ladies together. You look stunning. Your school uniform?"

"Yes, it is," Rina said. "Pleased to see you again. It's been too many years. And yes, now I'm perfect, just like my mother and sister, and you—and you must be Celinka. We're all beautiful and perfect."

Wit stared at Adri, his face twisted and reddening. "Adri? Is that really you? What the hell happened? Did they get to you as they did poor Salad? He looks like a special Great Lady but with no voice like Anala."

"It's me, Dad. Yeah, they got me, too. Knocked out by thugs and woke up like this. But I'm perfect and honoring my beautiful wife, showing her how proud I am of her by being one myself. Together, Rina and I show the world nothing's better than being a special Great Lady. I have to show solidarity with my beautiful Rina. I can't undo it."

"Good lord! What has become of our world? First, Salad, now you. Did they catch the thugs who did this? Why did they do it? Any clues?"

"No to those, Dad. No idea why. Rina and I are making the best of it. There's nothing we can't do. I want to learn the family business and split my time between teaching and the company if your offer still stands."

"We'll have to see."

With that, Adri pressed into Jona, our unique hug.

"You're looking more stunning every time I see you," Adri said, pressing into Celinka. "When do I get to meet your fiancé?"

She giggled. "At supper tonight. We will have a double wedding ceremony. Since you and Rina are doing it, Rufin and I moved ours up. Isn't this wonderful? But you're still a man, aren't you? Do those robots help as a real person would?"

He laughed and introduced the rest of us.

As Wit ferried us to their large home next to the Naraka mansion, he opened up a little.

"Old Salad is having an enormous difficulty adapting. Hell, he has no voice, like his wife. Sometimes he gets that video-voice gadget aligned right, but more often, he doesn't. He can't make a sound. They did a job on him."

"But Dad, that's the way Anala has been as long as I've known her. She's the perfect hostess—beautiful, poised, and always says the right things through her voice thing. You've said that a thousand times at their parties," Celinka said. "But I'm glad Rufin didn't want me to pick that option. Oh, Adri, do you like my new hair modification? I can feel with it. It's the latest thing. It's thick and shiny now. Been trying to convince Mom to get it done. You should, too, Rina."

Their home paralleled the Naraka home, and their side yards joined. I saw how much time the two kids spent together. There weren't other close houses. Like Salad's place, everything was on one main floor. That way our robots could help us. But, we soon discovered, Wit had his personal office in the basement, just like Salad. He kept it locked. That way, Jona or Celinka couldn't fall down the stairs. I made a note to check how Salad dealt with his basement office.

Wit said little during the afternoon but listened. Jona and Celinka chatted with Rina and me, asking how we managed schoolwork and life at the university while being special Great Ladies. Dirk and Adri allowed the women to dominate the conversation.

"So, how did you meet Dirk?" Celinka asked me.

I told her the truth—that we met in Space Navigation 101 class. I told her about many of the classes he and I took together, including piloting spaceships.

"You can fly a spaceship? And navigate, too?" she asked.

Her eyes opened wide. I'd just showed her what we could do.

"That's amazing. Dad, did you hear all that? We special Great Ladies can do anything, but I never dreamed such things were possible. I thought all I could do is be like Mom, look after a house and tell my assistant what to cook. I'm asking Rufin if I can go to the university, too."

"But Celinka, it's hard enough for us to manage our home. I can't imagine doing any of those things. Rufin might want you to manage your home and be the hostess for his business parties," Jona said.

"Little sister," Adri said, "you shouldn't let anyone dictate what you should or should not do. We are perfect. We can do anything we want, but we're dependent on our assistants."

"Seeing you and Rina, and her friends from Soros University," Celinka said, "makes me want to learn many more things. I hope Rufin won't mind."

Not approving the direction the conversation turned, Wit grumbled. "Celinka, dear, don't get too many wild ideas in your head. Your wedding is in a few hours. Then, you must adapt to being married, having your own home, and making Rufin happy, just like your mother has done for me these many years. She's always been the essence of perfection and beauty. Never let me down. I'm proud of her. You must make Rufin proud of you, unlike what happened to Salad's first wife. No offence, Rina. I'm skeptical Adri can run my business. Hell, I don't see how he can run an archeological dig anymore."

He let off his anger. "You're deluding yourselves—believing there's nothing you can't do. Celinka, you've met countless special Great Ladies at our parties. You, too, Jona. How many of them have ever done anything beyond instructing assistants in the running of their homes and hosting parties? None. Zero.

"Frankly, Rina, I'll be very surprised if the university keeps Adri once they see what he's become. All you special Great Ladies can do is talk. Your assistants are the ones who do these things for you. Be realistic. It's wonderful Adri had the good sense to marry Rina, but..."

Tears trickled down Celinka's cheeks, forcing her assistant to retrieve a handkerchief. Her fiancé's arrival broke the embarrassing silence. Lean, Rufin Klimek strode in wearing a tuxedo and carrying a bouquet of this world's equivalent of red roses. He handed them to Celinka's assistant, but only after Celinka sniffed them.

"Wow, so many of you," he said. "Delighted to meet this many special Great Ladies."

Distracted by the flowers and the reminder she was soon to be married, Celinka launched into the introductions. When she got to Adri and Dirk, she explained evil men had gotten to them, much as they had to poor Salad.

Jona said, "Let's change for the wedding. Afterward, I've a special meal arranged. Wit has hired a quartet of strings to play. Adri, you can show your friends and Rina to the guest rooms. My assistant has already taken their crates to their rooms."

Salad, Anala, and Lanka joined us for the ceremony and festivities afterward.

Celinka bubbled with excitement. "This is wonderful—both getting married together. Adri, how do I look?"

"Perfect, sis. Beautiful," he said.

"So do you. If you were a woman. Sorry, I can't help but see you that way now. Dad will walk me down the aisle."

"Dirk is my best man. Here we go. Just remember, I always love you. If you ever need anything, call. Don't let Dad get you down. We can do anything, I hope."

The brief ceremony united Celinka and Rufin Klimek while renewing Adri and Rina's vows. Anala and Lanka effused excitement, very pleased to see us again. Salad grumbled, at least that's what came from his voice machine. Jona presided over a meal that would make my chef son Bernardo jealous.

Wit took another opportunity to chastise Adri. "Son, if you didn't have those robots feeding you, you'd have starved. Stop kidding yourself. Check with the university and see if you still have a job."

Salad's lip reading device forced him to have to speak slowly, just as it always had Anala. He agreed with Wit. "Adri, we're helpless." After getting that out, he rattled off his implanted mantra so fast that the device couldn't reproduce what he said.

Anala noticed us struggling to listen and said, "Ignore him. He's just reciting the usual platitudes."

The musicians began, and we adjourned to their ballroom. Spiraling lights reflected from the silver streaks in the marble floor. Jona had the room filled with flowers, whose sweet aroma helped everyone relax.

Dirk and I, followed by Adri and Rina, showed the others how we held each other and danced. We put our chins over the other's shoulder. Soon, Rufin wanted to dance with me. Then, Wit took the opportunity. Before long, everyone danced with each other, except Salad who declined all offers. Anala and Lanka called him a party-pooper, but even that didn't get a rise from him. I wondered how the Third Invaders evaluated these, their experimental subjects. Would Salad mellow out in time as he learned to adapt to being handicapped? I admit it aroused my curiosity.

Towards the end of the evening, Wit took Adri aside. "Son, if you lose your university position and can't run my company, I won't leave you destitute. I'll see you and Rina have a nice home, servants, and a steady income fitting special Great Ladies, just as I will for Celinka."

Later back in our rooms, Adri told us what his father had said. Upon hearing that, Rina breathed a sigh of relief.

"I'd love to show you the geological wonders on Kali-D. But..."

"We'd love to, but another time," I said. "We have to meet the ID agent soon."

"Trouble is, I don't think we could do that," Adri said. "The ground is rocky and uneven; some have steep trails. Maybe Dad's right. We're very limited."

His implant kicked in. "But there's nothing I can't do..." His eyes glazed. Again, I cursed these damned implants.

Rina took me aside for a private word. "Since you're leaving, I have to tell you about what Adri and I have experienced. Rather embarrassing." Her face flushed.

"It's when we have sex. Since Adri became a special Great Lady, we always climax together. We experience a huge explosion of intense pleasure that goes on forever. Well at least several minutes. It didn't happen until we both became special Great Ladies. It's incredible. I asked Anala if that happened with her and Salad. Her description is identical to mine. Adri, she, and I agree this aspect is more than enough to make everyone want to become perfect special Great Ladies. We can't get enough of it. Thought you should know."

I thanked her. Later, I relayed this to Eve. She believed this might be one of the minor differences between Earth's Galactic Doll and the Great Lady mutation agents that she couldn't tie to an observable feature.

***

After goodnight hugs, we headed to our rooms, where our robots handled our needs. Throughout the evening, Bishop had remained in the room, preferring not to answer questions.

He said, "Molly, I've been giving the worm situation considerable thought. I might not be able to protect you from them."

"Don't worry. None of us know what's going on, but we soon will."

Since Wit promised Adri and Rina financial security, we took our leave the next day instead of waiting to hear how Adri fared at his university.

Anala said, "Molly, please come back for visits. It's always refreshing to talk with you and Dirk."

I promised we would. Many hugs later, Wit dropped us off at the spaceport. A day later, we entered my apartment in the Married Dorm. I called Wanda to let her know we were back.

As I drifted into sleep, I wondered what we had accomplished with these weddings. The well-being of Rina and Adri worried me. How different their lives would be had I been able to deliver a couple hundred hours of therapy, erasing the pain of the mutation, removing the force of the implanted words, and the myriad other emotional and psychosomatic aches they might experience. At least, I knew they'd not succumb. That mattered. I vowed to return and give them that boost if I could.

Only then did I realize what Adri meant about the geological wonders. With all the worlds I'd visited, I'd never had the time or opportunity to see those worlds in any kind of detail. I knew forced to wear these heels, hiking over any terrain that wasn't smooth was out. Bummer. I hadn't even seen much beyond a minuscule part of Cass-C.

Chapter 21 The Worms

October 1, 2368

Although classes started, Dirk and I got permission to skip the fall term. Dressed in black, we waited for Wanda to pick us up. We wore black blouses and pants, but the knee-high boots felt wonderful to wear, adding confidence to our walk.

With Bishop bringing our shipping crates, we met Wanda in the shuttle lot.

"Got a dozen sets of outfits for you, including the boots. Are you ready?"

"Thanks. Got our badges?" Dirk asked with a broad grin.

She attached them to our belts.

"Satisfied?" she teased.

During the fifteen-hour flight to Kali-D, we went over what little we knew, more speculation than fact. During the past month, the ID had uncovered a little information, scanty though it was. The last sighting lay in a suburb of Chicago called Peoria, about halfway to St. Louis. Now I worried.

Dirk said, "Didn't you say your relatives and friends live in Chicago?"

"Yeah, but some have moved to Domes. Not sure who's where. Been out of touch for six years."

Wanda said, "The worms come ashore from the river. Perhaps, these are aquatic worms. Anything like them native to Earth?"

"No. Never heard of them," I said. "There's a lamprey eel that latches onto fish with its mouth. But nothing like what's been described."

"Best theory ID can come up with," Wanda said, "is one of your deep space exploration ships ran into the worms and brought them back to Earth. They want me to bring a sample back for study—dead if it's too dangerous to bring back alive."

Wanda said nothing about us, but I picked up her thoughts. She had written us off as "worm food." A sober trip to Kali-D followed.

She received tower permission for a direct landing at the pad beside Salad's Genetics Laboratory. Wanda headed down the bay ramp at a fast clip, looking for our Third Invader member. Like snails, Dirk and I followed with our robots at the ready should we lose our balance. Once on solid ground, we spotted another woman coming out to meet us, shaking hands with Wanda. She looked human with short blonde hair and blue eyes though taller than me and fit.

Wanda said, "Captain Katya Binsk. She's been body swapped into a human clone for this mission."

"Captain," I said. "Your body is expendable?"

She laughed. "Precisely. Third Invaders aren't welcome on Earth. I can hardly show up in my body. Never say I did nothing for you and Dirk. This is a very dangerous mission. Your bodies will only get in the way, worm fodder as Wanda suggests. So, let's go inside. I have two new clone bodies for you two. They are still growing. You must eat a special formula, but they should perform well enough."

"Body swapping?" Dirk asked.

"Yes. They'll keep your current bodies in stasis pods until needed. In fact, we're taking them with us, along with a body swap machine—just in case. I'm bringing along a spare clone body in case something happens to Wanda's body.

"Also, don't worry about clothes, Wanda. I brought along new black outfits for the clones. You might need the clothes you brought. If these new clones get killed, you must swap back. Come; check this out."

211

I sensed pride mingled with a sense of superiority coming from the Third Invader. But I couldn't fault her logic or her brilliant idea of using throwaway clone bodies. That she had gone to this extreme suggested the dangerousness of this mission.

"That's me!" Dirk said, looking at the body in the stasis pod. "I get my body back. Thanks, captain."

"We best use only first names from now on. Katya, please."

I smiled. The clone of my body appeared the way I looked in Chicago before any of the mutations happened. But it wasn't the same clone body I'd bought months ago.

"Yes, thanks, Katya. This is a great idea. That's how I once looked."

Wanda chuckled. "I look years younger. Maybe I should get killed."

She and Katya laughed.

"They rushed construction of these two clones. Wanda, you don't want to eat the slop these two do. Yuck. The longer you stay alive, the less of this slop you'll have to eat. Okay, let's get the swaps done."

She signaled two genetic engineers. The process was identical to what Holly Ann had invented back on Earth. I laid down on a cot, the machine between me and the pod that held the new body. Engineers placed a head harness on both bodies and turned on the machine.

Nothing happened for a moment. Then I perceived that incredibly esthetic, pure white light. Basking in ultimate serenity. That's the best description I can give. I never wanted it to end. When the light faded, I felt something treasured had been stolen. I awoke in the stasis pod.

"Oh, I feel strange," I said.

An engineer lifted me up and out, sitting my naked body on the cot, while the other stripped my other body and laid it in the stasis pod. He stowed the clothing in a bottom compartment of the pod. I needed help to dress.

"Your body will feel stiff and sluggish for a time. It's rather like a baby getting used to its body," one engineer said. "Make sure you drink a gallon of the blue goo each day. It has the nutrients your body needs. After thirty days, you can eat non-spicy foods, bland items. In about six months, you'll have regained about half your strength. Takes a year before the process is complete."

I wore all black. I clipped on my new ID badge. My arms felt like putty, but I hoped I could fire my gun if only I'd brought it.

As if reading my thoughts, Katya said, "I brought along Earth-made guns for you and Dirk, based on what Bishop carries."

"Thanks. That's the one thing I missed. I used to be a good shot with my Glock."

Wanda said, "We have a small gun range on the ship. But won't the worms be too small to hit?"

"Dunno," Katya said. "I have the new shock guns our tech people made. Supposedly, they will force the worm out of the infected human body. We'll see. No guarantees."

Soon, Dirk joined me, flexing his arms. "I feel great. Okay, weak, but great. I'm me again. Let's get going."

Bishop wheeled a huge cart loaded with the blue goo onto the ship, while Wanda, Katya, and two staff brought out the stasis pods containing our other bodies. Then they brought one holding a Wanda clone and one with the real body of Katya. Next, crates of new clothes and a body swap machine joined us in the cargo bay, along with our no longer needed robots. Katya loaded many other crates but said nothing about them.

Wanda oversaw stowing the pods and gear we might not need. The robots powered down. After unpacking clothes in our new cabins, Wanda showed us the gun range in the ship's rear. From the number of cabins, the ship's crew ought to be close to twenty.

She saw me counting the cabins. "Yeah, I know. Regular crew is twenty. As I said, this is a suicide mission. Here are your new guns. Have at it while I get us on our way to Earth."

Katya joined us at the range, bringing along the new shock guns: a Taser on steroids. After shooting it into a dummy humanoid target, I doubted the human would survive the shock. Three clips later, my arms gave out, but I held the gun steady enough to get five kill shots. Pathetic.

Wanda joined us. "About a day to Earth. How do these shock guns work?"

Our bodies tired easily. After drinking blue goo, Dirk and I retired to our cabin.

He said, "Just so you know, I've lost my telepathy. Teos gave us Earth's version. But this body doesn't have it."

"Good to know. I still have my ability. It's a little lower power, but still there. I'm exhausted."

We dropped into a deep sleep. Circadian rhythms vanished for us as our bodies continued to develop. I know we woke and guzzled more goo several times, but we slept most of the trip to Earth. Only when Wanda landed the ship just outside Peoria did Katya wake us up with a mug of strong coffee.

We stepped outside to the fresh morning air. The ship parked on the east bluff of the river. The sprawling development below us contrasted with the tall modern buildings on the opposite side, Peoria proper. Soldiers rimmed these bluffs. To our right, I saw large field artillery cannons pointed towards the city. A tent city swarming with people lay below us, encircled by more soldiers with guns.

Walking up to us, an officer said, "You're from the Federation? Major Banker."

"Yes, from the Intelligence Division," Wanda said. "What's the situation down there?"

"The division has this entire regional area cordoned off. No one gets in or out. We established a refugee camp, but we're under orders not to let any of those who have been inside our perimeter line out. We're to shoot to kill anyone trying to leave. We have the worms contained to the greater Peoria area."

"But if the refugees aren't infected, why not let them leave?" I asked.

"Can't tell if they're infected or not. They appear normal until you expose their chests. I can brief you if you'll follow me to my command post."

Walking past the lines of well-armed soldiers unnerved me. Surely, the situation didn't call for such extreme measures. His tent held arrays of comm equipment. He motioned us to seats while he arranged a giant monitor.

"Okay, here's a video my techs spliced. As you can see, the worms fly up out of the water and attach their mouths to the person's chest. Here is one of the first methods we tried. Fishing boats and electrical charges brought fish and worms to the surface of the river. Other worms flew up and attacked the boat operators. We think we got a few of the worms, but it's always been a one shot attempt. The worms attack the boaters, sometimes before they can fire off the charges."

I watched as the worm flew up out of the water six feet and struck the chest of the fisherman. Like a lamprey, its mouth latched on. In less than a minute, it burrowed into the man's body, disappearing from view, leaving behind an ugly round scar of sorts.

"Once they take control of a body, they form a hive in the center of the city. Those who have access to weapons use them to attack us. Watch this segment."

Two men holding a pistol and shotgun approached a pair of soldiers. Both sides fired on the other. The worm-controlled men died, but the worms shot out of their bellies and attached themselves to the two soldiers. The men retrieved all weapons and moved out of sight back into the city.

"That's happened too many times. We think they're now well armed. The general ordered a drone strike on the central part of the town. Watch."

A drone's camera appeared. We saw it flying over the downtown area of Peoria, homing in on worm-controlled people. I watched twenty people get destroyed. But when the smoke cleared, the unharmed worms jumped six feet at a time, until attacking another twenty people trying to flee the destruction zone. Once attached, they moved back toward the center, disappearing into buildings.

"We have found a way to kill the damned worms. Watch."

A man carrying a child's baseball bat rushed out of a building and ran towards two soldiers who moved in too close to that building. The soldiers yelled, but the crazed man continued charging them. They fired their guns. The man died, and as expected, the worm crawled out and leaped toward the men. The worm needed two leaps to reach them. Both fired at the worm. Several bullets struck the creature, killing it. The men cheered.

"We can kill the worms. We've asked for more help, but the rest of the empire says we're on our own, that we brought these monsters to Earth via one of our exploration ships. Brass is looking into that. We're just trying to contain the infestation to this area."

"What about allowing those who aren't infected to flee?" I asked.

"Can't chance this spreading. We've no way to tell if a person is infected until it's too late. Watch."

We saw six men, women, and children running from a building. They saw the soldiers on patrol and headed their way while looking back over their shoulders. One soldier waved them on, hurrying them up. As they got close, a worm leaped from a child onto one soldier, creating havoc. A woman pulled a worm she'd held behind her and tossed it at the other soldier. The child and woman waited and then led the two soldiers back towards the building while the other civilians ran for their lives.

"The survivors are in the refugee camp. They weren't infected, just the two who you saw. Hosts can carry extra worms. And the real problem is we can't tell the infected until we're too close. We've tried to stop them. Watch."

We saw two men wearing biohazard containment suits marching toward the worms. The suits proved useless. The worms chewed through the suit in seconds while the men tried in vain to pull off the worms. Another pair wore bulletproof chest protectors. The worms attached themselves to the men's faces. This clip had no sound. Next, two soldiers in full body armor charged the worms. They killed a dozen worms before the worms cut through the armor at plate joints. In all cases, the worms took the soldiers' weapons and material.

"Where do we stand today?" asked Wanda.

"We've put in a request for a bombing run to destroy the heart of this city where the worms and hosts are at. If that doesn't stop them, then we've no choice but to nuke this whole area, fry every damned worm!" Major Barker spat out.

"What about the refugees? Others in the city who aren't infected?" I asked.

"Can't risk them spreading the worms beyond this twenty-mile zone," he replied.

"Have you figured out what the worms want? What's their objective? Where they came from?" I asked.

He shrugged. "We've seen them leaping up out of the river."

"How do you know there aren't infected people downriver or upriver?"

"Got remote sensors, drone patrols, and surveillance systems watching."

"Why here? Peoria?" I asked.

He shrugged.

"Is there anything strategic about this city? Does it have something valuable, special, useful? There must be a reason for invading Peoria. If the worms are in the river, I can't imagine why they haven't traveled far from here already."

"Who knows? One other fact. The worms haven't infected giants or dwarves."

"Let's go back to the ship and discuss our next move," Katya said.

Chapter 22 Investigating

"We need to discover what the worms want." I said.

"Where did they come from?" Dirk asked.

"Why this city?" Wanda asked.

"Why aren't they moving up or down the river or have they done that already?" Katya asked.

"Can they breed? How many more of them are there?" Dirk asked.

"Will the shock guns work?" Katya asked.

"We should get the refugees to real safety, but to do that, we need a foolproof way of determining if a worm is in them," I said. "Lots of questions. We need answers."

Dirk said, "Say, what about using the IR cameras or those on a satellite? If worms are warm-blooded, we might spot them. Even if they're in the river, maybe. I'll go check with Major Barker."

He returned and logged into Earth's satellite system, entering the code the major gave him.

"They're already using IR. Worm-infested bodies are a bit warmer, but there's not enough difference to separate people."

We saw many small wiggling things on the screen as Dirk focused on the river opposite the downtown area.

"Shit! That's a lot," Katya said.

Dirk said, "Can't tell a fish from a worm. Some wiggles are fish. Look here."

He focused the display up to where the river narrowed to a small channel.

"See that," he said. "That's a screen the engineers installed across the river. It lets water through and small creatures, but nothing the size of a worm. They have one downstream, too. They're hoping to keep the worms contained."

"Unless worms begin life tiny." Katya pointed out the obvious.

Just then Agent Wanda Hammerstein's comm center clanged, interrupting our tea-filled discussion.

"I've got a long distance call," she announced, "but it's for all of us. I can't believe this call. Anyway..." She flipped a switch, and the call echoed throughout the ship.

"Good. This is Commodore Irenka Bronislawa assigned as an aide to the Sol Empire's Admiral Rossi. Captain Binsk knows me as Rear Admiral Bronislawa of Home Fleet Two stationed around the Norma Arm."

Dirk, Wanda, and I looked at each other, blank looks on our faces. While Dirk and I couldn't be expected to know of such fleets, ID Agent Hammerstein should. But she didn't.

"Good rats! She's my superior officer," Captain Katya Binsk said. "You'd call her a Third Invader admiral. What's she doing breaking cover? Yeah, she's body swapped into a human female working with your Admiral Rossi."

"Don't worry, Captain Binsk. Once this transmission is over, Commodore Bronislawa will vanish. This worm affair has caused the worst catastrophe in a millennium. We ordered you to break cover and work with the humans. The worms are one of our scientific experiments gone wrong. We have exterminated that scientist. Anyway, the story goes, he found the worms and wondered what effect they'd have on human societies. He brought them to the Sol Empire worlds to see what they'd do. Now we have to clean up his mess. Home World is coming clean on the source of this experiment.

"Between us, they are terrified the wrong people might discover Third Invaders created the worms and retaliate with their unknown weapon—the one that seven years ago boiled thousands while they slept. That's why we're being up front

220

this time. Anyway, I've let Admiral Rossi know the precise location of the swamp planet where these worms live. We will let the Federation quarantine that world or destroy it."

Captain Binsk asked, "Why did you have me tell them all about Third Invader seeding human colonies?"

"Two reasons. First, Rina and Adri were about to expose those results. Second, another matter must be handled once this worm mess is cleaned up. I'll contact you and your human team later on. Admiral Rossi has arrived. I'm signing off. He wants to talk to you, especially Mrs. Parkinson. Later."

After a pause, I heard his familiar voice. "Admiral Rossi here. Who am I talking to? Is this call secure? Over."

Agent Wanda answered him.

"Good," he said. "The very people I want. Parkinson, I need your telepathic skills. Capture a worm and interrogate it. What do they want with human hosts? What are their goals? Why us? It's imperative we know.

"Bad news. The worms have infected all senators on Brussels, Tau Ceti, and the President and his entire staff on Pylon, Epsilon Eridani. The worm-infect humans tried to take over those worlds. They have killed all of them, including the worms inside their bodies. Those branches of the Sol Empire government no longer exist. Further, corporate execs who once demanded they have part of the rulers of the empire on their worlds now want nothing to do with either branch.

"I've ordered Earth's Senior Investigator and Senior Judge into hiding until this ends. The worms haven't found them, yet. The attacks on Pylon and Brussels were target-specific. But the worm attack on Earth is one of numbers. We need to know the worms' objectives. I'll give you twenty-four hours to find answers. After that, I've no choice but to exterminate the threat. I can't risk thousands of these worms breaking out of the Peoria area. They give their hosts superhuman strength, making them hard to stop.

"The Third Invaders told me ten thousand worms were released in Peoria, compared to the hundred on Brussels and Pylon. Considering the damage those hundred did, we cannot allow ten thousand worm-infected humans to run free on Earth.

"Detective Bennet, you're to rejoin your Galaxy Detective Squad at once. They're leaving to find the worms' marsh world. Once verified, we'll set up an official quarantine. That is all. Twenty-four hours, Parkinson. Over and out."

"Your people are behind the worms," Wanda said. "Damn you, Third Invaders! Hope the worms get you!"

"Hey, be glad Home World accepted responsibility and let you know. That hasn't happened in my five hundred years," Captain Katya Binsk said, glaring at Wanda.

"Hey, I wanted to be reinstated," Dirk said, "but can't it wait until we kill these worms? I'm supposed to help protect everyone."

"I know, Dirk," I said, "but Admiral Rossi ordered you. Best pack up and get going. We'll hang onto your old mutated body in the stasis pod."

"Hell, kill the damned thing. I sure don't want it back, not when I have a sound body, even though it's still weak. Guess I'll take a batch of that goo stuff with me," he said.

Once Dirk headed off to find a flight to Chicago's spaceport, we discussed how we could get me close enough to interrogate a worm.

"I need to use telepathy on a worm-infected human. But first, I'll try to detect the mind of a worm in the river."

From a mile away, I couldn't detect the alien worm minds, if they had any. Perhaps alone the worms didn't have a "thoughtful" mind. Either that or distance prevented my making contact. We three along with Bishop stood on the ridgeline, looking down on the tens of thousands in the valley pleading to let the soldiers allow them to flee the worms.

222

Ordinarily, I'd bask in the beauty of the scenic overlook. Then it happened.

As we watched, at least a thousand rushed across one bridge, racing towards the throng that continued to plead with the soldiers.

"Oh, shit! We don't run that fast," I said.

"They're making a break," Wanda said, drawing her weapons even though we were hundreds of feet above the chaos below.

Fear. Desperation. Those emotions swamped my mind, forcing me to block out the thoughts of others. Hundreds of guns, blasters, and disruptors fired. Those fleeing the charging worm-infested humans rushed up the hills and into the fire of the soldiers. Behind them, the infected fired their captured weapons at the soldiers and those fleeing. Bodies dropped like firewood before the line of soldiers broke. The fleeing rushed through, followed by the infected humans.

For several minutes, we watched from the safety of the hilltop. Then the onslaught reached us. I refused to fire on the fleeing victims, preferring to wait for the infected to arrive.

"Save your ammo," I said.

Bishop, like me, hadn't fired, though Katya and Wanda already had gone through at least a clip or two. While they reloaded, the desperate ran past us, moving beyond the ritzy homes along the ridge crest.

A few of the worm-infected charged up the hill. But most preferred to continue down the valley on level ground.

"We need one alive," I said.

"How?" asked Katya. "They don't stop when shot!"

We killed four before Bishop shot one in both legs, crumpling the man to the ground. Despite the pain he must have been in, he raised a captured gun to shoot. Bishop shot him in each arm. At last, Bishop had overcome the superhuman strength.

Before I could question him, a second wave hit us. I remember seeing a crazed man rushing up and tossing a handful of worms our way. One latched onto me. While I tried to pull it off, I didn't have the strength. I felt a sudden wave of pain shooting through my head. All went black.

I awoke, floating above the dead body's head. Bodies lay dead around mine. A great stillness pervaded the area. I saw the inert bodies of Wanda and Katya lying near mine.

That awe-inspiring white light appeared, commanding my full attention. So esthetic. Beautiful beyond words. I never wanted it to stop and tried to keep it from dying down, but failed. I gasped. No, my old body heaved. I saw Bishop standing over me, operating the body swapping device controls. He helped me sit up.

"Cleo's activated. He'll get you dressed while I recover Wanda and Katya. You can still interrogate the one I stopped. He's still alive," Bishop said.

Cleo dressed me in my ID black outfit with fancy boots. I stepped out of our ship to see the aftermath and find the one Bishop had for me. I heard Wanda's body gasping from inside the ship.

"Cleo, stand guard over me. I'll probe this one's mind."

While I had no idea what Cleo could do to protect me, it felt good to issue the order. I focused and entered the man's mind, ignoring the searing pain waves flooding its nerve channels. I floundered through the myriad thoughts firing in this dual mind, ignoring those that likely were the man's.

Alien images appeared. These I paid close attention to. But the man and worm died before I could probe the dual mind for details.

"Well, that sucked," Wanda said.

Jarred, I returned to the present. She joined me and looked down at her dead cloned body.

"Glad we used disposable clone bodies," she said. "Get anything useful from that dead one?"

"Alien images. Died before I could get a solid handle on them. Got a few concepts," I said.

"We can use Wanda's LD comm and let Admiral Rossi know," Katya said.

We turned to see her joining us. She had tied up her hair to disguise her distinctive Third Invader body's head.

"What did you get?" she asked.

"I think they had a symbiotic relationship with a humanoid race on their marsh world. The humanoids died off, leaving the worms isolated. They are trying to take over us as a substitute host. That's about all I got before it died."

"Wow. Interesting," Wanda said. "Best let Admiral Rossi know. Then, let's see what Major Barker is doing about the breakout."

While she reported, Katya, Bishop, and I avoided the dead and found the major's field tent. On his monitors, we saw soldiers racing after those who'd broken through their lines, trying to contain them as both normal people and the infected rushed down the valley floors on the east side of the river.

"Yes, send in another regiment," Major Barker barked into a phone. "They're leaving my soldiers in the dust. The worm-controlled men run twice as fast as us. Yeah, send them in about five miles down the various valleys."

Satisfied, he looked up at us. "What the hell happened to you?"

"Body swapped. The worms got to us," I said.

He rubbed his face. "I've lost half a regiment of soldiers today."

"Sorry to hear that. Many innocents died."

"Cursed worms," he said, picking up his phone.

We backed out of his tent, returning to the safety of the ship. My body seemed starving. Wanda's too. Lunch break turned into a lengthy break. Again, I had to depend on Cleo.

Bishop cleaned everyone's guns. He reloaded all magazines and recharged the disruptors and blasters.

During the meal, Katya patched our comm center into the video feed from drones hovering over Peoria and the river. We watched as worms hopped out of the river and moved overland in a series of six-foot hops, following the fleeing humans.

As we finished up, Katya said, "Look! Something's happening to the worms. Maybe they can't live long out of the water."

One by one, the worms appeared to die. One drone operator zoomed in on a deceased worm. Red spots dotted its skin.

I joked, "Looks like it's got the measles."

The drone's camera focused on worm after worm. All had red spotted skins.

While we pondered the significance, Major Barker's voice cut in on the drone feed. "Something's happened to the worms and the infected humans. I think they're dying. Drone Six, move out into the valley to the east. What's going on? I need a clearer picture."

One of the larger medical center complexes called Peoria home. Medical colleges, nurse training facilities, and actual med centers occupied half of the in-use buildings in the city. Drone images now captured many medical staff coming out of their buildings. They'd been hiding from the worms. Several carried white flags—a good idea considering the trigger-happy soldiers still here.

An hour later, we learned the worm-infected humans broke into a med center, which had been trying to contain a local outbreak of measles among grade school children. While the worms had ignored the kids, they had infected several staff members.

One doctor reported to Major Barker. "Sir, the worm-infected broke into the measles quarantine section. I'd swear the dead worms I saw on my way here have the measles, too. I'd like to get tissue samples."

"Go ahead, doc. Coordinate with my doctors. The general will want answers. And soon."

More troops arrived. An eerie silence fell, broken only by the soldiers removing the dead. For a time, we watched from our hilltop vantage point, but as night fell, we retired to the security of the ship.

On the morning news, scientists confirmed the fate of the worms. They'd died from measles, for which their immune systems had no defense. Wanda and I looked at each other.

She said, "Wow. That sure drives home how vital it is to follow strict decontamination procedures when landing on alien worlds. And getting immunity shots when visiting worlds. Do you know the Federation has a complete immunization grid? Yeah. You enter your home planet and the planet you wish to visit. It doles out the correct shots you'll need. All automatic. This sure emphasizes how critical it is. A tiny virus killed the invading worms."

I chuckled. "You don't have to tell me. I'm a licensed pilot and navigator. They drilled that into our heads our first day. Even on Earth, the doctors have automated it. I used to have two children working on deep space exploration ships. They'd land on strange new worlds. I always worried they'd contract an awful disease or something or they'd cause a pandemic by transmitting our germs to the natives."

Wanda said, "The ID has investigated several such incidents. It happens."

Just then, the voice of Commodore Bronislawa echoed around the ship from the comm center. I'd forgotten all about the second mess she'd warned us about. She hadn't.

Chapter 23 Robots

"Hi, Commodore," Captain Katya Binsk said. "We're receiving. Over."

We waited, counting the minutes, which reflected the distance between us. Twenty minutes passed, suggestive that she was about halfway between us and Cass-C. I surmised she was on the move since she had blown her cover by warning us about the worms.

When she responded, the commodore asked for a status update. Captain Binsk outlined the results, mentioning we'd lost our clone bodies to the worms.

"All right, mission handled. Now on to the second situation," Commodore Bronislawa said. "For over twenty millennia, we have been experimenting on your species, Homo sapiens as you call yourselves. Often our scientists set up a new colony on an uninhabited world. About a thousand humans per world. Our objectives varied, but often we wished to see how your societies developed over thousands of years. What form of government works best? What kinds of things get invented? How strong are religious beliefs? We've asked thousands of questions. In fact, your species is the most studied of any we've ever encountered in the galaxy.

"To the point here. One of your deep space exploration ships is approaching one of our experimental worlds. Your civilization knows it as the star Zeta Tucanae. The planet in question is the third out from the sun, called Bella by the natives. It's a fertile world, well suited for your species. We need you to intervene. We expect your people will want to incorporate this inhabited world into your Sol Empire. But you must exercise great care and understanding.

"Our people founded this world two millennia ago with a thousand humans who spoke the language then called Italian Latin. I'm sending you a download of their current dialect for your language translation units. Once installed, you'll be able to communicate with them. As of today, Bella's population approaches one billion with more women than men. The civilization is in the early stages of industrialization. The planet is rich in metals as well as gold and silver. Over."

"Okay. The language update came through," I said. "Katya is installing it in our language translation units. Why do you want us involved? Over."

I heard a chuckle as she responded. "Because of the uniqueness of this society. Mrs. Parkinson, you are well suited to interface between these people and your exploration crew. Why? In our Bella experiment, men don't have arms while women do. Further, the men have breasts comparable to your own Galactic Dolls. Men are the domestics. They nurse and raise the children. Women run Bella; men are subordinate to women. Second-class citizens in your terminology. The experiment has run for two thousand years. Our observers have documented their development. Incidentally, I suspect the Sixth Invaders might have gotten their ideas for their Galactic Doll mutation agents from Bella. We spotted one of their ships in the system a hundred years ago.

"Your job is to assist in the first contact situation, one that would shock the people on Bella. The exploration ship is the Voyager under the command of Captain Rich Bellflower. We estimate they will reach Bella in two weeks, giving you time to get there first, meet the ship, and coordinate the first contact. Over."

I cursed before calming down. "What kind of government do they have? Customs? Cities? Where should we land? Whom to contact? How about enough info so we can make intelligent plans? Over." The delay seemed interminable.

At last, Commodore Bronislawa's voice echoed. "Change of plans. The Voyager just landed at another location. We'll worry about Zeta Tucanae another day. Something more important has come up. Agent Hammerstein and Parkinson: you are to contact your ID Commander as soon as you return Captain Binsk to her ship. Captain, I have a new assignment. Over and out."

"Make up your mind." I joked, but neither laughed.

"Powering up the engines now," Wanda said. "Can you lay in the coordinates for at the spaceport Kistna, Kali-D?"

"I will," I said, following her to the front of the ship.

I sat in the navigator's chair, slipped off my heels, and used my toes to activate the menus. When Katya joined us, she verified them while Wanda lifted off.

"Activate hyperdrive," Wanda said.

Katya watched as I used a toe to flip the switch. She said, "Amazing, though Cleo could have done that for you. Okay, I'm hungry. To the galley."

Later, Katya woke me. "We're landing in ten minutes and dropping off the stasis pods and body swap machine."

By the time Cleo had me dressed, Wanda landed her ID transport beside the genetics lab. As Captain Katya Binsk prepared to leave, I caught her.

"Captain, thank you for your help. This time, Third Invaders have been our friends. I hope this can be the beginning of real relations between our people. I look forward to seeing you again."

"Home World did it to avoid retaliation with your secret weapon that boils people," she said, frowning my way.

"They did the right thing, and I thank you for that. Maybe our races are just the mouse and the scientist."

Katya's frown vanished. She chuckled. "Good one, Parkinson. Good one."

With that, she left. Wanda fired up the Long Distance communication array and contacted the ID Commander. I still didn't know his name.

"Ah, Agent Hammerstein, you survived. I heard measles wiped out the worms. That's the end of that. We have a far more critical case. Level Ten."

Wanda gasped. "That's the highest category. Hasn't been one of that level in decades!"

Because of the time delay, the Commander wasn't aware of her outburst and continued. "Go to Feldspar-B at once. Report to Chief Inspector Roscoe Raymond Risso in Marina. He'll fill you in on the latest details. We estimate you can be there in thirty minutes. I've fired off Strike Force One, but they won't get to Feldspar-B for about fifteen hours. Until they arrive, you're in charge. And take that Parkinson woman with you. Over and out."

Wanda stared at the LD unit, her eyes opened as wide as I've ever seen them.

"He—he didn't wait for my reply. Level Ten! Holy crap! I'm in charge for half a day?"

"What's Feldspar-B? Why didn't he tell us what's wrong? What are we supposed to do?" I asked.

"Don't have a clue. Come on. Let's fire up the engines. It's a nearby world. They manufacture all the sophisticated deep space exploration robots. They have a monopoly on them. I think they might have made Cleo. Fantastically wealthy planet. Something must be horribly wrong for them to send me. I think the Commander thought I wouldn't be returning from the worm mission."

While she powered up her ship, I used my nose to scroll through the menu choices of the nav unit. Once I found Feldspar-B, I tapped it, entering it as our destination. Wanda glanced at the display to verify it, and we lifted off.

After the jump into hyperspace, I said, "Ten minutes to Marina. You're pouring it on."

Wanda grinned. "Damned right. I aim to beat his time estimate. Level Ten. My gods, are they being invaded or attacked? Something huge must be happening."

We lost a few minutes getting permission to land at the spaceport outside Marina. But once we landed, a police officer rushed up, got us through customs, and drove us into the city to meet with Chief Inspector Risso. But the officer knew nothing about the urgency. He followed orders.

Via the viewport of the small shuttle, I watched the city fly by. The man flew far too fast. Much became a big blur. But I saw a clean, modern city, filled with gleaming skyscrapers, though gray smoke rolled upwards from many tall smokestacks that appeared at random locations among the buildings. Sun rays reflecting from the skyscrapers often blinded me. I needed sunglasses but hadn't brought any with me.

We landed on the roof of a skyscraper. When I stepped out of the shuttle, hundreds of shuttles darted about the skies. Thousands parked on the surrounding rooftops, reminding me of Chicago. Plus I spotted what had to be robot-like machines darting about the skies. Their purpose: unknown. As we descended in the elevator, I concluded this civilization had evolved a notch above ours, but I found the similarities striking. The man led us into Interview Room One.

"Ah, here you are. I'm Chief Inspector Risso. Have a seat. That will be all." He dismissed the police officer who'd brought us here. Taller than me, he could lose some weight. His black mustache showed faint traces of gray.

Another woman sat at the table. She had shoulder-length blonde hair and a round face accentuated with piercing blue eyes. Her bright red dress displayed too much cleavage for my taste. Her nails got my attention—three inches long and painted to match her gown. Only then did I notice four rings on her fingers. She wore tall heels that matched her dress.

The two stared at me, but I expected that, as I pushed a chair out enough so I could sit. Cleo moved up beside me. Wanda and I still wore our black ID outfits though I wore the tall-heeled black boots.

"Thank you for responding quickly," he said. "This is Dr. Alessandra Scala, the CEO of Robotics 4 All."

Wanda introduced us. "My Commander sent us here on a Level Ten crisis. He didn't mention what's happening. What is the crisis?"

The Chief Inspector nodded to Dr. Scala, deferring to her.

"What do you know about our world and products?" she asked.

"Nothing," I said.

"Then, I should provide you with background. Feldspar-B is the Federation's foremost robotics manufacturer." She grinned. "We made your robot assistant, though that's an older model. Our main thrust is the design and construction of planetary exploration robots for which we have a monopoly."

She flashed a nail. That motion activated a 3d holographic projection. A strange spaceship appeared in the center of the table.

"This is the Mark One. A total exploration package. Enter the coordinates or launch it from your mothership and it travels to the new star system. There, it surveys the system, logging the number of planets and moons. For each, it sends down a robot probe that analyzes the object, relaying everything a human observer would note if they were visiting. Mass, temperature ranges, distances from sun or planet, period, and whether habitable by humans are among those observations.

"If it is habitable, more probes search for intelligent life forms. Are radio waves detected? Are there cities? If so, are they illuminated at night? Do they have air travel? Space flight? Our sophisticated robots and computers answer countless vital questions. The mothership has a positronic brain, which controls all aspects of the ship and subordinate robots.

"If it detects no life forms or primitive humanoids, then it launches another series of robot probes. These analyze both its geography and geological properties. It identifies critical raw materials, such as titanium, silver, and gold, for example. Our survey probes can detect thirty different materials, outlining their location and potential quantities. If you're looking for rich rare earth deposits within this new star system, the mothership will report back such locations and expected amounts. This is invaluable for miners.

"So, I hope you can see how valuable our manufacturing operations is to the entire Federation."

"Okay, thanks. Makes sense. What's the problem?" I asked. *Can I get one of these ships for Earth?*

"Something weird is going on. Dr. Marco Moretti is our top robot designer. Last week, he stopped working on the new proposals. He claimed he needed to go help our miners dig more titanium. Baynard Smelters refines the rutile rock or TiO_2. They convert it into titanium chloride and then reduce it to titanium using either magnesium or sodium. Titanium is a key metal used in all our robots. Dr. Moretti's action makes no sense. He left his high-paying designer job for the ridiculously low-paying miner's job. Dr. Moretti won't even talk about it to anyone. Keeps talking about how we need more titanium. Our doctors think he might have developed a mental problem.

"Then, two days ago, our CFO, Dr. Karl Von Stroebel, abandoned his position, joining Dr. Moretti in a titanium mining operation. We think he's gone nuts, too. One, I can see, but not two of our top people. I checked further. This morning, I got the results. During the last month, four hundred key workers have abandoned their jobs to become miners. Something is going on here. I called our Senior Senator who

234

relayed the situation to the Intelligence Division on Cass-C. I didn't expect such swift a response."

Chief Inspector Risso said, "Since this involves our top CFO, I've requested an audit of the entire world's financial records. I'm told that will take time."

Wanda looked puzzled. I said, "First, I'd like to visit these two doctors. Talk with them."

He said, "That's a problem. During working hours, they won't talk to anyone. They work at a frantic pace. Best talk to them during meal breaks or at night."

"Sooner, please," Wanda said.

"I'll arrange it. You must travel to the Los Gato Mine. That's about an hour's flight from here," the Chief Inspector said. "We'll leave in two hours. Meanwhile, Dr. Scala can show you their offices, if you think that's important."

"Call me Alessandra," she said. "If you'll follow me."

Ten minutes later, I gasped. "Wow!" We had entered one of the robot factory plants. I gazed out upon what must have been at least a football field space, filled with robotic arms and other machinery. The automated facility built robot probes, all with no human intervention.

"Yes, it is impressive," Alessandra said. "Dr. Moretti's office complex is this way, twenty stories above here. The plant you're seeing is ten floors tall."

"I recognize some of those robotic arms," I said as we walked. "Took several robotics classes at Soros University."

Alessandra smiled. "What do you think of my field? Are you going for a doctorate? Always use new minds here."

"I hate to be ignorant of a field. That's happened too many times. I've been taking a wide variety of classes. Where did the others work before they headed to the mines?"

"I don't know. Is that important? All lived in Marina, but our population is seven million at the last census."

"Could be."

We entered an office complex, which looked much like the CEO offices of Galactic Defense back in Chicago. White walls, LED lighting, stainless steel furniture, and drafting tables. Giant photos of robot probes and machines lined two walls.

"Everything is as he left it," Alessandra said, flicking her claws towards the desk and tables. "This is Fifi, his assistant."

A floor-length, white lab jacket covered her red dress. She, too, had very long nails painted to match her dress. Like Alessandra, she wore tall heels, professional looking. I sensed Wanda felt out of place in her black shirt, pants, and soft-soled shoes. In fact, as we toured the facility, the women we encountered dressed in similar outfits. Here, long nails and tall heels formed a fashion statement among the professional women.

The men, in contrast, wore business suits with colorful sashes for belts. Later, I learned the color of women's dresses and men's sashes reflected their clan affiliations. I didn't know how important this detail might be.

A thirtieth-floor walkway allowed direct access to another skyscraper that housed the management offices of Robotics 4 All.

As we entered Dr. Scala's office, she said, "I oversee this world's twenty-five robotics companies or corporations. Dr. Karl Von Stroebel dealt with their combined finances. True, each one has their own CEO and CFO and a myriad other officers, but we provide top-level oversight for robotics of our world. Yes, we have people working in the agricultural arena, but their job is to provide food for everyone else. Every person on Feldspar-B focuses on achieving our goal of providing the finest in robotics."

She flicked a finger, and lights turned on. "We automate everything. One person controls the entire manufacturing assembly line that makes helper robots, like your Cleo. One

236

person runs the farming robots that produce our food. Our world is the penultimate in automation and robots."

She led us into her meeting room where her secretary brought in refreshments. Sandwiches and tea. As she sat a plate before me, I noticed she, too, kept her nails long. Her red dress suggested she and Alessandra belonged to the same clan, whatever that meant. For a moment, Dr. Scala watched to see how I could eat. Cleo performed his routine job.

"I see even these older models work well," she said.

"I was made here," Cleo said, "and I can recall rolling off the assembly line."

Until now, Bishop remained in the background. Only now did I have to introduce him to Alessandra.

"Yes, it's wise for you to have a bodyguard. We didn't design the Model 1 for that purpose."

Once we finished eating, she took us to the rooftop where Chief Inspector Risso waited for us beside another shuttle, this one with police markings on it. Another woman who wore a white blouse and black skirt stood beside him, a grin on her face. I'd never seen her before.

"This is the Federation Inspector General Katya Verney, from Robotics Central Division. She insists on being part of this investigation," he explained.

Katya nodded. I touched her mind. A broad grin lined my face. "We meet again, Katya," I said, hoping Wanda would pick up on this.

"Indeed. Small universe," Katya said. "Agent Hammerstein. Good to see you again."

Wanda's grin suggested she realized this was Captain Katya Binsk. Her new assignment involved us. Why wasn't I surprised?

Katya asked, "Is your first move to visit with Dr. Marco Moretti?" I nodded. "He's one of their finest designers. Why he would abandon his vital position to dig for titanium ore is a mystery. Let's go get answers."

Chief Inspector Risso chuckled. "He and hundreds more have abandoned their jobs to take up mining. Feldspar-B has never had such an upheaval in its job market. The mad scramble to fill those abandoned positions has been wild. I even lost two officers. It's crazy. At first, we believed they'd contracted some undefined illness. But our doctors ruled out medical issues. Strap in. It's a two-hour flight to the mine."

Chapter 24 Discoveries

We flew over crop fields tended by robot machines though a human controlled them from the background. Forests and rolling hills gave way to barren, jagged mini-mountains. While not officially mountains, mining operations stripped these hills of their cover, including forests.

"Ahead is Los Gato Mine," Chief Inspector Risso said.

Giant robot machines chewed up giant chunks of rock and soil, spewing it out onto conveyors that transported it to more machines. We landed near the largest building not surrounded by robot equipment. Several men scurried about on the level gravel outside the building.

Crap. These heels and gravel don't mix.

Cleo said, "I cannot navigate across that."

"I figured, Cleo. Bishop, steady me. Let's go meet this doctor."

Chief Inspector Risso led the way. "This is the human complex. Their sleeping quarters are on the second floor. Kitchen, dining room, and lounges fill the first floor. Follow me."

A dozen men wearing dirty overalls sat at tables, shoveling food into their mouths. One of these men was the highly educated Dr. Marco Moretti, but as I entered, I couldn't tell them apart. Chief Inspector could, leading us to the side of a thin, middle-aged man. Black dirt stained his face and hands. Did he ever wash? Or was mining this dirty a job?

"Dr. Marco Moretti, Federation Inspector General Verney, ID Agent Hammerstein, and Mrs. Parkinson are here to talk to you," he said.

I pushed a chair out enough so I could sit across from him as he continued to shovel food into his mouth. Wanda and

Katya sat on either side of me. At first, I said nothing. As I expected, he glanced up several times before his glazed eyes focused on my body. My lack of arms got his attention if only for a moment.

"Dr. Moretti, I'm Molly Parkinson. Can you tell me why you—"

"Can't talk. Have to eat and get to sleep. I'm tired. I have to mine more titanium. Mining titanium is the most important thing I can do. We must have much more titanium. Feldspar-B depends on titanium. I have to do my part. I must devote all my waking hours to mining titanium for my world. You're keeping me from my work. I have to go now."

With that, he rose and headed up the corner stairs. Several others mumbled similar words and followed him.

Another miner slid his tray over to our table. "Don't mind them. They're off their rockers. I'm Gil. Worked here all my life, but these new fellows—well, they're just maniacal about mining more titanium. Just ask Josh, the boss. We're producing twice as much titanium ingots since those six arrived a couple weeks ago. Yeah, we're getting richer thanks to them. Still, they're fanatical. Pay them no mind. What's a pretty young thing like you doing out here in the sticks?"

"Hi, Gil. Just checking on those fanatics. Makes little sense they'd abandon their usual work to mine ore," I said.

"It's easy work. Robot machines do all the work. We watch over them, control them, and maintain them. We used to run the mine with just four of us. But now we're making double wages because of the extra ingots we ship to the factories."

Four other men came down the stairs, yawning and wiping sleep from their eyes.

Gil said, "Here come the night crew. These four are like that doc fellow, fanatical about making more titanium. We didn't use to run a second shift of mining, but with these new arrivals, Josh didn't have a choice. Only so many robot controllers."

The four filled trays and sat down to eat. The aroma of strong coffee jarred my senses. After thanking Gil, I tried to chat with these new arrivals. Next to impossible.

"No time to talk. Shift starts now. Have to mine more titanium. Really important. We must have more titanium. Robots depend on titanium. Got to do my part. Go away."

Those who talked to me said much these same words as they gobbled up hearty breakfasts and downed mugs of coffee. Within minutes, we sat alone in the room.

"Guys, I know what happened to them. How about you two?" I asked.

"They're crazy. Fanatics," Katya said.

"Note their eyes," I said.

"Yeah, glazed over like Adri's and Rina's," Wanda said.

"What does that tell you?"

"Oh, hell. Implants? How? I mean how can that be?" Wanda asked. Her face lightened while frown lines appeared.

"How can you tell that from talking to them?" Katya asked. "I get it. They're insane, but how does that mean implants?"

"What are you three talking about?" Chief Inspector Risso asked, rubbing his face. "If you've seen enough, let's head back. I don't want to miss my supper."

Once airborne, we continued sharing observations.

I said, "Yes, glazed eyes are an indicator. But what Dr. Moretti said convinced me. Someone has implanted this behavior in those men."

Katya said, "But I thought that was only used with the special Great Ladies to prevent their wild reactions upon waking from their comas."

"What are you talking about?" Chief Inspector Risso asked.

"Someone has intentionally installed this fanatical behavior pattern into their minds. One way is to use a combination of severe pain and/or drugs while someone repetitively reads a script that tells the victim what he's to do."

"But with the special Great Ladies, they're in a coma. No pain. No drugs. Their bodies are just listening to the desired behavior script," Katya said, pulling on her cheeks.

"Beg to differ. Bodies are in great pain while in the mutation comas. Intense pains. What locks in their behavior pattern after they wake up is all that unconscious pain. If they try to go against the words, that overwhelming underlying pain surfaces, forcing them back into following the script," I explained.

"But these men weren't mutated," Wanda said. "I doubt just hearing the script a lot of times would turn them into fanatics. Hell, we listen to songs all the time and don't go nuts because of just hearing the words many times."

Katya nodded her agreement. The Chief Inspector looked at me and nodded, encouraging me to say more.

"That's true, Wanda. But there's another aspect to implants. Esthetic waves. Electronic waves operating in the kilo–yattohertz range. Those are what's used in the body swap machines. An incredibly beautiful white light you can't resist. Bombard the person with esthetic waves and lay in the commands you want followed. Presto. Implanted behavior. True, if the person endures great pain, such as a mutation, the process is almost foolproof. Without my sister's therapy, those heavy-duty implants with esthetic waves and pain can't be undone. Soros University Professor Heli's machine takes the edge off heavy implants, but it doesn't erase them. And they soon recharge."

"How do we cure Dr. Moretti and the others? Is it even possible?" Wanda asked. "You know that'll be the uppermost question they'll ask us."

"I can try by using Celeste's therapy methods. But the more important questions are who did it and how did they do it?"

"And why?" added the Chief Inspector. "We have to stop whoever is doing this before they wipe out more key people."

"When we get back, let's visit Dr. Moretti's workplace and home," I said. "We must discover how they did this. Since hundreds of others have been implanted, we must examine their workplaces and homes. Then, we can have the police step in and guard everyone."

Wanda said, "We have a full ID strike force arriving in a few hours. They can help us find these answers."

While the Chief Inspector handled our landing, Wanda whispered, "Are you sure they implanted Dr. Moretti? Glazed eyes can have other causes."

"I looked into his mind," I whispered. "He's sitting in the middle of the incident, surrounded by that white light. He doesn't want it to go away. Too beautiful."

"Shit!" Katya whispered. "Damn, damn, damn. Someone's figured out that bit of technology. I thought that was only the province of Third Invaders."

"Sixth Invaders made heavy use of it on Earth," I said.

"Body swap machines are available on many planets," Wanda said. "It's not surprising others figured out how they work. We had better be careful or we could get implanted ourselves. I don't relish spending the rest of my life running dirty mining robots."

"Darn good point, Wanda. We best be careful."

"Are they using plates like they did at Salad's lab?" Wanda asked.

"That's one way of doing it," I said, "but the Sixth Invaders did it from a drone flying overhead while we slept. Beamed the esthetic waves and commands down on us."

"That tech is known, too?" Katya asked. "What's this universe coming to?"

"Did your people invent the esthetic wave implanting?" I asked, picking up on what she said.

Katya flushed. I had my answer, but she said, "Well, yeah, we did, eons ago. Still..."

"An overhead drone isn't as likely in this case," I said.

"Why?" asked Katya.

"Because it appears as though they are targeting specific people. The overhead drone approach implants all people within its energy beam cone. We need to identify the hundreds of others. Could be specific targeting and drone area approach."

When we landed, the ID Strike Force One rushed us. A dozen men in full battle armor and loaded with weapons dashed towards our ship. Intimidating, yes.

"I'm Captain Fritz Dengler. I'm taking over from you, Agent Hammerstein. You must be that Parkinson woman. Pathetic. And you, whoever you are. There isn't a Federation Inspector General, Robotics Central. But they ordered us to cooperate with you, whoever you are."

"Katya Verney, if you please."

"What have you learned?" he asked.

I said, "They've been implanted."

I didn't expect his reaction though I suspect Wanda did. He roared with laughter.

"Okay, men. Let's go visit this Dr. Moretti ourselves. Wanda, you and your accomplices, stay out of this. We got this."

With that, he forced Chief Inspector Risso to take them back to the Los Gato Mine. He wasn't too pleased. I heard him curse under his breath.

When they left, Wanda said, "Well, so much for that. Guess we're done here."

"Hardly," I said. "Let's go see Dr. Alessandra Scala again. I want to see if we can find radiator plates in Dr. Moretti's lab or home."

"Right. Let's," Katya said.

Though night had come, we found Dr. Scala still at her office.

"So, did you get anything from Dr. Moretti?" she asked.

I explained my working theory while she led us back to his office. I told her what we wanted to do next, gather information on all the victims. Meanwhile, since looking for metal plates exceeded what I could do, Wanda and Katya poured over his lab, focusing on the ceiling and floor tiles.

"How does this implanting thing work?" Dr. Scala asked. "I've not heard of it."

"Several ways," I explained the process, beginning with the pain, drug, words version before describing the esthetic wave version. "I think Dr. Moretti fell victim to the wave version. Now we have—"

"Got it!" Wanda yelled. She held up a metal plate with a device attached to it she'd pulled from the ceiling. One of the ceiling tiles lay on his office desk. "Now we need an electronics person to figure out how it works, how to disconnect it, and where it comes from."

"Let me look at it," Katya said, dashing over to Wanda who stood on Dr. Moretti's desk, holding the device. She jumped up and examined it. "We didn't make it!"

"I didn't think you did," I said. "Best leave it hanging there. Put up a sign warning everyone to stay away from this room. I don't think its range is much beyond his desk area."

"Fingol's Donkey!" Dr. Alessandra Scala said, her hands up to her mouth. "We've been invaded!"

"That's a big leap. Can we check out the CFO's office next?" I asked.

After she led us there, she dashed off to alert security and get signs installed. Katya and Wanda found the second device in two minutes.

"We know what to look for," Wanda teased.

"Oh, my! Another one!" Dr. Scala said. "If there are two, there could be hundreds. No room is safe! We must pull down every ceiling tile everywhere. Fingol's Donkey!"

She headed off yelling for security.

"Let's get something to eat. Besides, I'm falling asleep," I said.

We returned to Wanda's ship. I watched as she and Katya fixed supper. Wearing these fancy boots, I couldn't do anything to help, and Cleo would be in their way. I felt pangs of helplessness again.

Over dinner, Wanda asked, "How can we figure out who's behind the implanting? Or should we check on the other cases first?"

"Someone is benefitting," I said. "I wonder what happens to all the titanium ingots. Where have they gone? That might provide us with answers."

Katya said, "I won't spend much time inside their buildings and risk getting implanted and spending a thousand years in that filthy mine. Everyone knows implants can't be undone. That's the whole point." She looked at me. "Well, not easily. I've never heard of one being erased as you say."

The next morning, we awoke to someone banging on the side of Wanda's ship. She opened the bay door and faced Captain Dengler.

"I thought I told you I was in charge of this operation!" he said.

"Parkinson got results," Wanda defended us. "We've proved her theory. Someone has implanted Dr. Moretti and Dr. Von Stroebel."

He frowned. I sensed he hated to acknowledge our success. "Must admit it's a wild theory. Best your group joins us for a planning conference. Now."

Fritz turned, his boot digging into the tar of the landing pad. He strutted back to his black ID strike ship. We followed behind him though Wanda forced herself not to laugh. Katya didn't bother and roared.

He assembled his dozen men and us in a meeting room so small that Cleo and Bishop had to wait outside at the door.

"Okay, we're dealing with electronic implanting tech," Captain Fritz Dengler said. "Parkinson called this one. You've seen the two devices. I have to decide how to proceed."

Not trusting him, I spoke up. "Several angles should be traced. Some, I hope your people are better equipped to handle."

"Like what do you mean?" Fritz said, glaring at me.

"We might get a lead on who is behind this by tracking where the extra titanium is going. Someone should go over the CFO's computer system. I always say follow the money trail. It's probable that someone has been messing with the overall finances. I hope you've got someone knowledgeable in that area. Then, we must identify the hundreds of others who've been implanted and find where each was attacked. I fear they're using a drone. Or perhaps it's done at a gathering place, like a diner or pub. What do these hundred have in common? And find those devices. I think Dr. Alessandra Scala is about to go on the warpath tearing out ceilings everywhere."

Everyone chuckled.

Fritz said, "Tom, you check out the two devices. Disable them. See if you can track their origins. Sam, you're on the finances. Get Dr. Scala to give you the passwords to his finance system. George, coordinate finding the others who've been implanted. Find what's common and find those damned devices."

"What do you want us to do?" Wanda asked.

He looked at us. "I would say stay out of this, but we're supposed to include you. Why don't you try to track what happens to these titanium ingots? We'll meet here at lunch for a progress update."

Katya said, "Hey, be alert. Don't get implanted yourself."

She received many dirty looks. After we returned to Wanda's ship, we had breakfast before heading off to discover what happened to the titanium.

Dr. Alessandra Scala met with us. "It's a primary metal used in all robots. We have a central storage facility in Morrison. That's a town about fifty miles from here. It's home to every company's warehouses. You want Building T-1. Take a shuttle. I'll call ahead and get you clearance."

Chapter 25 Intrigues

Teslenko sent an electronic signal to Podrova. "It's that infernal Molly Parkinson human. Again. She's interfered too many times. Parkinson ruined my operation on Cass-C. We put a bullet through her brain, but she's back. That human just won't quit. Hasn't been but a day in Marina and she's uncovered two of our implant stations. She's trouble. We must see she stays dead this time."

Teslenko looked indistinguishable from any other human in Marina, but that was by his choice. He and Podrova changed their exteriors to fit in and not draw the slightest attention to themselves.

Podrova sent back, "The Cass-C operation yielded a hundred sixty top-of-the-line positronic brains. That kept us from having to get them from Feldspar-B. We don't want to draw much attention. The assembly project is moving along according to our calculations. But I agree. Parkinson has to go. Why doesn't she stay dead like that husband of hers—that Ted Billings human? Trouble is, she doesn't go anywhere without that Bishop bodyguard."

Teslenko sent, "He's the one who kept her alive. The bullet should have killed any human. We must separate her from her bodyguard. Otherwise, the odds are Bishop will keep her alive after we kill her again."

"What about the ID humans from Cass-C?" Podrova asked. "Should we kill them, or implant them to work for us as the others do?"

"Make them work for us. Wasteful of human resources to kill them. Another detail. Parkinson is the only recent human who can identify us as human-form robots from Chicago. How she can do that is unknown. Years ago, that

249

weird Aaron Strawn man detected me in Hoffdorf. Later, that Bonita woman and the detectives got too nosy."

Podrova asked, "Are your connections on Cass-C still valid?"

"Yes. I fooled them. Do you have a progress report from Glinski? How many and how soon will we have increased our numbers?" Teslenko asked.

"Ten will join us in a week. By twelve weeks, Glinski will have a hundred fifty ready to activate. We're right on schedule," Podrova said. "Braniski is still searching for an ideal base. Kimko reports the armaments will be ready in eighteen weeks. Getting spaceships is the remaining problem. Say, I have an idea how we can separate the bodyguard from Parkinson so we can kill her. What about this?"

***

Dr. Alessandra Scala finished her call. "There. You have total clearance to all the warehouses in Morrison, not just T-1."

We thanked her and headed towards her office door.

She called after us. "Implants. Who could do this? Poor Dr. Moretti. Of all the people on Feldspar-B, he's the only one who can't be replaced. He's designing the Deep Space Explorer Model V. No one else knows what he does. If only implants could be undone..."

She sighed and shook her head from side to side. I turned and faced her.

"Given enough time, I might be able to erase that implant," I said. "My sister developed a therapy that can do that, but it often takes days."

She looked up, her eyes drilling into mine. "Really? Fingol's Donkey! If you can do that for Dr. Moretti, I'll give you a kingdom. Dr. Von Stroebel, too. But focus first on Marco. He's a dear friend of mine. I'll have him brought here from the mines right now."

"All right. I'll try."

250

Katya asked, "Do we know how many titanium ingots are supposed to be in Building T-1?"

"Perhaps you can work that out from Dr. Von Stroebel's records. I'm sure they have a log at the building, but now I fear there might be a big difference between 'supposed to be' and 'is'. Maybe we can uncover the 'supposed to be.' Come with me. Oh, Lil, take Mrs. Parkinson and find her a room she can use for her therapy thing."

Cleo and I followed her secretary to a tiny room. It held a small desk with a single chair on either side. No windows, but the soft lighting worked for me.

"This is perfect. Thanks."

"Do you think you can get rid of Marco's insanity?" Lil asked.

"I will sure try. I think I can."

She exhaled deeply. "Oh, thank you."

I couldn't help touching her mind. "You like Dr. Moretti?"

"We're in love. We hoped to get married one day. His wife died, you see. We fell in love. Sort of just happened. I lost all hope when he left. The doc said he had gone crazy. Had a mental breakdown. But I knew he hadn't. I just knew it."

"I'll do my best. Now, lead me to the others. It will be a couple hours before Marco gets here."

We joined the others, crowded around Karl's large desk. His computer displayed its 3d holo screen four feet tall centered on his desk. An ID man operated the controls while the others asked questions and watched the fancy display.

Alessandra said, "Yes, that's right. We use about one hundred thousand tons of titanium per year. How do we figure how many ten-pound ingots are in the warehouse?"

(Note: she used local units of measurement. I converted them to units I'm familiar with, though rounding the numerical conversions.)

"Well, that's what's confusing," the ID man said. He manipulated the dozens of accounting sheets he had on the display. "Mines produce more while manufacturing consumes them. It looks like you should see about one hundred sixty thousand ingots in the warehouse, based on last year's average monthly storage."

"Thanks," Alessandra said.

"But that's not what's there today," the ID man cautioned. "By my calculations, there should be ten times that number. There's been a huge titanium production increase."

Katya whistled. "You mean we should see one and a half million ingots? How can we ever count that?"

The ID man laughed. "Glad that's your problem, junior agents. I'll follow orders and deal with this computer system."

Wanda let out a protesting moan. We all laughed.

He said, "The system is troublesome. It'll take time to conduct this financial audit. Best leave me in peace."

"Well, I don't relish trying to count those ingots. No hands. Besides, that'll take days. Dr. Moretti will arrive in two hours. I'll stay here and wait on him. Maybe I should send Bishop with you, just in case it turns out to be dangerous."

Bishop said, "With all the security men running around tearing out ceiling tiles, you should be safe here. There might be trouble at the warehouse. Why make ten times the normal monthly quantity only to store it? This is an entire year's needed amount."

Wanda started to protest but must have thought better. "You're welcome to come along, Bishop. But I doubt we'll need protecting. I'm sure they've got plenty of security around the building. What with that much pure titanium lying there."

***

Two strong men carried the struggling and yelling Dr. Marco Moretti into the tiny room, forcing him into the seat opposite

252

me. Dirt smudges covered his face, hands, and overalls. He continued to rant.

"Let me go! I have to mine more titanium. Mining titanium is the most important thing I can do."

"Step outside, but don't let him leave," I said.

The men nodded while looking at how dirty they'd become by handling him.

Cleo sat at my side. The table held two glasses of water. I focused my full intention and said, "Marco, close your eyes."

Yes, he continued rattling the implant words, but he obeyed.

"I want you to return to when you first saw that incredibly beautiful white light."

After a few more "can't talk's," he said, "Oh, yeah. Wonderful light. So pure."

"Good. Now go through what happened and tell me what you're seeing, feeling, hearing."

"It's beautiful. I'm at my desk, but I can't think. Only stare at it. But where is the light source? Can't tell. Oh, my eyes are shut. I hear this voice. I ignore it. I marvel over the angelic light. Wish Lil could see this."

"What is the voice saying?" I asked.

Slowly at first, the recorded words appeared. An hour later, he'd relayed all the words. I had him return to the incident's beginning and go over it again. I figured it should erase. We had all the words, but it didn't.

"My head hurts. I'm going to throw up. Pain. Shooting pain. The voice speaks again. Wait, this is another day!"

After a dozen more passes, the whole incident appeared. He'd been blasted with the implant procedure on ten different days. In the middle of each attempt, the device stimulated pain receptors in his body. Marco believed he felt an excruciating pain. Once the implant finished, he had two choices. He could disobey the implanted behavior and experience horrible, continuous pains throughout his body or he could go mine titanium.

When he spotted this, the incident blew. Laughing, he rattled off the implanted words. "How silly. Now we have ten years' worth of titanium on hand. Ha. Ha. Ha."

I couldn't get him to stop laughing. I ended the session, a smile on my face.

"You can let us out," I said to the guards on the other side of the door.

Marco continued to laugh. He noticed me. "You don't have any arms."

"Nope, not a trace of them. It's well past lunch. You can lead me to wherever there's food."

Still laughing, he said, "Follow me. Oh, isn't that one of our older robot helper models?"

"Cleo? Yes, works very well."

Lil heard the laughter and joined us. Marco picked her up and twirled her around, all while laughing. As we headed to the cafeteria, Dr. Alessandra Scarla must have heard his laugh; she joined us.

"Glad to have you back, Dr. Moretti!"

"What a nightmare. What the devil are we going to do with a ten year supply of titanium?" Again, he roared with laughter.

That's when I realized the ability to project my intention had skyrocketed. I'd just cut through the man's insanity, reached the being himself, and gotten him to confront what had happened, pain and all. Intention to reach. I amazed myself.

Wanda and Katya hadn't returned, but I didn't worry. I had no idea how they could count that many ingots. The ID man joined us for lunch.

He said, "I'm finding many minor anomalies in the accounting. Not sure what it means yet. I wish we had Dr. Von Stroebel here to query."

I said, "Dr. Scala, if you can get him brought to me after lunch, I'll see if I can erase his implant, too."

And that's how I spent my afternoon, sitting across another filthy man who yelled about mining more titanium. He spouted the same verbiage as Marco. Once more, I began by facing him, confronting the man, and putting in my intention. It cut through the insanity of "have to mine more titanium. Mining titanium is the most important thing I can do. We must have much more titanium."

We finished up close to suppertime. They had implanted him a dozen times while he sat at his desk. After the twelfth time, he couldn't disobey the commands any longer and had abandoned his life for the northern mines. Laughter accompanied the erasure of his implant, too.

At supper, Captain Fritz Dengler and his crew joined us. Over the meal, Fritz said, "Tom, what have you discovered about the devices?"

"Not commercially made. Built from parts available at any electronics outlet. There are three components. One generates an intense white noise in the kilo yattahertz range. That's the signal used in the body swap machines, Captain. Another component delivers a voice recording repetitively. The third one I'm not sure what it does yet. Generates a wave, though, very low frequency. Still working on that one. No clues who made them. The same person likely made both."

"It generates excruciating pain throughout the body," I said. "That's the other detail I learned while erasing their implants."

Fritz glared at me. "Everyone knows implants can't be erased."

I retorted with a snicker. "Tell that to Dr. Moretti and Dr. Von Stroebel."

If his eyes could have shot the pain waves, his would have. He changed the topic. "Sam, what about the finances?"

"Anomalies for sure. Now that Karl is himself, we're making progress. He had uncovered several strange entries and began a document. We should have something more concrete tomorrow. Can't rush finances." He chuckled, but no one got his joke. I presumed he meant it that way.

George said, "We've been all over the city tracking down the other victims. Done in a pub—whatever this world calls them. The other victims frequented two bars. We ripped the devices out of the ceilings there. Tom's verified they were made by the same person who made the ones Parkinson found. What's more important is that we've rounded up video. We're hoping we've captured the person installing the devices. Tomorrow, we'll go over hours of security recordings. So, Parkinson really can erase implants?"

"Ask Karl and Marco," I said. "Any word from Agent Wanda and Inspector General Katya?"

All shook their heads. Now, I worried. It wasn't like them not to check in. Worse, I couldn't call Bishop. Our comm devices depended on Earth satellites.

Captain Dengler said, "Not tomorrow. Get on it tonight. All of you. We have a crisis going here."

"What do you want me to do?" I asked.

"Hey, don't be ridiculous. You can't *do* anything."

I glared at him.

"She can come and help us with the video surveillance," Tom said.

"Yeah, go ahead," Fritz said, shaking his head.

I followed Tom and six others. They set up a video review center in one large room. A dozen 3d holo displays appeared hanging in space, eye-level. Cleo and I stood near the back. I could see all twelve. I pushed a chair there and watched, glancing from display to display. From my PI days, the only action more boring than watching hours of surveillance videos is an all-night stakeout. The ID men broke the monotony by sharing observations about this case.

Several hours passed before Sam joined us. "Hey, Karl and I just found huge anomalies. Someone has been stealing the titanium, gold, and silver, too. There's a trail of fake purchase orders marked paid in full, but there's no actual deposit of those funds. Clever banking scheme. Someone's got a thriving black market going on. You guys found anything?"

I noticed a security man standing at the door listening in.

"Hey, this might be something," Tom said. "I keep seeing this man going into Marco's office. You guys get him entering Karl's office? Can't make out what he's carrying."

"Date-time code?" another asked. He synched his display to that date. "Hey, yeah. There he is going into and then out of Karl's office. Look, he carried something in but came out empty handed."

Shit! Then, it hit me. I recognized the man. He was the guard standing at our doorway. But he was also the robot on Cass-C who had murdered people! I turned. Instant recognition on both our parts.

"That's him!" I said. "At the door. It's the robot who's been murdering people on Cass-C!"

Fritz tried to say it didn't look like the description of the robot that the ID had gathered from the incident on Cass-C, but the agents reacted fast. Men whipped out various guns. I marveled at their "quick draws." The robot ducked out of the line of sight. ID men charged after it.

When I poked my head out, I saw the ID men darting about the hallways. The robot gave them the slip. I suspected it activated an invisibility shield.

Minutes later, one reported to Fritz. "Lost it. Used an invisibility shield. Now what?"

Captain Dengler said, "Seal off this building. Fan out. Alert Dr. Scala. Find that damned robot. Shoot to disintegrate it!"

Me, I stayed in the video room, figuring that would be the last place the robot would go. Questions bounced around my mind. Why did the human-form robot come here? It did make sense. Feldspar-B was the robot center of the entire Federation. But what could that robot want? More positronic brains? I'd seen the cost sheets on the fancy robot deep space ships—the one that controlled the whole remote operation. The cost of its positronic brain dwarfed the value of all the extra titanium being mined. They couldn't steal those. But were they trying to make more human-form robots? Every life organism desired to procreate. Were robots immune to wanting a future?

Later, Captain Dengler gave the all-clear signal. The robot had escaped yet again. Thankfully, Fritz had to explain about the human-form robot to Dr. Alessandra Scala, not me. Without a word, Cleo and I headed back to Wanda's ship for the night. I hoped they'd be there, but the ship was a silent ghost.

Chapter 26 Captured

While inside Building T-1, Podrova sent an electronic signal to Teslenko, who was milling around inside the skyscraper that housed Dr. Scala's office. "That ID Agent Hammerstein and Inspector General Verney are here counting titanium ingots. Bishop is with them. Parkinson isn't here."

Teslenko sent back, "Last I saw, she was with Alessandra. Let them count for a while. Something's going on here. I'd like to interrogate them. Find out how Parkinson can detect us. That is the key to our survival. We must discover how she does it and devise a way around it. Prepare a knockout shot. Let's not deal with Bishop. He's not worth bothering with. Mere security guard. I'll contact you later. Meanwhile, prepare the ships. We might have to leave on short notice."

"I can get rid of Bishop. You're right. We need answers before they get on to our operation. Keep watch on Parkinson."

Podrova glanced at the three, two focused on counting stacks of titanium, gold, and silver ingots. Bishop stood near the door, a bored look on his face. Podrova appeared to be an unremarkable warehouse employee with no discernable traits or habits. He pretended to get a phone call, faking alarm.

"What? How many? Oh, dear. No. I don't have any security guards here. They've been summoned to Marina. Something about implanters, whatever that is. Oh, that's bad. Really bad. Wait. Maybe I can help."

He laid the comm device down and hurried over to Bishop. "Sir, are you a security guard?"

"Yes."

"Could we have your help? It seems a huge fight has broken out up at Los Gato Mines. Men are trying to steal titanium ingots, but our security guards are in Marina. Dr. Scala summoned them there to help search for bad people. Can you go up to Los Gato Mines and help secure the mine? I don't know who else we can send."

"You should go," Wanda said. She had overheard the discussion. "We're safe here. We'll be counting all day. Boring."

"As you wish," Bishop said.

"Oh, thank you. Thank you. I'll arrange a shuttle to take you there right now." Podrova rushed back to the comm device and pretended he'd found a security guard. "Yes, I'll send Mr. Bishop up at once. Over and out."

He yelled over to Bishop. "I'll be back. Have to arrange your shuttle. Keep watch."

Minutes later, he returned to fetch Bishop. "Here is your shuttle. I've programmed the nav system. Just press Activate. Its automated system will take you to the conflict. Do be careful, Mr. Bishop."

Bishop nodded and entered the ship. A minute later, the shuttle lifted off. Podrova smiled. He'd jammed the nav controls with a magnet. By the time Bishop discovered he wasn't at Los Gato Mines, he'd be out of fuel halfway around the planet.

The huge warehouse housed his private spaceship parked behind a shield where it had been for six months. Podrova slipped inside, retrieved his tranq gun, and cocked it. He ambled over to the two women who didn't even notice him. Podrova prided himself on that. Humans always seemed to not see him. A perfect disguise.

Puff. Puff. He fired twice, once at each woman, hitting them in their necks. By the time their fingers felt the dart, they slumped to the floor.

Podrova picked up a woman in each arm, carrying them into his back office close to his ship. There, he tied each woman to a chair and gagged them. Satisfied, he then waited for them to regain consciousness.

Katya recovered first. She mumbled and struggled against the ropes.

"I'll remove the gag as long as you keep quiet. Holler and it goes back."

Katya nodded, and he removed it.

"How is Parkinson able to detect the human-form robots as she did on Cass-C?"

"I don't know."

Wham! He slapped her across her face. Not hard enough to injure her frail human body, but enough to sting. He asked again with the same results. Annoyed, his next hit broke her nose. Blood splattered about, just as Wanda woke up and struggled.

"How is Parkinson able to detect the human-form robots as she did on Cass-C? Answer me," Podrova said. "Next time, I'll break your legs."

"I don't know. I don't, you beast. Wait til Bishop gets back."

He slipped the gag back into her mouth, removed Wanda's gag, and asked her the same question. After slapping her around with no results, Podrova put his hands on Katya's upper arms, close to her shoulders. "One last time, how is Parkinson able to detect the human-form robots as she did on Cass-C?"

Both women shook their heads, refusing to answer. Podrova squeezed his hands tight. A sickening sound of crushing bones echoed. The gag didn't dampen Katya's screech. He moved to Wanda and put his hands in similar places.

"They'll have to remove those arms. I've shattered six inches of her bones. If you don't want to join her, answer me. How is Parkinson able to detect the human-form robots as she did on Cass-C?"

Wanda blurted out, "Telepathy. She has telepathic abilities. The robots don't have a mind to detect. Now get her medical attention right now!"

"That's better. Interesting." He slid her gag back and then crushed her upper arms, too. Both women passed out from the pain. Podrova carried them into his spaceship, depositing them near huge stacks of platinum ingots. He then sent a message to Teslenko telling him what he'd done and found out.

"Telepathy? I should have known. Damn. Killing her will not work. We tried that years ago in Chicago. All those telepaths almost got us. Wait. The special Great Lady mutation. That's the answer. According to Ashton Soros, that mutation removes telepathic ability. Parkinson is the last telepath around. We mutate telepathy out of her, and ·we're safe from that meddling human. We'll take those two with us. Keep them unconscious for now. I have to capture Parkinson without drawing attention. Our operation isn't blown yet. We can recover from their meddling."

"Acknowledged. I will be ready for liftoff. Over and out."

***

After Cleo handled breakfast for me, I checked up on Wanda and Katya. Since no one had heard from them and no one answered the communications, Dr. Scala lent me a shuttle.

"It's automated. Cleo can run the menus. I haven't been able to reach the warehouse manager. When you get there, have him call me. The situation just keeps on getting worse. Stolen gold, silver, titanium. Where's it going to end? Thank you for saving my two key men. I owe you for that. Bye. Remember to have him call me."

I walked up the ramp while Cleo rolled up beside me. We almost ran over a gangly man wearing all black.

"Oh, hi, there. Agent Otto Stein," the man said. "Captain Dengler ordered me to come along. I'm to upbraid

262

Agent Hammerstein for not reporting in. And escort you. Someone has entered the destination already."

"Glad for the company. I'm sure there's a good reason they haven't been able to call. I can't reach Bishop either. No comm relay satellites on our frequencies."

"Agent Hammerstein has a comm link that should reach our ship. Strange she hasn't used it. You heard the Commander almost fired her because those two agents died?"

"Yes, but she wasn't at fault. The obnoxious men forced her to stay out of it while they charged in like bulls. Wanda said you put in a good word for her."

Otto smiled. "Yeah, I did. Some ID personnel emulate the Commander. I think they think that makes them better agents and can move up the power ladder. Wanda and I believe agents should focus on doing a good job and bring confidence of the ID to others."

He strapped me in and Cleo pushed the Activate button. The readout showed an hour flight time. I settled back to think how we could find that human-form robot before it killed anyone else. I could detect it. The best idea I had was for Alessandra to parade all her people past me while I touched each person's mind, verifying they weren't a robot. But the robot wasn't dumb. It would detect that plan as soon as it started. No, I needed something better. But what?

"Hello? Is anyone here?" I called out. We'd landed. Otto, Cleo, and I walked the short distance to Building T-1 and entered a spacious cavern. High overhead LED lights illuminated the space, reflecting off the huge stack of titanium ingots on the far left and the gold and silver stacks on the right. I spotted a dozen automated moving carts. That bit of automation I liked. I could drive one.

"Katya? Wanda?"

"Oh, hello," a voice said from behind me.

I turned and noticed a pleasant looking man, one I'd never seen before. Unfortunately, he held a strange looking gun and fired. A dart stung my neck. Otto drew his gun, but a dart struck him, too.

"What's going on?" I said.

A surge of weakness swept over my body, like a tidal wave coming ashore. I slumped to the ground and darkness came. I slipped out of my body's head. Stacks of titanium, gold, and silver lay surrounded me. Otto, Katya, and Wanda lay beside me. I touched the women's minds and recoiled. Massive pain. Something looked wrong about their arms, but my non-body vision has never been very good. Had their arms been broken? Katya had dried blood on her face. Her nose looked crooked. At least, that's how it seemed. I regretted not having practiced out-of-body vision before I realized such seldom happened.

I thought of nothing for a time. Then, I remembered Bishop. Where was he? I looked around as best I could, but didn't see him. Since he had no mind, I had no way to contact him.

Time passed, but I couldn't estimate how much. Motion. I spotted motion. There was that human-form robot again, the one from Cass-C. Beside him stood the other man, the one who shot me.

Wait! That's not a man either. It's another human-form robot from Chicago! What are they doing? Loading ingots? It looked like they might be talking, but I couldn't hear voices.

***

"Okay, we've enough for now. Let's get going," Teslenko sent.

"Coordinates are laid in. Engage cloaking now. Powering up," Podrova sent back. "Stealing this stealth ship has been one of our better moves."

Minutes later, Podrova said, "Cleared Feldspar-B. Enter coordinates. Destination?"

264

"Kristna, Kali-D. We're paying Salad's genetic lab a visit. We're about to end Parkinson's telepathic ability to detect us. When she awakes, we'll be safe again."

"Could just kill them."

"No, that isn't optimum. We don't want the entire Federation's ID forces scouring the galaxy for us. They'd do that if we kill them. Humans hold grudges. They seek revenge. We'll make sure Parkinson can't detect us any longer. Flight time: fifteen hours. Sure they'll stay knocked out that long?"

"I'll check. Even if they wake, they can't do anything. Parkinson doesn't have Cleo, and the other two women's upper arms are shattered. I have the ID man tied up. Relax, Teslenko."

Fifteen hours later, they hovered over Kristna, Kali-D where it was noon local time. Thus, they parked in a high orbit until local midnight. Then, they descended and landed in the lab's lot. Still cloaked, they lowered the bay door, and Teslenko activated his invisibility shield. Minutes later, he rendered the night guard unconscious and verified no one else was present, except for the clones and bodies in stasis pods, that is.

"I need one of them invisibility shields," Podrova sent.

Both robots imitated a smile before carrying the four inside. While Podrova stripped them of their clothing and laid them in stasis pods, Teslenko fiddled with the menu-driven controls, dialing up special Great Lady doses. He rejected using the voiceless option. No need to silence them. But he chose the neurons in hair choice, believing that might cause them sensory overloads. He brought four doses back to Podrova. They injected Wanda and Katya first, followed by Otto.

"Ah," Teslenko sent, "it's taken hold already. They've slipped into comas. You can tell from their eyes. Now to prevent Parkinson from ever bothering us again."

He injected her in a leg. Nothing happened. He fetched three more syringes. One by one, he injected them. Podrova checked her eyes a minute after each injection.

He sent, "Is she immune to this? No, wait. Maybe something's happening."

I couldn't hear them, but even with the fuzzy vision, I knew we were in Salad's genetics lab. Re-injecting me. Ha. It will not work. Bishop had to use a huge dose last time. How many are they using?

Teslenko returned with three more. On the sixth injection of the special Great Lady mutation agent, my vision turned off. My body had slumped into a deep mutation coma, bringing me in with it. My last thought: what happened to Bishop?

***

"I've been tricked," Bishop said. He'd watched the land fly by, but the ship never seemed to arrive. He checked the fuel gauge. Half empty. He ended the flight, landing in a meadow. He scrolled through the menu choices until he found one for Marina. A minute later, he lifted off, hoping he had enough fuel to make the return trip. Hours passed.

The shuttle made an emergency landing just outside the large city. Lacking any local comm device or currency, he jogged back to Dr. Scarla's skyscraper. He stopped for directions several times. After walking into the building at suppertime on the day that I was abducted, he went straight for Dr. Scarla's office. There, ID agents were briefing her on the discoveries they'd made today.

"Bishop. There you are. Parkinson wanted to see you," Captain Dengler said.

"I've been tricked," Bishop said. He outlined what had happened.

266

That triggered an immediate response. Captain Dengler fired off half his men to pay a visit to that building. Bishop went with them. When they entered with guns drawn, they found the place empty of people.

Sam said, "There aren't enough titanium ingots in here. But where are the women?"

The men fanned out. Several minutes later, one called out, "Fritz. Over here. Blood on the floor."

Captain Dengler ordered a sample taken and compared to known DNA. Bishop calculated the man thought it might belong to Agent Hammerstein. If so, her abduction or killing would be on him.

Bishop continued to observe. The ship he'd spotted earlier wasn't there. "Hey, Captain, there used to be a spaceship parked here. See the marks on the floor. Theory: the human-form robot kidnapped the women and fled, taking a lot of ingots with it."

Fritz cursed.

Sam whispered. "No sign of Otto either. This one's on him, not us." Several others nodded.

With only speculation remaining, Bishop headed back to Wanda's shuttle. After charging, he placed an LD call to my sister Eve.

"Oh, hello, Lara. Is Eve there? Over."

After a thirty-minute delay, he heard. "No, she's in Kristna, Kali-D at Salad's Genetics Lab. She's checking on Molly's clone body and those of Wanda and Katya. Over."

Since he didn't have a way to contact her there, he left a message for Fritz and took Wanda's spaceship on a fifteen-hour flight to Kristna.

***

"Morning, Eve. Come see what's happened last night. Someone shot our security guard. We have it on video. Our guards are looking into it now. But three women and one man are in mutation comas. Their bodies are lying in pods, but

267

they're not hooked up yet. We found a pile of used syringes beside them."

A minute later, Eve gasped. "That's Molly. That's ID Agent Wanda Hammerstein. That must be Katya's human clone body. Crap. They're wearing earbuds."

An engineer walked up. "Boss, we've examined the syringes. All contained a dose of the special Great Lady agent with hair neurons."

"Thanks. That tells us what's playing through the earbuds," the manager said. "I suppose we should leave them hooked up. Otherwise, they'll panic when they wake."

Eve said, "But isn't the panic better than the implanted behavior?"

"No, not at all. Look how well Adri adapted. That man's amazing. I would have predicted he would have gone insane when he woke. Instead, he's married and doing well, as far as we've heard. Since Molly's your sister, you can remove the earbuds if you think that's best."

Eve did so. She tried to convince them to remove the earbuds from Wanda and Katya but thought better of removing Otto's. The manager refused. Eve noted the date, estimating when they'd waken from the mutation comas. Eve suspected Molly's coma wouldn't last eight days.

Next, she joined the manager along with many local security men, reviewing the video of the previous night. No one recognized either man. At Eve's request, that afternoon, the manager fired off the details to the ID on Cass-C, requesting a full investigation.

As soon as she'd finished the call, Bishop landed Wanda's ship in the lot outside the lab. Security men swarmed around him, leading him before Eve and their manager.

"Molly's been abducted by the human-form robots. Otto, Wanda, and Katya are missing," he said to Eve.

"Relax. They are here. In mutation comas. Seems they injected them with the special Great Lady agent," Eve said. "What the heck happened?"

Bishop attempted to display great relief on his face for the manager and the security guards' benefit. "Long story." He spent an hour bringing them up to date. When he finished, they showed him the video.

"That's him. That's who watched the ingots at the warehouse. He arranged the shuttle for me and sabotaged it. I calculate he did that to sidetrack me so he could get the women."

Eve said, "You can thank him for that. Otherwise, you might wake up to find yourself a special Great Lady like they are."

"He didn't want to kill them? I can't compute their motives," Bishop said.

Eve shrugged her shoulders. "Neither can I. Another thing, he must have tortured both Wanda and Katya. He crushed both their upper arms."

"Pulverized, I'd say," the manager said, correcting Eve. "It's a blessing they're becoming special Great Ladies. With such severe injuries, I'm sure the doctors would have had to amputate their arms. This way, they'll be beautiful women."

Eve rolled her eyes. Bishop nodded before speaking again. "They were there to count the ingots. By my estimate, most of the excess ingots weren't in that building. If he tortured them, what did he want them to say? Did they say anything to him? And why bring them here and mutate them?"

"Can't answer those," Eve said. "Walk with me, Bishop."

They strolled out to the landing pad, out of earshot of everyone. Eve said, "I could use telepathy to contact them. Try to find out if you think it's critical. Otherwise, my guess is Molly will awaken in a day or two. Her body hasn't much to mutate. We could wait and question her then. The others will

269

be in comas for eight days. Trouble is, if I try to contact them, they're in the middle of a very severe and painful trauma."

"Best wait on them. I will stand guard over Molly all the time. But I calculate you will have a problem with the three. Otto and Wanda will awaken and believe their lives are over. Katya's body being mutated is only a clone. But they can't body swap her back into her Third Invader body, not with the implant being recorded."

Eve said, "I know, Bishop. I tried to get them to remove the earplugs. No go. They believe they are helping the women by easing the transition when they waken. Might be the case with Otto."

"Like Adri," Bishop said.

"Yes. If we can keep Katya calm enough in her mutated clone body, Molly or I can try to erase the trauma and the implanted behavior. If we're successful, then she can body swap back into her own body."

"But Otto and Wanda are in trouble," Bishop said.

"They have been growing a clone body for Wanda, but it won't be ready for six months. I suspect they could stick her in it sooner. But Otto..."

"But she'd be like Dirk and Molly when they headed off to fight the worms on Earth. Eat lots of that blue goo," Bishop said. "Maybe Adri can help Otto adjust."

Eve nodded. "And be very weak. The clone body isn't fully developed yet. Wanda will be stuck as a special Great Lady for several months at least. I've sent word to Lara Axehead. When she gets here, we will analyze their DNA and see if any of our cures can work on them. It's a shame Ashton's version isn't compatible with this Kali-D strain. Otherwise, we could re-mutate them with it and then apply the cures we developed for the sixteen hundred. It's never easy, is it?"

"No, it isn't. Still, you have eight days to find any cures for Wanda."

"Right. We'll just have to see. I've got them compiling their complete DNA sequences. Even though the mutation isn't complete, I hope to gather clues in advance. I called Celeste and asked her to come and help with therapy. I'm hoping with enough therapy, the three can somehow manage and adapt."

Bishop said, "Good. Still, I can't escape that fact it's my fault for getting tricked by that man. They might be well if I hadn't fallen for his subterfuge."

"Don't blame yourself. I'm sure Molly isn't. Analyze what happened and see if you missed any sign it was a trick. Do better next time. That's part of being human. We're never perfect. We make mistakes. The trick is to learn from them so they don't happen again. Keep watch over them. I'm off to check on the DNA results."

Chapter 27 Recoveries

I stirred. "Oh, my aching head. What happened? The robots!" I struggled into a seated position. "I'm perfect. Where am I? Bishop? Cleo?"

"You are on Kali-D in Salad's genetics lab," Bishop said. "Otto, Katya, and Wanda are here, but in heavy mutation comas. Eve and Lara are here working on cures. The robots have escaped along with a large quantity of titanium and some gold and silver ingots."

"Oh, I've lost my hair again. I've all these tactile sensations from my hair. Ah ha. Mutated again into a perfect special Great Lady. Crap! Did I get implanted? I have these words rolling around my throbbing head. Cleo, get me dressed."

As Cleo dressed me, I asked, "Are Otto, Wanda, Katya mutated, too?"

"Yes, the engineers confirmed the special Great Lady agent."

"Boy, do we have trouble. This will devastate Otto and Wanda, and we don't dare swap Katya back into her Third Invader body. Wish my head would stop thumping."

"Eve is trying to find a solution. You've been unconscious one and a half days. We expect them to wake in six days. I'm to get you fed and take you to Eve."

"Keep an arm around me, Cleo. I seem to be wobbly. Lead on, Bishop."

We entered a side office reserved for Eve and Lara.

"Wow, Celeste! Good to see you. Who's this?" I asked.

Celeste with her flaming red hair blushed. "My husband, Will Reynolds. From St. Louis. Years ago, he was one of the mutation victims. We ran my therapy on him. Turned him into a believer. He's been delivering therapy sessions and running my St. Louis practice. We planned to invite you to the wedding, but you were off on a secret mission to Kali-D. Anyway, let's get you fed and into a therapy session. Before the ID men arrive to grill you."

Celeste ran a bang-bang session, wasting no time. Considering the thousands of hours of her therapy I had had, I blew through the pain of this recent mutation. Mostly, I had head pains, that infernal throbbing wouldn't quit. She asked for something that happened earlier. After a minute, I spotted it. A painful birth that squashed my head. After re-experiencing it several times, the throbbing head vanished. I felt rejuvenated and thrilled to be alive. Total session time: one hour. Nice.

Next, we met to plan what to do when the three woke.

I said, "We'll need a place to stay, where food is available, and where we can deliver therapy sessions. We can check if Adri and Rina have bought a home. I'm sure they'd welcome us. They could help us hire personal assistants for the three unless you think we can handle their physical needs."

"But Adri and Rina are implanted," Eve said. "We'll be erasing the same implant they received. Won't that upset them? Should we try to erase their implants, too?"

"I want to do that," I said. "That's always been my intention. Didn't have the time before."

Will said, "Based on my experience, Rina and Adri will get upset if they see us erasing the implant they believe helps them survive. Best to rent a suite in the hotel. Handle Rina and Adri after we handle these three."

"And do we work with Salad?" I asked. "What about Adri's mother Jona and Anala, Salad's wife? Do we work with them, too?"

"Salad and Anala don't have voices, right?" Celeste asked. I nodded. "They will be challenging. I suppose I should meet them and see how well those lip reader voices do."

"I should work on Katya since she's a Third Invader," I said. "I hope your therapy works on that race."

Celeste and Will left to find a workable hotel suite in Kristna. Meanwhile, Captain Fritz Dengler and his ID crew arrived and questioned me.

He said, "I guarantee agents Hammerstein and Stein will get commendation medals and a pension. With luck, it will be enough credits for them to live on since they can't work or be in the Intelligence Division."

I glared at him. Such callousness. "What about the robots?"

"Ah, we have a huge problem. With a hundred sixty or more positronic brains and all that titanium, gold, and silver, my guess is they want to build more of themselves. We've requested all the documents your Galactic Robotics Chicago has on the construction of human-form robots. They'll need laboratories in which to fabricate the robots. Our Commander is recommending a Federation-wide alert about these robots and the threat they pose. I'm sure we'll get them soon enough."

"Have you worked out what their goals might be? They could have killed the four of us. Instead, they mutated us," I said.

"Agents Stein and Hammerstein are out of action forever. Might have been kinder had they killed them, especially Otto. He was a good man. I'm sure we'll track those rogue robots down soon."

With that, he left. I had no confidence they'd find the robots on their own. But I felt a little responsibility for the robots. Earth researchers in Chicago created them. My people.

With days to wait, that evening, I visited Adri and Rina. Bits of their implanted words continued to infiltrate their conversation. With his father's help, they'd bought their first home, a small mansion a few blocks away. The two radiated happiness.

"Oh, you must see our new home," Rina said. She led me on a tour. It included a small formal garden and a large swimming pool. As we stood beside it, Rina sighed and said, "I haven't been brave enough to try swimming yet. We're perfect and can do anything. It's just—well, you know—scary. Anala has promised to show us how."

"What's important," Adri said, "is the university hasn't fired me. In fact, they've hired Rina. They should since we're models of perfection. We're both teaching in the History Department. But I lost my archeology position. Can't dig, they said. We can do anything. We're perfect, but they had a point. I can't show my students proper digging techniques. I can still do academic research in my field. That's something."

"Are you learning your dad's business?"

"He's coming around. Slowly. Special Great Ladies can do anything, but he must see how we can. Can't blame him. But it's hard."

I spotted his eyes watering. Rina's too.

She swallowed. "We can do anything, but it's hard. I keep trying to do things with my hands, and they're not there. Never will be. But that makes us perfect though."

Both their personal assistants had to dab the moisture from their faces. I changed the topic and explained what brought me back to Kristna.

"Oh, it's wonderful Wanda's a perfect special Great Lady," Rina said. Her enthusiasm returned. "We should encourage her."

Adri said, "Otto will need plenty of support, even though he'll be perfect, too. He'll see nothing's better than being a special Great Lady. He'll be a role model for others."

"We should get them proper clothes," I said.

"We can go shopping on Saturday. I have to teach tomorrow. It's hard, but there's nothing I cannot do. I depend on my personal assistant. She's the greatest."

Her silent assistant smiled. I suspect she appreciated the kind word.

Eve talked to Ashton Soros and arranged for three more robot assistants. They arrived late Sunday. The hotel suite Celeste rented had four bedrooms and a spacious living area with an attached small dining area, perfect for our use. When the three woke from their comas, we had everything ready for them. The new robots stood beside each stasis pod, along with that person's new clothing. We waited.

Wanda woke first, followed by Katya and Otto. Screams and terror filled their first minutes upon awakening. We allowed them to vent. As expected, within a few minutes, their implants took hold. Each recited the words that played non-stop into their heads for two hundred hours.

Perfection versus flawed. Happy versus terror. Wonderful versus awful. The dichotomies formed an energy manufacturing engine. Tears accompanied fake smiles. Fear and terror accompanied by self-pride and self-worth. We had three insane people to help. Their new robot assistants dressed them. Then, we led them to our shuttle. Minutes later, we had them sitting in three bedrooms in the hotel suite. All the while, they continued to recite the implant words. We said little, following Celeste's guidance, only what was necessary to get them to the hotel.

Next, room service brought up meals. Even though we knew their knotted stomachs might not keep food down, we had the helper robots feed them. Should we give them a day to adjust and get a good night's sleep or just dive in with therapy session? Celeste decided for us.

I pushed a chair in front of Katya, who sat on the bed. "Close your eyes." Thus began her first session. I had her

276

return to the first moment when she sensed something was wrong. As she moved through the intervening hours, she told me what she was seeing and feeling. Since she was an alien body swapped into a human, I didn't know if the therapy would work on her. Katya's mind might obey different laws than human minds.

Her constant recitation of parts of the implanted words compounded the uncertainty. Still, I heard bits that made sense, if you ignored the implant banter. We continued all afternoon before stopping for dinner, having gone through the incident several times. She hadn't contacted the intense pain of either the mutation process or the crushing of her arms. But she relaxed. After being fed, she fell asleep.

When I checked with Celeste and Will, they reported similar progress with Wanda and Otto.

Will said, "I hate implants, but in Otto's case, the implant is forcing him to want to live. How unlike those waking up from the terrorist attacks on Earth. When I woke up and found myself much like Otto, I kept begging for someone to kill me. Otto hasn't even suggested dying. This is the first time I can say anything positive about implanted behavior."

The trouble we had trying to help someone who's just been implanted is time. After six days of sessions and countless passes through the lengthy painful incident, all three contacted the buried mutation pain. Excruciating pains shot through their arms as they withered on their comatose bodies. Once Otto re-experienced that pain, the entire implant and mutation incident erased, leaving him cheerful but helpless.

Wanda and Katya needed another day to face the pain caused by the robot's crushing their upper arms. Once Wanda faced that, she erased the whole thing, becoming cheerful, too.

Over dinner, Wanda said, "I thought I'd betrayed you when broke down and answered the robot interrogation question. I blurted out you detected the robots via telepathy, and he crushed my arms anyway." She laughed, free of that burden.

I said, "Wanda, by telling the robot that, you saved our lives. I suspect that's why the robots injected us with the special Great Lady agent. They tried to get rid of my telepathic ability. It's true. The Sixth Invaders' armless Galactic Doll agent turns on telepathy as part of the mutation. But I got mine after having thousands of hours of Celeste's therapy sessions, not from a genetic mutation."

I think she appreciated hearing I thought she'd saved us all. But at the end of that day, Katya's pain hadn't erased; I had to ask for another incident that was similar and had happened earlier.

The following morning, I had her make one final pass over the past nine days before I asked her for something earlier. After several minutes, she found it.

"I see a silver thing. Oh, it's the inside of a saucer. We're flying. I'm in command. No, I'm being thrown out of an airlock. The pain!"

We went over it five more times before she opened her eyes, and a huge smile appeared. "I was betrayed! My second in command mutinied. That's what I felt when the robot crushed my arms. Betrayed. Wait. That was a different lifetime. Oh! I have lived before. Just like you said. Wait. Your therapy thing. It worked on me, a Third Invader." She laughed and then couldn't stop laughing.

"You've saved my life, Molly Parkinson. I was insane. Even if you'd body swapped me back, I would have been insane. Forever. We don't have any way to erase implants. That was an implant for sure. Wow. Do I ever owe you one, human Parkinson. I'll never forget this." She laughed for hours.

The next day, we body swapped her back into her Third Invader body. She hugged me and left for Cass-C and her next assignment.

When I returned to the hotel, Will and Celeste had Otto and Wanda in therapy sessions. Bishop said, "They're erasing other unwanted feelings and emotions. She said you'd understand."

At supper, an ID agent arrived and tried to hand the two their medals. Red-faced, he handed them to Will.

"They've posted your monthly retirement pensions into your bank accounts on Hoffdorf. Here are your current benefits statements." Again, he handed them to Will. Hastily, he left.

"We made him most uncomfortable," Otto said, "freaky me."

We all laughed.

He then said, "This therapy thing of yours is fantastic. I really have lived before. Several times that I've seen. It's remarkable how these weird emotions and feelings have a painful trauma behind them if only you can find it."

"And erase it," Wanda added. "I kept feeling helpless. Celeste got me over that one today. It sure wasn't coming from this life, either. This therapy thing is incredible—most valuable thing ever."

Celeste said, "Thanks, guys. We won't stop until we've eliminated all these unwanted feelings, emotions, sensations, and aches and pains. We have lots of time."

After dinner, Rina and Adri dropped by to visit us. For me, it became a study in contrasts. Wanda and Otto thought clearly, even though they still felt helpless.

Adri said, "Pleased to meet you, Otto. We have a lot in common. We're perfections of beauty. I'm honored and proud to be a special Great Lady. I see you're happy, too. I'm being a role model for others at the university. Rina is too. We're both faculty, teaching History, though it is hard. We know there's nothing we can't do. Heck, I'm even learning my dad's business. But we must depend on our personal assistants. We've got Soros University robot helpers, but we prefer our human assistants. Right, Rina?"

"Yes, absolutely. You should hire human helpers. We can help you with that if you wish. Do you like the gowns we picked out for you? They're imported from Molly's world. Her sister makes them. They're just as perfect as we are. Adri and I are content. He's right. We're being role models, showing everyone how wonderful it is to be a special Great Lady. You both are just perfect, too."

Wanda laughed. "Yes, but we're helpless without these people around us and the robot helpers. I'd not say we're perfect or content with what's become of our bodies, especially Otto. He spooked the ID agent who just came to give us our medals and pension statements. We're no longer ID agents. Kicked out."

"Well, they're crazy," Adri said. "We are perfect. There's nothing we can't do. Okay, I admit we depend upon our personal assistants."

Rina said, "I've not yet gotten brave enough to try swimming. I used to be a good swimmer. Soros U has a great pool. While I know there's nothing we can't do, I'm still spooked by the pool. I'll get over it. We're perfect, after all. Don't you both feel just perfect?"

"Anyway," Adri said, "you are invited over to our new home Saturday night for a barbecue. Drop by around six. We'll party 'til we drop, as we used to say in college. Otto, nothing's better than being special Great Ladies. You'll see."

Rina said, "Have to head home. We have to prepare tomorrow's lecture. We take hours to do that. There's nothing we can't do. Until Saturday."

After saying they'd provide everything, they left.

Wanda said, "God, they're still saying those damned words, aren't they? The implant words."

"It's nuts to think we're any of that," Otto said. "I look like a freak, and we're helpless. Even the ID tossed us out. Who are they fooling?"

"Themselves," Celeste said. "Molly, they should have the implants erased. But Eve wants to know about clone bodies for them. Wanda, they have a clone body growing for you, but as I understand it, the body won't be fully developed for six months. Salad's genetic engineers can grow a clone for Otto."

I said, "Eve checked. Otto's DNA isn't on file. Wanda's clone body isn't a perfect copy, though it's close. She said they can grow a male clone for Otto, and he could choose the male model from the DNA database."

"But it wouldn't be my real body, would it?" Otto asked.

"No."

Wanda said, "I'm worried about taking over my clone body. I mean, it isn't me, is it? This is the real me. That one is a fake me, a copy. I know how helpless I am, but I'm not sure I want to always be in a fake me body. It makes my skin crawl. But I can tolerate a clone body for a short while, but forever? No, too creepy."

I said, "Well, Eve and Lara are famous for developing cures. Give them enough time and they'll likely come up with a cure. Look how they cured Dirk. He looked much like Otto. Now he looks like he did before any mutations. Otto has the Kali-D version, but I'd bet Eve and Lara will come up with a cure in time."

Wanda sighed. "But how long will that take? Months, years?"

"I'll admit they took four years to undo all the mutations done to males. But they did it. Dirk and eight hundred men are back to being themselves. It takes time. The question for you two is are you willing to deal with your handicaps and wait for a cure?"

It's a credit to Celeste and Will's therapy sessions. Both Otto and Wanda agreed to deal with life as it is, counting on Eve and Lara's eventual cures.

"In that case," Celeste said, "Will and I will keep working with you two until we can't find anything else to erase."

"Thank you," Wanda said. "It's saved our lives and is the most valuable thing I've ever experienced."

"Right," Otto said. "Most valuable thing ever. Is it hard to learn how to do your therapy? Can I learn or do I need hands?"

"Heck, no hands are needed. I'd love to teach you how to do it. Say, why don't you handle Rina and Adri as your first patients? We can do your therapy during the day and have you do theirs in the evenings. Molly, when we visit them Saturday night, see if you can set it up with Rina and Adri."

The next day, Dr. Alessandra Scala requested I return to Marina, Feldspar-B, for a major conference. Several Federation representatives insisted I come. Bishop made the travel arrangements. I took Cleo and Bishop with me. I figured Celeste and Will could work things out with Rina and Adri.

Chapter 28 A Short Flight

I let Bishop handle our ID cards and tickets as we went through Kali-D spaceport customs and security. When we arrived at our gate, we spotted our deep space passenger liner parked outside.

"Awfully small," I said.

"Few are going to Feldspar-B today," Bishop said. "This was the first available flight. They use larger ships on the weekends. At least I didn't need to buy Cleo a ticket on this flight. They said I would if we took the larger ship. The why of that eludes me."

We chuckled as we walked up the ramp into the passenger liner. Each side of the main aisle held one seat—cramped at that. A man and girl had already boarded.

As we moved up to sit near them, the girl said, "Oh, look, Pappa. She's just like me." She turned and said, "You don't have any arms either. Are you a Great Lady? I'm going to be a Great Lady. When I grow up that is. I'm Kasi. I'm five. That's my Pappa."

"Why, hello, Kasi. I'm Molly. Molly Parkinson."

She wore a pink, sleeveless dress and matching tall heels. Little children shouldn't have to wear such high heels. Just as I was about to glare at her father, he turned. Wow. What a handsome man.

"I hope she's not bothering you. Balin Khan. My daughter Kasi. Her mother was a special Great Lady, but she died last year. Kasi loves to talk."

"Oh, I'm sorry."

"Thanks. It's been hard on both of us. I was devoted to her, such an incredible woman. I don't know what she ever saw in me."

"Oh, Pappa, don't be silly," Kasi said with a frown on her face. "Mamma loved you. She told me so. Only now I miss her."

"Looks like we're it. The only ones going to Feldspar-B today," he said, changing the topic. "I'm a spaceship designer. For robots, that is. Unmanned deep space ships. For Robots 4 All on Feldspar-B. I'm taking my latest design. Security and all."

He raised his other hand and had a briefcase handcuffed to his arm.

"After this sale, I will retire and devote my life to raising Kasi. She is all I have left."

"My youngest daughter is attending Soros University on Cass-C. We adopted older twins. One is a famous linguist and is on Domes, and Bernardo has his own fancy restaurant in Chicago, Earth. Sol Empire."

"And Mr. Parkinson? What does he do?" Balin asked, glancing at Bishop.

I chuckled. "Bishop is my bodyguard. I've lost two husbands. Murdered by rogue robots."

"Pappa, she's the one we saw on the news. Isn't she? The telepath who saved everyone." She looked at me and said, "Can you read my mind?"

I smiled. "I could but I wouldn't. That would be prying. You wouldn't want a stranger to know every secret you have, would you?"

"Well, no..."

"It's a real pleasure to meet you, Mrs. Parkinson. I didn't make the connection. You've been all over the news. You unraveled the robot plot on Feldspar-B and the evil men at Salad's Genetics Laboratory. You're amazing. See, Kasi. She is a really special Great Lady."

"I want to be like you. When I grow up," Kasi said. "Pappa will help me learn everything. The school won't let me

284

in. No arms. Pappa said arms don't learn. It's in our heads and minds. I don't see why they wouldn't let me in. I play with other boys and girls. Sort of. It's hard to keep up. My shoes. If I'm not careful, I fall down. Does that happen to you?"

"Yes, keeping our balance is hard. Don't you have a personal assistant?" While I asked her, my focus was on Balin. Why didn't he provide her with one?

"She's too young. After her mother's death, I don't trust leaving Kasi with one. I look after her. Children are our future. That's why I'm retiring after I deliver these plans. I can devote all my time to her. She loves hearing stories."

This young man appealed to me. My heart raced. I took a deep breath.

"That's a remarkable attitude to take, Balin. Impressive. My second husband, Sam, was wonderful with our two children."

"Do you know any stories?" Kasi asked. "Is that your robot helper? Pappa, can I have one? Then, you wouldn't have to retire."

"Kasi, you shouldn't bother strangers."

"Oh, that's all right. Its name is Cleo. I know many stories, but most are for grownups. But Nikita always liked this one. When she was about your age." I launched into the fairy tale with a captivated audience of one. After we dropped into hyperspace, the pilot announced we'd arrive in ten hours and that they would serve a meal in five hours.

Cleo plugged himself in to keep fully charged. Bishop pretended to doze.

As I told the story, an odor I'd smelled before registered. I looked up. A slight yellow haze filled the cabin. I watched Balin slump in his seat, followed by Kasi. The last thing I recall is Bishop snatching my phone from my dress pocket. Blackness surrounded me. My last thought was "not again."

I struggled to shove myself out of my body, to turn on my "being" vision but had no luck. Knocked out again.

"Molly! Molly, wake up."

Bishop's voice. I recognized it. Eyelids weighed a ton. Vision turned on. I coughed.

"What happened? Knocked out?" I blinked several times trying to water my dry eyes.

"I recorded it on your phone. Watch while I wake Kasi and Balin."

Cleo rolled up, took the phone, and pressed Play. I watched our pilot enter the cabin unaffected by the knockout gas. He pulled out a syringe from a pocket and injected it into Balin's arm. Then he ripped the handcuff off his hand, crushing Balin's wrist and hand. He walked past me while carrying the briefcase and injected Bishop with a second syringe. After that, he left the camera's field of view. Bishop played knocked out. Later, I heard air hissing. Bishop turned the camera. I saw the red message "Airlock In Use" flashing. Then, it cleared, and the video ended.

"What happened?" Kasi asked. "Pappa's hand is bleeding."

Bishop wrapped a towel around it, stopping the bleeding. He checked Balin's eyes, before bringing me the syringe. I looked at both syringes.

"Are those—"

Bishop said, "Yes. That's Salad's Genetics Laboratory's symbol. I believe it's the special Great Lady agent—the one used on Wanda and Otto. But I can't be certain. He's in a mutation coma. Someone stole his spaceship designs and left the ship."

"Why doesn't Pappa wake up?" Kasi asked.

"You must be very brave for your Pappa. I should check on our pilot. Cleo, you help Kasi."

286

"Hi, Cleo. Something's wrong with Pappa." She and Cleo chatted while I made my way up front.

I pushed the door to the crew area open and entered. "Hello?" Deserted. We had no pilot and no crew. Worse, the ship had dropped out of hyperspace but was stationary. Where were we? My stomach knotted. I headed back to the cabin.

"Bishop, we're motionless with no pilot or crew. Just us."

"That's what I calculated. Now what? Should we call for help?"

"Depends on where we are. First, let me gain control of the ship. Find our location."

"Are we lost?" Kasi asked.

"No, we're right here. But we don't know where here is compared to where we want to go. I'm a trained pilot and navigator."

"But you don't have arms. How can you fly us?"

"Easy. You can learn to be a pilot. First thing is to figure out our location by recognizing the stars."

When I opened the small observation dome, the star field looked different from any I'd seen in my training. I had Bishop look. His attempt at a baffled appearance told all.

"Well, that will take observations," I said. "Best check our fuel levels. Can you check on our supply of food and water?"

A half hour passed before I satisfied myself. I had manual control of the ship though I kept us at rest. Three-quarters of our fuel supply remained—a very good sign.

"Molly, there's ten gallons of water onboard and enough food supplies for ten passengers for one day. If we ration it, we should be able to survive for many days. Suggest we discuss options."

I glanced at Kasi. While I sensed her worry, she and Cleo bonded, chatting about spaceships. Bishop and I returned to the front.

"Until we have our location, I don't dare use fuel. That had to be a robot pilot. The gas didn't knock him out, and he wore no mask," I said. "Once we have our position, then I can estimate our chances of returning to known spaces."

"I wish Trevor Jones was here," Bishop said. "He is a master at navigation by star fields. I focused on ground actions."

"I know. You've saved me too many times. Okay, my province. I've had five courses in navigation. It's time I put it to use. Might take a while."

Where had that robot taken us? Likely light years off course if not parsecs. I studied the star field but found no clues. I used the thrusters to rotate the ship and studied this field. Still, nothing looked familiar.

"Bishop, see if you can find the nav star charts. No ship is allowed to travel without a complete set."

A half-day later, he found the charts. Kasi's worry over her father grew, especially when I had Bishop undress him and lay him in the rear seat in a prone position and covered with a blanket. I had to get her attention off her father.

"Come with me, Kasi. You can help me figure out where we are from the star charts Bishop found."

I squeezed her into the cramped nav seat with me by sitting her on my knees. I used a foot to flip star charts, which now lay over the smashed coordinates display.

"Is that busted?" she asked.

"Yes, the evil robot smashed it. We don't know where we are."

"Do we need it to get home?"

I sighed. No sense in lying. "I'm not sure. It depends on where we are. I can fly the ship. That's the pilot's seat over there. But if we need to use hyperspace, we have no way to enter the coordinates or read them."

"Are we going to die?"

"Not if I have anything to say about it."

"Is Pappa going to die? Like Mamma? He isn't waking up. If Pappa joins Mamma, will you be my new Mamma? Please? You are nice."

"No, he won't die, but his body will change. He'll still be a man, but his body will look like mine and what yours will be when you get older. That's why he will need lots of help from you. And if something bad happens to Balin, I'll be your Mamma. Okay?"

She smiled. "Okay. But he won't have arms?"

"No, he won't."

"How can I help him? I don't have arms. He's always helped me."

"By using our feet as hands."

She brightened up. "Oh, yeah. That's what Pappa has me practicing. Be independent, Pumpkin. That's what he calls me. Pumpkin."

"He's right. You and I will practice together. Now here's what we must do."

I explained how we needed to find a star field on the charts that matched what we could see from the observation dome. If the ship had a spectroscope, that would have helped because we could pick out stellar types.

As days passed, Kasi watched her dad's arms wither into husks while his bosom swelled ever larger and his hair grew longer. Bishop rationed our food, but each time as we passed by Balin on our way to the galley area, Kasi checked on him.

On the sixth day, Kasi found our location on a star chart. What an inventive mind she had.

"Molly, look at this." She pointed with her toe. "It's like we're looking at it sideways."

My eyes went from the star chart to the sky and back several times. "Incredible! Kasi, you're right! Very well done! Now we know where we are! Yahoo. Let's go tell Bishop."

"We must make a hyperspace jump to return to the vicinity of our worlds," he said. "We're in the Perseus arm, not the Sagittarius arm of Feldspar-B or our own Orion Arm. But we can't enter the coordinates because it smashed the display."

"Exactly. I can fly us there at sub-light speeds. But..."

For Kasi's sake, I didn't finish the thought. At sub-light speeds, we'd need many years to return to our arm.

"What about pointing the LD antenna towards known worlds and sending out a distress call?" he suggested.

"Last resort," I said. "The ship burns fuel maintaining life support and gravity. In theory, we can hold out until a rescue ship came. It's food and water that are our enemies."

"Are we going to die?" Kasi asked.

"Not if I can help it. On Earth, we say: where there's a will, there's a way. Stop and think how. That used to be my husband's and my motto. Think about how you can get something done using your feet and toes. There's always a way, but sometimes you have to invent it."

She giggled. "I like that. Stop and think how. Oh! Pappa's waking up."

Together, we headed to the rear. My stomach tightened anticipating Balin's terrified and wild reaction as he awoke to his new reality.

I reminded Kasi. "Remember. Be brave for Pappa."

As we approached him, memories haunted me. I'd seen thousands of men and women waking from this hideous mutation. Terror and deafening screams couldn't be forgotten. Ever. If Balin reacted similarly, Kasi might be emotionally scarred for life. In a flash, I realized I faced a test of sorts. Just how good was my intention? I recalled Empress Kalindi Amandani of Indrani-C and her incredible power of intention. She told me I had that ability too and should be the Empress of the Sol Empire. I'd forgotten all about that. Was this my test?

I focused and projected an aura of calm over Balin as he awoke from the mutation coma. While Kasi was upfront with me, Bishop had dressed him in my clothes that almost fit his new shape. Kasi wouldn't see him naked and neither would he, at least at first. Still, shock spread as his mind grasped what happened to him. I sensed a tidal wave of fear rising and re-enforced my flow of calm over him.

"What's happened to me?" His voice trembled, but he didn't shriek.

"The evil robot attacked us, Pappa," Kasi said. "Stole your briefcase."

I said, "He injected you with the special Great Lady mutation agent. But Kasi decided we should call you a special Great Man since you're not a lady."

Kasi giggled, pleased with her suggestion.

Telepathically, I sent him, 'Be brave for Kasi's sake. How you react will have a monumental effect on her well-being.'

"I feel so—vulnerable." Still touching his mind, I knew he meant to say helpless, but changed it. His mind held onto an image of Kasi. She had become his rock. "Yes, Kasi. Special Great Man. I'll need lots of help, too."

"I'll help you, Pappa. Molly's been showing me how to use my feet. I'll show you."

"I feel strange," Balin said. His voice still trembled. "My mouth—dry."

Bishop held a bottle of water with a straw up to his lips.

I said, "Don't drink too much until your stomach settles down. You're doing amazingly well. Right, Kasi?"

"Yes, Pappa. Now we're the same. I like that. Molly promised to be my Mamma if you joined Mamma. I worried because you didn't wake up. Been days. Hasn't it, Molly?"

"Yes, eight days have passed. Let's get you up front. Bishop, a hand."

Bishop helped steady him. The area around Balin stunk from his body's excrements during the coma period. We had no way to clean it up.

Kasi said, "Small steps, Pappa. Remember. That's what you told me."

A fleeting smile appeared on Balin's taut face, as I continued to project an aura of calm over him. While clutching a mental image of Kasi, his thoughts continued to repeat. Be brave. Be brave.

Once sitting down in his original seat, his muscles relaxed a little. Kasi sat across the aisle, smiling at him while I stood in the aisle.

"See, you made it, Pappa. It'll be okay. Molly says so. I found where we're at. From the star charts. Tell him, Molly."

He looked up at me. "No easy way to break this bad news to you, Balin. One of those human-form robots was our pilot. It released knockout gas, ripped your briefcase off your hand, and injected you with the mutation agent. It injected Bishop but goofed the injection. Bishop wasn't affected. The robot smashed the nav display unit before dropping out of hyperspace and powering down. We're on life support and gravity at the moment. It left via the rear emergency airlock.

"I'm a licensed navigator and pilot, but I didn't recognize the star field. We searched for days trying to find our location. Kasi's brilliant idea did it. She saw we were looking at a start chart from its side. Now we know where we are. Trouble is, we're in a catch-22 situation."

"Catch-22?" Balin asked.

"We're in trouble no matter what we do. We're almost out of food. Still have water though. Without the nav display, I can't enter hyperspace coordinates. Without hyperspace, we can't get back to our part of the galaxy. We're in an outer arm. The robot tried to make sure we'd never return."

292

"Can I see the damage?" Balin asked. I picked up his thoughts. 'Be brave. You must help.'

I led him up to the front, sitting in the pilot's seat while he sat in the navigator's chair. Kasi followed and stood in the aisle between us.

"It's smashed, Pappa."

"I can see that, Pumpkin. Pappa's got to fix it."

"But how, Pappa? The evil robot took your arms. But Molly says we have to 'stop and think how.' She's letting me use her motto now. You can too, can't he, Molly?"

"Yes, that's what my first husband, Ted, taught me. Stop and think how. There's always a way to do something. Be inventive. But Balin, I don't know how we can fix it. The robot destroyed the display."

Balin chuckled, surprising me. Had he cracked up? No.

"Molly, that's the smartest thing anyone has ever told me. Kasi, that's perfect for us. Stop and think how. Incredible. Molly's as smart as she is beautiful. I have to think."

Bishop helped him back to his seat.

Kasi and I followed. She said, "Pappa is thinking. That's how he looks when he's doing it. We must be quiet. I'm hungry."

We headed back to the galley. Cleo said, "We are down to the emergency blue goo rations." It filled a cup for Kasi.

She slipped off a heel. Using her toes to grip the spoon, she fed herself. I ate, too, planning to save the rest for Balin and Kasi, who needed the nourishment more than I did.

We finished when we noticed Balin standing in the galley doorway.

"Kasi, you're feeding yourself," he said. "Wonderful."

She beamed. "You can, too, Pappa. Can't he, Molly?"

I nodded but sensed Balin wanted to speak to me. I said, "Run along and play with Cleo. Your dad and I want to talk."

293

She headed off to do just that. Balin entered the galley, but instead of sitting as I expected, he walked over to a wall unit I hadn't noticed before.

"Just as I thought. This model spaceship has a small nav display in its galley to alert the flight attendant. Anything entered on the main console is echoed back here. That is if the circuitry isn't destroyed. If someone could enter a coordinate number up front, I can see if it's reflected in the display back here. If it is, we have a way you can set the coordinates, though you can't see any menu options."

"Balin, you saved our butts!" I pressed my body into his. "Thank you! You're a genius. Let's go home."

Chapter 29 Returns

My first step: get the coordinates of a known location. One didn't memorize these long series of numbers. Rather, we depended on menu entries. With the display destroyed, the menu choices couldn't be displayed. Calling someone for them wasn't possible. Our location was too far from any world we knew.

"Scavenger hunt, everyone," I said. "Scrounge every corner of this ship. Find me something with coordinates on it."

As I meant this for Bishop's benefit, he attempted a chuckle. "Molly, I know the coordinates for Earth and for Kali-D."

Balin emanated a sigh of relief.

I expected to set up a yelling relay system from the display in the galley to the nav seat up front. But Balin pointed to the intercom. I felt a tad foolish.

"Since I can't press the button, perhaps Cleo can do it. I can read off the numbers while you enter them," Balin said.

Bishop and I headed to the cockpit. While I sat in the pilot's seat powering up the drives, he sat in the nav seat, pressed the intercom button.

"Ready up front," he said.

"Ready back here," Balin said.

Thus began a lengthy exchange of numbers. Bishop entered a digit and waited for Balin to confirm it took. What would have taken me about fifteen seconds to enter our destination of Kali-D took fifteen minutes. I had no intention of taking off until they verified the coordinates. Twice. We only had one shot at getting back into our part of the spiral arm. One tiny goof and that would end us.

I said, "Okay, everyone strap in for the short flight home. I hope."

I waited until Bishop returned to the nav seat, having helped Cleo fastened their seatbelts.

"If anything goes wrong, take the controls. Okay?"

Bishop nodded. I increased the throttle. When we reached an eighth the speed of light, I activated the hyperspace jump, holding my breath. We sensed the slight lurch. The star field vanished, replaced a black void.

Bishop returned to the galley to read the display. He spoke loud enough to be heard throughout the ship. "One hour to Kali-D."

Never had I heard a prettier sound. I relaxed. We'd survived.

I slipped out of my seatbelt and returned to the cabin. Kasi had fallen asleep. My heart skipped a beat when I saw Balin looking at me.

"Balin, well done. You are the most impressive man I've met in ages. I can't believe how well you've held it together. My sister developed a therapy that helps anyone erase the traumas they've experienced, removing their harmful effects. As soon as possible, I want to give you and Kasi that boost. Before we left, we did it to Rina, Adri, Wanda, and Otto. It's safe to say it's salvaged Otto's life and Adri's too."

"I'm not sure you need to waste your time on me. My life's over, though I have to make sure Kasi is cared for. I can't see how I can even care for her now, let alone myself."

"Don't be so hard on yourself. Terrorists struck my last husband, Sam, with almost the same mutation agent they used on you. They got my first husband, too. Sam's physical limitations were the same as yours are. Yet, Sam raised our two children, who also had no arms, and continued to work at his job as a librarian. Yes, we're handicapped, compared to

296

normal people, but we aren't helpless. We take longer to do things and have unique ways to do them."

Balin said, "When I'm around you, I'm relaxed, so calm. I've never felt this way with anyone. You're giving me hope I can somehow provide for Kasi. I had no idea how frightening it is to be a special Great Lady. She gave no hint..."

"No, not if they installed their implanted behavior when she underwent the mutation process," I said.

"Huh? I don't know what you mean. Leya always seemed cheerful, happy, and contented. But I'm anything but that. Now I look like a real freak. How can I even show myself in public? I hoped to remarry, to find a kind woman for Kasi, who deserves a mother. But now I look like a mother, a special Great Lady. I'm not one."

"No, but you have both subjective and objective reality on what Kasi faces. That alone is a gigantic benefit for Kasi. And you are a handsome man."

He snickered. "Get real, Molly. I'm a freak."

"Perhaps in some eyes you are, but not in everyone's. Your face hasn't changed. That's what first attracted my attention. Balin, I'm interested in the person, not their physical attributes. You have more potential than any man I've met in the last six years. Look at how you handled this mess. When you woke, you didn't scream, beg to die, or traumatize Kasi. You have mettle. I want to get to know you. Besides, I'm sure in time Eve and Lara will invent mutation cures for you and the others.

"You must have a zillion unwanted emotions, fears, thoughts, and aches. As soon as I can, I'll give you as much of Celeste's therapy sessions as you want. That will make a huge difference. It won't regrow arms though."

He grinned. Damn, his smile is infectious. I'd already fallen for this man. Then, the five-minute warning light flashed.

I called out. "Prepare for landing."

Balin watched my every move as I and my feet landed the space transport in the designated spot. After touchdown, security men and an emergency response team rushed towards us.

Bishop lowered the bay door.

A man yelled. "What happened to this flight? You've been lost for over a week. Anyone injured?"

I let Bishop deal with them. Ground crews unloaded our baggage while a maintenance crew assisted us off the ship and checked on the damage. I had to file an official ID report. But I ensured no one talked to Balin and Kasi. Then, Celeste, Eve, and Lara arrived.

Eve said, "My God, Molly, we thought we'd lost you this time. The company couldn't locate the spaceship and presumed all passengers were lost in a catastrophic explosion or something. Hey, good news. The vogelmenschen are a real humanoid species and not genetic engineered humans like they told us. Celeste discovered the human victims were body-swapped into captured vogelmenschen bodies. Presumably their human bodies then terminated. We're cloning the victims human bodies, but it'll be a year before they're ready. Are you okay?"

"Wow, that's good news. Yes, we're safe. The robot mutated Balin but failed with Bishop. Please, get us to the hotel. All of us in one room. Then, I'd love to have you and Lara find clothes that fit Balin. He will need lots of therapy. Kasi lost her mother. That needs to be handled."

Celeste laughed. "Leave it to Molly to find trouble. Do you realize you had half the Sol Empire's space fleet out looking for the remains of your ship?"

I flushed. "No, if it hadn't been for Balin's clear thinking, we would have never made it back. But first, I need tea and a bath. Oh, and a decent meal."

An hour later, they ushered our baggage and us into a large suite at the hotel near the spaceport. Efficient hands took over. Each got a much-needed bath, our hair washed, and a nourishing meal. Pampered? Yes. It felt good to relax. Lara picked up several outfits for Balin in his favorite color, blue, with matching heels.

Since we weren't tired, Celeste took Balin into the bedroom for his first therapy session, while Eve handled Kasi and the loss of her mother. I dealt with numerous authorities who dropped by, insisting on the full details. I learned the actual pilot and flight attendant were discovered bound and gagged in their rooms. That was four hours after the flight departed, the attack long over.

An LD message arrived from Feldspar-B. Dr. Alessandra Scala expressed her relief I was safe and how sorry she was for the mutation of Dr. Balin Khan. She suggested the meeting be rescheduled for November 1. That pleased me since that gave Balin time to adapt and to receive many therapy sessions. I sent word to Ashton Soros that we needed two more robot helpers. In a subsequent message, he agreed since he had thousands now in storage.

That evening, Cleo got a workout getting three of us ready for bed. For practicality, I said, Balin and I would sleep in one bed while Kasi took the second bed in the adjoining room. We tucked Kasi in. She looked forward to getting her own robot.

While I said it was easier for Cleo to handle us if we slept together, who was I fooling? I wanted this man. We kissed. Wow. I recalled something Rina and Adri had told me. I caressed his empty shoulders. Instant physical reactions. Best lovemaking ever!

Afterward, we lay side by side.

"That was incredible," he said.

"I'm never letting you go, handsome, sexy Balin Khan."

"Guess we better do something about that, Molly Parkinson. Only I have to consider Kasi."

"She's already asked me to be her mother. That's handled. I'd be honored to be her step-mother. Or adopt her if you prefer."

In the morning, Cleo again wore down his batteries getting the three of us dressed, fed, and ready for the day. Thank heavens for room service.

When Celeste arrived to give him more therapy, I heard him say, "Yeah. I feel helpless."

I smiled. That would soon vanish. I spent the morning with Kasi. Together, we practiced doing things with our toes. At lunch, Eve and Lara dropped by.

"Okay, kids. We've invented a way to get your feet and legs back to normal. You'll be much more stable wearing flats," Eve said.

"Yahoo. Yes. Oh, Balin, Kasi, there will still be times when have to wear these heels. We should continue to practice wearing them. Yes, life will be easier with normal feet."

The next day, I let out a cry when my feet snapped back into their normal shape, delivering a pair of sharp pains as they did so. What a difference in stability. Kasi dashed around the suite happy as could be. That our feet had been restored gave Balin much needed hope for the future.

That night, Balin told me he had lived before. He discovered his feeling of helplessness didn't stem completely from his mutation, but from a very painful incident in an earlier life.

He'd been a fighter pilot on a battlecruiser when his ship took a direct hit. Shrapnel shattered his spine. He awoke to find himself a quadriplegic. For the next forty years, all he could do was talk. "Now that was helplessness!" he said.

Each day, Celeste worked with him. More inhibiting emotions and feelings vanished. What a pleasure to wake to his cheerful mood each morning. The arrival of two more robot helpers made quite a difference. Still, we three took every opportunity to practice doing things by ourselves. Balin got a crash course in special Great Lady survival techniques. Our departure date loomed, and he'd have to face traveling to Feldspar-B and more. I wanted him as prepared as possible.

Although the robot stole his spaceship designs, those were working copies for Feldspar-B engineers. He had a backup copy on a storage device disguised as his belt buckle. Bishop retrieved it and made another copy for Balin to give to the engineers, completing his last design contract.

As we sat on our bed stuffing clothing into bags for the trip, Balin said, "Carrying things is the most challenging thing, isn't it?"

"Definitely. I use bags with straps over my shoulders. Have to be very careful because they keep slipping off my shoulders. Annoying. Hope you're ready for this trip."

He sighed. "As long as they don't laugh at me or stare at me, I can handle it. How do you take all the stares?"

"By imagining I was in their shoes looking at a most unusual person. When I understand their point of view, it's not that bad. Come on. We best get going. At least, this time they're bringing us there in a battlecruiser."

Balin laughed. "Yeah. Let's see the robot take out that ship. Do we have to wear the heels?"

"It's what's expected in society from a Great Lady," I said. "We'll get less flak that way."

Chapter 30 The Meeting

The battlecruiser transferred our bags to one its shuttles and landed us down close to our skyscraper destination.

"Wow! What a welcome," I said as we walked down the shuttle's ramp.

A column of security guards in parade uniforms stood at attention. Each was well armed, impossible to miss. The personnel we'd met on our last trip stood in a tight group around Dr. Alessandra Scala, but I recognized uniforms of Sol Empire space fleet. Admiral Rossi looked many years older than I last remembered him. Sunlight reflected from large golden lip disks of Senior Ambassadors. I recognized Senior Ambassador Sanura Fenuku of Zahra-C, but the others I did not.

We endured hugs. Many, beginning with Admiral Rossi and Dr. Scala.

"Wonderful to see you again," Senior Ambassador Sanura said, her voice coming from her language translator box around her waist. "You look smashing as ever, though I would have loved to see you in your black ID agent dress."

News traveled fast around Cass-C. I'd spent six years there and had never paid any visits to the Senior Ambassadors of any system.

"Who are these charming people?" she asked.

I noticed most had inquisitive looks. Hence, I introduced Balin and Kasi. "He's brought copies of his new design for you, Dr. Scala."

Senior Ambassador Sanura Fenuku said, "You have eclectic tastes."

Dr. Scala said, "This way. First, we'll conduct official Feldspar-B business. Then, we'll conduct Federation business. Last, the Sol Empire wants to meet with you. Promises to be a busy day."

We entered the same meeting room, only with additional chairs. I let Balin handle his business first. His robot handed the belt-buckle storage device to Dr. Scala.

"It's all there. The robot stole the actual blueprints, but anyone can print another set from that. I'll be retiring ship design after this. But if any of your engineers have questions about this latest ship, they can contact me."

"What is critical about this ship design that the rogue robots risked so much stealing it?" asked Senior Ambassador Sanura Fenuku. Many other heads nodded.

"It's designed for Feldspar-B robot deep space explorers. It won't carry people. Minimal life support except for gravity and enough heat to keep robots from seizing up in the cold. I streamlined this model. It has better flight characteristics in upper atmospheres while traveling twice as fast through hyperspace as your current models do. But, Senior Ambassador, I don't know what that rogue robot wanted it for. It can only be useful for Feldspar-B exploration drone robots."

Her lip plate masked any observable response.

Admiral Rossi frowned. "These robots killed humans. Warlike is a valid description. With five robots, this isn't a problem—"

"But it is," I said, interrupting him. "We know they've purchased about a hundred sixty of the most powerful positronic brains. They've stolen a huge quantity of titanium, gold, and silver, all components used in the internal framework of these human-form robots. My guess is they are building or have built a hundred sixty more of themselves."

Gasps. Mostly from those not present before.

Dr. Scala said, "Please, let's hold this discussion for the second part of the meeting. As promised, we've transferred your payment, Dr. Khan to your usual account. I hope you'll reconsider your early retirement though I can understand your predicament. I'm thankful you had the designs completed and weren't killed, though perhaps you have different thoughts. Anyway, moving on. Mrs. Parkinson, our world owes you a huge debt. Had you not exposed the robots, who knows how much more they could've stolen.

"We know your fledgling Sol Empire has only recently explored more distant star systems. We are giving you five complete deep space exploration robot packages. Each comes with all the robots and drones to enable your people to visit remote systems in search of life, minerals, and habitable worlds. Each one retails for about a billion of your Sol credits. Again, please accept our heartfelt thanks."

"Wow. Yes, thank you! You don't need to do this. I only wanted these robots terminated."

"We shipped the five to your Chicago Spaceport," Dr. Scala said. "Now for the Federation business. Dr. Khan, you can take your daughter on a tour of our facilities. Perhaps Bishop can go with you."

I suspected Balin wanted to stay, but Kasi didn't. After they left along with two helper robots, several scooted their chairs apart. Senior Ambassador Sanura Fenuku began the conversation.

"As we hinted, it's likely these human-form robots pose a serious threat to Federation security. Until now, the ID on Cass-C hasn't been involved. Only a few murders."

If I had hands, I might have slapped her for making little of the deaths of Bonita, Ted, and Aaron. I glared at her, but she didn't see it.

"But one hundred sixty more poses a problem. Except for Molly here, no one has detected one of these human-form robots. They look like us. Might I ask how she can detect them?"

Others agreed with her, nodding and looking at me.

"They don't have minds, not as we do," I said. "I can sense their lack of a mind." I didn't mention telepathy on purpose. That was a mess I didn't want reopened. Sometimes what you want isn't what you get.

"Do you mean you use telepathy to detect them?" Admiral Rossi asked.

"Yes."

"Does Balin and Kasi have telepathic abilities, too?" Senior Ambassador Sanura Fenuku jumped on my answer.

"No. Two different genetic mutations produce similar looking people. The Kali-D version is called the special Great Lady. That mutation doesn't give anyone telepathic abilities. The Earth version is the armless Galactic Doll, and it gives the person telepathy. That's why the robot injected me with the special Great Lady version in the hopes I'd undergo that mutation and lose my telepathic ability."

"And did you?" She continued to probe.

"No."

"Can't we devise a mechanical way to detect them?" Admiral Rossi asked.

"Once we capture one. We can disassemble it and see," another admiral said.

"Well, that hasn't happened yet," Senior Ambassador Sanura Fenuku said. "Are we all agreed these robots pose a very serious threat to the entire Federation?"

Admiral Rossi said, "That already was the conclusion of the Admiralty Roundtable, Ambassador."

"So, shouldn't we consider creating a Telepathy Division?" she suggested. "If these robots are only detectable by telepathy, then in our own defense, we need an army of telepaths. Hell, one of these robots could already have infiltrated your Admiralty Roundtable."

That caused significant mustering.

"Are you saying you want to make an army of people as handicapped as Mrs. Parkinson is? Turn men into—he's not here. I'll just say it—turn men into women, just to make a telepath?" Admiral Rossi asked. "Good lord, not again."

Dr. Scala said, "Perhaps genetic engineers can isolate what gives these armless Galactic Dolls telepathy. Then, introduce that mutation into normal people who would still appear ordinary. Then they'd not be freaks or helpless, dependent upon Soros University robot helpers or expensive personal assistants. We can see just how valuable a real telepath is."

Senior Ambassador Sanura Fenuku coughed. "While that is a humane notion, it will never happen. Why? One couldn't tell if the person next to them was a telepath. No state secrets, business secrets, or Federation secrets would ever be safe again. Anyone could spy on anyone, and no one would even know it happened. Nothing would be safe. No, the Federation long ago dictated a real telepath must be recognizable in any situation. A person lacking arms and with Molly's distinctive body shape—that fits the bill. Trouble is, even that option isn't available any longer, what with the special Great Lady version."

"That version's been around a hundred years," I said. "Until now, that hasn't been a consideration. I don't want people to think little Kasi has telepathy or Balin either. It's not fair to all those on Kali-D and other worlds." I thought of Rina's mother. Perhaps some special Great Ladies moved to other worlds. "A person who lacks arms should not fear someone abducting them under the mistaken belief they have telepathic skills."

"Don't forget the massive problems we had on Earth with that," Admiral Rossi said. "Besides kidnapping them, unscrupulous men and women infected innocent men, women, and children just to make telepaths they could then sell to the highest bidder. You almost destroyed Earth to stop that practice if you haven't forgotten." He was livid.

Senior Ambassador Sanura Fenuku countered. "But back then, we didn't face such a serious human-form robot threat. Now we do. We must use proper safeguards. Perhaps dress all our new telepaths in black, like those in the ID. We can't tolerate a telepath looking like an ordinary person. My world fears these robots. If they've infiltrated Feldspar-B and Cass-C, what other worlds are they on?"

"But having a telepath isn't any guarantee," Admiral Rossi said. "Molly was on that commercial flight and didn't detect the robot pilot."

"He has a point. Do people inspect everyone onboard every commercial flight to see if he or she is a robot in disguise?" I asked. "Even if I had, how could I stop it? Kick it? I can't even hold a gun. It's a bitch trying to open a closed door."

Senior Ambassador Sanura Fenuku countered. "But we must act and soon. Look at the damage five robots caused. How long will it take them to make one hundred sixty more? I can't imagine the damage that many of these could cause across the whole Federation. Look, if you admirals don't act on this, I'll bypass you and go straight to Seven and the ID about this. We must have an army of telepaths or a foolproof way of identifying these robots. Do we know who invented them? Someone at Galactic Robotics Chicago?" She glared at me.

"They were built there, yes. My first husband, Ted, died at the hands of a robot while he tried to answer that question. The Sixth Invaders controlled Galactic Robotics in secret for thirty years. If I had to guess, I'd say they developed them. The why is anyone's guess."

Admiral Rossi asked, "You don't suppose these human-form robots and the Sixth Invaders are working together? To conquer the galaxy?"

"Now that's a chilling thought," Senior Ambassador Sanura Fenuku said. "So, take my proposal back to the Admiralty Roundtable. Acquire samples of Earth's armless Galactic Doll mutation agent. Under tight controls, duplicate it in enough quantities and store it in top-secret, tightest security locations. Then get volunteers to become telepath ID agents and see they're highly paid with a personal assistant to help them meet their physical needs. Post them in all critical Federation areas, along with heavily armed soldiers. If you don't take that to them, I promise I will present this to Seven himself."

Admiral Rossi chuckled. "Assuming you can even find that man."

She glared back at him. His smile evaporated. I made one last argument.

"Hold one second. Armless Galactic Doll genes are dominant. If any parent, male or female, is one, any child inherits it. If you're not careful, soon the majority of any population would be armless Dolls. And it's not fair to fix it so they can't bear children. That's inhumane."

"We can deal with children," she said.

I tried, thankful Admiral Rossi was on my side. Still...

"Another possibility," she said, "would be to hire Molly to visit the worlds within the Federation, searching for more of these evil robots. Pay her a handsome salary. Let her bring her family with her. Unless you know of another real telepath in the Federation?"

"Not gonna happen!" I said.

Senior Ambassador Sanura Fenuku took another approach. "Mrs. Parkinson has a valid point we must consider. When we make our needed telepaths, some unscrupulous individuals might go after special Great Ladies, believing they have telepathic skills. We must protect them and any other person who could be confused with our new armless telepaths.

I suggest, Admiral Rossi, that you include in your request that the Federation creates a special Great Lady registry. That way, they'd be protected from kidnappers seeking a telepath."

I countered her. "What about men like Balin? A special Great Man registry? And what about ordinary people who've lost their arms through a birth defect or an accident? An accident registry?"

"Point taken. Perhaps only one registry. The non-telepath registry. That would do. If we protect these people, the way is then clear for us to make our army of telepaths to protect us from these human-form robots," she said. "Having a hundred sixty-five of these things roaming Federation worlds is more than alarming. We must act."

I said, "Be careful what you wish. Once telepaths are widespread, no secret will be safe."

She glared at me but said nothing further.

Just then, six ID agents burst into the room, guns drawn. Everyone seemed shocked by their sudden appearance. I concluded this wasn't planned. Admiral Rossi rose.

"Sit down, Admiral. You too, Ambassador. Parkinson, come with us now," one said.

Several protested, but the man cut them off.

"Shut up. We'll return Parkinson after a while. Take your supper break. This way." He motioned with his gun. I thought about protesting but realized they could pick me up and carry me off. I obeyed, saying nothing.

They led me out of the building and into one of their black ID space shuttles. I entered a small meeting room where two men sat. One motioned me to the only other chair, the one on which a bright light shone. A light touch of their minds satisfied me neither man was a robot. One wore a uniform with markings showing rank though I didn't know what. The other wore ID black in the form of a suit. I sat down and stared at them.

The uniformed man spoke. "I'm Captain Styles. This is Dr. Gomez, one of the Federation's best genetic engineers. We had a hidden microphone in that meeting room and heard everything. We're interested in the ability to make telepaths. This rogue robot situation must be handled. You and I know the only method of detection is via telepathy. And yet some years ago, the Federation outlawed Earth's mutation agent that made them. Dr. Gomez..."

"Ah, yes, Parkinson. The woman's whose DNA is one grand mess. For your benefit, I invented most of the mutations and cloning that Salad's uses on a grand scale, at least those within the last fifty years. My finest achievement was the Vogelmenschen mutation. Anyway, you're here to continue the discussion about making telepaths. Earth's armless Galactic Doll agent is the only known method of making a telepath.

"We've tried several experiments. We made a clone of you, taking a DNA sample when others knew you had telepathic ability."

Shocked, I interrupted. "You think making an illegal clone of me would make a body that had telepathic ability? How did that work out?"

Yes, I snarled at him. The audacity of the man.

"We had a perfect body that should have telepathy. We body swapped many test subjects into it. None displayed telepathic ability, and we don't know why."

"Shows me you don't understand what a person is. Body, mind, being or spirit. Fool. Telepathy springs from the being and their mind. The body is only a minor medium."

He said, "Except you can't see this so-called being or spirit. And you can't see the mind. While we can transfer the mind and its consciousness into other bodies, our conclusion is that cloning is out. We must make telepaths the way Earth made them. By using the armless Galactic Doll agent. But..."

310

"Ah, the 'but.' There's always a catch. Isn't there?" I said and snarled at him.

"Well, yes. I've studied mutation subject reactions on Earth. Perhaps you could offer firsthand evidence. Some who woke begged to be killed. I read they screamed."

"Yes, their terror screams still haunt me. Many refused to live, especially men who looked like women, helpless, too."

"You did save or salvage some if I read that right."

"By using Celeste's therapy, we salvaged some, but it took at least eight long days of therapy just to get them to stop wanting to die. After months of therapy, they stabilized and became useful people again."

He said, "Ah, yes. As telepaths on deep spaceships. That's documented. Your daughter and son were telepathic linguists, paid handsomely according to Earth's records."

"That's true."

"Well, we can't spend months getting them able to work. From the records, there were thousands. What happened to so many?"

"Terrorists exposed random populations to the agent. The people we salvaged had higher IQs or had more vitality. Many had low IQs, and they had huge problems when they developed telepathy. They had no control over it. Imagine walking down the street and the thoughts of every person screamed into your mind simultaneous. They couldn't bear it and found ways to die just to end the chaotic shouting in their minds. If you're making telepaths, be careful who you mutate." I hoped this would dissuade him.

"Thank you. That fact was omitted from the documents. A valuable insight. We need to mutate sharper people. We should get the person's agreement to be mutated into a telepath, correct?"

"Absolutely. We had people who wanted to become a telepath. That's when it first began. Offers of a million credits per year for their services. Those who became one had a terrible time adapting to a handicapped life."

He changed topics on me. "Kali-D has the special Great Lady mutation, except such women have no telepathic ability. Salad's Genetic Labs invented their programmed script they play into the patients' ears during the lengthy mutation comas. From all indicators, the script is highly effective. We paid close attention to Salad's reactions when he woke to find himself a special Great Lady. Adri and Otto, too.

"No hysterics. No terror screams. They've settled down within minutes and are doing well. The implanted behavior modification works. Has worked for fifty years. Earlier records suggested they had a wake-up problem with newly made special Great Ladies freaking out for days.

"So, Parkinson, wouldn't a similar implanted script alleviate the myriad problems your victims faced there on Earth? Just change special Great Lady to 'powerful telepath.' You've been around several as they wake from these special Great Lady comas. Doesn't that implant solve such problems?"

"No, it makes them more insane. Go spend time around one of those special Great Ladies. Listen to their speech. While they appear to display no terror or fear, all that is buried in their minds, and they run on a manic behavior pattern, one that's not rational. Go to one of their parties where dozens of these special Great Ladies gather. Listen to their talk. Discuss issues with them. You'll see bits of those implanted phrases coloring everything they say. I've never met a sane person who believed being handicapped is wonderful and perfect. If you do that to a telepath, then those implanted words will be constantly echoing in their minds, dwarfing any real ability to pick up other's thoughts."

"Hum, we hadn't thought of that. We will check on that aspect. It sounded very promising. What suggestions do you have for us to make telepaths?"

"The solution to today's problem will become tomorrow's problem to solved." I sighed. "Okay, I realized a telepath is likely the only way you have to detect these human-form rogue robots. Your best approach is to get willing volunteers, offer huge incentives for them to become one, support them afterward. But I'm warning you. There's nothing more dangerous to a society than rogue telepaths. They can implant any thought into anyone's mind. They can extract secrets from any mind. Nothing is safe. A telepath can span an entire world. If you make telepaths, they could well turn out to be your worst nightmare. Thank heavens they destroyed Earth's proposed Telepath Division before it took hold."

That ended the meeting. Two agents ushered me back, and I joined the others who were finishing their suppers.

Chapter 31 Earth's Demands

An aide of Admiral Rossi ushered me to him. We met in another of Dr. Scala's offices, only this one held us two. A small desk separated us. No room for Cleo who waited outside.

"I've had this room cleared of any electronic bugs. What we say is between us. I'm retiring soon. Admiral Carr of Epsilon Eridani replaces me January first. Before then, I want to meet several goals. Let's discuss what you discovered at Salad's Genetics Laboratory on Kali-D."

"I hate to see you retire. You've always done well for the empire. What do you want to know?"

"Were the Third Invaders really running it?"

"Yes, they body swapped into the two top administrators. Over the years they've created several batches of a thousand human clones."

"Okay. Do they have a copy of Earth's DNA database?"

"I believe they do. They had a copy of my own DNA from before any genetic mutations happened. I can't see how else they could have that."

"And they can clone anyone whose DNA they have?"

"Yes, as I understand it. The process takes about a year to complete the clone body, though one can use it sooner, but it's weak and must eat the blue goo."

"We've gone through official channels to get them to share the cloning process. Having this technology is vital for our empire. Not for people to live longer lives, but for security. Imagine what can happen if someone cloned me and then inserted the clone into our society as me. Will the real Admiral Rossi please stand up? You get the picture."

He saw my grimace and continued.

"We've seen how valuable having a clone body can be. Witness the recent worms attack. Sometimes I must send soldiers off on a dangerous mission. If I could send them off body swapped into clone bodies..."

He said nothing for a moment. I didn't need him to complete his thought.

"Where was I? Oh, yes. We need a copy of that tech for the Sol Empire. Since official channels failed, I'm taking other means. I won't bother you with them. Rather, I need your focus on these human-form robots. I used to employ one. Major Airla Baker. Years ago, she and I realized you were in far more danger than I ever was. I sent her off to watch over you."

I smiled. "She's saved my life many times, sir. Thank you."

"Yes, I've heard of that. Another one, a Travis Jones, has been my deep space eyes and ears. He brought us our first contact with the Federation of Planets and thereby saved us from the Sixth Invaders. But you know that. Three others exist, but I've had no knowledge of them or their purposes.

"But the five rogue robots. Now their actions are in part on us or Galactic Robotics Chicago to be more precise. I had hoped to exterminate them before I retired, but that's not happening. With the latest developments—a hundred sixty more of them—I can't ignore this mess any longer. I'm getting ahead of myself.

"Years ago, I set up a team to look into ways of detecting the human-form robots, based on their positronic brains. That has failed. They shield those brains to prevent harm to nearby humans. Until we capture one and dismantle it, we have no certain way to identify one. Weight might be. X-rays might reveal their titanium alloy skeletal frame. From all we've seen, the modern robot construction methods involved mimicking the human bone structure. That's got us nowhere. Perhaps if we dismantled one..."

He sighed. "No, as the others pointed out, the only certain detection method belongs to you, Molly. Telepathy. They aren't human and don't have a mind as we do."

"I had hoped someone would have already figured out a better way of detecting them," I said. "Something that's automatic, like the bomb searching scanners at the spaceport."

"Yes. I'm convinced we need to be proactive on this one. The damage a hundred sixty-five can wreak is huge. Makes the Sixth Invaders' robot soldiers on North Continent, Brussels, look like gnats. Worse, the infiltration factor. No installation in the empire would be secure. This is a security nightmare."

"I can see that. I take it you have a proposal?"

He chuckled. "Astute as ever. Yes, I do. I've already made arrangements. The Sol Empire wants to make its own telepaths, based on the armless Galactic Doll mutation agent. Look, back then, we experienced a few successes, such as your own daughter, Isabella. Records show that out of that incredible fiasco, twenty-five had very successful stints as telepaths.

"We've collected, refurbished, and stored all those machines the Sixth Invaders created for us—the hair-nail machine, the dressing machine, and the maid cook. We've thousands in storage, along with all the laptops with the hours of how-to videos on them. Plus, we've just signed a contract with Soros University to get a dozen of their helper robots like Cleo. We aim to help them be comfortable and independent while they are being telepaths for us.

"My select team has interviewed Isabella, Bernardo, and the two dozen others who had successful times as telepaths. We've isolated the personality traits and IQ levels needed for a successful stint as one. The program will be very tightly controlled. We will accept only those who meet this rigid profile. They'll be well-paid, of course. Oh, yes, an important detail: officially, they'll be called special Great

Ladies, since they are widely known not to be telepaths. That might help protect them.

"To further those ideas, we're beginning a special Great Lady program on Earth. We'll be advertising that mutation, but I don't expect many will request it. That will give cover for telepaths."

We both grinned.

"What about the trauma they'll experience when they wake from their comas?" I asked.

"This is where your sister's therapy comes into play. We're signing a contract for her workshop in St. Louis to give whatever therapy sessions the new telepaths will need. Humane all the way. At the end of the telepath's contract, we'll provide the genetic cures. That way they can resume a normal life again and be wealthy."

"This is the best I can do to protect our empire, Mrs. Parkinson. Once the program gets going, I'd like you to oversee it. Offer suggestions. But I'm getting ahead of myself again.

"The recent worm attack can't have been an accident. Someone sent the worms to all ruling bodies of the Sol Empire and on several planets, too. You've probably heard, but in case you haven't, we've no official rulers. Again. The senators charged with making our laws are dead. All those in the executive body who enforced the laws are dead. The worms did a job on them on both Pylon and Brussels. I saved the Senior Investigator and Senior Judge who were on Earth at the time of the attack."

"Ward Tilman and Ashley Peterson?" I asked. Years ago I had recommended both for the positions.

"Yes. Already Ward has launched a full investigation. No results so far. I've had serious discussions with the CEOs of Galactic Expansion, Galactic Defense, and several other corporations. I've talked with them from all member worlds and moons. It seems after the fiascos of the last half-century, no one wants to host a new ruling Senate. GPan officials wish to return to the way the empire was initially run. From their offices, naturally. As we are an expanding empire that makes sense.

"I've worked out a compromise. We'll keep the Senior Investigation office and the Senior Judge branch. They've agreed there must be a single leader over all the myriad GPan offices, coordinating them, but as usual, they can't agree on who gets that much authority. We've reached a compromise. They've agreed to set up an Empress/Emperor of the Sol Empire who coordinates GPan and other corporations' plans, handled defense and other similar matters.

"I received help from Empress Kalindi Amandani. She convinced the many CEOs that having an empress is the best way to oversee an expanding empire. Further, the choice for the first empress is unanimous. Congratulations, Empress Molly Parkinson. The job is yours. The only stipulation is the GPan executives insist you keep your current body form until you retire from office."

"They want an armless telepath?" I asked. Why didn't this surprise me? In the past, most top leaders figured we were darn near helpless and thus couldn't abuse our positions.

"Yes. The executives required this because they thought no one in their right mind would want to body swap into your body to take over your position."

I doubled over roaring with laughter. After a minute, I regained control.

"Makes a strange sense. That the Sixth Invaders body swapped into our two top CEO positions and ran our empire for thirty years isn't easily forgotten."

He grinned. "Precisely. I'm sure that's the reason behind their insistence the empress/emperor be handicapped. Still, your authority is supreme over the ruling corporations. You should coordinate with the Senior Judge to delete now-obsolete laws the Senate passed. I'm told in recent years, they bickered and didn't pass much.

"Empress Kalandi Amandani told me to remind you of her final words to you. And that she's doing fine. If you take the position, she will set up a direct communication line to her. You can get expert advice. Her words."

"She's an expert. No doubt about that. How long am I supposed to be the empress?"

"Nothing has been decided. As it stands, as long as you wish."

He laughed and said, "Until you make too many rulings against them. You know CEOs."

I did and laughed with him.

"Your top priority is to make sure these rogue robots are not manufacturing more of themselves on any Sol Empire world or moon or using any of our resources as they did on Feldspar-B. I'm sure your new admiral will insist on that detail.

"Next topic. Thanks to you, we have normalized relations with the Sixth Invaders. Can they be trusted? And what about the Third Invaders? If they are to be believed, they've seeded many nearby worlds with humans, conducting experiments on us. Yet, they warned us about the worms and helped us destroy them. Can we trust the Third Invaders?"

"As far as I can throw them," I said, chuckling. "I trust Ambassador L'Grina. She's changed since she pretended to be CEO Hardy. I can't say anything about other Sixth Invaders. I met one new Third Invader, a Captain Katya Binsk. She's okay, too. Helped us defeat the worms in Peoria. Other Third Invaders? I wouldn't trust them. Two of them ran Salad's Genetics Lab. Lord knows the mischief they caused there. Plus, they have a long history of experimenting on humans, going back many millennia, if what they've told me is true. Their supposed help with the worms may well have happened because they feared another secret attack like the one which boiled thousands of their people. They don't know what that weapon was or who attacked them.

"Plus they wanted me to intervene when one of our deep space exploration ships discovered a planet housing a two-millennia-old human experiment of theirs."

"Yes, I was informed of that, but then that ship discovered another hot prospect world and changed course. Still, I presume you'll be needed there soon," he said.

"Why do these CEOs want me to be the empress?" I asked the gnawing question I had and hoped the Admiral would give me an honest answer. I trusted him more than other leaders.

For a moment, he sat silent, pulling on his chin. "Well, I've wondered that myself. I know the various member worlds' CEOs can never agree on anything. They don't trust each other—not for the last two dozen years. While you were on Cass-C, the Senate and Executive groups got totally out of their control, passing crazy laws that none of the corporations backed. I think the CEOs believed their power had been usurped. I sensed they wanted a telepath in charge. When they meet with you, you can tell if one of them is being honest with the group. And I think they respect you for how you exposed the Sixth Invaders."

"Thanks. That's more or less what I assumed. If I get married, how will my mate fit into this ruling picture? Emperor? What authority will he have?"

"He or she won't have any position or authority or title. But you can give them a position in your executive branch. They want to deal with one telepath only."

That made sense. Less to coordinate. We chatted and then they returned me to the others. A transport ship waited to return us to Kali-D. Sleep came readily.

Chapter 32 On Heading Home

Balin, Kasi, and I stepped off the transport in Kristna, Kali-D, with our robot helpers rolling along behind us. My sisters and Lara waved. But another special Great Lady called out to Balin.

"Vinata?" Balin asked. His brows rose. I sensed disbelief.

"Mamma!" Kasi squealed in delight.

"You're dead! I buried you," Balin said.

"It's me, Pumpkin. The stupid engineer at Salad's forgot to tell you they body swapped me into this new growing body. When I fell, I hit my head and died. But when they got me to the hospital, they swapped me into this new clone body. I woke up only a week ago and found they forgot to tell you."

Kasi pushed her body into her mother's. Balin's mouth hung open.

Me? I felt a sledgehammer crushing me.

"Balin, you look different. But we're perfect. We must depend on our personal assistants. I had to get a new one. Where's Kasi's helper and yours?" she said.

"Robot helpers from Cass-C. I thought you were dead. We're trying to move on with our lives. Oh, gods."

He looked at me and then at Vinata. He looked helpless at that moment.

I swallowed hard. "This your wife? She's beautiful. Kasi, it's wonderful you have your Mamma back."

"Er, yeah. Vinata, this is my savior Molly Parkinson. This is confusing."

Celeste hugged me, pulling me apart from the three. Eve and Lara joined us, putting space between them and us. I needed that space. What an unexpected shock.

I looked back at Balin, watching him as he pressed into the woman wearing the bright red gown. Kasi continued pressing into her legs.

I needed a distraction. Celeste provided it.

"Let's get you through customs. Lots of news. Wanda and Otto finished up Rina and Adri's therapy sessions. They discovered their DNA is in Salad's DNA database, and Salad's engineers are cloning new bodies for them. They must get by for a year before they can be swapped into the new bodies."

"Terrific," I said, though I found it hard to muster enthusiasm at the moment.

"Plus, I tried my therapy on Salad. Been quite the challenge. I've got the implant desensitized and hope to erase it in another couple of days. He's long had a new male clone body in a stasis pod. Once he's erased the implant, he'll get body swapped. His wife insists he does that."

"What about Wanda and Otto?" I asked.

Eve said, "We've repaired their feet.

"I think we're close to being able to regrow arms on the victims," Lara said. "Even if that works, Otto will continue to look like a Great Lady. Lots to do. I can't believe how messed up your DNA has become."

I chuckled. "Didn't want your job to be too easy, Lara."

The dwarf gave me an appreciative hug, nearly crushing my ribs. We laughed, and my tension eased.

With an apologetic look, Balin came to me. "Molly, I don't know what to say."

"I do. Kasi has her mother back, and you have your wife back. That's one incredible miracle. You go home and enjoy them both. We'll chat later."

"But..."

He sighed and did as I suggested. Thus ended what I had hoped would be a wonderful union.

While Eve and Bishop gathered my things, Celeste said, "It's a loss. We'll handle it soon. But I'm not sure what to do about Wanda and Otto."

I knew she wanted me to think about something other than the surprise loss of my fiancé. Still, I allowed the diversion.

"Wanda has this thing about a clone body not being her body. Otto, too, but to a lesser extent. Eve's retrieved their original DNA from the ID on Cass-C. Seems they stored it in case they needed to identify their bodies from DNA only. Eve said it's possible to make clone bodies for both. Be a year before they are ready for the body swap."

"Otto is willing, but Wanda isn't?" I asked.

"Yes. Both are becoming excellent therapy givers. They want to move back to Earth with me and work in my St. Louis clinic," Celeste said.

"But if they got clone bodies, in a year they could be back working for the ID as agents."

"Neither wants to return to the ID. I think Wanda is holding out, hoping for a cure."

Once in the large hotel suite, I told them what had happened, specifically my meeting with Admiral Rossi.

Eve sighed. "Well, they need a way to detect the rogue robots. But someone will pay an awful price."

My sisters gave me a bath and washed my hair. Room service brought us our dinner. After that, Wanda and Otto came by for a visit, along with Rina and Adri.

"We just had to see you and thank you," Rina said. "We can't stay long; we take forever to get the next day's lectures prepared."

"You like your new teaching job?"

Rina beamed. "You bet I do. It's more challenging than I ever imagined. I keep reaching for things with my hands. Adri, too."

"We're still adjusting," Adri said. "But a year from now, things will change. My dad is pleased and has accepted me as heir to his company. And I found a way to thank you for saving our sanity if not our lives. Your own deep space transport. One from Dad's company. It seats twenty people and carries enough fuel to cross half the galaxy. I had a guy park it on the tarmac close to your hotel."

"Wow! Thank you. I could really use my own ship."

"Lot's safer, too," Adri said.

We talked about his surprise gift until they headed home to finish preparing tomorrow's lectures. Since I wasn't tired and the hour not late, Celeste took me aside.

"Close your eyes. Okay. I want you to return to the moment you had any idea you were about to lose your fiancé."

"Well, hell, Celeste. I just found me another man I could respect and love when his dead wife shows up. Can't deny him that nor Kasi her mother, now can I? Okay. Okay. I'm there, stepping down the ramp, and I see everyone welcoming us."

An hour later and some tears, I erased that chain of loss and trauma. Seems several hundred years ago, I'd made the mistake of having an affair with a married man who promised he would leave his wife. When I pressured him, he bashed my head in. Not one of my finer hours. But I had a clarity of mind.

As I drifted into slumberland, an idea flashed. The next morning, I used the hotel's complimentary computer to search for synthetic flesh. Curious, Bishop looked over my shoulder.

"Ah, ha," he said, emulating a surprise reaction. "You are on to something. Probably want the largest manufacturer. That one, Velos-9. It's in the Sagittarius arm, more or less on our way home. Shall I arrange a visit to Skins-R-Us?"

"Yes, Bishop. It struck me last night. If these rogue robots are going to make more like themselves, they'll need a large amount of synth skin. Med centers use it on severe burns. I read it beats the terrible scarring and ugliness of human skin grafts."

"I wish I knew more about my own manufacturing. Perhaps I could be of more use."

"You're highly useful as it is. Say, will I need lessons to fly my new transport? Any chance you can fly it now?"

Bishop displayed a smile for me. "I expected that. While everyone slept, I studied all ten operations manuals. I should be able to pilot it. You should be able to handle the navigation console. It's almost the same as the Federation standard nav console. You should study the manuals before you try to solo."

"Excellent. Check what arrangements we'll need to visit Velos-9 and this company. I'll let the others know we're taking a slight detour on our way home."

We couldn't leave until all the therapy sessions finished. That delayed our departure for a week. In fact, everyone gathered around the stasis pod holding the Salad clone while his engineers performed the body swap.

"My gods! I'm me again! I can talk. This is truly a miracle. I don't know how I can ever thank you enough for what you've done."

I've seen happy people before, but Salad's exuberance infected us all. My sisters must have discussed this beforehand. Celeste asked him about his company's cloning process.

He said, "I understand the special Great Lady implant now. If they hadn't given it to me and I didn't have this new clone body waiting for me, I would have found a way to kill myself. Instead, I went insane trying to be one while knowing I had a clone replacement waiting but one I never could use. But if I had, I would have insisted on undergoing the mutation a second time. Insanity. You've saved me. How can I ever thank you?"

"We could use this system of cloning back on Earth," she said.

Eve explained the awful results of the terrorist attacks. "You possess our original DNA database," she said. "If we had had your cloning system, we could have created clones for the male victims and saved their lives. Many died rather than live like one of your special Great Ladies."

"Consider it done! Yes, that's what I can do to thank you. Let's go talk to my manager and chief engineers. I'm sure we can get you a smaller version of the cloning process. It's separate from the genetic mutation side of the operation," Salad said. "But first, I need to hug Anala. Come here, my dear, you beautiful woman."

Eve and Lara stayed behind to receive the smaller cloning machine and related equipment. Thus, Bishop, Celeste, Wanda, Otto, and I headed to Cass-C. I wanted to talk to Nikita before heading home. Wanda and Otto needed to retrieve things from their apartments before moving to Earth.

While Celeste and Bishop helped the two retrieve what they wanted to keep and tossed the rest, I visited my daughter. She looked grown up. Where had the years gone? We had a long talk.

"I'll miss you, Mom," she said, hugging me as we said our goodbyes.

Then, with the required vaccination shots for Velos-9, we departed the spiral arm's bar region, bound for the Sagittarius arm, about halfway to Sol.

***

After fiddling with the language translator units, we answered the customs man's questions, and he, ours. We had landed at a spaceport close to Minoit City. Because of the stares we got, Wanda and Otto remained on the ship, while Celeste, Bishop, and I visited Skins-R-Us.

The yellowish-skin people resembled those of Asian descent on Earth. Similarity of names struck me. Could the Third Invaders have populated this world? Modern, sleek.

That's how Celeste and I described our first view of the city as we exited the terminal and found the shuttle rental kiosk. I let Bishop make our arrangements.

The computer-controlled ship activated as we entered, asking about our destination. I spoke via my translator unit, but it took two repeats before the computer worked out I had a bad accent. After repeating our destination, it asked for flight confirmation. Once okayed, the shuttle lifted off, heading for the manufacturing plant. The glass-steel skyscrapers reminded me of Hoffdorf, but frequent patches of green told of a love for open parks.

After landing, we joined others on the streets, as we walked the short distance from the lot to the sprawling building. They dressed much as ordinary Chicagoans did. I relaxed. We entered a lobby area, well lit. Banks of doors lay to our left. A kiosk-like desk blocked forward progress. Well, we could have walked around the imposing desk.

"Hello. Welcome to Skins-R-Us. How may I help you?" the receptionist asked.

"I'd like to talk to someone about synthetic skins. A large amount of it," I replied, trying to ignore the young woman's stares.

What did I say? Her smile vanished. I saw her hand press a button. A dozen armed guards wearing blue uniforms and carrying blasters pointed at us charged out from side doors. A man dressed in a black uniform hastened up behind them.

"Miss Cho?" he said.

"They were asking about synth skins, a lot of it," she said.

"You three, come with me. We have questions for you."

He waved his blaster toward one side door. We entered a sterile office that smelled of disinfectant. Stark white walls ceiling, and floor, steel chairs, and a giant desk with a cushioned chair occupied the room. Intense white light flooded the room. I wished I'd brought sunglasses.

"Sit," he said, though he holstered his blaster.

We did. He flipped open a folder on his desk as he sat. Our chairs left everything to be desired. I squinted at the man and touched his mind. Human. I relaxed a little.

"I'm Captain Lu. What do you know about the theft of ten million credits of synth skin?"

"Er, nothing. We're here to find out if you are missing any synthetic skin," I said. "Rogue human-form robots stole vast amounts of titanium ingots as well as gold and silver from a company on Feldspar-B. Before that, these rogue robots purchased a hundred sixty of the best positronic brains in the Federation. I suspect they are trying to build a hundred sixty more of themselves. To do that, they'd need synthetic skin. I searched and found your company is the top producer in the Federation."

"Yes, we've been informed by the Federation's ID to be on the lookout for these robots. Are you the person they claimed can detect one of these robots? Do they really look like humans?"

"Yes, Captain Lu. They are indistinguishable from you and me—well if I had arms that is. I helped foil their plot on Feldspar-B. What can you tell me about the theft?"

"It's not so much a theft as a disappearance of stock. We have tight quality control here. Everything is logged in and double counted. Our computer system always knows the precise amount of product in storage. When we heard about the robot mess on Feldspar-B, our CEO ordered a complete visual check of our stock and computer records. That's when the discrepancy was discovered. There you are, you see.

"Missing stock?" I asked.

"Wait a moment. I'll summon our CFO. Mr. Zhou. He can explain it."

Another man in a business suit entered. Captain Lu pulled one of these uncomfortable chairs around for him. Then, he explained the situation.

"Well, it's a clever ruse. Via the computer order system, someone entered fictitious orders. The system filled these orders, packaged them, and shipped them off to the customer, whose payment received was logged into the system. Marked paid in full. Yet, no actual funds ever appeared in our accounts. The product was definitely shipped. We're out ten million credits worth of product. My ass is on the line here. There you are, you see."

I didn't see but smiled. "Have you caught the person responsible?"

"Well, no. Now if the stories coming out of Feldspar-B are true, perhaps we have one of these rogue robots working for us," Mr. Zhou said.

"Do you have surveillance video? Who can enter those orders? I assume Captain Lu has done a full investigation," I said.

"I could find nothing amiss," Captain Lu said. "There you are, you see. We have a huge theft and no suspects. I presumed whoever was behind it would come looking for more large amounts of our product. Hence, you were flagged. I still have to verify you are who you say you are."

"I detected the rogue robots on Feldspar-B for them. If you like, you could take me on a tour of your facility. I can look for one of the rogue robots."

"How many of them are there?"

"Five. I've met two myself," I said.

"Will you need to bring your equipment in here? I must have our engineers examine such, you see. You could be saboteurs or worse."

I grinned. "No equipment. Just me."

"In that case, let's do it. I'll lead you around. You check for your rogue robots," Captain Lu said. "My men will accompany us. Shoot to kill. There you have it, you see. We'll get this rogue robot. If there actually is one that is. Mind you, I don't honestly believe you."

I made a mistake. Expanding my awareness, I touched Captain Lu's mind and sensed utter disbelief. But when I reached for CFO Zhou's mind, I found nothing at all.

"Mr. Zhou isn't human," I said. "It's a robot disguised as Mr. Zhou."

Ten seconds flashed by.

"Teslenko said he mutated you hoping you'd lose your telepathy. I see he's got it wrong," Mr. Zhou said.

With that, he rose and slammed a fist into my head, knocking my body halfway across the room. It followed that by swinging its other hand at Captain Lu, knocking him backward. Fortunately for him, his chair had rollers. Much of the blow's force transferred to rolling backward into the wall. Mr. Zhou rose, flipping the giant desk over, pinning Bishop and Celeste against the wall I'd smashed up against. It left no doubt it was a robot because it ripped the door off its hinges. He then plowed through the startled security guards milling around the hallway. I blacked out.

***

Celeste took charge. "Do it, Bishop."

"How could Mr. Zhou be a robot? After him. Shoot to kill it!" Captain Lu said, rushing into the hallway where his guards scrambled to their feet.

Left alone, Bishop injected my leg.

"How big a dose?" Celeste asked.

"Six times overdose. Last time it took five doses. Looks like it crushed her face. It wanted to kill her. Conclusion: last time, they tried to make her lose her telepathic skill to detect them. Failing that, they want her dead."

"Not if we can help it, Bishop. We'll get her to Kali-D fast and into a stasis pod."

He lifted my eyelids. "Ah, working. She's drifting into the mutation coma. I'll carry her to the ship. Perhaps you should stay and see what else you can find out. I'll be back as soon as I get her in a stasis pod. Couple of days at most."

"Right. Take good care of my sister."

He left, carrying my comatose body back to my new transport. Later, he told me that while explaining what had happened to Wanda and Otto, he handled the pre-flight checks. Then off they went to Kali-D and some stasis pods.

Captain Lu returned to his office. His face had turned back and blue. He looked downcast.

"He got away. Afraid he killed your friend. Who knew it could be that strong? You see what it did to my steel door? I've sent a search party to Mr. Zhou's home. He's probably dead. Thanks to her, we've found our thief. I've sent word to our CEO and others. We'll hold a meeting soon. Too bad it killed her."

"Bishop put her into a mutation coma. She's not dead, captain. I'm sticking around to answer questions and find out what damage this robot has done," Celeste said.

Later, Celeste viewed the shipping records. "Looks as though it sent most of the stolen product to Earth. We're headed there next. Bishop and I will see if we can find the trail. Maybe return some stolen product to you."

"Excellent. There you are, you see. The robot mess comes back to where it started. You're lucky our CEO has decided not to bring the Sol Empire up on charges of inventing rogue robots," Captain Lu said.

With several days to kill, Celeste toured the facility and got to touch a synthetic skin sample.

"It feels like real skin. Has that texture," she said.

That done, she spent two boring days in a hotel close to the spaceport.

***

Damn. Killed by robots twice in the same year! I woke to a fabulous headache while lying naked in a stasis pod. I knew what must have happened. Celeste noticed me rousing and came to my side.

"Wake up, Sleeping Beauty," she said.

"Again?"

She chuckled. "Yeah. Again. Thank heavens for Bishop. Took six times the maximum dose. Got the job done. Eve claims your DNA is even more screwed up. Not her scientific words though. Let's get you dressed."

"What happened? I mean after the robot bashed my head."

She outlined events while dressing me.

"We're staying in our usual hotel suite. Let's get you out of here and cleaned up."

"Rats. My feet are messed up again. They didn't get the rogue robot, and it stole mountains of synthetic skin. Geesh. Doesn't anything stop them?"

"Well, I gathered data for you. I've copied the shipping destinations of their stolen products. All are Earth-based. Some in Chicago even. When we get back, you'll have plenty of leads to check on. Meanwhile, I forwarded that to Admiral Rossi who promised to get the Senior Investigator and his staff on it. No rush for your return. We need to get you cleaned up, fed, and then erase this latest trauma."

"Maybe I should have a dozen clone bodies made. Lots of spares."

We both laughed.

The therapy session this time captured my interest. In many lifetimes, I had received a fist in my face and had punched other people's faces. The time that hung up all the others happened when I angrily lashed out and smashed a person's face only to discover she was innocent. I'd attacked the wrong person. Boy, did that one ever hang me up. After

332

that, my face and I became a magnet for people's fists. If I ever got enough, then the scales of justice would balance.

As we packed up to head to Earth, Eve and Lara observed Salad's engineers loading their new cloning equipment into my new transport.

Eve said, "For once, we'll own innovative equipment. We're starting Axehead's Genetics Lab in Chicago. Earth won't be backwaters any longer. We're bringing along your new clone body, but just don't get killed for another year."

I laughed.

"It's true," Lara said. "State-of-the-art in the Federation. Besides, your DNA has become so confused that we're no longer sure how to cure anything for you. Except for your feet. That's been the only constant bit of genetic material. We introduced that cure while you were healing. Your feet should be normal in a day or so."

"Thanks. Both of you. Thank you."

As she loaded the last of our crates into the transport, Celeste said, "Molly, you have a remarkable knack for finding the next rogue robot nest. I mean out of all the companies in the Federation that make synthetic skin, you picked the one the robots used. Amazing. Are you sure you don't get insider information?"

We chuckled. "No," I said, "I have a knack for getting myself nearly killed. It's vital I keep Bishop around at all times."

Even Bishop smiled, adding a human reaction.

"Their ad said they made the finest skin and are the Federation's largest manufacturer. That's why I visited them. Now I have more questions. It's obvious they are amassing the materials to make more robots like themselves. My questions revolve around where are they constructing them? They have to turn their raw materials into titanium alloy and such. I wish Ted Billings wasn't dead. He would know what the robots needed to do next."

Celeste said, "Admiral Rossi implied he would raid the places that received the synthetic skin. Perhaps that will stop the robots. On the other hand, you are returning with major gifts for the top corporations. That should make them more inclined to accept you as their empress and let you help them run the Sol Empire."

"If that isn't enough on my plate, I still must deal with the Third Invader world of Zeta Tucanae-C or Bella. They sure messed up their genetics and biology this time. I'm not even sure how we can annex them into the Sol Empire. I sure wish the Third Invaders didn't practice genetic mutations on humans."

The End.

A Favor to Other Readers

How about helping other readers? Many readers rely on reviews to make the decision whether to buy a book. You can help them make their decision by leaving your opinions and viewpoint in a short review of the positive things of this book. Writing the review and expressing your opinion only takes a few minutes, and other readers will appreciate your efforts.

Click this link: The Sol Empire Volume 5 Genetic Engineering
https://www.amazon.com/dp/B097LTCDB3
scroll down to Customer Reviews; click on Write a Review, and enter your review. Thank you.

Author Information

Visit My Amazon.com Author Page
Vic Broquard Author Page

Follow My Blog
Vic Broquard's Blog

Follow Me on Social Media
Facebook
LinkedIn
YouTube

Other Books by Vic Broquard

Without Warning (fantasy)

The Trident Series: (fantasy)
Volume 1 The Trident and the Book
Volume 2 The Trident and the Scepter
Volume 3 The Trident and the Resurrection

The Adventures of Elizabeth Stanton Series: (science fiction)
Volume 1 The Evolution of the Path
Volume 2 The Great Messiah
Volume 3 Of Kings and Queens and Troubadours
Volume 4 Chaos in the Aftermath
Volume 5 Power Plays
Volume 6 Age of Exploration
Volume 7 Abducted
Volume 8 The Emperor and Empress
Volume 9 A Job Worth Doing
Volume 10 Degradation
Volume 11 The Second Crusade
Volume 12 When Worlds Collide
Volume 13 Dark Ages

The Lindsey Barron Series: (fantasy)
Volume 1 The Rod of the Apocalypse
Volume 2 The Board of Governors
Volume 3 The Crown of Moses
Volume 4 Dominus for President
Volume 5 The National Health Care Program
Volume 6 States Justice
Volume 7 Cross and Double-cross
Volume 8 Down the Dragon Hole

The Sol Empire Volume 5 Genetic Engineering

Zoran Chronicles Series: (fantasy)
Volume 1 A Dragon in Our Town
Volume 2 Dragons, Power, Courts, and War

Planet of the Orange-red Sun Series: (science fiction)
Volume 1 When Kingdoms Fall
Volume 2 Dark Ages
Volume 3 Age of the Towers
Volume 4 Difficillis Exitus
Volume 5 Age of the Lords
Volume 6 The Renegade Tower
Volume 7 Rebellions
Volume 8 The Aliens Return
Volume 9 Power Struggles
Volume 10 Guilds, Genetics, and Gods
Volume 11 Magi, Witches, Swords, and Superstitions
Volume 12 The Voyage of the Eagle's Seed
Volume 13 Eagle's Seed and Origins
Volume 14 Justifications
Volume 15 Responsibilities

The Return of the Wizards: Twelve Companions – The Making of Wizards (fantasy)

Slow Comes the Dark Series: (science fiction)
Volume 1 Creeping Darkness
Volume 2 Serendipity
Volume 3 Darkness Descends
Volume 4 Perversion Incarnate
Volume 5 Extermination Wars

Reclamation Series: (science fiction)
Volume 1 For the Want of a Pill

Vic Broquard